TH

SPARE

ROOM

THE
SPARE
ROOM

LAURA STARKEY

First published in Great Britain in 2024 by

Bonnier Books UK Limited
4th Floor, Victoria House, Bloomsbury Square, London, WC1B 4DA
Owned by Bonnier Books
Sveavägen 56, Stockholm, Sweden

A CIP catalogue record for this book is available from the British Library.

ISBN: 9781471414954

This book is typeset using Atomik ePublisher

Embla Books is an imprint of Bonnier Books UK
www.bonnierbooks.co.uk

For Emma and Liz – never forget that you're
the business.

Misery acquaints a man with strange bedfellows.
William Shakespeare, The Tempest,
Act 2 scene ii

You will love again the stranger who was your self . . .
Sit. Feast on your life.
Derek Walcott, Love After Love

June

Chapter 1

As Rosie Butler dug around in her underwear drawer for a pair of stomach-squashing control knickers, she reminded herself that it wasn't every day she was asked to attend a swanky eight-course dinner at a posh central London hotel.

If she was honest, she'd have preferred the invitation to have been delivered a little earlier and a *lot* more clearly – but she pushed this thought aside, suppressing the spark of annoyance she felt in the same way her very large, very tight pants would soon be compacting her tummy and backside.

It was the day of James's work summer party – an annual event at which employees and their dates were invited to eat, drink and make merry. Her boyfriend of almost a decade had his eye on a major promotion, and he'd repeatedly stressed the need for the two of them to show up smiling and ready to schmooze.

Somehow, though, he'd left it until Rosie had showered and started smearing moisturiser on her cheeks to mention that the event would involve a formal sit-down dinner. The dress code, he had blithely explained, was super smart – without so much as a hint of casual.

Dismayed, Rosie had eyed the pretty cotton sundress and sandals she'd planned to wear, laid out neatly on their bed. It was the same outfit she'd shown him two days ago, and which he'd given an absent-minded thumbs up while typing something on his phone.

'You're telling me I need *evening wear* for this thing?' she'd asked, panic-stricken. 'A cocktail dress? Heels? And you're mentioning this *forty-seven minutes* before we need to leave?'

James had merely shrugged. 'It's at a high-end hotel in Covent Garden. I thought it was obvious.' The notion that Rosie – whose wardrobe largely consisted of well-worn jeans, favourite t-shirts and casual Chuck Taylors – might need time to put together a suitably elegant look had entirely passed him by.

Rosie had sat in silence as she applied blush, lipstick and mascara, valiantly resisting the urge to bring up the fact that last year's summer party – a relaxed affair involving Pimm's, chicken kebabs and posh burgers in brioche buns – had been held in the garden of *the very same hotel* they were going to tonight.

Aware that she had to be in a cab in approximately fifteen minutes, Rosie stood in her fluffy pink dressing gown and riffled through her wardrobe. She watched James shrug into the custom-made suit his parents had bought him for his brother's recent wedding, and sighed heavily. It wasn't fair; dressing up for a posh evening do was so much *easier* for a man.

She pushed aside an array of coat hangers that, in the main, offered her nothing more elegant than yoga pants, oversized jumpers and hoodies. Finally, she dug out a red, vintage-style pencil dress she hadn't worn in at least five years. Made of scarlet shot silk, it was beautiful but very unforgiving. She prayed she could still pour herself into it.

Taking care not to smear her makeup or muss her blow-dried blonde hair, Rosie pulled the dress over her head and smoothed it down her body. *There*. She'd managed to get her hips into the snug, wiggle-style skirt without splitting a seam or giving herself a hernia. Now she could only hope that the dress would do up.

Delicately, she pinched together the two flaps of crimson fabric that hung below her right arm. With a little effort and a *lot* of breathing in, she pulled the zip all the way into position, then fastened the hook and eye that sat above it.

Emitting a (shallow) sigh of relief, she slipped her feet into the black high-heeled shoes she'd bought for the funeral of Mr Bettini, their old landlord and the former occupant of their building's top-floor flat. The shoes had been purchased at short notice for an event that would mainly involve sitting down, weeping and looking respectful, but they were the only appropriate ones she owned.

Rosie shuddered, somehow already able to feel blisters forming on her toes. She was an ungainly disaster in any footwear that wasn't flat. Prone to clumsiness at the best of times, she'd suffered several near-death experiences while wearing stilettos in her younger years, and had given them up entirely after spraining her ankle so severely it swelled up like a balloon.

She smiled as she remembered Mr Bettini's despair at her 'mannish' trainers and boots. He'd been a bad-tempered, seventy-something curmudgeon, but she'd liked him – and her natural warmth had worn him down until they became friends as well as neighbours.

She eyed her reflection in the bedroom mirror and realised she didn't look anything like herself. The sensation was weird. Discomfiting.

The red dress was snug and exposed the curves Rosie usually sought to conceal. It highlighted the fullness of her backside, the hip-to-waist ratio that belonged in another century and the sizeable bosom that (at least in this outfit) could best be described as 'heaving'.

On the other side of the room, James looked ostentatiously at his watch. 'You almost ready?'

'Yeah,' she said. She glanced self-consciously at her behind. 'Do I look all right?'

'Fine,' James said. 'Nice. But I wouldn't worry, it's not as if you're going to be the centre of attention anyway.'

'Oh, great. Thanks a bunch,' Rosie said wryly, forcing a smile.

He risked a *don't be dramatic* eye roll and muttered, 'You know what I mean.'

Under the circumstances, she thought she'd scrubbed up fairly well – but the tight set of James's jaw reminded her that this evening wasn't about her, and she exhorted herself to be supportive. Nodding mutely, Rosie brushed dust from a little black clutch bag she'd found lurking at the back of a cupboard, and slipped her keys, phone and bank card inside it. A car horn sounded from the street outside.

'That'll be the taxi,' James said. '*Shit*. He's early. I need to find the invitation or they won't let us in.'

'Seriously?' Rosie wrinkled her nose. She hated this sort of pretentious nonsense – pointless gatekeeping for the sake of making self-important people feel more so.

'We *can't* risk going without it,' James muttered. 'There'll be people on the door. Can you go and tell the driver I'll be out in a minute? Make sure he doesn't bugger off?'

'All right.' Rosie sighed. She turned her back on James and wobbled past the spare room, cursing the shoes that seemed tighter than ever and thanking the universe that their flat was on the ground floor.

As the irritation and stress of the past hour was finally given leave to flare in her chest, she flung the flat door aside with more force than was strictly necessary – stomping out onto the threadbare carpet in the corridor in the hope that it would release a little of her frustration.

It took only a second for Rosie to realise this theatrical gesture had been a mistake. As the heel of her left shoe caught on an ancient loop of acrylic pile, she understood with sudden but perfect clarity that she was going to fall over.

Would her too-tight red dress tear as she tumbled to the floor? A small part of her actually hoped so; it would give her the perfect excuse for bailing on what she was increasingly sure would be a rotten evening.

As she tipped forward, unable to pull her shoe away from the carpet or right herself, she heard her own voice shout, 'Bollocks!' and screwed her eyes shut.

Beneath her yell came the sound of the building's front door closing. Then the heavy tread of feet, moving at increasing speed.

She slammed into something solid and noted that, whatever it was, it wasn't the floor. In the few seconds before she opened her eyes again, she registered that it was warm and soft against her cheek. It smelled of soap, or maybe washing powder, and a little bit of *man*.

'Oh-my-bloody-god,' she said in a breathless rush, her words muffled by the faintly fragrant fabric. 'I'm so, so sorry.'

Two large hands were planted on Rosie's bare upper arms, steadying her as she backed away from what she now understood was a chest.

She lifted her head, sure that her cheeks were flaming the same colour as her frock. Then she lifted it a little further, craning her neck in search of a face. The owner of this chest was tall.

He was handsome, too, with inky-black hair, olive skin, a sharp, stubbled jawline and deep brown eyes. He was looking down at her with evident concern, his full-lipped mouth unsmiling.

'I'm sorry,' she said again, thoroughly flustered. 'And, er . . . thanks. For stopping me from hitting the deck, I mean.'

He shook himself slightly, as if he too had been thrown off balance, then slid his hands towards Rosie's elbows before lifting them from her skin altogether. She felt like the air around her had thickened – as if she was suddenly underwater.

Without saying a word, let alone explaining what the movement meant, the man bent down and rested his full weight on one denim-clad knee. Utterly confused, Rosie's brain short-circuited and began playing a reel of all the romantic proposals she'd ever seen in films and on TV.

'Ha ha ha, it's a bit soon for an engagement,' she babbled, 'we only met thirty seconds ago.'

She'd been aiming for jocular but, as the words left her

lips, she came to the horrifying conclusion that she sounded deranged.

Of all the idiotic things she could have said, why had she chosen *that*?

But also . . . what on earth was he doing?

He glanced up at her through long lashes, a flicker of amusement briefly dancing in his eyes. Still silent, he gently lifted her left foot, unhooking the heel of her shoe from the scrap of carpet it was stuck to.

After placing it back on the floor, he stood up. He seemed confused about what to do next, unsure of where to look.

His eyes darted around, eventually coming to rest on Rosie's face. She suddenly felt as if her skin, as well as her dress, were a size too small. And why was the hallway so *hot*, all of a sudden?

Rosie wished powerfully that she was wearing something less tight. Less *revealing*. She felt an odd certainty that this man was the sort of person who *saw* things – noticed fine details that passed most others by. It was intimidating.

For a second, she thought she detected a slight flush – a pink glow that hadn't been there before suddenly decorating his high cheekbones.

'Well,' Rosie said. 'Sorry again. And thanks. Again. Erm . . .'

Dear lord, she was an idiot. In fairness, though, this wildly handsome stranger seemed to have had the power of speech knocked out of him by her earlier impact – and surely *someone* had to speak?

His gaze caught hers and held it for a moment that seemed to stretch on, extending into hours. He opened his mouth like he was *finally* about to say something, and Rosie felt her chest tighten in anticipation.

An insistent honking cut through the oddly charged atmosphere.

'Bloody hell, Rosie,' James yelled from inside the flat. 'I thought you were going out there. Look lively, will you?'

As the tall stranger stepped aside and Rosie moved further into the hallway, James appeared behind her. 'Come *on*,' he said irritably, ignoring the random man entirely and propelling her by the waist towards the front door. He glanced back as he shut it behind them, then manoeuvred Rosie into their waiting cab.

'Who was that?' he asked, as the car pulled away from the kerb and headed south-west. 'New neighbour?'

'Oh. Yeah. Probably,' Rosie agreed, remembering only now that there'd been a backpack and several boxes stacked on the staircase up to the building's first and second floors. They'd been mostly obscured by the very large, very mysterious and weirdly intense person she'd just crashed into.

James threw her an exasperated look. 'Well, you met him, didn't you?' he demanded. 'Did you not find out if he was moving in?'

Rosie shook her head.

'For god's sake, what are you like?' James laughed, relaxing by degrees as they sped towards their destination. 'What's his name? You asked that, surely?'

'No,' Rosie told him, her head spinning. She wondered what on earth was wrong with her. 'I've absolutely no idea.'

September

Chapter 2

Towards the end of a boring Thursday several months later, Rosie glanced at the time display in the bottom right-hand corner of her computer screen. She sighed inwardly and concluded that her chance of leaving work on time this evening was approximately zero.

It was 5.56 p.m., and her ten-hour shift was supposed to finish at six.

The customer she was currently dealing with – a Mr Geoffrey Bathurst of Eastgate Close, Whitchurch, Shropshire – did not seem ready to face facts, preferring instead to rant down the phone at Rosie in the mistaken belief that she had some power to alter them.

He blustered on relentlessly about Cover 4 U's 'erroneous, *unconscionable*, frankly OUTRAGEOUS' decision not to pay his recent car insurance claim. The firm had rejected it on the grounds that his wife – the named driver on the policy – was apparently *not* the main user of the gigantic Range Rover Velar that had been backed into a neighbour's garden wall. In fact, the neighbour in question had informed Cover 4 U's investigator that the diminutive Mrs Bathurst was a rather nervous driver – terrified to get behind the wheel of what she alternately referred to as 'her husband's pride and joy' and 'that ludicrously expensive penis extension'. By all accounts, she was barely equal to pootling around their village in her own Mini Cooper – let alone tackling country lanes in a car not much smaller than a minibus.

Thanks to six years' experience as a Cover 4 U claims handler, Rosie understood that this was a classic case of fronting: fibbing about who drove a vehicle most frequently in order to secure insurance at a lower price.

She had so far refrained from using the word 'fraud' during this evening's conversation with Mr Geoffrey Bathurst, as she strongly suspected he wouldn't care for it. However, fraud *was* the operative term here – as well as Cover 4 U's justification for not buying Mr Bathurst a new back bumper or replacement brake lights.

'I'm sorry you're disappointed, sir,' Rosie said into the mouthpiece of her headset, seizing the opportunity to speak when the man took a moment to draw breath. 'Unfortunately, our investigators found that the information you gave us when you took out your policy wasn't accurate. That means we're unable to pay your claim.'

'This is unacceptable!' Geoffrey Bathurst bellowed. 'Shameful! I've paid the premium *every month*! This is not on. Not cricket. Not *British*!'

'I'm sorry, sir, but there's nothing more I can do,' Rosie said calmly. 'Your claim can't be taken any further.'

She hoped very much that if she continued to repeat this mantra, Mr Bathurst would demand to speak to her manager. Rosie wasn't allowed to suggest it herself – and didn't dare to in case the call was being recorded – but passing this guy on to Martin would kill two birds with one stone.

First, it would mean she could get out of here for the night – something she was keen on doing as quickly as possible, not least because she was meeting Niamh for dinner. Secondly, it would reroute Mr Bathurst's warpath in the direction of her smarmy, self-satisfied boss.

Martin was universally disliked among his team of claims handlers, and justifiably so: he was a small, mean-spirited man for whom the mere suggestion of power over others was intoxicating. When he'd refused a perfectly reasonable holiday request from Ellie last week, the act had affected him like a shot of tequila. He'd spent the whole day with a smug smile on his face that Rosie – as well as the rest of her colleagues – had longed to wipe off it.

'Not good enough!' Mr Bathurst continued, bringing her back to the here and now. Rosie winced as his volume increased in direct proportion to his outrage, causing her cheap plastic headphones to vibrate.

'Isn't it your job to solve this problem? To sort this *out*?' he demanded.

Rosie raised her eyes to the polystyrene-tiled, fluorescent-lit ceiling and swallowed a groan. It was 6.06 p.m. 'My job is to process claims, sir, which has now been done. As I said before, I'm sorry you're not happy with the outcome but there's nothing further I can do.'

'*Not happy* is something of an understatement,' Mr Bathurst barked. 'Do you have any idea how much spare parts for this type of vehicle cost, young lady?'

Oof. *Young lady*. If this conversation continued much longer, Rosie would score a full house on the Problem Caller Bingo card Ellie had given her at last year's Christmas party – a joke present that Martin had made clear he 'did not find funny in the slightest'.

Rosie resisted the urge to inform Geoffrey Bathurst that she was thirty-two years old. Nor did she point out that she had no idea how much Range Rover parts cost, though she imagined they were extortionate – on which basis, *she* might have avoided reversing into a stationary obstacle that stood a clear metre off the ground . . . especially in a car that doubtless had both cameras and sensors designed to prevent such mishaps.

'I suppose your silence means you have *no concept* of how much this is going to cost me,' Bathurst went on. 'Well, I can tell you I'll be making a complaint. You – JOBSWORTHS like you – you're part of the problem, you know. No common sense, no proper education . . . it's all *computer says no*. YOU'RE what's wrong with this country.'

This, Rosie couldn't help thinking, was a bit rich. She'd

done well at school, worked hard and paid her fair share of tax. Perhaps more pertinently, unlike the man on the other end of the line – who she now imagined was a red-faced, Barbour-wearing boomer – *she* was fundamentally honest.

Rosie was also kind to strangers, would do anything for the people she loved and (though she'd never admit it to her boyfriend) regularly fed the stray cat that lived in the alley behind their flat. However, because she was well-practised at not rising to the bait from irate customers, she kept this to herself, merely explaining: 'You'll find the complaints procedure you need to follow on our website, Mr Bathurst. Or if you'd prefer, I can send you the relevant forms in the post first thing tomorrow.'

The man spluttered incoherently, wrong-footed by Rosie's refusal to defend herself or argue with him.

'Is there anything else I can help you with today, sir?' she asked, keeping her voice light, pleasant and dignified.

'*No*. I don't imagine there is!'

'Then thank you for calling us today. Have a lovely evening,' Rosie said sweetly.

She clicked to end the call and breathed a deep sigh of relief.

'That sounded rough,' Ellie said from opposite her, smiling over the flimsy partition between their workstations. 'I could hear him blow-harding at you from over here.'

'I've had worse,' Rosie said, shrugging. 'At least he didn't swear at me. He was just your typical "obviously in the wrong but determined to dig in" kind of caller. He owns a car worth at least fifty grand, yet lied when he took out the insurance for the sake of saving about seventy quid. Now he's pissed off about the price of the spare parts he'll have to shell out for.'

Ellie made a face. 'What a knobhead.'

Rosie nodded, laughing as she removed her headset and logged off her computer. Ellie's Lancashire accent, which Rosie adored, rang with casual disdain in a way her own Essex twang never could.

'You here late tonight?' she asked.

Ellie nodded and grimaced, her pretty face contorting in dismay. 'On till ten.'

'Ugh,' Rosie said. 'Commiserations. The good news is, there are doughnuts in the break room. Just avoid the ones masquerading as chocolate-filled – they're coffee-flavoured and unspeakably disgusting.'

Ellie laughed, then asked: 'You in tomorrow?'

'Yeah. Short shift, ten till four. You?'

'Same, see you then. Now get out of here while you can. *Save yourself.* Martin's stomping about upstairs with a face like a smacked arse. If I were you, I'd disappear pronto.'

Rosie shuddered, briefly wondering what fresh hell awaited them at their next 'quick team catch-up'. Shaking the thought away, she pulled her coat from the back of her swivel chair and shrugged into it.

'See you tomorrow,' she said to Ellie as she headed for the exit.

''Night,' Ellie said, pressing a button to pick up a new call.

As the office door swung shut behind her, Rosie heard her friend brightly utter the words that punctuated their work days: 'Thank you for calling Cover 4 U Insurance. How can I help you this evening?'

About half an hour later, Rosie tumbled into a booth in her favourite Italian restaurant, sweaty and dishevelled from rushing. It was a small, family-run establishment just off Wanstead High Street – a no-frills diner that offered delicious, freshly made fare in old-fashioned but comfortable surroundings.

'Sorry I'm late,' she told her best friend, who was already sipping from a large glass of red wine. 'I got stuck on a call and then the bus took forever to turn up.'

'Not a problem,' Niamh said, waving a hand. 'Let's get you a drink, shall we?'

'Please,' Rosie sighed, shoving off her navy-blue coat and

thinking, not for the first time, that it had definitely seen better days.

Niamh – fashionably attired in a loose jersey minidress that subtly highlighted her height and slenderness – caught the attention of a waitress, beckoning her over so Rosie could order a glass of iced water and her own red wine.

'So,' Niamh said as the drinks arrived a moment later. 'Is it safe to assume you were dealing with a less-than-satisfied customer?' Rosie loved Niamh's voice – she still sounded unmistakably Irish, despite the fact that she'd spent nearly twenty years in the UK.

'A classic,' Rosie nodded. 'Some rich old duffer who'd lied when he took out his policy, ranting at me because it wouldn't pay out . . .'

'I've no idea how you put up with it,' Niamh said.

'It pays the bills,' Rosie shrugged. 'And I don't *hate* it.'

'Hardly a ringing endorsement.' Niamh's eyebrow arched as she looked at her friend.

'Come on, now, we can't all be high-flying marketing-slash-events innovators.'

Rosie put air quotes around the final four words, grinning widely as Niamh cringed.

'You know that isn't what I call *myself*,' she argued. 'It's just what they put on the company website.'

'Did *they* put it on your LinkedIn profile, too?' Rosie asked, raising an eyebrow mischievously.

'Oh, shut up,' Niamh laughed, and threw a piece of breadstick at her.

'I will if you will,' Rosie told her, deftly plucking the breadstick from the front of her stripy t-shirt so she could point it at Niamh. 'I don't want to talk about work all night.'

'Because you don't want the standard lecture on how you're too good for that place?'

'Precisely.'

'But you *are* too good for that place,' Niamh argued, her dark brown eyes wide. She swept her long braids, some of which were decorated with shining silver beads, over one elegant shoulder. 'You're six years into a temporary job, Rose. Whatever happened to going back to uni? Pursuing your dreams?'

'*Niamh*,' Rosie moaned, not wanting to dwell on her aborted attempt at getting a degree. 'Life happened. Rent. Grocery shopping. The gas bill. And I'm not sure I ever really had a dream beyond not living with my parents.'

'So that's it. Life goal achieved?'

'Maybe. God knows, James's new job is swish enough for the both of us. "Chief Information Officer" sounds impressive, right? And I daresay I'm as happy as the next person – though I'll be happier still when I've got a massive bowl of pasta in front of me.'

Rosie prayed this clumsy attempt to change the subject would work. She and Niamh had known each other since they attended the same sixth form and, although their lives had taken quite different directions, remained incredibly close. They could talk to one another about anything, but Rosie's career – or lack thereof – had long been a sore point between them.

Their waitress reappeared to take their order, and both women requested the day's special: penne pasta with shredded courgette, chilli, pecorino cheese and toasted pumpkin seeds. Rosie asked for a side of garlic bread for good measure, ignoring the dire voice in her head that warned against eating so much refined starch.

'Double carbs? Nice work,' Niamh said. 'Do I take it there's still a moratorium on them at your place?'

'Sadly, yes,' Rosie confirmed. 'I can barely remember the last time I ate a meal that wasn't designed to perfectly reflect James's macros.'

'Sounds like a giant pain in the arse,' Niamh said, 'mainly for you, since I assume you're the one cooking dinners devoid of rice, bread and potatoes?'

'Well, yeah – you know James isn't the best in the kitchen.

And as far as giant arses are concerned, I'm pretty peeved mine hasn't shrunk in the past couple of months, despite almost daily consumption of kale.'

'Your arse is lovely just the way it is,' Niamh told her, laughing.

'It's really not,' Rosie replied. 'I feel worse than ever about it just lately – and the rest of me, too, of course.' She gestured at herself, her fingertips sweeping up and down to indicate her head, chest, stomach and everything else currently concealed beneath the Formica-topped table.

Niamh frowned. 'You are *gorgeous*,' she said. 'I hate hearing you shit-talk yourself – I thought you'd vowed to stop doing it.'

'I know,' Rosie mumbled. 'And I *have*. But I suspect body positivity is easier for those of us who've never been above a size eight.'

'You can't live your life worrying about whether you meet other people's bullshit expectations,' Niamh said sagely. 'I might be slim, but have you any idea how many times I've rocked up to meet a client I've spoken to on the phone, only to witness their shock that I don't look like one of The Corrs? Somehow, nobody imagines an Irishwoman who's less Enya, more Zendaya . . . Anyway. What I'm saying is, anyone worth bothering with will appreciate you as you *are*. They won't fixate on what you're not.'

'All right,' Rosie said. 'Point taken. It's just hard with James constantly quaffing protein shakes and droning on about CrossFit. At least he's stopped trying to convince me to do it with him.'

Niamh guffawed heartily at this. 'Sorry, sorry . . . It's just the idea of you trying to lug a tyre around or do that thing with the ropes . . .'

'I know,' Rosie agreed, giggling too. 'Though to be fair the idea of *James* doing it would have been ridiculous a few months ago. For the first nine years of our relationship, *I* was the healthy one: walking everywhere, the occasional park run . . . actually eating foods that grew in nature and didn't come in foil trays from Deliveroo. Until recently, James's only form of regular exercise was strolling to the corner shop when we'd run out of Coke and crisps.'

'D'you think it'll stick?' Niamh asked. 'I mean, not to be negative, but I remember his "I'm going to learn to ride a motorbike" phase. And that time he got obsessed with brewing his own beer. *And* the several weeks he spent insisting he could play the ukulele.'

Rosie shook her head and grinned. 'Who knows? He seems pretty committed at the moment, and the healthy eating thing is broadly a *good* development – but I won't be sorry if he rolls it back a bit and allows bread in the house again at some stage.'

Niamh laughed again. 'So is he looking all ripped, now? Has he developed muscles in places you'd never previously suspected they might lurk?'

'Er. Not really, no. I mean, he's lost some weight, obviously – but it's not like he's turned into Magic Mike over the summer.'

'Pity . . .' Niamh said, spearing a piece of penne with her fork the second their food arrived. 'I wonder what brought on this fitness mania, though? Health scare? Midlife crisis?'

'We are *not* middle-aged,' Rosie insisted.

'Did you hear from Gather yet?' Niamh asked suddenly, remembering that her friend had been awaiting feedback on a volunteer position she'd interviewed for. Gather was a charity helpline for under-25s, and Rosie had applied to answer calls for a few hours each week – an easy investment of time now James spent so many mornings and evenings at the gym.

The organisation helped young people navigate issues with relationships, education, family and housing by lending a kind, non-judgemental listening ear. It was the sort of work Rosie had once imagined she'd do professionally – and it was exciting to think she could find some fulfilment of an old ambition without completely upending her life. She might not have the psychology degree or counselling training she'd hoped for, but she could still make a difference to people in need.

'I did!' she said, unable to stop herself from gushing. 'I'm in! I'll start my training in January.'

'That's brilliant!' Niamh cried through a mouthful of pasta. 'Ah, Rose, I'm made up for you.'

'Thanks,' Rosie said, grinning. 'Believe it or not, the day job helped. I've spent a lot of time connecting with people on the phone . . .'

'Excellent. What did James say when he heard the news?'

Rosie took a sip from her wine glass and considered how best to respond. Niamh tipped her head to one side, regarding her quizzically.

'Er. Well. The whole thing had sort of slipped his mind,' Rosie said eventually.

A line appeared between Niamh's eyebrows and the corners of her mouth turned down.

'OK,' she said, seeming annoyed. 'So he can remember the exact mix of different nutrients in his favourite brand of protein powder, but he can't remember *this*? It's a big deal for you.'

Rosie tore a corner off her garlic ciabatta and chewed it thoughtfully. 'Not ideal, I agree. But he has had *loads* going on lately. He's been in his own head a lot.'

Niamh scoffed at this, and Rosie sensed she was reining in a major rant.

'I've actually started to wonder if, with the promotion, and the eating, he's started to think about the future more. *Our* future.'

'Do you mean . . . you think he's finally going to propose?' Niamh's jaw seemed to slacken with shock.

'I dunno. Maybe? Fingers crossed, I guess,' Rosie said. 'It is our ten-year anniversary next month. And I seem to recall you telling me Brendan got all weird when you went on that holiday to Barbados, right before he asked you to marry him.'

Niamh smiled indulgently at the memory. 'He did, the absolute plank. I freaked out on the last day because I thought he was going to dump me – he'd been so *off* the whole time we were there . . . I was screaming at him about how he'd never find anyone better, and he said, "*I know*, that's why I'm trying to work up the courage to propose to you." And then he showed me the ring. He'd been carrying it around for almost a fortnight, trying to find the perfect moment.'

'So romantic,' Rosie sighed, glancing at the glittering emerald on her friend's left hand.

Niamh snorted. 'Romance is in pretty short supply in our house these days,' she said. 'As is sleep.'

Rosie wasn't surprised that Niamh hadn't asked whether she'd accept James's proposal, should it materialise. The answer was obviously yes.

Rosie had spent the past few years wondering if and when James might feel ready to take what, for her, had always been the next logical step in their relationship. After getting married, she hoped they'd have children – even though Niamh's recent experience of pregnancy and early motherhood had been intense to witness, never mind live through.

Niamh and Brendan, her husband of three years, had ten-month-old twins. Eva and Rory were Rosie's honorary niece and nephew, and she loved them to pieces – but she didn't envy her friends the prolonged period of broken nights, blurry days and endless bottle feeding they'd been through in the months since the twins' arrival. Niamh was back at work now, trying to navigate a new normal, but the babies still weren't good sleepers. Rosie inspected her friend's face as they ate, noting the shadows beneath Niamh's eyes and the new, enhanced sharpness of her cheekbones.

'How is everything, with you being back at work?' Rosie asked.

'Oh, it's fine,' Niamh said airily. 'All good. An adjustment, but everyone will get used to it.' Rosie noted her firm and final tone, and elected to hold back her questions about how Niamh was managing, for now.

The waitress returned to clear their plates, and two portions of tiramisu were ordered.

'I know what I've been meaning to ask you,' Niamh said a few minutes later, through a mouthful of espresso-soaked sponge, chocolate and cream. 'What's the latest on Nameless Neighbour?'

'He isn't *nameless*,' Rosie said, rolling her eyes. 'We just don't know what he's called.'

'He's so mysterious,' Niamh murmured. 'So enigmatic. So . . . *fit.*'

Rosie laughed. 'You literally saw him for about thirty seconds in the corridor.'

'Which was plenty long enough to determine that he is, objectively, the best-looking man I've ever seen in real life.'

'What about Brendan?!' Rosie demanded, scandalised.

'Oh, Brendan's handsome, he's lovely, I adore him, blah blah blah. But your man in the flat upstairs? He's *Hollywood*-hot. What is it that's written on his post again?'

'Everything I've ever seen comes addressed to "A. Thomas",' Rosie said.

'And you've no idea what the "A" stands for, even though he's lived upstairs since June? That's, what . . . three months?'

'Correct. James regularly speculates on the A, naturally. Could it be Arsehole? Axe-murderer? Adolf?'

Niamh sniggered. 'He's still pissed off about the bike thing?'

'Very,' Rosie nodded. 'Though to be honest, I never thought the Post-it was "passive-aggressive". It was perfectly polite, and A. Thomas was probably right about the bike blocking the front door and being a fire hazard. Plus all the dirt it tracked onto the carpet for the cleaner to clear up.'

She smothered a smile as she remembered how mad James had been when their neighbour insisted the offending mountain bike be stored in the shed to the rear of their flat, rather than left leaning against the post table in the hallway. He'd complained about it for days, conceding only because Rosie pleaded with him not to cause trouble. After the death of their old upstairs neighbour and landlord, Mr Bettini, the building had changed hands – and Rosie didn't want the property investment firm that now owned it to have any cause for an early review of their tenancy agreement.

'So A. Thomas is a safety-first, fire-aware neat freak, as well as crazily handsome . . .' Niamh said dreamily, tapping her credit card against the reader their waitress had brought over. 'Interesting.'

'Stop it,' Rosie ordered, grinning and wagging a finger at her friend. 'He just wants to be left alone. And you are married. With twins.'

She paid her half of the bill and the waitress moved on, leaving behind a silver tray stacked with after-dinner mints. With some effort, Rosie resisted the urge to eat one and sweep the rest into her handbag.

'Balls. I'd almost forgotten about them,' Niamh groaned. 'I suppose I should be getting back. What are the chances Brendan's managed to get both kids bathed and into bed, d'you reckon? I'm thinking slim to none.'

'I couldn't possibly say,' Rosie told her, holding both palms up. 'But I'm rooting for him – and you.'

'I know you are,' Niamh said, grasping Rosie's hand across the tabletop and squeezing it tight. 'And I'm in your corner too, you know. Always.'

'I'll let you know if James does pop the question,' Rosie said. 'You'll be the first person I call.'

For a split second, Niamh's smile seemed to falter – perhaps, Rosie thought, because of what this said about her friend's difficult family relationships.

'You do that,' Niamh told her, recovering her composure and grinning brightly as they made their way out of the restaurant. 'Keep me posted.'

Chapter 3

Rosie decided to catch the bus back to Walthamstow, where she and James lived. Niamh hugged her goodbye at the stop, then set off to walk the short distance back to the four-bedroom Victorian town house she shared with her family.

Theirs was the kind of home Rosie had once thought existed only in films or interiors magazines: all elegant bay windows, original wood floors and real, working fireplaces. Brendan – a successful barrister who specialised in intellectual property law – had built up a sizeable nest egg before meeting Niamh at a corporate event she'd organised for his firm. He'd immediately fallen head over heels in love with her, and two years later they'd married, then bought the house as a dilapidated shell. Costly, extensive renovations were completed not long before the twins were born.

By contrast, Rosie and James's rented flat was modest – but Rosie adored it, having spent the past six years sanding, painting, decorating and loving it back to life. Mr Bettini, who'd first rented it to them as a soulless box, had been happy for Rosie to renovate it to her liking. In fact, he'd kept their rent below market value in exchange for her tasteful work on the place. The discount had been enough to dissuade James from pushing Rosie on buying somewhere of their own for now – a compromise she was glad of, since his dream of a sleek, suburban new build clashed horribly with her love of period features, vintage furniture and quirky textiles.

Privately, Rosie suspected that theirs wasn't the only rent the landlord had kept low. Val and Pat, who occupied the first-floor flat that lay between what used to be Mr Bettini's place and their ground-floor residence, had lived in the building almost as long as he had. A female couple that he'd referred to as 'close companions', they were both in their fifties and semi-retired from teaching careers. Their long-standing presence in the house, as well as that of Mr Bettini, gave the place an unusual sort of homeliness. The old man would never have admitted it, but Rosie got the sense that the occupants of his building felt a little like found family.

She'd been deeply upset when Mr Bettini died – and not just because it put the ownership of her home in doubt. He'd had no other friends or relatives that she knew of, so – taking her cue from Val and Pat – she'd popped in regularly with cake and biscuits she'd made, or books she thought he'd enjoy. Once he stopped pretending to complain about these 'unsolicited visits', the two of them had grown close.

His funeral had been a pretty bleak affair. It had been organised in accordance with the funeral plan he'd set up many years before, but attendees were scant – consisting only of Rosie, Val and Pat, gossip-hungry Mrs Beaumont from next door and a few people from the local bridge club.

James had gone to work as normal. He thought Rosie's sentimental reaction to Mr Bettini's death was sweet, but told her she'd regret wasting a day of annual leave on an event that was really nothing to do with her. As she'd wept hot, salty tears in an empty church pew, however, she'd felt a strange sort of satisfaction. It was right that *someone* should cry, that someone should mark and mourn Mr Bettini's passing. Rosie couldn't think of anything sadder than leaving the world unnoticed, unremarked and unmissed. She'd helped to ensure that didn't happen to a person who, in a small but significant way, had mattered to her. The thought still gave her comfort.

As she got off the bus, taking her nose out of her book and making her way back up William Road, Rosie noticed there was a light on in what was now A. Thomas's sitting room.

She'd feigned a level of disinterest she didn't truly feel when Niamh had mentioned him earlier, and wasn't entirely sure why. When she examined her motives, she realised that admitting her own intrigue about 'Nameless Neighbour' would feel somehow disloyal. Since the day he'd moved in, James had grown to genuinely hate the man – though Rosie didn't think his behaviour, stiff and standoffish as it was, justified such loathing.

She'd never mentioned the fact that he'd saved her from falling over in the corridor – possibly even from breaking a bone or two, given the shoes she'd had on at the time. For some reason, she'd even kept the story from Niamh.

But A. Thomas's conduct in that moment had convinced Rosie he couldn't be the surly, misanthropic bastard James insisted he was. OK, so he hadn't actually *spoken* to her – but there'd been a kindness about him, a sort of warm humanity. He'd helped her without making her feel like an idiot – though in the end, she'd done an admirable job of that all by herself.

What was the word Niamh had used to describe him? *Mysterious*. A. Thomas was definitely that. In addition to not knowing his name, Rosie and James had no idea what he did for a living, where he was from or what his voice sounded like. Even for London, this was a pretty impressive level of distance to keep from two people who lived under the same roof he did.

While she'd never concede the point, Rosie also agreed with Niamh about A. Thomas's good looks. He was handsome in a way she found almost far-fetched – like the brooding male lead in a perfectly lit period drama, or the smouldering star of a *Vanity Fair* photoshoot. The fascination A. Thomas inspired in her was akin to how she felt about exotic zoo animals: she was drawn in by their beauty and wondered about their secret inner lives, but was quite content to admire them from afar.

She opened the heavy front door of the building – old,

with peeling red paint and a tarnished brass knocker and letter box – then made her way to the flimsier internal door that led to her flat. As she passed the occasional table in the hallway, she noticed that on one side – *their* side – it was still piled high with post.

There was a large, messy stack that Rosie assumed consisted mainly of unsolicited junk mail, all addressed to James Gardiner. She felt a brief prickle of irritation at his untidiness.

Once inside the flat, she eyed the detritus of James's solo evening in: the PlayStation controller and protein bar wrappers on the coffee table, the whirring dishwasher and the dirty wok and chopping boards piled up in the sink.

James himself was nowhere to be seen. Rosie checked her watch: 9.47 p.m. She'd been hoping they could catch up and chat about their days over a cuppa, or at the very least take in an episode of something funny on TV before turning in for the night.

She pushed open the bedroom door softly, in case he was asleep. In fact, James was sitting up in bed, two pillows nestled between his back and the antique wooden headboard Rosie had rescued from a street market five years ago. She grinned as she remembered how she'd had to hire a six-seater taxi to bring home the slab of intricately carved dark wood James was leaning against.

James's legs were bent triangular under the bedclothes, a thick book resting on his knees. Rosie's eyes swept its cover, and she made out the words *Paleo Perfect: A lifestyle bible for the modern caveman*. She felt her eyebrows shoot up and tried not to laugh.

'All right?' James said, looking up and running a hand through his dark-blond hair as she bent down to kiss him hello. He was boyishly handsome, Rosie thought – if a little more aware of it than he used to be. There were moments when she missed the somewhat scruffy student she'd first fallen in love with, even though this version of James was more polished, more financially solvent and better acquainted with shampoo.

'Whoa, are you trying to ward off the local vampires or something?' James exclaimed, wincing theatrically as Rosie stood up again.

She smiled and rolled her eyes. 'I *might* have eaten some garlic bread this evening,' she said, more sheepishly than she'd intended to. 'And some pasta, which probably also contained industrial quantities of garlic. Although there definitely wasn't any in the tiramisu . . .'

She had no idea why she was confessing this evening's food choices, but the urge to do so was irresistible. It was as though she were a penitent and James some sort of diet shaman, armed with the unique power to forgive her food sins. It hadn't always been this way, but his recent conversion to 'pursuing wellness' had come with side-effects Rosie could never have foreseen.

'Yikes – so much starch,' James went on, in a contradictory echo of Niamh's comment about double carbs. 'And sugar. The twin enemies of all body goals.' He arched a brow and smiled at her, but the expression didn't quite reach his eyes. After a few seconds, his gaze drifted away and settled on the page he'd been reading before Rosie came in.

For a moment she felt hurt – as if he'd poked an angry bruise. James knew as well as she did that she'd tried every imaginable weight loss regime in the time they'd been together – and that she'd spent long years wishing away the curves that had suddenly appeared around her thirteenth birthday. He also knew that, even before then, she'd been dubbed 'Roly Poly Rosie' by her stick-thin younger brother, Michael.

On her best days, Rosie felt zen about not being thin. She was satisfied she'd reached her body's natural set point. Increasingly, she was convinced that the things she really wanted in life had little to do with the waist size of her jeans – even if comments like this one made her worry James was no longer so sure.

Her thoughts drifted to the spare bedroom – the only space in the flat that Rosie hadn't painted, furnished or decorated. She cherished the unspoken hope that, at some point in the not-too-distant future, she might be able to fit it out as a nursery.

A sudden rush of tenderness doused the spark of irritation James had ignited – smothering it before it could burn its way up Rosie's throat and take form in words that would inevitably cause a row. He just wanted the best for her, she told herself. And he'd certainly left her in no doubt when they first met that he considered her attractive. She liked to think she hadn't changed too much; she'd felt *chosen* that night – thrilled and amazed that she was preferred above every other woman in the room. He'd laughingly told her she had the face of an angel and a rack to die for – which, while teasing and crude, was unquestionably flattering. If the changes James was making felt like a comment on her lifestyle and appearance, maybe that was her issue?

'Cup of tea?' she asked him, keen to chat but hoping to avoid any further discussion of macronutrients or the 'body goals' James apparently thought she should have.

'No, thanks,' he said, frowning slightly at her offer. 'Caffeine at this time of night's probably not the best idea.'

This, Rosie supposed, was true – though she reasoned it would take more than a mug of PG Tips to stop her from nodding off when her head hit the pillow this evening.

'OK,' she said, refusing to be cowed or to sound in any way resentful. 'Well, I'm going to have one – watch the news, maybe. I'll see you in the morning? Love you.'

''Night then,' James nodded, burying his nose in his tome again. 'Don't stay up too late.'

Chapter 4

When Rosie awoke the following morning, James had already left for the gym. Pale sunlight was streaming in through a crack in the bedroom curtains, illuminating a sock and a pair of boxer briefs that for some reason hadn't made it all the way to the laundry hamper.

She didn't have to be at work until ten, so she scooped them up, threw them into a basket she'd begun filling the previous night and took it to the kitchen. On the way, she noted a crate of protein supplements and energy bars that had been unceremoniously dumped in the spare room. Rosie needed to speak to him about this habit, or she knew the whole space would soon be given over to storage of James's gym stuff – but she didn't relish the prospect of bringing it up.

As the kettle boiled, she put two slices of wholemeal bread into the toaster, loaded the washing machine and flipped the switch on the radio. Rosie hadn't intended to tidy up after James, but nevertheless found herself binning his rubbish, putting his console controller away and running hot water into the sink so she could wash up the dishes he'd forgotten all about. They were emitting an odour that Rosie knew would permeate the whole flat if she ignored it much longer.

The kettle clicked off and she threw a teabag into a mug, opened the fridge and pulled out an empty carton of semi-skimmed.

Rosie had a momentary vision of James gulping ice-cold milk like an overgrown teenager. She sighed. Not for the first time, she asked herself what sort of person puts a container *with nothing in it* back in the fridge. Then she put a stop to her internal rant and made a snap decision. Her toast would have to wait.

She stuck her feet into the sliders next to the back door, grabbed her handbag from the countertop and threw her coat on over her pyjamas. Rosie *had* thought she'd have plenty of time for getting ready and doing a few chores this morning – but that advantage would be lost if she faffed around and tried to make herself presentable before popping to the corner shop.

Besides, it was only a couple of minutes' walk away. The sole person likely to see her was the thick-spectacled, monosyllabic man behind the counter, and he never seemed to recognise his customers from one day to the next. She could probably go in there naked and he'd just say, 'Six pounds ninety-eight, please,' as he handed over her groceries. Shuddering at the idea of being nude in public, Rosie shook this thought away and headed for the door.

Just over ten minutes later, she was on her way home from the minimart with four pints of milk, six apples, a packet of bagels and a bunch of bananas. At this point she found herself wishing she wasn't wearing her book print PJs. Not only were they loud – jade green, with bright, multicoloured texts adorning them in a splatter pattern – they were *thin*. Summer still clung to the start of September, as it often did in England – but the chill in the air reminded Rosie that autumn was on its way.

She picked up her pace, also regretting the bright pink, plasticky footwear she only usually wore in the flat's little scrap of garden. She felt tension building in the stretched handles of the flimsy bag she was carrying and slowed again, in spite of her cold feet. It struck her that the contents weighed rather too much for a single carrier to cope with.

Sure enough – mere seconds before she reached the front door of her building – the bag split. It did so in deadpan fashion, unceremoniously dumping everything Rosie had just bought onto the garden path.

The heavy milk carton hit the ground first, its top dislodged by an aged concrete slab that was rapidly turning white.

'*Bollocks*,' Rosie shouted, righting the container in a bid to stop the leak and then realising that her apples were rolling away, back towards the road.

She turned to set about retrieving them, then felt her semi-bare foot connect with something cool and squishy.

Marvellous. She had quite literally stepped on a banana.

She closed her eyes, turned her face upwards and took a deep breath. This was *fine*, she told herself. At least – just this once – there were no witnesses to her klutziness.

As she exhaled and her eyes fluttered open, it became clear how wrong she was. Amid the devastation before her was A. Thomas, bent down and scrabbling for an errant apple before it could spin into the path of an oncoming Fiat 500.

Rosie swallowed. Hard. She felt embarrassment crawling up her spine, and her face was suddenly hot.

Her upstairs neighbour – who had now rescued all six of her fruits – came to stand in front of her, clutching them in large, lightly tanned forearms.

Oh god oh god oh god. Why was this happening? Why was she in *nightwear*? And why, almost every time she saw this person, was she doing something inelegant and humiliating?

Biting her lip, she opened her bucket-sized handbag and nodded at him, wordlessly signalling that he could drop the apples into it.

As he did so, she allowed herself a brief look at him. Annoyed, she conceded he was as ridiculously tall and handsome as he'd been last time she saw him. Even worse, his standard aura of self-contained serenity only sharpened Rosie's awareness of how flustered and clumsy she must seem.

This morning he was in running shorts and a slightly sweaty t-shirt that seemed determined to stick to his chest. It was attire that signalled his status as a well-organised, fully functional, 'exercise in the morning' sort of person – a striking contrast to her own look, which screamed 'shambolic hobo who couldn't be arsed to get dressed'. Rosie's cheeks flamed.

As A. Thomas retreated slightly, his eyes drifted to her jazzy pyjama bottoms and she thought she detected a smile trying to form in the corner of his mouth.

'I always dress to impress when I go to the minimart,' she heard herself blurt out. 'Feel like I should make an effort, you know?'

What. Was. She. *Doing*?

Her stomach rolled over as she remembered what she'd said the last time she had a run-in with A. Thomas: the stupid comment about him proposing to her that had spewed forth as he pulled her high heel free from a knot of carpet.

Something about his demeanour unnerved her, she realised. She felt a bizarre need to fill the silence between them before it could get too heavy – which apparently resulted in her saying extremely stupid things.

On this occasion, at least, Rosie's idiocy earned her a short, deep laugh. Her neighbour was regarding her quizzically, now – the way he might look at some strange, potentially dangerous species of animal he'd never come across before. He was probably trying to work out whether she was having some sort of acute psychological incident, Rosie thought. In all honesty, she couldn't blame him.

She pulled the banana she'd squashed from beneath her right foot and threw it into the food waste bin that was stored just off the narrow path. The remaining intact bananas went into her massive handbag, on top of the apples she now feared were so bruised they would have to end their days as compote or crumble.

A. Thomas was still hanging back, watching her movements from his position at the road end of the path. Was he transfixed by her bad taste pyjamas? No doubt his girlfriend was the sort who wore a silk negligee every night.

When he inclined his head in her direction, however, it hit Rosie that he was simply being polite – allowing her time to gather her wits, and her groceries, instead of barging past her so he could get into the building first. At the same moment she understood this, she noticed there was a glob of sticky, pulverised banana flesh on her big toe. Good *god*, the indignity was unbearable.

Desperate to end her mortification – not to mention fearful that she'd do or say something else ridiculous if she stood there much longer – Rosie picked up the dented (but still mostly full) carton of milk. She drew her shoulders back and tried to channel cool, calm confidence before she opened her mouth.

'Well,' she said after a moment. 'Thanks. For your help, I mean. I'm Rosie, by the way.' A. Thomas tilted his chin in acknowledgement of this introduction but didn't offer one of his own. What was *with* this man?

'I don't know why you only ever see me at my clumsiest,' Rosie rambled on. 'It's very unfair . . . I prance around Walthamstow like a ballet dancer most of the time, ask anyone!'

Urgh. Mouth one, brain nil.

Also: lies.

Cringing, Rosie walked away from her still-silent neighbour towards the old red front door, realising too late she'd have to fumble for her keys one-handed unless she put the damaged milk container down again. Before she could do so, A. Thomas stepped around her and deftly put his own key in the lock. She caught a waft of the same clean, soapy scent she'd smelled on the day he stopped her from falling over in the corridor. She instructed herself not to inhale it.

He held the door open so she could go through ahead of him and she shuffled inside, taking care not to get banana on the carpet. She couldn't quite believe he'd still said *no words* to her in the whole time he'd lived in the building – despite having stepped in to help her on two awkward occasions that might ordinarily involve at least a little speech.

Maybe he had chronic laryngitis? Rosie thought. Or was in some religious order that permitted living solo in an east

London flat but forbade all talking? Then again, it was more likely he had simply determined to avoid socially interacting with someone who he'd probably concluded was a walking disaster.

Not expecting any kind of response, Rosie mumbled, 'OK, so . . . thanks again,' as she opened her flat door.

'No problem,' A. Thomas murmured as he began to climb the stairs – his voice so soft and low she could easily have missed it beneath the scrape of her key in the lock.

There was an accent there – a hint of something pleasant, interesting and definitely not southern – but before she had a hope of identifying it, he'd disappeared.

Utterly befuddled, Rosie went inside, deposited her groceries on the table and tore a piece of kitchen towel off the roll that stood next to the sink. Wincing, she wiped her foot clean of mashed banana, restarted the toaster and set about making the cup of tea she now needed more than ever.

A short while later, as she looked out of the kitchen window with a much-needed second cuppa and ruminated on her fresh humiliation, Rosie spotted the large silver tabby cat she sometimes fed. He – Rosie was *sure* it was a he – was sauntering along the wall that separated their tiny scrap of garden from Mrs Beaumont's.

The cat was long-haired, with scruffy, abundant fur that gave him the look of a well-loved, slightly mangy cuddly toy. He had a pointed, intelligent face with wide-set eyes, above which a series of dark grey vertical stripes conspired to give the impression he was wearing a permanent scowl. Rosie found this equal parts hilarious and adorable – and impossible to resist.

She opened a cupboard and dug through all the tins, packets and jars to the very back, where a box of cat food and a saucer were concealed. Smiling at her subterfuge, she unlocked the back door and propped it open, then placed the food on the old concrete step just outside.

Within seconds, the cat had bounded over and was devouring the noxious-smelling jellied meat with gusto. Rosie finished her tea, then sat on the kitchen floor in the hope he'd condescend to let her stroke him once he was done eating.

To her delight, he stepped cautiously through the open door the second his food was gone – sniffing her outstretched hand suspiciously, the way he always did on the days he was brave enough to get close to her.

'It's OK,' Rosie whispered. 'You know me. I'm not going to hurt you.'

Seeming to decide he believed this, the cat nudged her fingers with his soft, stripy head until she began gently smoothing the fur between his ears. He started purring as Rosie scratched beneath his chin, closing his huge yellow-green eyes in contentment. Rosie's heart swelled, feeling suddenly full and heavy in her chest.

'I wish I could keep you,' she told the cat. 'But James says you've probably got fleas. And he's allergic.' She laughed wistfully and shook her head.

From somewhere in the back of her mind, a small, treacherous voice pointed out that James was barely here at the moment – that in fact, Rosie might be spending more quality time with this allegedly flea-bitten feline than with her boyfriend.

She told the voice to shut up, then glanced at the time display on the oven and sighed. She needed to unload the washing machine, shower and start getting ready.

'Sorry, mate,' she said, giving the cat a final stroke and standing up. 'Duty calls.' He sat primly on the tiled floor and stared with watchful eyes as she piled wet laundry into the basket, before following her outside and gazing at her as she hung it out to dry. As she pegged a last sock to the rotary washing line, he rubbed his soft face against her left leg – a rare, overt plea for more affection that Rosie couldn't ignore.

Wondering whether he'd tolerate it, she bent down to pick him up. To her surprise, he didn't scratch or scramble for release; he purred again, letting her bury her face in his soft fur as though he were a teddy bear come to life.

As the sound of the radio's 8.30 news bulletin drifted through the back door, Rosie set the cat back down. 'I really do have to go now,' she said.

He mewed at her resentfully, licked a paw and rubbed it against his nose. Seconds later, a blur of white and grey fluff streaked across the tiny lawn, then scrambled over the fence into the alley behind the street.

To her own surprise, Rosie felt the loss like an ache. She was still reeling from the morning, and how ludicrous she must have looked in front of her intriguing neighbour. The whole episode, and especially his silent chivalry, had been so surreal she was starting to wonder whether she'd imagined it. The cat's presence had calmed her frayed nerves, and his forthright demands for affection had soothed some internal pain she hadn't known she was nursing. She quickly decided not to think about that for now.

In any case, James was right, she supposed: feeding the neighbourhood stray could only lead to trouble later down the line. She'd fall in love with him but be unable to adopt him, and the whole business would simply make her sad – even more so than she felt right now.

As she swiped at her inexplicably prickling eyes, she heard a sound from above – a phone trilling insistently, demanding to be answered. She glanced up just in time to see a dark head shrink back inside through an open top-floor window.

A. Thomas had been watching her, she was almost sure of it. She could only hope he wouldn't spill to their landlord about the cat.

Chapter 5

After a mercifully short and sweet six-hour shift at Cover 4 U, Rosie snapped shut her laptop and felt an unexpected surge of Friday feeling as she prepared to head home.

She'd been supposed to go for a drink with Ellie, but the plan had been rain-checked because her seven-year-old son, Finn, had a temperature. While sympathising with her friend, Rosie found herself thinking that she couldn't remember the last time she and James had had a proper night out. The golden September sunshine filled her with confidence that she could drag her health-conscious boyfriend to a pub garden, and maybe even beyond. It felt like exactly what they needed. When Rosie walked into the flat about forty minutes later, wondering if she could get away with displaying her slightly stubbly calves in an old faithful midi dress, she was immediately greeted by the tinny sound of computer game gunfire and realised James must be home.

She had expected to have plenty of time to freshen up and message him about where they should go – teasing him about the detoxing opportunity an old-school Friday night would present. Recently, he either worked late or did long sessions at the gym on Friday evenings. Perhaps, Rosie mused, the unseasonably warm weather had squashed any urge to remain virtuous, and she'd find him more amenable to her plan than she'd thought.

Her surprise at his presence quickly gave way to an appreciation that she could be sipping something cold and delicious in the evening sunshine in under half an hour. She burst into the sitting room, where he was perched on the edge of the sofa, ready to cajole him into action. He was hunched over the PlayStation controller, his narrowed gaze fixed on a Nazi zombie he was trying to kill. Vaguely, Rosie wondered if you *could* kill a reanimated corpse – and if not, what the point of this computer game purported to be.

As she dropped her handbag onto the couch, James turned to face her, startled. Evidently, engrossed in his virtual mission, he hadn't heard her open the front door or enter the room. 'What are you doing home?' he asked, in a strangled sort of voice. 'I . . . I thought you had plans with Ellie.'

'I did,' Rosie said, tempted to jokily ask whether he had another woman hidden behind the sofa. 'Finn's sick,' she explained. 'We decided to do it another time. I was thinking we could go out, just us? It's a gorgeous night.'

'Ah,' James said, releasing a deep breath. He turned back to look at the TV. The words GAME OVER were writ large across the screen. With a clatter, he set down his controller on the walnut coffee table. The noise seemed to slice through the charged silence in the room.

Rosie suddenly got the distinct sense that he'd had important plans her unexpected arrival had disrupted. Her heart began to thump wildly. Could this be it . . . ? Had James devised some scheme to set up a romantic scene in the flat, then propose to her when she arrived home later this evening?

Rosie cast her eyes around for evidence: candles, flowers, chocolates, ice-cold champagne. Her eyes snagged on his massive gym bag, abandoned on the floor next to the flatscreen, but aside from that she could find nothing – which perhaps explained his alarm at her sudden appearance.

The quiet between them stretched on, becoming taut. Rosie's whole body thrummed with anticipation. She noticed a muscle working in James's clean-shaven jaw and saw the high, rigid set of his shoulders. He was *definitely* nervous. She suppressed a smile as she remembered Brendan's proposal to Niamh . . . perhaps a little encouragement wouldn't go amiss.

'James . . . ?' Rosie said, her voice soft and reassuring. 'Is everything OK? Is there something you wanted to talk about?'

Relief flooded his features, though his face remained pale and clammy. He looked almost shaken – like he was willing himself not to panic.

'It's all right,' Rosie murmured, sinking down next to him on the sofa and slipping her hand into his. 'You can talk to me.' His hesitancy was charming, she thought – a sign that, while he wasn't the most proactive of partners, he didn't take her for granted in the way she occasionally worried he might.

James sighed and she saw a tiny drop of sweat drift past his temple, then disappear into the dark-blond hair above his ear. His blue eyes were darting around the room, like he was scanning for an escape route.

'I . . . I do need to talk to you,' James finally mumbled, focusing intently on a wood knot in one of the floorboards.

'I'm listening,' Rosie said, smiling at him and squeezing his hand.

James took a huge breath, then looked up at her, his sand-coloured eyebrows high in his forehead. His eyes were wide, now: round with apprehension.

He opened his mouth to speak and Rosie's stomach rolled over.

This was it. The start of the rest of her life. The moment she'd remember forever.

'It's . . . it's us,' James eventually managed. 'You and me.'

Rosie nodded gently, making it clear he should go on. She felt almost sick with excitement.

'I can't . . .' James faltered. 'I can't do this – *us* – anymore.'

The words *Yes! Of course I'll marry you!* stuck in Rosie's throat a second before she uttered them.

She froze in shock, as if a jet of cold water had hit her full in the face.

James had robbed Rosie of the power to speak, to *think*, leaving her able only to gape at him in horror. She couldn't make sense of what he'd just said – the words she thought she'd just heard.

'Er . . . what?' she said, after what felt like an eternity.

James pulled his sweaty hand away from hers, and she felt as if he'd slapped her.

'*Fuck*,' he groaned, clawing at his hair in despair. 'I just . . . I can't do *this*.'

He flapped his hands, gesturing at the space between them, the room they sat in and, obliquely, their relationship.

Something inside Rosie begged her not to set off the bomb that was primed to detonate. She knew that the thing James was steeling himself to say couldn't be unheard once spoken aloud, any more than a lobbed grenade could be unexploded after blowing up a building. Nevertheless, her need to understand what was happening squashed the urge not to ask.

'Tell me what you *mean*, James. Say it with words. I don't get it,' Rosie cried, and her eyes began to swim with tears as the lie left her lips.

She might have quit university after only a term, but she was plenty smart enough to know where this discussion was heading – even if she didn't want to think it possible. In recent weeks, she'd convinced herself James's nervous behaviour might mean marriage was imminent. Now, his edginess made a different sort of sense. She cringed at her own stupidity.

'I just feel like we're not good together anymore,' James murmured, his ashen face desperate and pleading.

Rosie had seen enough break-ups in soaps and TV dramas to understand how this was supposed to go. There should be shouting. Swearing. Maybe some smashing of china or glassware thrown into the mix.

As it was, she felt too winded to scream or get violent with James. She was numb, immobile, incredulous – even though there was no reason to doubt that he meant what he was saying.

'So, what? You're unhappy?' Rosie asked, feeling tears rolling down her face.

'Not unhappy,' James said in a rush. 'Just . . . not ready. You know I've made a lot of changes lately. I realised I wasn't living my best life – that there might be more out there for me, and that I didn't have to . . . plod on with things as they were.'

The words were a volley of punches to Rosie's gut.

'Plod on? *Not ready*?' she repeated. 'We've been together almost ten years, James. Am I supposed to believe you felt ready after five years, or seven, but not now? It makes no sense.'

'I don't want to settle down,' he said.

Rosie leapt to her feet and stared at him. She was furious with him for making her extract this confession as though it were forced and untrue, proffered only under torture.

'You've got a funny way of showing it,' Rosie spat back, anger finally flaring. 'I've spent the best part of a decade washing your underpants and buying your mother's birthday cards.'

James seemed to shrink back into the sofa cushions, intimidated by her ire. 'I'm sorry. Really, I am.'

'You still haven't told me *why*. And I need to know. Help me make sense of all this.' She felt the words *I thought you were about to ask me to marry you* dancing on the tip of her tongue and bit them back. She felt humiliated enough as it was.

'Surely you can feel we've grown apart over the last few months,' he said. 'We don't want the same things anymore – we don't have as much in common. I've been concentrating on . . . building a better me, I suppose. That's the journey I'm on now.'

Rosie ground her teeth. Beneath the sting of the clear implication that she was not committed to her own self-improvement, a sad voice in some recess of her mind whispered, *Building a better me? The journey you're on? And here was I thinking we were on that journey together.*

Out loud, she said: 'We have *everything* in common. We live together. I'm the person your office rang when your appendix burst and you had to be rushed to hospital. You've bought me tampons from the corner shop. We jointly own a tumble dryer, for fuck's sake!'

James deflated a little, as if this barrage of banal facts had knocked the wind out of his sails. After a moment, he drew himself up to look at her and said, 'I don't think I want those things anymore. I don't want a "tumble dryer" kind of life.'

'What the fuck does that mean?' Rosie said, exasperated. 'You don't want a life where you can get clothes dry in the middle of winter?'

Not, she thought bitterly, that James would ever consider such a thing. She genuinely couldn't remember the last time he'd done a load of washing.

'I want a life of adventure!' he cried, somewhat lamely. 'This is precisely the problem! I don't want to be focusing on this kind of stuff.'

You don't *focus on 'this kind of stuff'. You don't have to,* Rosie thought – realising with a sickening jolt that the care she took of him was not only under-appreciated, it apparently went entirely unnoticed.

It astounded Rosie that James seemed convinced she was holding him back in some way, when in fact she had enabled so much of his life. It cut her to the bone that he saw her presence as no more interesting or necessary than that of a standard domestic appliance they'd bought in the January sales two years ago.

'So *I'm* the reason your life feels mundane?' she asked, stifling a sob. Rosie's heart throbbed. Every bad thing she'd ever thought about herself, every admonishment for not being slim or beautiful enough, every failed diet and every life-changing routine she'd abandoned . . . They all weighed on her so hard in this moment that she felt like she'd punctured a lung.

'No!' James cried, without conviction. 'But you're *content*. I'm not.'

With his accusation ringing in her ears, Rosie noticed James's eyes move towards his gym bag. With another lurch, she understood that he hadn't simply dumped it on the floor on his return from a workout – he'd packed it in readiness for leaving her.

An icy fist squeezed her insides as she realised she hadn't asked the most obvious question – that it hadn't even occurred to her until now. 'James, be honest with me, please,' she said. 'Is there someone else?'

'*No!*' he said again, his voice almost a yelp. 'This is about me. About where I'm at and what I want.'

Rosie laughed bitterly. 'More like what – and who – you *don't* want.'

Her eyes roamed the room, seeking comfort in the familiar. She found none as she took in the framed photograph of them on holiday in Crete, the wine rack full of 'special occasion' bottles and the bookcase that housed her most treasured novels, as well as his handful of non-fiction favourites. Everything she looked at spoke of their comfortable coexistence: of two lives woven together over long years, in a way she had never imagined unpicking.

As she turned back to look at James, Rosie noticed for the first time that there was an envelope on the sofa seat next to him. Her name was written on it in his haphazard, almost childlike scrawl.

She felt cool sweat begin beading on her skin, soaking the back of her neck. Her heartbeat drummed in her ears and her breathing grew shallow. She already knew the answer, but she asked the question anyway. 'What's that?'

'Oh. Ah. It's nothing,' James said, extending a protective hand to cover it.

'It's not nothing. It's an envelope,' Rosie said, 'and it's got my name on it. Give it to me, please.'

'Rosie, honestly – you don't need—'

'Don't you *dare* try and tell me what I need,' she warned him, cold rage ringing from every word. 'Give me that envelope or so help me I will come over there and take it from you.'

He handed it to her. She held it between a quaking fingertip and thumb, the way she'd have handled a dirty tissue.

'What will I find out if I open it? What does it say?'

'Rosie, *please*—' James begged. His eyes were alight with alarm.

Realising she didn't need him to respond, she said: 'You were going to leave me a *note*. You were planning to move out without saying goodbye – without even *speaking* to me – and let me find a letter when I got home. After *ten years*. What the fuck, James?'

Shivering with hurt and shock, and seized by a strange urge to laugh hysterically at how crazy this all was, she glared at him. James hung his head but said nothing, silenced by Rosie's unflinching – and entirely accurate – assessment of his intentions.

'So, where are you going to stay?' she asked, nodding in the direction of his bag.

'With a friend from the gym. Nobody you know. Just for a week or two, probably, while I sort myself out.'

This brief mention of practicalities seemed to pull James from a stupor. He stood up, then shuffled awkwardly from foot to foot like he was waiting for permission to leave. How very like him, Rosie thought: even now, he needed her to be the one who took action – dealt the final blow.

'*Nobody I know*,' she parroted. 'I'm not sure I even know *you* anymore, James. How could you do this? I mean, who are you?'

'I'm still me,' he said, in a quiet voice that, to Rosie's ears, sounded far sorrier for itself than it had any right to.

'You're not,' she informed him. 'Yes, the James I knew always tried to avoid confrontation, but this . . . it's pathetic. Cowardly. More than that, it's cruel. I'd never have believed you capable of it.'

Still he stood there, staring at his feet like a naughty child facing dismissal from the head teacher's office. Rosie noticed he was already wearing trainers, ready to make his getaway.

As he glanced at the fitness watch on his wrist, Rosie couldn't resist spitting: 'Waiting for something, are you? Got somewhere urgent to be?' Her voice was so hard it sounded strange to her own ears. James flushed scarlet.

'I . . . oh god, I don't know,' James answered. 'Er . . . I suppose there were things I wanted – *needed* – to tell you. I didn't want to end it like this.'

Something like pride flamed inside Rosie then: a powerful, self-preserving urge to take back some agency in a situation that had totally blindsided her. She wiped her face free of tears with her fingertips and willed herself not to cry anymore.

'I'm sure there's nothing you need to say that isn't written in your letter,' she quipped. He flinched at her sarcasm.

'Seriously, don't let me keep you,' she went on. She gestured for him to follow her towards the flat door.

'Don't forget your bag.' She pointed at it, all too aware that it would be standard James behaviour to leave it behind, then have to come back for it later.

She marched up the corridor and he moped after her so pathetically that an unversed onlooker might have believed Rosie had dumped him, rather than the other way around.

As Rosie reached for the latch on the door so she could open it and hustle him out, the buzzer sounded. There was someone at the main entrance of the building, wanting to be let in.

'Who on earth is that?' Rosie demanded.

James bit his bottom lip, but said nothing.

She picked up the old plastic intercom and said, 'Yes?'

'It's Ali here. I have your pizza,' explained the person on the other end of the line.

'My what?'

'Your *pizza*,' Ali repeated, audibly annoyed by her slowness. 'Sides, too. And dips.'

'Fine,' Rosie said, and pressed the button that would open the outside door for him. Then she turned and fixed a steely glare on James.

'Please correct me if I've got any of this wrong. You came home early from work so you could play *Kill the Nazi Zombies*—'

'*Call of Duty*,' James put in, without thinking. Rosie stared daggers at him and he said, 'Sorry,' under his breath.

'You wanted to play *Kill the Nazi Zombies* for a bit,' Rosie ploughed on, 'because you knew you wouldn't fit your PlayStation into the overnight bag you've packed SO YOU CAN LEAVE ME. You're sadder about saying a short-term goodbye to your games console than you are about the end of our relationship – which you intended to finish by *leaving me a letter*, like we're in Year Nine and you've decided you don't want to snog me behind the bike sheds anymore.'

James looked at her almost imploringly. He didn't want to be the bad guy, Rosie realised – or at least, not *this* bad a guy.

Too fucking late, she thought.

There was a knock at the door.

Rosie opened it and Ali, their Domino's delivery driver, handed her a large box upon which several smaller ones were stacked. She took them from him, checked they'd been paid for and thanked him.

'And perhaps worst of all,' she said, turning back to James after the door had closed again, 'you ordered pizza to eat while you played your games. PIZZA. With actual DOUGH. For fuck's sake, how many of those cauliflower-based abominations have I suffered through while you've been committed to eating less gluten?'

'I . . . I know it's bad,' James mumbled, his face flaming. 'I think I ordered it so I could stress-eat.'

Rosie felt her face tighten into what she hoped was the most withering look she'd ever given anyone. 'Oh, I'm sure dumping me by letter after a few rounds of your favourite shoot-'em-up adventure would have been *super* stressful,' she said, derision dripping from every word.

James heaved his bag off the floor. Leaving a healthy gap between them, Rosie reopened the flat door and stood aside for him. Head bent low, he slunk through it almost as though he was trying not to be noticed.

Before she could shut the door behind him, James turned. There was something like hope in his eyes, and it made Rosie's blood boil. Instinct, plus a decade's worth of experience, told her he was perilously close to suggesting that, after a little time, they could still be in each other's lives platonically.

'Don't tell me we can get over this, James,' she said. 'We can't. If you go now, there's no coming back – not even as friends.' She knew she meant it, even though everything she'd hoped for – her vision of the life she thought they'd live together – was caving in on itself like a dying star.

Then she noticed that James's eyes were fixed on the hot, slightly soggy takeaway boxes she was still clutching.

'Oh my god,' Rosie breathed. 'You *weren't* going to say we could stay close. You were going to ask if you could take your pizza with you.'

James recoiled as Rosie advanced towards the open doorway. Finally overcome with shame, he shifted his gaze to the floor at the same time as he raised his hands, ready to receive the long-forbidden contraband carbs he'd ordered. It made Rosie think of a Catholic churchgoer awaiting communion.

She took a long, hard look at him and wondered how she could have got so much so wrong. She'd put this man on a pedestal at the centre of her life – yet he'd been prepared to walk out of it without doing her the basic courtesy of telling her, to her face, that their relationship was over.

'Goodbye, James,' she said, praying that every scrap of the contempt she felt for him at that moment was clear in those two icy words. He backed away in shock.

Allowing herself one last look at him, Rosie nudged the flat door towards its frame. 'Thanks for dinner, by the way!' she called, as it clicked decisively into place.

Chapter 6

As Rosie munched on a large slice of Pepperoni Passion, a number of questions began to take shape in her mind.

First among them was how she'd ever allowed James to convince her they should no longer order takeaway on a Friday night. Even in these dire circumstances, the combination of melted mozzarella, spicy sausage and squishy bread base was heavenly.

More uncomfortable was the question of how she could have misread the state of her relationship so catastrophically. Had it been in terminal decline for months, or even years? How long ago had her idea of what she and James *should* be to one another parted company with the reality of how things were?

More prosaically, how would they divide up ten years' worth of stuff? She felt nausea seize her as she contemplated what might happen to the flat, though there'd surely be some time to work that out.

Then again, James might even change his mind about leaving – think better of it and beg her to forgive him. She'd said there was no way back for them after this, but now the heat of the moment had cooled, she knew she might waver if the alternative was saying goodbye to the man she'd thought she'd marry *and* losing the home she loved.

Briefly, Rosie considered digging out the ancient bottle of whisky that she knew lurked in the drinks cupboard – but the sound of the door buzzer intervened before she could start searching.

She pressed the button to open the building's main door since she already knew who was there. She opened the flat door, too, only to see A. Thomas pushing a collapsed cardboard box into the recycling bin beside the post table. He had his back to her, and she was momentarily transfixed by the smooth movement of muscles beneath his white t-shirt.

It seemed he'd unpacked some garment made from a material Rosie could only describe as 'rubbery-looking', then draped it over one shoulder while he disposed of the wrapping. What on earth *was* that?

She locked eyes with Niamh, who had just appeared at the other end of the corridor. Her best friend threw a glance in A. Thomas's direction, then mimed fanning herself as best she could with a bottle of wine in each hand.

Seconds later, an entirely oblivious A. Thomas straightened up and turned to acknowledge Rosie.

'All right?' he said to her in his still-unplaceable accent, then inclined his head politely towards Niamh.

'Hi,' Rosie managed. 'Yeah. I'm good! Great! Thanks.'

She marvelled at her own inarticulacy – not to mention what her mouth had just said. *Great?* She was anything but.

As A. Thomas disappeared up the stairs, Niamh winced and shook her head despairingly at Rosie. Once they were inside the flat, she said: 'I suppose I should be pleased that, even in this situation, you're not beyond being flustered at the sight of a gorgeous man.'

'I am not *flustered*,' Rosie insisted, taking a bottle of pale, chilled rosé from Niamh and leading her towards the kitchen. 'I'm in a general state of shock.'

'Of course you are. Come here,' Niamh said, depositing her own bottle next to Rosie's on the counter and pulling her in for a hug. 'For the record, though, it is one hundred per cent normal to come over all unnecessary when someone that hot is sighted in possession of a wetsuit.'

'A what?' Rosie asked, stepping back and frowning.

'A wetsuit. That thing he was carrying. A skintight garment for swimming, surfing, diving . . . Emphasis on *skintight*.' She grinned lasciviously.

Rosie rolled her eyes and laughed a little, grateful for Niamh's indefatigable commitment to smutty jokes.

'So . . . what the fuck happened, Rose?' Niamh asked, more serious now. She uncorked a bottle of wine as Rosie thrust the pizza box in her direction, then placed two glasses on either side of it. They pulled out the two stools that sat just beneath the worktop, sinking down to sit on them.

Rosie was surprised to discover that, despite its inevitably seismic consequences, the story of James's departure took her mere minutes to recount.

'Oh my god,' Niamh said when she'd finished, her words filtered through a mouthful of cheesy garlic bread. 'I'm fucking *rabid*. I don't think I've ever been angrier.'

Rosie managed another laugh. 'Really?'

'Yes!' Niamh cried, waving Rosie's disbelief away and picking up another slice of pizza. 'I'm plotting James's slow and painful death as we speak. I cannot believe he's done this to you.'

'Can't you?' Rosie asked. She wasn't quite sure why she'd said it, but the silence that followed her question struck her as significant.

'I'm shocked,' Niamh eventually said, after what Rosie concluded was a fortifying gulp of wine. 'Truly shocked that he's behaved so brutally. I mean, writing you a letter and leaving it for you to find . . . What is he, twelve?'

Rosie shook her head sadly, eyeing the sealed envelope that she'd left on the coffee table. She'd told herself that reading it was hardly a matter of urgency; that tearing it open would elevate its importance, giving its contents a gravity they surely didn't deserve. Besides, what could it possibly say that she didn't know already, or that would make her situation worse?

'I sense a "but" on the horizon,' Rosie said, turning back to look at her friend.

'OK. I'm not entirely surprised something's kicked off between you,' Niamh admitted. 'I'd never have expected him to be *such* a spineless wanker, but . . .'

'But . . . ?' Rosie repeated.

'Look, I don't want you to hold this against me in the event he turns up tomorrow, admits what an utter twat he's been and begs for forgiveness. But I've been convinced for a while that he doesn't appreciate what he's got in you. He takes you for granted, Rosie. As his body's shrunk, his head has swollen. He's mistaken having an amazing, supportive girlfriend for someone who's *weighing him down* or *hampering his potential*.' Her voice dripped with sarcasm.

'Ouch,' Rosie murmured.

'However, it won't be long before he realises that life without you is a lot harder and *much* less exciting than he imagined,' Niamh insisted hotly. 'Tosser.'

'You think so?' Rosie asked, her tone involuntarily brightening.

'Absolutely,' Niamh said, sounding considerably less happy at the prospect. 'Do you want honesty here, Rose?'

'I think so . . . yeah,' Rosie said, summoning courage.

'Well then, I think the question isn't *whether* James will come back to you, I think it's *when* – and, more importantly, if you'll let him. You need to think about how he's treated you. Ask yourself whether you could ever really trust him again after this. I'll hold my tongue on that point for now, but should you decide you want the full Ted Talk, you know where I am.'

'I do,' Rosie agreed.

'I guess the pressing question now is practical: what's the deal with this place?'

Niamh gestured at their lovingly renovated surroundings, and Rosie felt moisture pool in her eyes. 'I've no idea. Which is why I suppose I should read his letter.'

After blinking away tears and wiping her sticky fingers on a piece of kitchen roll, she padded back to the sitting room and picked up the envelope.

Inside it was a single sheet of paper covered in James's

haphazard script: one stream-of-consciousness paragraph that felt insultingly brief. The fact he hadn't put much time or effort into his 'Dear Rosie' missive compounded her hurt that it existed at all.

It stated that, in hindsight, the break-up had been 'inevitable' for some time; that James felt he and Rosie had drifted into being housemates or friends rather than lovers. On this, she could grudgingly admit, he had something approaching a point. Their sex had hardly been on fire recently – but that was as much down to James's relentless exercise regime as any disinclination on Rosie's part.

He wrote that he wasn't sure they wanted the same sort of future anymore, and conflated this with his new-found commitment to 'health and wellness goals'. Implying that her refusal to eschew rice in favour of quinoa was the reason why he couldn't commit seemed nothing short of absurd. Rosie swore out loud as her eyes swept over the words, and – though it must have cost every scrap of her self-control – Niamh resisted the urge to ask why.

Eventually, Rosie placed the thin piece of A5 next to the half-eaten, rapidly congealing pizza and put her head in her hands. The sudden wetness of her cheeks and chin alerted her to the fact that she was crying.

She felt torn open by James's letter in a way she hadn't by their face-to-face discussion. It was as if the written word had a power his clumsy, garbled reasoning had lacked when spoken aloud. Between James's carelessly scribbled lines was the message: *I think I can do better than you, and I've decided to try.*

He didn't want her anymore, and seemed certain he didn't need her. Apparently, he didn't think she was good enough, attractive enough, *anything* enough to stake his future on. Rosie had given James her heart, had put everything she had into making them a home and would have promised to take care of him for the rest of her life. Yet he'd walked away as if the love she offered him was cheap or trivial.

Would this have happened if she'd been prettier, sexier or skinnier? Would James have done this if she'd agreed to join him at weight training or willingly committed to the keto diet? Rosie didn't think so, and a part of her took vicious aim at what this revealed: a failure to value someone who loved him for what lay beneath the less-than-perfect surface – a laser focus on the superficial that she'd never seen in him before. At the same time, however, the truth *hurt*. It kicked her in the too-fleshy stomach she'd spent half her life desperately trying not to hate.

'Rose . . .' Niamh said softly, bringing her back to the present. 'Rosie, love, let me at you.' She'd stood up, and now covered Rosie's shuddering, hunched-over body with her taller, leaner frame. She soothed and stroked her friend's light-blonde hair, shushing her until Rosie's flash flood of tears had abated.

Once they were both seated again, Rosie steeled herself and read the worst passage aloud. It pertained to the division of her and James's things, as well as the small matter of their joint tenancy agreement.

I know you're very attached to the flat. Sorry if me leaving means you have to move but I can't carry on spending on the place now I'm no longer living there. As we've just paid rent for next month, you should have three weeks to work out what you want to do. Guess that's find a flatmate to take the spare room or move on? I'll come by at some stage to collect the rest of my things, but I won't take furniture, etc. Goes without saying, that's your stuff . . .

'What the hell?' Niamh shouted. 'Selfish *bastard*. Is it even legal for him to just piss off like this?'

'I have a horrible feeling it is,' Rosie sighed.

'It can't be, surely?'

Rosie massaged her temples. She could feel a headache forming there, either from the wine – she and Niamh were now well into the second bottle – or the sheer stress of her situation.

'If I remember right, we're jointly and severally liable for the rent.'

'And what on earth does that mean?'

Rosie snorted, almost amused. 'Aren't you married to a lawyer?'

'Yeah, but I'm a marketing-slash-events innovator, remember? I don't read legal documents – there's a guy at head office who does that for me.'

'It means,' Rosie explained, 'that the landlord – whoever they may be – can pursue *me* for both halves of the rent if James doesn't pay. So I either stump up the cash, find someone to take the spare room or move out.'

Her valiant effort to sound matter-of-fact and in control backfired as her voice cracked on the final two words. Out loud and uttered to another person, they sounded far worse than they had in her head.

Rage and despair fought for supremacy inside her. *Three weeks.* That was all the time she had to piece together a plan for keeping the home he knew she loved.

And he was planning to take next to nothing with him – to pick himself up and relocate to god knew where, as if he were some sleek, modernist sofa that made no sense in the shabby chic life they'd shared. If she'd been in any doubt about James's lack of affection for the flat, she wasn't now.

'Does he seriously expect you to believe he can't afford to stump up another month's rent?' Niamh demanded.

'So it seems,' Rosie said, her voice flat.

They both knew how much he earned, and it was roughly three times Rosie's salary.

Three weeks. It was nowhere near enough time to find and vet a potential flatmate, and James surely knew there was no way she could afford to keep the place on by herself. What was more, he hadn't considered that, even if she contacted their faceless new landlord and explained her intention to leave the property today, she'd need to give a full calendar month's notice.

'What does he expect you to do?' Niamh ranted, standing up from her stool and pacing angrily around the kitchen.

'Ask my parents for money, probably,' Rosie said. That was certainly what he'd do in her shoes. Mr and Mrs Gardiner were solidly middle-class retirees who lived in a detached period cottage in Cheshire. Though James had never admitted it, Rosie was sure they regularly injected his old childhood savings account with spare cash. Her parents, while by no means poor, were far less able to throw money at her problems – and nor were they inclined to.

Colin and Julie Butler had never understood why their daughter wanted to live in London in the first place. Neither Mum nor Dad had managed to make sense of the sudden 'independent streak' that had seen Rosie depart the family home after her grandfather's death and move in with Niamh.

Rosie could perfectly predict what would happen if she asked them for assistance. They'd consider it throwing good money after bad and encourage her to move back home instead – only to end up reminding her on a daily basis how sad it was to be single and still living with your parents at thirty-two.

She shuddered at the thought. Going back to Braintree to live with them – as well as thirty-year-old Michael, whose continued presence in their suburban semi somehow never attracted the same opprobrium hers would – was not an option.

Sighing, Rosie heaved herself up and – in the absence of any better ideas – decided it might be time for bed. Perhaps some bright, shiny solution to her problems would appear overnight, revealing itself in a dream just as the melody of 'Yesterday' supposedly came to a comatose Paul McCartney.

'You should head home,' she said to Niamh, glancing at the oven clock and realising with horror that it was almost one a.m. 'You have that spa break tomorrow – you'll want to get on the road early so you can make the most of it.' Niamh and Brendan had organised an overnight getaway – a chance to fully relax after her first month back at work – and Rosie knew how precious 'couple time' was to them now they had the twins to take care of.

'Are you *sure* you're OK?'

'I will be,' Rosie promised. 'Dinner this week? I could do with something to look forward to.'

'Definitely,' Niamh said. She stood up, then tapped at her phone to order an Uber. 'How about Thursday again? And Rose, call me any time you want to talk. I don't care if it's the middle of the night. Let's face it, I'm probably going to be awake anyway. You're not alone in this – I'm with you every step of the way.'

Rosie swallowed the golf ball-sized lump that had risen in her throat. 'You're bloody amazing, you are,' she said. 'I love you. It means the world to me that you dropped everything to come over here tonight.'

'It was nothing,' Niamh said, smiling. 'Don't mention it. Honestly, the cab fare was worth it just for another sighting of Nameless Neighbour, who – let the record show – actually *spoke to you* this evening.' Rosie rolled her eyes, instructing herself not to blush or wonder what A. Thomas might look like in that wetsuit.

A short while later, as she brushed her teeth, she caught her own reflection in the mirror above the bathroom sink. Her skin was blotchy and her eyes were swollen – the lids angrily pink and puffed up, like she was experiencing some severe allergic reaction.

Perhaps she was; maybe her body was literally rejecting the idea of being single again after all this time. The green of her irises clashed violently with their bloodshot surroundings, and her lips were ghostly pale. *I look like a reanimated corpse*, she thought – *like a creature from one of James's video games*. How was that for irony?

And if she was single, that made James her ex-boyfriend. It sounded strange – like it couldn't be real. The only ex Rosie had ever had before was Liam Brody, a boy she'd dated for eight months at sixth form. That she now needed to count James alongside him – consign them to the same sparsely populated category in her romantic history – was both unbelievable and unmistakably clear.

She collapsed into bed, willing sleep to come for her. There were the usual household chores to do tomorrow, not to mention the small matter of beginning the search for a new flatmate.

At least, she reasoned, the spare room was empty – a deliberately blank canvas that someone could move into immediately. She suppressed the thought that she'd hoped to soon brighten it with wall art, picture books and soft toys. The room would have to become something else now, Rosie told herself – and so would she.

Chapter 7

'Easy, Roly,' Michael warned as his sister reached to pluck another crispy roast potato from the serving dish, 'that'll go straight to your hips.' He used Rosie's hated childhood nickname in full and gleeful awareness that she'd be needled by it.

Beneath her mother's dining table, she balled her hands into fists so tight that her nails bit into her palms. Sunday lunch at Mum and Dad's house was a monthly custom so sacrosanct that it rarely occurred to her to swerve it. Today, Rosie had reasoned that while feigning illness might earn her a temporary reprieve from facing her family, it could also arouse suspicion. The last thing she needed was to spend the day fending off enquiries as to whether she was pregnant. Defiantly, Rosie forked a tiny spud with edges so crispy they looked crystallised, then popped it into her mouth. It tasted like heaven, but she couldn't quite manage to enjoy it – and she didn't miss the despairing look that crossed her mother's face as she chewed. Julie had downed eating tools some time ago, ever conscious of the threat all foods posed to her obsessively maintained, ultra-petite frame.

'What time are you expecting James back?' she asked, her gaze still trained on the cutlery in her daughter's hands – seemingly willing her to put it down and stop eating.

Not for the first time that afternoon, Rosie asked herself why she'd decided to lie about James's whereabouts. Perhaps she lacked the savagery needed to obliterate her family's strong affection for him – the killer instinct that would see her lay bare his selfishness and cowardice, then dare them to try and absolve him.

Yet it wasn't quite that simple. Deep down, Rosie didn't trust her parents and brother to be unequivocally on her side. They'd pity her loss, rather than reassure her she could move on and survive without James. Even worse, they might deflect blame for the break-up onto her. Rosie still remembered the precise order and tone of Julie's words when she'd told her that Liam – away at university in Plymouth – had finished with her over the phone. 'It's a shame, darling, but I have to admit I saw this coming. We're your family, so we have to love you – but you're never going to be everyone's cup of tea. He's probably found some skinny girl who likes all those water sports he's into.'

Buried beneath Rosie's lack of faith in her parents lay an uncomfortable truth she was trying to ignore. Despite how hurt and angry she was, she didn't want to assassinate James's character so comprehensively that it was beyond saving. If she trash-talked him today, she'd have some serious explaining to do if they got back together in a fortnight's time – and a part of her still wondered whether James might think better of leaving and ask if he could come home again. It was the same part that couldn't swear she'd reject him if he did.

'Earth to Rosie . . . ?' Julie said, laughing. 'I asked you what time James would be home tonight.'

'Oh. Sorry. I've no idea,' Rosie said, shrugging. It struck her that this was the first fully honest thing she'd said since arriving at her parents' 1970s-built semi several hours ago.

'What is it he's doing again?' Colin asked, helping himself to another slice of roast beef.

'Sorting out some IT crisis at work,' Rosie told him.

'Ah,' he said, 'he's a good lad, isn't he? The sort you can trust in these situations. Hope he's being paid overtime on a Sunday, mind.'

Shame at her own dishonesty and indignation at the phrase 'good lad' mingled hot in Rosie's chest.

'I suppose you don't have to deal with insurance emergencies at the weekend,' Colin went on. 'They'd be above your pay grade, ha ha.'

Rosie cringed again and forced a smile. 'Definitely.'

She knew that her dad didn't intend to make her feel small or disparage her job. It would simply never occur to him that she might want a role with the sort of responsibilities James had – fictional though today's work crisis was.

Colin's disinterest in Rosie's career prospects came from the same place as her parents' bewilderment that she'd stayed on at school for A-levels and applied to university. They hadn't discouraged her, as such, but they'd been more than happy for her to shelve the idea of getting a degree – not least because the prospect of borrowing thousands of pounds for the privilege of studying felt extraordinary to them.

'Great roasties, Mum,' Michael said, as he bit messily into the last one, not bothering to ask anyone else if they'd like it first.

Rosie glanced at him across the table. He was as tall and wiry as ever, though he had the greyish, dull complexion of someone whose acquaintance with vegetables was casual at best.

'Ahh, thanks, love,' Julie said, smiling at him.

Rosie, who had been entirely responsible for cooking what she had to admit were *stellar* roast potatoes, gaped at her mother's audacity. Julie winked at her daughter surreptitiously – a gesture that Rosie guessed was supposed to imply gratitude.

Typically, Sunday lunch prep was dumped on Rosie the moment she arrived at her parents' house, while Colin and Michael were free to watch whatever football match was on TV or slope off to the pub. It wasn't unusual for Julie to disappear entirely, too, feigning some vital errand that couldn't wait until after the roast was ready.

Today it had been the 'urgent' delivery of the latest TrueYOU catalogue to a neighbour. Rosie's mother had recently begun capitalising on her reputation as a local glamourpuss by selling makeup and skincare products that promised to render the wearer 'empowered, enlivened and irresistible – at any age!'. Julie's success at hawking lipsticks, moisturisers and anti-ageing serums to the more mature women in their neighbourhood – not to mention encouraging them to join her 'team' of vendors – came as no surprise to Rosie. However, it was also clear that while TrueYOU believers styled themselves 'network marketers', the set-up was worryingly reminiscent of a pyramid scheme.

Julie Butler was perfectly capable of hard work and efficiency, but tended not to bother with either when her daughter was around. To some extent, Rosie couldn't blame her for this. A lifetime spent running around after Colin and Michael meant Mum seized on any opportunity to slow down a little. It had always been the same: from a fairly young age Rosie had helped with housework and cooking, and then had taken the lead on looking after Grandpa George when he'd unexpectedly moved in with the family during her ill-fated first term at university.

He'd broken his hip while out playing bowls with an old army friend, and – while his wits remained as sharp as ever – his physical health had deteriorated with alarming speed. Rosie was shocked at the sight of him when she came home for the Christmas holidays. George's recovery from hip replacement surgery was slow, and at the end of December the family was informed he'd need knee operations, too. Then came a cancer diagnosis. What should have been a brief stay at his son and daughter-in-law's home would likely become permanent.

As the time drew near for Rosie to head back to her hall of residence, Colin and Julie began discussing care home options – and with no pause for internal debate, she told them to stop. Grandpa George had always been kind to her, seeming to think rather more of her than her own parents did. He'd often said that Rosie, with her silvery-blonde hair, curvy figure and green eyes, was a beautiful throwback: the image of his late, much-loved wife, Margery, whom Rosie had never met. While she'd laughed this off, it had meant something to her that he cared for her so deeply, and thought her capable of 'making something of herself'.

She couldn't – *wouldn't* – allow him to be shunted into some sterile, unknown place to be looked after by overworked, underpaid strangers. She'd press pause on getting her degree, she told herself: postpone it until the time was right to pick it back up again.

Rosie still couldn't bring herself to regret it, even though the temporary suspension of her psychology studies had stuck. The only thing she felt bad about was the fact that she'd broken her promise to her grandfather. Having assured him she'd head back to university as soon as she was able, she'd let the idea drift until it felt vague, distant and eventually impossible. On the rare occasions she let herself stop and think about it, she knew this would have disappointed him.

'Do you three want some pud?' Rosie heard her mother ask – the fact of her own, upfront refusal to eat dessert implicit in the question. Michael and Colin answered in the affirmative as Julie rose from her seat and passed from the small dining room back into the kitchen. Though Rosie hadn't asked for any, when her mother returned she plonked a large helping of shop-bought vanilla cheesecake in front of her.

Rosie didn't even *like* cheesecake – she never had – but she picked at it anyway, unable to bear the prospect of her mother's beaming approval should she reject it. No doubt Julie would assume she was dieting if Rosie pushed her plate away untouched; perhaps her mother would even ask if she was trying to slim down in advance of wedding dress shopping.

The thought made Rosie's lunch jump around in her stomach. Determinedly, she forced down a final bite of the fluffy-textured, synthetically sweetened confection before setting her fork down with a clang.

At the same moment, her dad and brother abandoned their empty plates and made for the sitting room. It had never occurred to either of them that their help with tidying up after a meal might be appreciated, so Rosie was unsurprised that the revelation didn't strike now. She stood to help her mother clear the table, collecting crockery, cutlery and condiments for transfer to the kitchen.

'I hope James isn't out too late,' Julie said, showing very little interest in helping Rosie clean up. 'I don't like to think of you by yourself in that flat of an evening. You're not in the best part of town, are you?'

As Rosie rinsed congealing gravy from a plate, she felt her temper threaten to flare. She'd spent more evenings by herself lately than she could count, but she'd never once felt uneasy or insecure. In every way that mattered, she felt safer, happier and more settled in her little ground-floor flat than she ever had in this house. The home she'd made for herself was a safe space: somewhere she could live, not just exist, without feeling as though she would inevitably disappoint someone or end up the butt of a joke.

Besides, while Walthamstow wasn't perfect, it was far from the urban hellscape her mother imagined. Like many parts of the capital, it had become increasingly gentrified in recent years. The presence of a health food store that sold loose-leaf herbal teas at £12 a jar made it clear the area's demographic was shifting.

'You don't need to worry,' Rosie told her mother, her tone final. 'Believe it or not, our street's quite sought-after these days.' She thought fondly of Mr Bettini, who could easily have raised the rent on the flat to reflect its rising market value. He never had, but Rosie's stomach swooped as she remembered that sooner or later her new landlord was bound to reconsider the sum she should be paying each month.

She'd spent the previous afternoon sending out speculative emails and texts to various friends and acquaintances who might need somewhere to stay, without spelling out the reason for her sudden desire to let the spare room. She'd also listed it for rent on various 'find a room' websites, not at all sure how she'd tell a potentially psycho applicant from a non-threatening normal.

Once she'd stacked her parents' dishwasher and set the hot tap running to fill the washing-up bowl, Rosie pulled her handbag from the coat hooks by the back door and dug out her phone. She hadn't had any responses this morning, but maybe some had come in since then.

Yes! There were three.

To her dismay she found that all the messages she'd received were from men – despite her advert's clear, bold type statement that she would only consider a female flatmate. One guy had asked what she looked like, and another had attached an image to his note of introduction.

Fearful that it might contain a shot of some bodily appendage she had no desire to see, Rosie forwarded the message to Niamh, who'd always been stronger of stomach. She put three question marks in the subject line.

Seconds later, Niamh responded:

😭 DO NOT LOOK. Definitely not a candidate for cohabitation. Block him without answering – though god knows you could be forgiven for asking why he's showing *that* off as though he has any kind of bragging rights.

Rosie heard herself snigger.

'Is that James?' her mum asked, nodding her head towards the phone in Rosie's right hand.

'Yeah,' Rosie said. The lie felt like ashes in her mouth. Then inspiration struck: 'He's on his way home, so I should make a move soon.'

Julie looked around the kitchen, taking in the crusty baking trays and used saucepans stacked on the worktop. She looked dismayed.

Rosie shook her head, her resolve to flee the scene crumbling. She pulled on a pair of rubber gloves. 'Fine,' she said, eyes locked onto Julie's, warning her not to try another disappearing act. 'I'll wash if you dry.'

Chapter 8

As Rosie approached the office on Monday morning, she felt her spirits wilt. Cover 4 U was based on a purpose-built business park made up of austere, warehouse-like buildings. Even without taking the firm's worst clients and staff into consideration, it was a grim place to work. The desks and chairs were cheap and insubstantial, the lighting harsh and the heating unreliable. Even the break room felt unwelcoming, with its ancient, limescale-clogged kettle and pinboard full of 'important notices', most of which were edicts issued by Martin.

In several spots around the claims handlers' area were potted cacti, presumably put there by some well-meaning, naively optimistic HR consultant. Any long-term member of staff would have understood that even succulents seemed unable to thrive in this environment, drooping and yellowing as though death might be preferable to living here.

Rosie arrived at her workstation and waved hello to Ellie, silently nodding in acknowledgement that her friend was already engaged on a call. Ellie threw her a sarcastic thumbs up, but smiled in greeting as she listened to whoever she was dealing with.

'Hey up,' Ellie said a moment later as she removed her headset, pleased her call had ended. 'You all right? You look a bit peaky.'

'I'm fine,' Rosie assured her, glowering at her computer. It was yet to boot up successfully, despite having been switched on several minutes ago.

'Well, you won't be when you check your emails,' Ellie

groaned. 'Martin's booking in one-to-ones with the whole team. He wants to discuss *efficient use of company time*. I've got an appointment first thing tomorrow.'

'Ugh,' Rosie sighed. 'What does that even mean? It's not as if we're sat here reading celebrity gossip or scrolling social media all day – half the websites on the internet are blocked. I couldn't even check the weather forecast the other night . . . Who thinks MetOffice.gov.uk represents a major distraction, for god's sake?'

'Martin,' Ellie said, grimacing. 'He's relentless. I think he was an evil Victorian in a former life – one of those blokes who sent terrified children up chimneys for profit. He stopped me one day last week and demanded to know how many times I'd been to the toilet.'

'No way,' Rosie said, trying not to laugh, all thoughts of her own problems receding as she imagined this tableau.

'Yes, way,' Ellie insisted with a smirk. 'He regretted it, though. I asked him how many times he thought it was acceptable for me to change my tampon during an eight-hour shift.'

Rosie hooted.

'*Then* I innocently suggested we might want to seek HR advice,' Ellie went on. 'See if there was any kind of official guidance on loo breaks for menstruating women. At which point his face went a bit purple and he buggered off upstairs.'

'Amazing,' Rosie said. 'Top-quality work.'

'Wasn't it just?' Ellie smiled. 'I'll make us a brew,' she told Rosie, standing up with a yawn. 'At super high speed, obviously, for maximum, Martin-standard efficiency.'

As Rosie's computer came slowly to life, she switched her mobile to silent and then absent-mindedly checked her social media feeds. Twitter, or whatever she was supposed to call it these days, was typically full of political screeds. She clicked away, on the basis that she was already angry enough.

Instagram offered her nothing of note – just several acquaintances' weekend snaps, plus a reel of a cute kitten chasing a catnip toy. Facebook, it turned out, was the network she should have avoided – and if it hadn't been for her ancient laptop's struggle to load the CRM database, she would have.

Just moments ago, James had been tagged in a photograph at some outdoor sporting event. Based on the greyish sky and the mud spatter on his trainers, legs and shorts, Rosie thought it must have been held yesterday.

He was at what looked like a finish line, with his arm slung around a slender, dark-haired woman. Her taut, toned arms were tanned, exposed in a sleeveless, skintight running vest. Rosie recognised her as a member of James's gym. She had one of those 'hot girl' names that Rosie had always admired, but which she felt too plain and ordinary for herself. Was it Dara? Delilah? No. *Dylan*.

With a jolt, Rosie remembered James had told her this. The woman in the photo had been named after Bob Dylan, her parents' favourite singer-songwriter. Rosie recalled that James had said he thought it was cool – he'd explained that this woman somehow pulled off having a name that sounded as though it should belong to a man. Rosie had smiled at the time, nodding as she thought how nice it was that James had some new, like-minded friends to chat with about his health and fitness.

She felt the breakfast cereal she'd eaten earlier curdle in her stomach. *No, no, no*, she told herself. *Calm down. You cannot throw up all over your own desk.*

But the siren that had begun wailing inside her head wouldn't shut up: *he lied, he lied, he lied*, it sang. Rosie couldn't work out whether she felt devastated, livid or like the world's biggest idiot for taking James at his word – for believing there was nobody else involved in their break-up.

Common sense told her this single image wasn't *absolute proof* he'd cheated – but the adoring expression on his face, which was tilted in Dylan's direction, said otherwise.

'Are you sure you're OK?' Ellie asked, back from the

kitchen and now gazing down at Rosie with an anxious expression on her face. 'You look like you've seen a ghost.'

She placed a large mug of steaming tea on the desk beside her friend, clearly awaiting a response.

'I'm all right, I promise,' Rosie said, managing a shrug. 'Just a bad case of the Mondays.'

Ellie didn't look convinced. The claims line began to ring, and she pointed a finger at Rosie before she could pick up the call.

'I'll get this,' Ellie said. 'You look like you need some caffeine – or maybe a couple of uppers – before you're expected to deal with members of the Great British public this morning.'

'Thanks,' Rosie said sincerely, trying and failing to resist having one last look at the picture of James and Dylan.

She swiped to unlock her phone, only to see a 'sorry, that content no longer exists' message in place of the offending image. Someone had untagged or deleted it within two minutes of it going online. Rosie felt sure she knew why.

Later that day, Rosie made her way upstairs to the first floor of Cover 4 U's two-storey building. She'd been allotted an afternoon slot for her talk with Martin, which she'd accepted in lieu of having any reasonable excuse to avoid it.

The decor up here was no plusher than at ground level, but instead of a series of open-plan workspaces, it boasted several meeting rooms and a clutch of tiny offices. These belonged to team leaders and high-level administrative staff, with one set aside for the firm's rarely seen managing director.

One of the doors bore a shiny nameplate with 'Martin Bell' written on it. Resisting the reflexive eye roll this inspired – Martin had surely bought and attached the thing himself, since none of the other offices had them – Rosie knocked and waited.

A moment later, his voice reached her from inside. 'Enter.'

She shook her head in distaste, twisted the doorknob and went in.

Martin's office was orderly and stark. The blandness of it surprised Rosie, even though she'd been in here several times before. There was precious little of anything personal to be seen, despite the fact he'd occupied the space for as long as they'd worked together. Even Rosie's tiny desk, which she sat at only in shifts, had her favourite pens, a pretty coaster and a half-eaten packet of Hobnobs on it.

Martin's clothes were similarly nondescript: grey slacks, black shoes and a white shirt that, unfortunately, was a little more transparent than Rosie would have liked. She cringed at the realisation that she could see his chest hair through it.

Martin also wore a charcoal-coloured tie – the sort a provincial bank manager might have sported in the 1980s, but which was completely unnecessary in the here and now. He was quite short – only a little taller than Rosie, who was five feet five – and for the last two years had sported what Niamh would have called 'seriously ill-advised facial hair'. This took the form of a wispy goatee that did nothing to strengthen his weak chin.

'Miss Butler,' Martin said, breathing stale coffee fumes in Rosie's direction. 'Please sit.' He gave the statement the same gravity that a High Court judge might employ when instructing a clerk to bring out the defendant.

She sank onto the stiff, unyielding couch on the other side of his desk, but said nothing. Martin's affected formality grated on her, making her feel defensive even though, as far as she knew, she'd done nothing she needed to worry about.

If anything, Rosie felt quietly confident that she was good at customer service – charming, even, compared with some of her colleagues, and by no means a shirker. Nevertheless, she braced herself.

'I'm speaking with all team members about the need to ensure time-wastage is minimised,' Martin began, steepling his fingers and bringing them to rest on what Rosie couldn't avoid thinking of as his surprisingly hirsute chest.

'I'm sure you can appreciate that every minute lost to unproductive activity represents a cost to the company,' Martin went on. 'These are costs we can ill afford in this economy. This issue is of significant interest to senior management, and I've been tasked with creating a strategy that will tackle our budgetary "black hole", shall we say.'

Rosie felt her eyes start to glaze over.

'I see,' she said, not seeing at all.

'Very good,' Martin answered. 'Then you'll also understand, Miss Butler, why I took the decision to review all claims handlers' recent recorded calls. My aim was, of course, to assess them for efficiency.'

'Right,' Rosie nodded, wondering why Martin's speech was modelled after a member of *Downton Abbey*'s landed gentry. If Ellie's intel was correct, he'd been born and brought up in Edmonton.

'I have some concerns about several of your recent calls,' Martin pressed on, frowning. 'No doubt you're aware of what I'm referring to.'

Rosie felt her breath catch in her throat. Was this about Mr Bathurst and his unsuccessful claim? She *had* sort of hung up on him, she supposed – though only after asking if she could help him any further and receiving an emphatic no in response.

'I . . . er—' Rosie mumbled. 'Sorry. No.'

'Indeed? Allow me to explain,' Martin said, shaking his head at her in apparent disappointment. 'First of all: last week you spoke with Mrs Edith Green – a customer based in Coleshill, Buckinghamshire. Your conversation lasted twenty-two minutes, eight of which consisted solely of the lady wittering on about her husband's cataracts.'

'What?' Rosie asked, nonplussed. Even if Martin's close analysis of the timings was correct, she didn't see how they reflected on *her*.

'*Cataracts!*' Martin barked loudly, as if Rosie were hard of hearing rather than baffled by the turn this discussion had taken. 'In what way does allowing the woman to drone on about her other half's eyesight advance us towards our CHIM target? How does it contribute to the growth of our business? More to the point, how does it relate to her claim for a storm-damaged greenhouse?'

Rosie racked her brains, unable to remember what on earth the CHIM target was. She *hated* these stupid acronyms . . . Then, in a flash, it came to her: *Claims Handled In the Month.* 'Well . . . it doesn't,' she said, finally. 'Not directly, anyway. But isn't Cover 4 U known for its excellent customer service? The strapline on all our ads is "low prices, high standards and a human touch".'

Rosie stifled an embarrassed shudder as she quoted this, wondering under what circumstances anyone would ever let *Martin* offer them a 'human touch'. 'The poor woman had just been told that her husband needed surgery and was worried sick,' she pressed on. 'She was overwhelmed – dealing with a load of different problems at once. She needed to talk, and telling her to zip it didn't seem like the best way to proceed.'

'There's good customer service, *then* there's letting a customer talk at you relentlessly while you coo in sympathy,' Martin said triumphantly. 'There's also the matter of your directing the customer to the NHS website for reassurance,' he continued. 'Hardly your job, Miss Butler.'

Rosie took a deep breath and tried to quell her rising annoyance. 'I felt it was the best way to calm her down and get the conversation back on track,' she said. 'I was very aware of the lady's old age. If I'd upset her, it would hardly have reflected well on the company, would it?'

'This meeting is about inefficiency, not Cover 4 U's brand health,' Martin ranted. 'That call, in my judgement, was highly inefficient.'

Rosie swallowed and said nothing, furious as well as mildly nauseated by the phrase 'brand health'.

Martin took her silence as humble acceptance of his

'judgement' and continued: 'Next – your conversation with a Miss Shivani Sharma regarding her car insurance claim.'

Rosie listened as he outlined all the ways in which he believed she'd mishandled the call. Again, she'd supposedly given the customer's worries 'too much airtime'. She'd also been 'overly reassuring' and 'too quick to imply we'd pay out' when she explained that millions of people had bumps and scrapes in their cars – that such incidents were the reason why insurance policies existed.

Rosie remembered this conversation: a panicked call from a twenty-year-old girl who'd grazed the side of her mother's car against a wall in a badly designed multistorey car park. Shivani Sharma had cried as Rosie asked her to explain the incident, struggling to articulate what had happened through her sobs. Only someone with a heart of stone could have stopped themselves offering her a little comfort.

And so it went on. Martin listed four more conversations that he felt Rosie had allowed to 'drift off topic', or during which she'd 'wasted time being unnecessarily pleasant'.

Unnecessarily pleasant? Her mind boggled.

While Martin was capable of separating the speed at which Cover 4 U handled claims from the impression its staff left on customers, Rosie knew this to be a wilfully stupid feat of doublethink. Yes, conversations would move more quickly if she, Ellie and the rest of the team were prepared to be rude, pushy and unsympathetic. However, it was absurd to pretend such briskness wouldn't have consequences for the firm further down the line – especially with the older generation, who were high-value, brand-loyal customers, as Martin might have put it.

How, Rosie asked herself, had she ended up here? Spending the majority of her time in this dreary building, mostly surrounded by dreary people. She was brighter than this, *better* than this, as Niamh so frequently tried to tell her – but she'd believed none of that mattered as long as her home life was happy.

Unnecessarily pleasant. She considered the words again and wondered whether it was possible that hell had frozen over, because – possibly for the first time ever – Martin had said something that resonated with her.

As he ranted on, Rosie thought again about James, and the woman she now suspected he was sleeping with. Perhaps had been sleeping with for a while. He'd talked about her at home – had even seemed a little starry-eyed about her – and his ever-supportive girlfriend hadn't suspected a thing.

The betrayal had hidden in plain sight. Rosie's sheer *niceness* had made it easy for James to do whatever he wanted, from taking motorcycle lessons to setting up a home-brew kit in their garden; from spending all hours exercising to eating his own body weight in chickpeas. Apparently he hadn't drawn the line at consuming colossal amounts of soluble fibre just lately; the aphrodisiac effect of so much roughage had led to him boffing another woman.

'Altogether, Miss Butler,' Martin now said, his tone so swollen with self-importance that it made Rosie feel ill, 'I think you need to be more *focused* in your dealings with customers, as it were.'

The sour coffee smell found Rosie's nostrils again, and she fought to stop her nose wrinkling in distaste. Surely, she thought, nobody so proud of themselves had ever had so little to boast about. Martin was a narrow-minded, patronising arsehole who clearly – and inaccurately – considered himself a cut above his 'less intelligent' team. She felt anger coursing through her blood like venom as he stared across his desk at her, expecting contrition.

'What does "more focused" actually mean? In plain English, if you don't mind?' Rosie demanded.

Martin's brow furrowed. 'Quicker to press on with the relevant claims processing questionnaires,' he said. 'Rather less optimistic that we can help. *Much* more willing to shut down irrelevant waffle.'

'Irrelevant waffle like this, you mean?' Rosie said, the words erupting like lava before she could stop them.

Martin's eyes grew cartoonishly round. He spluttered, evidently struggling for something to say.

Eventually he managed, 'There is *nothing* irrelevant about my new ACE metric: Average Call Efficiency will now be checked weekly and considered at all claims handlers' quarterly appraisals. I don't know what has come over you in the past few minutes, Miss Butler, but I'll thank you to keep a civil tongue in your head.'

'A few minutes ago you were telling me I'm too nice,' Rosie said hotly, her temper suddenly at snapping point. 'You were very firm about the need for me to shut people down when they're *droning on* or *talking at me*. Am I to assume you're exempt from the rule?'

Colour was rising in Martin's face. His ears were turning pink, as if to signal their outrage at what they'd just heard.

'I expect you to know your place – to remain polite when speaking in the workplace with *any* superior,' Martin spluttered indignantly.

It was the word 'superior' that did it. Or maybe the phrase 'know your place'.

Rosie had spent most of her life pandering to other people's needs and expectations – and where had it got her? She was single, stuck in a dull, uninspiring job and probably about to lose her home. It was years since she'd fully lost her rag, but now seemed the perfect time.

'How dare you?' she demanded, seeing red. Standing up.

She loomed over Martin, emanating the sort of righteous anger usually associated with rousing wartime speeches – ones that started with words like, 'My fellow Americans', or ended with 'we shall never surrender'.

'You are *not* my superior in any way,' she informed him. 'And for the record, I'm very good at my job – certainly better at it than you'd be. It must be nice, sitting up here in your little office and finding fault with the way other people handle difficult real-life conversations. You wouldn't last five minutes if you were let loose with a headset and had angry customers in your ear all day.'

Martin pushed his chair back from his desk. His whole head was now a luminous shade of magenta. There were sweat patches beneath his armpits, their moisture now rendering his white shirt almost totally transparent. Rosie refused to look at the abundance of body hair this revealed.

He opened his mouth, then closed it again. He looked as if he was quite literally boiling with rage. He had the appearance of a lobster, turning pinker and pinker in a pan of steadily simmering water. It seemed he was so close to spontaneous combustion he could no longer form sentences.

'As for knowing my *place*,' Rosie went on, 'I don't think this is it. I've spent six years here, and I've just realised that's probably long enough.'

'Now see here,' Martin puffed out, 'this sort of insubordination is a disciplinary matter. Consider this a formal warning. I'll have no choice but to terminate your employment here if you cannot show me the respect I'm due.'

'Respect?' Rosie scoffed. 'That works both ways, and you've got no respect for me or anyone else below your pay grade. And you can stick your warning where the sun doesn't shine. You can't terminate me – I'm leaving.'

With that, she turned and marched out of the office. Martin was vainly bellowing something about notice periods and contract clauses as she stormed down the stairs. She paid him no attention.

When she arrived back at her workstation, Ellie was already staring at her.

'Did I just hear shouting?' she asked.

'You did,' Rosie confirmed, picking up the few personal possessions that littered her desk and dropping them into her handbag.

'What's happened?' Ellie said. 'It's like you're channelling

Boudicca – are you about to lead an uprising and lop the heads off some Romans?'

'Martin and I had our *chat*' – Rosie put air quotes around this word – 'which culminated in me quitting.'

'You're leaving? Right now?'

'Yep,' Rosie said, flying high on adrenaline as she scraped up her belongings – feeling almost drunk with the thrill of refusing to eat the bullshit sandwich she'd been served by her boss.

Ellie whistled. 'I've always liked you, Rosie, but now I think you might be my hero. I'm going to miss you, but you go for it. Get out there. Keep in touch though, yeah?'

'For sure,' Rosie said, stepping around her own, already empty, desk to give Ellie a tight hug goodbye.

'I'm off, then. Have a nice life, everyone,' she said to the room at large. 'I absolutely intend to.'

Chapter 9

By the time Rosie got home, the thick red mist of her rage had lifted.

As she riffled through her handbag for her keys, she discovered the almost empty Hobnob packet she'd picked up from her desk had split. The few biscuits left inside had disintegrated into a coarse, sweet-smelling powder that now coated everything from her iPhone to her cache of emergency tampons.

She opened the front door of the building and the intoxicated, fizzy feeling that had seized her as she erupted at Martin finally gave way to cold, creeping dread.

What had she just *done*?

Yes, Martin was completely detestable, and yes – her job was pretty rubbish. But throwing the mother of all tantrums in her boss's office, however justified, had added 'unemployment' to her growing list of problems.

The scant contents of Rosie's savings account, which housed the last vestiges of the money Grandpa George had left her, would see her through a few weeks at most – and she still wouldn't have solved the conundrum of having double rent to pay, or a new home to find, if she didn't sort herself out with a flatmate soon.

She closed her eyes and shook her head, almost tempted to laugh as she remembered her foolish hope that the small sum of money she'd put aside might represent the beginning of her wedding fund. Sighing, she put her key into the flat door, turned it and pushed.

Nothing happened.

She tried again, nudging the bottom of the door with her foot this time to see if she could shift it.

It refused to budge even a millimetre. *What the hell?*

For a second, Rosie wondered whether she was using the wrong key. But that couldn't be it; it had slid into the lock the same way it always did, and she'd encountered no resistance when she tried to move it.

She stepped back and looked at the door, as though staring at it might reveal the reason for its intransigence. Surprisingly, within a few moments, it did.

Rosie's stomach dropped as her eyes caught on the keyhole for the deadlock she and James had almost never used. It was old and prone to sticking, and in the early days of living together they'd had more than one hairy moment of thinking they might need a locksmith to get them back inside the flat. They'd given up on using it after a few weeks, and it had been so long since they'd bothered with it that Rosie no longer carried the key.

James must have been here, she realised – probably to collect more of his things while she was at work. He'd obviously been so keen to shut the door on their life together that he'd double-locked it for good measure – and in typical James fashion, it hadn't occurred to him that this might present a problem for Rosie.

She felt an angry sob begin working its way up her throat. Chief among the array of things she was feeling right now, she realised, was exhaustion.

Rosie was *tired* – ground down by the various disappointments and disasters of the past few days. She turned, put her back against the front door of the flat and sank down into a sitting position. Cradling her head in her hands, she decided to allow herself a few minutes of pure, unrestrained misery before – yet again – she would have to pick herself up and work out what to do.

Tears flowed freely down her face, and – too late – she understood that letting herself melt down might have been a mistake. Her chest burned and her throat ached with the effort of trying to regain control. Her nose was running, and when she swiped the sleeve of her jumper across her cheek, it came away grey – stained with mascara.

Then came the unmistakable sound of the old wooden door to the building pushing open; the tread of large feet on the thin corridor carpet.

A. Thomas was level with her in seconds, and he pulled up sharp as he noticed her. He stood, suddenly motionless, one foot still slightly aloft – as if he were playing a game of musical statues and someone had paused the party tune.

Rosie looked up at him.

From this vantage point, he was taller and broader than ever. His expression was wary, with a healthy dose of alarm.

Seeming to decide that he couldn't simply keep walking, he set both feet on the floor and put down the shopping bag he was holding.

After a beat of silence that felt like it lasted six months, he said: 'What can I do? Can I help you somehow?'

Rosie felt her mouth drop open in astonishment. Not only was the man talking, he'd come out with something she'd never have predicted. Most men, she thought, would have asked the obvious but fundamentally stupid question, 'Are you OK?' when confronted with a sobbing woman they didn't really know. This guy had skipped straight to offering practical assistance.

'Probably not,' she told him, 'unless you're skilled in the art of breaking and entering, or know someone who can get me into my flat without bankrupting me.'

'Are you locked out?'

Rosie nodded her head and swallowed back a fresh wave of tears.

'Sorry,' A. Thomas said, cringing. 'That was a daft thing to say.'

'No . . .' Rosie said, pulling herself back up to stand in front of him. 'At least you bothered to stop and ask.'

'Don't sound so surprised.'

She brushed at the wetness that still lingered under her eyes, then cocked a brow at him. 'I think I'm allowed to be a *bit* surprised. You've lived upstairs for three months without ever properly speaking to me. I don't even know your name.'

'It's Aled. Aled Thomas.'

'So *that's* what the "A" stands for,' Rosie said, brightening a little in spite of the mess she was in. 'I'd never have guessed.'

'You were . . . guessing?' His mouth was doing that thing she'd noticed the other morning: a twitch of the lips that suggested a smile, but didn't quite stretch to one.

'Kind of. Sometimes,' Rosie said. 'Aled didn't occur to me, though. It was all, maybe it's Alex, or Andrew, or Adam . . . and then sometimes I'd imagine totally outlandish things like Alvin or Anakin.'

Shut up, shut up, shut up. It was bad enough that this preternaturally good-looking, perfectly self-possessed individual only ever saw her tripping over her own feet, scrabbling around for dropped shopping or sobbing and covered in snot. Why, every time she ran into him, did she have to affirm her idiocy by *talking*?

'You thought I might be named after a chipmunk or a Sith Lord, but it didn't occur to you that I might be Welsh?' Aled asked. His lips were quirking again.

'Apparently not,' Rosie admitted.

'Well. I am.'

'I see that now,' she told him. 'I *hear* it, in fact. But the funny thing about people never talking to you is that you can't detect their accent.'

Rosie was properly smiling now, her own facial muscles stretching in a way that felt unfamiliar after days of stress and misery. Ribbing Aled for his reticence felt irresistible, for some reason. It was like his quietness sparked her curiosity; it made her want to see whether she could ruffle his feathers. Dimly, she wondered what it would take to make him laugh so hard he cried – whether that were even possible.

'I suppose that's fair,' he said, squinting at her.

For a few seconds, they simply looked at one another. Then Rosie said: 'Right. I suppose I'd better ask Google who I can call to come out and get this door open . . . Then consult my banking app and see how big a dent this is going to leave in my budget.'

She bent to pull her crumb-coated mobile out of her handbag. When she straightened up again, Aled was frowning at her. Biting his bottom lip.

Bemused by his silent scrutiny, Rosie dusted off her phone and swiped to open it.

'Don't bother about a locksmith,' Aled told her, the words seeming to burst out of him after some internal debate. 'There's no need. I can get you in.'

Taken aback, Rosie pocketed her phone and turned to him. 'Hmmm,' she said, sizing him up. 'You certainly look as if you *could* break the door down – and it would definitely save me a few quid – but I don't think it'd make me very popular with the new landlord, whoever they may be. Thanks, though.'

Aled was gnawing on his lip again. 'I wasn't planning to break the door down,' he muttered.

A little exasperated, Rosie said: 'OK. So what *were* you going to do? Stare menacingly at it until it dissolved?'

Another classic. Why the hell was her mouth saying words before her brain had signed them off?

This latest gaffe prompted Aled to make a sound that could almost have passed for a laugh. He regained control of himself and said, 'No. I have the key you need to get in.'

'Er . . . ?' Rosie stared at him, staggered. She remembered James saying once that he thought their neighbour had 'handsome-but-probably-a-serial-killer' vibes.

Should she be scared? She *was* a little scared. What possible explanation could there be for this man having access to her home?

'Oh my god, no – it's nothing creepy,' Aled said in a rush, realising his mistake. 'You've no need to freak out.'

'Well, then . . . what? How?' Rosie asked.

Aled sighed and raked a hand through his dark hair.

'*I'm* your new landlord,' he told her, his voice heavy and reluctant. 'I own the building. I've got keys for every floor.'

Rosie gaped at him. 'But I thought some property investment group owned the place nowadays? How can that be *you*?' she asked.

'When I found out I'd inherited the building,' Aled said, 'I got some financial advice and it was suggested to me that I set up a company.'

Rosie merely stared at him, still struggling to process what he'd told her. Had he just said *inherited* . . . ?

'Wait here,' Aled said. 'I'll go and get the key. I'm assuming it's the deadlock that's the problem?'

She nodded dumbly and he headed up the stairs, taking two at a time. Rosie eyed his shopping bag, which was stamped with a logo that read 'Red Fox Deli'. Wondering idly what it contained, she peeped over its thick paper rim and spotted a bottle of what looked like very good olive oil, a loaf of sourdough wrapped in greaseproof paper and a richly fragrant packet of ground coffee. Her stomach rumbled.

A moment later, Aled was back, an elderly-looking key clutched in his hand. It was a *huge* hand, Rosie noted – probably twice the size of her own – but it was nice: long-fingered and clean, with short, neatly trimmed nails.

He waved the key at her, almost apologetically. 'Do you want to . . . or shall I . . . ?'

'Go ahead,' Rosie said. 'The lock's a bit dodgy, which is why we stopped using it. At least until today . . .'

She stepped out of the way to give him easier access to the door. After a few seconds and a little energetic jiggling, the key rotated and she heard the lock snap open.

Seeming to sense that it would be presumptuous to open the door himself, Aled moved back and allowed Rosie to do it.

'OK, then,' Aled said, reaching for his shopping. 'I guess I'll—'

'Oh, no you don't,' Rosie interrupted, cutting him off before he could say 'go'. The sheer randomness of the day's events had left her feeling reckless, and far from ready to be on her own. 'I have questions about this whole "I'm your landlord" revelation. You owe me an explanation. And I'm pretty sure *I* owe *you* a cup of tea for helping me open the door.'

'I . . . oh. OK, then,' he agreed, half nervous, half gratified. He followed her inside, past the bedrooms, the bathroom and into the open-plan living and kitchen area. Rosie noted again how tall he was. He seemed to take up more space than James ever had, yet at the same time he was less expansive – in no way overbearing.

'Wow,' he said, looking around him at the packed bookshelves, hotchpotch of vintage furniture and gallery walls. 'This is lovely.'

'Thanks,' Rosie said, warmed by the compliment but stung afresh at the thought that she might soon have to move out.

'How long have you guys lived here?' Aled asked. His accent really was something else, Rosie thought: lilting and musical, in a way that made even mundane questions sound borderline poetic. His voice was deep and resonant, too – it made her think of stage actors and radio plays, and Richard Burton narrating *The War of the Worlds*.

'About six years,' Rosie said. She filled the kettle and switched it on, then threw two teabags into a pair of mugs. 'Mr Bettini let me decorate it – it was a bit of a fixer-upper when we first moved in.'

'You knew him, then?'

'He lived upstairs. Of course I knew him,' Rosie said pointedly, softening the barb with a smile. 'I liked him – he was a bit grumpy but he had a good heart. I used to visit him a few times a week – make sure he wasn't lonely. Val and Pat did the same. How d'you take your tea?'

'Just milk, thanks.'

Rosie placed a mug in front of Aled, then gestured at the

stools that were tucked beneath the kitchen counter. 'Have a seat.'

He nodded his thanks and did as he was told.

After taking a sip from her own cup, Rosie said: 'So . . . inherited?'

Aled rubbed a hand across his forehead and sighed. 'It's not as interesting as it might seem. I was contacted about six months ago by a company that specialises in tracking down the relatives of people who've died intestate.'

'What's that?'

'It's when people pass away without making a will. When there's property or a lot of money at stake these firms try to find the people who should get it. In exchange for a fee, naturally.'

Rosie drank some more tea. 'So . . . you're saying you're *related* to Mr Bettini?'

Aled took a sip from his mug, then nodded his head. 'Yes. He was my grandfather. But I didn't even know he existed until he was already gone.'

Rosie looked across the worktop at him, wide-eyed. She felt shocked, yet somehow not completely surprised by Aled's story.

Now she thought about it, there was definitely some physical similarity between the man in front of her and the elderly friend she'd lost. Rosie had always thought Mr Bettini must have been a looker in his youth. He'd first come to the UK from Italy in his twenties, and she could imagine he cut quite a dash with the ladies of 1960s London. And there was a deeper resemblance, too, Rosie decided: Aled's steadfast reserve had a similar flavour to Mr Bettini's practised grouchiness. Perhaps the standoffishness was genetic.

'So, that means . . .' Rosie said, her mind racing as she considered the possibilities.

'My father – who I had absolutely no relationship with – was his son.'

'I see.'

Rosie winced. The word 'was' hadn't been lost on her. Whatever might have happened between Aled's parents during his childhood, it seemed clear that his dad had been out of the picture – and that he'd predeceased Mr Bettini. Yet the old man had never mentioned a son, much less one who'd died.

Aled looked uncomfortable, and Rosie quickly changed tack. 'So, why didn't you say anything when you moved in? Did you not want the residents of the building to know who you were?'

'It wasn't so much that,' Aled said. 'I'd have felt embarrassed knocking on your doors and telling you all, "Guess what, I own your homes now." And I didn't want to make anyone feel uncomfortable, either. Like they had to be worried I was watching them – checking to see whether they were knocking holes in the walls or damaging the carpets.'

This made sense. Rosie could certainly imagine that James would have hated the thought of a new, possibly more involved, landlord living just a few metres above them.

'Your turn,' Aled said.

'What d'you mean?'

'I answered your questions, so it's only fair for you to answer mine,' he explained, with another almost-smile. 'What were you upset about just now? I don't think it was only the lock.'

His words reminded Rosie of the likely state of her face: blotchy and smeared with the remnants of this morning's makeup. *Great.*

'Finding myself locked out was kind of the last straw,' Rosie admitted. She sighed. 'I've had a pretty shocking few days.'

Aled nodded but stayed quiet, concentrating on his tea. A slight incline of his head signalled that he'd listen if she wanted to say more.

Suddenly, she did. Telling a relative stranger about the mess she was in somehow seemed easier than giving those close to her the gory details.

'Well,' she said, 'in no particular order, I've been unceremoniously dumped by the man I thought was about to propose to me, and who I now suspect has been sleeping with someone else. I also had a horrible lunch with my family over the weekend. They already think I'm a total sad case, so I didn't have the guts to admit to them that James had left me.'

'Yikes,' Aled murmured, grimacing.

'Also,' Rosie went on, 'my vile boss picked today to inform me that he thinks I'm "inefficient" – no, wait, "unnecessarily pleasant". So I informed *him* that I was quitting, packed up my stuff and left.'

Aled let out a low whistle.

'Finally, unless I find someone to move into the spare room within the next couple of weeks, I'm going to have to move myself . . . Which I suppose is pertinent to you, since it turns out you're the landlord. I love it, but I can't afford this place on my own, and James – despite having plenty of money – says he's "not able" to keep paying rent while I sort out a long-term solution. So there you have it. Discovering I was locked out was actually the least of my troubles.'

'I . . . er . . . *god*,' Aled said, eventually. 'That's quite the catalogue of catastrophes.'

'You must think I'm a walking disaster,' Rosie cringed, draining her teacup and setting it back down on the worktop.

'Not at all,' Aled told her, a sympathetic half-smile now vying for full possession of his face. 'Accident prone, perhaps. A tad unlucky.'

'Let me guess,' Rosie said. 'You work in PR. Or you're some kind of spin doctor for dodgy politicians.'

'No, nothing like that,' he said, shaking his head.

This, Rosie thought, was the point at which anyone else might have said, 'In fact, I do such-and-such for a living.' Aled, however, chose not to elaborate. She sensed he was trying to rein himself in – that he'd already given away far more than he'd ever intended to.

They sat in silence for a few minutes, and Rosie willed herself not to break it. To her surprise, the quiet wasn't uncomfortable. Perhaps by sharing the terrible truth about her situation, she'd made it more bearable. And as confidants went, Aled appeared to be the living, breathing equivalent of the lockable diary she'd had as a teenager: apt to hear news of her woes without interrupting, and unlikely to breathe a word of them to anyone else.

'I'm sorry about James,' Aled said, apropos of nothing. 'Had you been together long?'

'Nearly ten years,' Rosie said. Then, before she could stop herself, she added: 'And, after all that time, he was going to dump me by leaving me a *note* instead of telling me face to face. I just came home early and happened to catch him before he could do a bunk.'

'You're joking.'

'Nope. I imagine I'll be able to see the funny side at some point . . . I think impending homelessness, to which I've now added joblessness, is putting a dampener on my sense of humour.'

'You're on the hunt for a flatmate, then?' Aled asked.

'I am. I can't bear the thought of leaving this place, on top of everything else – I've made it *mine*, you know? Even though it's obviously not.'

'I get it,' Aled said. 'It feels like a proper home, especially compared with upstairs. I don't think my grandfather was much bothered about decorating or mod cons . . . I'm actually going to be moving out myself as soon as I find somewhere else to crash. I was planning to speak to you about it – I've already apologised in advance to the ladies on the first floor for the disruption it'll cause. They've decided to move out for a while and live on their houseboat.'

Rosie started in surprise, then nodded.

'It was their own idea – and it goes without saying that I won't be charging them rent while they're gone,' Aled added hastily, keen not to come across as some Dickensian miser.

She smiled at him. 'You have major plans, then?'

'It needs a new bathroom, a new kitchen . . . a total renovation, basically,' Aled said. 'It'll be far easier to sort out if I'm not living there while it's all done. The builders are waiting for me to vacate.'

Rosie nodded again. Having been up there frequently, she felt pretty confident that Mr Bettini's flat had last been worked on sometime before she was born.

She wondered where Aled worked – *if* he worked – as well as what he did. She wondered whether he'd look for somewhere local to rent, or move to a different part of London entirely.

The questions jockeyed for position on the tip of her tongue, but all were swallowed away as an outlandish – but potentially logical – idea occurred to her. She looked up at him and understood immediately that he'd had the same thought.

'What if . . .' he said, speaking slowly – as if the words were leaving his lips at the precise moment he was thinking them. 'What if *I* took your spare room? Just for a few months, while things are sorted out upstairs. As you've probably guessed, I'm pretty quiet – a good quality in a housemate, I believe. And I don't have a lot of stuff to store, so it's no issue if the room is small . . .'

Rosie found herself nodding. In less than an hour, she'd gone from not knowing this man's name to contemplating living with him.

She forced herself to stop moving her head up and down. This idea was crazy. Absurd. *Completely* ridiculous. Yet it made a strange, irrefutable sort of sense; so much so that she and Aled had both come up with it.

'I . . .' Rosie faltered. 'Well. I was originally looking for a female flatmate. But I've got to admit, I haven't had much luck with that so far.' Impressed with her own restraint, she resisted the urge to tell him she'd now received several dick pics as a result of advertising the room.

'I completely understand,' Aled said, looking abashed. 'It was just a notion.'

He sounded almost relieved that she hadn't jumped at his offer – and in a contrary kind of way, this made it more appealing.

'No,' Rosie said. 'I'm going to think about it. It's a surprisingly decent idea. Can I let you know in a day or two?'

'Sure,' Aled said, standing up. 'That's fine. And no worries if someone more suitable comes along in the meantime. I'd better get going, anyway. Thanks for the tea.'

'Thanks for letting me back into my flat,' Rosie said, following him down the corridor so she could see him out. 'I appreciate it.'

He regarded her as he stood in the open doorway, his large frame almost filling it. 'You're welcome. And it was a pleasure to meet you properly, Rosie Butler.'

'You too,' Rosie said, smiling. 'I'll see you around, Aled Thomas.'

Chapter 10

'So let me get this straight,' Niamh said on Thursday evening, swirling her red wine around her glass before taking a sip. She and Rosie were back at their favourite Italian, awaiting two portions of mushroom risotto.

'Your plan – if this madness can be called a plan – is to let a man you've had precisely *one* conversation with move into your spare room. A man who, while insanely attractive, you know almost nothing about, and who you have referred to alternately as "Nameless Neighbour" or "the sociopath upstairs" for the past three months.'

Rosie felt her nose scrunch up in an involuntary expression of distaste. '*James* referred to him as "the sociopath upstairs", not me,' she corrected.

Niamh held her gaze for a few seconds, then said: 'That's how you justify this idea? *That's* the sum total of your defence? This could just as easily be the start of a horror story as it could a romcom, you know. "Mysterious-yet-hot stranger appears" foreshadows murder as often as it precedes amazing sex. Occasionally it prefaces both.'

'I didn't realise I needed a *defence*,' Rosie mumbled, screwing a paper napkin into a tight ball and trying not to look at her best friend. 'In case you've forgotten, I don't exactly have a plethora of options here. In two weeks' time James is going to stop paying his share of the rent. From then on, it's down to me to cover the lot – and there's no way I can afford it on my own.'

'You don't think Whatshisname would just . . . I don't know . . . like, give you a couple of months to get straight?

Let you have some time to sort things out? He owns the place outright, doesn't he?' She took another gulp of Shiraz, then narrowed her eyes again. 'Which, by the way, is *also* weird. Bordering on creepy. Why did he never mention he was your landlord?'

'It isn't *creepy*,' Rosie said, exasperated. 'He said he felt awkward about it, which I can actually understand. He didn't want to make anyone uncomfortable – he was worried that we'd feel like he was keeping an eye on us the whole time. And for reasons I never did fathom, James hated him from the moment he moved in, and never bothered to hide it. Aled turning around and saying, "I own the building, boyo," was hardly going to help matters, was it?'

His name still felt weird and unfamiliar in Rosie's mouth, and she sipped her drink to cover the sensation. Niamh's gaze stayed on her as she swallowed. 'As for the idea of a temporary rent reduction,' Rosie went on, 'it'd feel wrong . . . Like some sort of favour I'd have to repay later.'

Niamh snorted with laughter. 'Sounds like a storyline out of a spicy romance. You know – something with a half-naked couple on the cover and a title like *Renting from a Rake* or *In Debt to the Duke*.'

Rosie rolled her eyes. 'I'm starting to feel like I need to stage an intervention. When was the last time you read a book that didn't include explicit shagging?'

'You will pry my Kindle from my cold, dead hands,' Niamh said, throwing her a wicked grin. 'We married mothers need to get our kicks somewhere.'

'I don't want to be in any kind of debt – to *anyone*,' Rosie argued, determinedly bringing them back to the point. 'At least this way he and I both get something we need out of the arrangement. Aled has a place to stay and I don't have to worry about finding a proper flatmate immediately. I can take my time to decide on someone and move them in when he goes back upstairs. It's a straightforward business transaction.'

Niamh shot her a sceptical glare, so she continued: 'Also, I really don't have much choice about it unless I move back in with Mum, Dad and Michael – which I definitely *do not* want to do.'

Niamh frowned and shook her head. She looked murderous. 'Fuck. Ing. *James*,' she said darkly. 'I can't believe he's walked away and left you to deal with all this on your own. I mean *his* name's on the tenancy agreement too, isn't it?'

'Yep,' Rosie agreed, sighing heavily.

'If I ever see that man again, I'm going to staple his balls together,' Niamh growled.

Rosie winced, a now-familiar blend of rage and desolation rising inside her as she struggled to reconcile hating James with mourning the life she'd hoped they could have together. For all those years . . . She tried to breathe through the horrible, tight sensation in her chest that accompanied contemplating how stupid she'd been. It felt like her heart and lungs were being shrink-wrapped.

Niamh picked up the wine bottle and splashed more into their glasses. She threw Rosie a soft, anxious look.

'You're sure this guy isn't a psycho then?' she asked, her tone gentler than before. 'I mean, I know he's gorgeous, but you're sure he isn't going to murder you in your sleep?'

'I'm as sure as I can be.' Rosie shrugged. She didn't bother mentioning that her faith in her own judgement was pretty much shot to shit. Just days ago, she'd still believed she and James would be together for the rest of their lives – so it seemed fair to say her instincts were somewhat out of step with reality.

'OK,' Niamh said, slurping more wine. 'Time for another question you won't like. How confident are you that you're not going to end up sleeping with this man?'

'What?!' Rosie spluttered, her face suddenly hot.

'Don't bullshit me, Rose, I've *seen* him. He looks like the love child of Monica Bellucci and Ross Poldark.'

'Have you lost your mind?' Rosie cried. 'That doesn't even make *sense*. Two minutes ago you were worried for my safety, and in any case Poldark is *fictional*—'

'That's not the point, and you know it.' Niamh pointed a long, elegantly manicured finger at her. 'The man is hot as hell. Are you seriously telling me you're going to be able to share a bathroom with him and not think about him naked?'

'Believe it or not, that is *precisely* what I plan on doing,' Rosie said primly. 'And I refer you to your earlier point about how unfeasibly good-looking he is. The idea that he'd have *any* romantic interest in me is straight up laughable.'

'Total rubbish,' Niamh scoffed. 'You're beautiful – and just because you don't see it, that doesn't mean *he* won't. I think you're being wilfully naive.' She arched a single suggestive eyebrow.

'And I think you're massively underestimating how *not* interested I am in finding a new boyfriend,' Rosie retorted.

'Who said anything about him becoming your boyfriend?' Niamh demanded. 'I'm merely suggesting that living in close proximity to this person could lead to some inadvertent – but no doubt enjoyable – riding.'

Rosie opened her mouth to protest, but Niamh held up a hand to stop her. 'I'm only saying what everyone else is going to think,' she insisted. 'To anyone who doesn't know better, it'll look like you've kicked James into touch and started doing the nasty with your fit neighbour.'

Rosie gaped at her friend across the table and tried to muster a convincing response. Before she could say anything, though, Niamh clapped a hand to her forehead and her eyes went wide with shock.

'Oh-my-god,' she said in a rush, 'tell me this isn't about making James jealous. Tell me it isn't some crazy attempt to get him back.'

'No!' Rosie cried. 'Of course it isn't!' But guilt gnawed at her gut, as she wasn't being one hundred per cent truthful.

While she didn't expect that news of Aled moving in would

bring James crawling back to beg her forgiveness, she was certain it would piss him off. And she felt a grim kind of satisfaction at the prospect of James hearing that she was living with another man.

The promise of wrong-footing him – shocking him by doing something as unexpected as moving in with a virtual stranger, especially someone he openly loathed – made something inside Rosie glow with vengeful delight. James thought he knew her, upside down and inside out. He was so sure he could predict what she'd do from one day to the next, from one *year* to the next. She couldn't help thinking: *we'll see about that.*

As though she could read Rosie's mind, Niamh tipped her head to one side. Her eyebrows pulled together in an expression that said, *I'm not angry – just a little disappointed.* 'I can understand why this whole thing is tempting, but I vote no,' she said, her voice kind but firm. 'I'm bringing out the Best Friend Veto. This is a disaster in the making.'

'This isn't a referendum on how I'll pay my rent, Niamh,' Rosie informed her. 'I'm not sure you get a say – especially if you can't come up with a better way to cover the £650 a month shortfall I'm going to be facing in a fortnight's time.'

To her horror, Rosie heard her own voice wobble slightly. *Do not cry*, she instructed herself.

Niamh reached across the table for her hand. Rosie discarded the balled-up serviette she'd spent the past few minutes squeezing into a pulp, then let Niamh grasp her fingers.

Their food arrived, and Rosie was grateful for the opportunity to regain control of her prickling eyeballs. She took several steadying breaths as the waiter sprinkled freshly grated parmesan on her dinner.

After he'd retreated, Niamh said: 'Brendan and I can help you with the money. I know you don't want charity, and I know you don't want to get into debt – but I love you, and I also know you'll pay us back whenever you can.'

Rosie nodded her thanks as she chewed on a mouthful of richly flavoured rice. Sensing victory might be imminent, Niamh pressed on.

'Letting the random sexy guy from upstairs – who also happens to be *your landlord* – move into your flat would be a bit mad at the best of times. But doing it, even in part, because you know it'll wind up your ex . . . ? It *screams* drama, Rose. And the last thing you need right now is more drama.'

Rosie couldn't argue with this. Niamh took her hand again and squeezed it. 'You're going to be OK, you know.'

Rosie blinked away a fresh wave of tears before they could fully form, squeezing Niamh back.

'Now,' Niamh said. 'We're going to stop talking about this and order some more wine. Tomorrow, you'll wake up with a headache and a mouth like Gandhi's flip-flop and you'll agree that I'm right. *Then* you'll agree to let me help you with the rent.'

Rosie shrugged – not refuting the point, but not quite conceding it either.

'All right – one more glass,' she said, waving politely at a passing waitress.

She couldn't quite bring herself to say she'd take Niamh's money, but she could definitely agree to another drink.

The following afternoon, after doing a YouTube yoga class, stress-cleaning the flat and baking a batch of banana and chocolate-chip muffins, Rosie decided to go for a walk. She hoped that a dose of clear, bright autumn sunshine would lift her mood and clarify her thinking.

Her tidying marathon – usually guaranteed to provide cheer – had only served to remind her how attached she was to her home. As she'd dusted it, she'd replayed the memory of finding the sitting room's well-preserved Victorian fireplace behind a strip of plywood – a treasure revealed as she scraped off sheets of tobacco-stained 1970s wallpaper.

She was no further forward with finding a viable flatmate. Several more 'I'm interested' messages had landed in her inbox, but they all came from people who didn't meet the criteria she'd set. Every applicant sounded either unreliable or borderline deranged.

Niamh's offer to lend her some money was still on the table, but Rosie felt no less reluctant to accept it now than she had last night. She and Brendan had a sizeable mortgage on their family home, and costly bills that now included two sets of full-time nursery fees. In any case, borrowing money that she'd ultimately need to repay was hardly a long-term solution to Rosie's predicament.

She strolled through Lloyd Park, taking in the pleasantly fresh chill in the air, the play of low light on late-summer flowers and the reddening leaves of the trees she went past. While she couldn't deny that letting Aled move in seemed mad – or that her motives were at best a little blurry – it still looked like the least-worst option.

As if she'd summoned him by thinking about the idea, she suddenly saw him strolling towards her down the park's central tarmac path. This was weird, but it would definitely be weirder to pretend she hadn't seen him.

'Hi,' she said when they reached one another. 'You all right?'

'Yeah,' he said, 'just on the way home.'

Rosie glanced at her watch and realised that daylight would start fading pretty soon. For all its gentrification, she didn't fancy wandering around Walthamstow in the dark.

'I'll walk with you,' Rosie said, colouring as she realised that he hadn't mentioned wanting company. 'If that's OK, I mean.'

'Sure,' he nodded. They began walking towards the park exit, Aled slowing his pace slightly to match hers.

'So . . . how are you?' he asked after a few moments of silence.

'About the same,' Rosie told him.

A tiny line appeared between his dark brows, and though he cleared his face of the expression quickly, she registered confusion. 'Why d'you ask?'

'I thought . . . I thought you'd patched things up with James,' Aled said awkwardly.

'Hardly,' Rosie snorted. 'What made you think that?'

Aled chewed on his full bottom lip, apparently considering how best to answer this question. 'Well?' Rosie pressed.

'I saw him last night,' Aled finally admitted. 'I was on my way out and he was arriving in this big, shiny car.'

Rosie felt her stomach lurch, though it wasn't news to her that James had been round. He'd obviously assumed that, as on most Thursdays, she'd be out with Niamh, and had scheduled a ransacking of his wardrobe – and no doubt his spare room stash – for a time slot that wouldn't involve facing her.

A car, though? And a posh-sounding one, at that. James didn't drive, despite Rosie's repeated attempts to convince him to get behind the wheel of her reliable old VW.

Rosie reminded herself that two plus two always equalled four, and there was no profit in being wilfully dim about this. 'Did you see who was driving?' she asked Aled, already wincing in advance of his response.

'Um . . . not really. It was dark.'

'Not *really*?' Rosie repeated, surprised to hear a note of wry amusement in her voice. He was obviously uncomfortable and trying to spare her feelings. She felt almost as sorry for him as she did for herself.

'Go on, you might as well just tell me,' she said bracingly. 'Was it a woman?'

Aled sighed. 'I think so. I thought it might be a relative? She had dark hair. I wondered if she was dropping him off – if perhaps he'd come round to try and sort things out with you.'

Rosie allowed this to sink in. Aled's physical description of the woman he'd seen tallied with what she knew Dylan looked like . . . And if Rosie were the betting type, she'd happily have put money on Dylan having an expensive 'look at me' car to go with her Lululemon wardrobe.

'Rosie?' Aled said, and she realised she'd stopped walking.

Her shoulders sagged as she admitted, 'James doesn't have a sister. He's the younger of two brothers.'

'Oh, shit,' Aled murmured, his face falling in dismay. 'I'm so sorry. I'm an idiot.'

'You're not,' Rosie replied briskly, and started strolling again. 'But James is.'

She felt the full truth of this as she said it. 'I'm pretty sure that's the woman he's sleeping with – maybe even living with, come to think of it – although he hasn't admitted as much.'

'Seriously?' Aled sounded outraged. 'What an insanely thoughtless thing to do when you've just broken someone's heart . . .'

In honesty, Rosie's heart felt rather more bruised than it did broken – a fact she'd filed away for closer consideration later, when her more pressing problems had been solved. Nevertheless, she was struck by this astute analysis of James's casual disregard for her feelings.

'It's definitely crap behaviour, but I can't say I'm surprised by it,' she quipped. 'As far as selfish slip-ups go, it might not even make his top five.'

'Wow.' Aled's dark eyes widened. 'Should I take it you're not pining away in sorrow, then?'

They walked along quietly for a minute or two while Rosie collected her thoughts.

'I mean, I'm gutted,' she said. 'Hurt and sad and all the usual feelings. But I think I'm too pissed off to be full-on devastated. He's made me so angry the pain is tempered somehow, you know?'

Aled nodded, before adding, 'I can empathise with the anger a *teeny* bit . . . Did you know he once refused to sign for a parcel for me? It ended up at some depot near Billericay. Took me half a day to go out there and collect the thing.'

'Oh my god, *no*,' Rosie said, giggling. 'That's awful. Sorry. I know I shouldn't laugh.'

'It's fine.' He gave her the half-smile that she'd begun to understand was a significant gesture.

'I don't think he ever forgave you for making him put his bike in the shed, to be honest.'

'I'm sure he didn't,' Aled agreed. 'But Michelle – the cleaner who comes in once a fortnight – was *very* grateful.'

Conversation lapsed as they traversed main roads, then residential streets and eventually arrived back at the house. Left to her own thoughts, Rosie couldn't help turning James's betrayal over and over in her mind; she'd examined it from every possible angle, and there was no denying it looked worse than ever.

She'd been so quick to shrug off his bringing Dylan to their home, as though she were impervious to the insult – like a kid at the park jumping up and insisting her hideously grazed knee was fine, even though the wound was full of gravel and quite possibly needed a stitch. This was what James had done to her – or maybe what she'd allowed him to do. She'd minimised, tolerated and excused things she should never have put up with for the sake of keeping the peace. For the sake of keeping *him*. Laid bare, his disrespect was staggering.

She remembered again what he'd written in his goodbye note: *Sorry if me leaving means you have to move.* But he wasn't sorry at all. For the first time, Rosie truly understood that James hadn't considered, even for a moment, what it would mean for her to lose her home, as well as her partner, within the space of three short weeks. He simply hadn't cared enough to think about it, despite it being the likely outcome of his departure.

Anger, and something deeper, stirred in Rosie as she looked clearly at the facts of their relationship – perhaps for the first time. Well, bollocks to James and the car he rode off in. Bollocks to giving up the flat and going back to her mum and dad's. Bollocks to borrowing money she had no idea how she'd ever pay back, and bollocks to taking her chances on some random weirdo she might find on the internet.

Aled was kind of stiff and unsociable, and Rosie still didn't know him from Adam – but she felt as comfortable with him as she was likely to with anyone she'd only just met. Letting him move into the spare room would solve her housing problem immediately – and if James heard about it and it put a dent in his oversized ego, so much the better.

'Aled,' she said, as he unlocked the front door to the building and held it open for her. 'Are you still looking for somewhere to stay?'

'I am . . .' he said, 'but I don't want you to feel under any pressure. It was daft of me to suggest—'

'No, it wasn't,' Rosie put in. 'It was a good idea.'

'You think . . . ?'

'Yes, I think. How about we say you'll take the spare room any time from now until the end of the year. That gives me a while to find a permanent flatmate, and your builders enough time to do the major work upstairs.'

'Are you sure about this? Won't James go mental if he finds out?' Aled paused. 'Or is that the point?'

'Yes, yes and no, in that order,' Rosie said, not entirely truthfully.

She opened the front door to her flat and left it ajar, waiting for Aled to respond.

'Is that . . . can I smell *baking*?' he asked, inhaling deeply. The scent of Rosie's banana and chocolate muffins, which she'd left to cool while she was out, was wafting into the corridor.

'Oh. Yeah,' Rosie laughed. 'I made some cakes before I left earlier. Tempted?'

'Overwhelmingly,' Aled said. 'Irresistibly.'

His voice was low and deep. Rosie was torn between trying to ignore the goosebumps that had immediately erupted on her (thankfully covered) forearms, and laughing at the thought that he sounded like he belonged in one of Niamh's Regency bonkbusters.

'Sorry,' she said, giving in to a sudden, powerful urge to tease him. 'They're for flatmates only.'

'In that case,' he replied, folding his arms and raising his inky eyebrows at her, 'when can I move in?'

Chapter 11

On Saturday afternoon, Aled moved his things from the second-floor flat into Rosie's ground-floor residence. She offered to help him, but he insisted he could cope on his own – and as she sensed he'd rather not have company while he shifted his few possessions downstairs, she made herself scarce for a few hours and left him to it.

Obviously Rosie had removed all potentially embarrassing items from the property's communal areas before giving him unfettered access to it. She'd relocated her facial waxing strips from the bathroom cupboard to her bedroom, thrown away an ancient tube of haemorrhoid cream that she assumed must actually have been James's, and buried several cringeworthy magazines at the bottom of the recycling bin. Aled seemed serious and smart; she didn't want him to assume she was neither on the basis that she occasionally read speculation about which Hollywood actors were indulging in illicit, off-camera trysts.

Something like nervousness, or maybe excitement, fluttered in Rosie's belly at the thought of being around this attractive, interesting person. It was irrational, she knew, and she tried to tamp the feeling down. In the end, however, the fact remained: she wanted him to like her.

Sunday morning saw Aled heave his heavy, disassembled bed into Rosie's starkly blank spare room. It was a warm day – the last gasp of what the BBC weather team had termed the year's 'Indian summer' – and Rosie struggled to stay composed as she watched him lift the heavy dark-wood bedframe onto its side, then set about screwing the headboard into place. His biceps strained with the effort, pulling his t-shirt sleeves taut. It struck Rosie that – for all James's efforts at the gym – *his* arms had never looked like that.

While Aled definitely seemed warmer and chattier than he'd ever been previously, he still seemed to want to keep Rosie at arm's length. She left him surrounded by screws of varying shapes and sizes, his face creased in an expression of confused determination as he tackled reattaching the bed's legs.

A short bus ride later, Rosie arrived at the brunch spot Niamh had picked out for them. It was a cafe that served decent coffee, bougie breakfasts and boasted a kids' play corner where – fingers crossed – the twins could amuse themselves for a while.

'Here's Auntie Rosie,' Niamh said, her tone flush with relief. Within seconds of her friend's arrival, she handed Rosie a child across the table where she'd already set up camp. It was strewn with abandoned bottles of formula milk, a stone-cold, half-drunk cappuccino and a toasted teacake that had barely been touched.

Rosie frowned at the evidence of this aborted attempt at breakfast – Niamh was slimmer than ever just lately, to the point of looking a little drawn – then examined the sweet-smelling bundle she'd just been passed. This was Rory, she realised. Eva was sitting on a soft foam mat to the side of their chairs, chomping on a large plastic building block.

'Ugh, teething again,' Niamh said, attempting to switch out the block with an appropriately sterilised chew toy that – rather oddly, to Rosie's mind – was shaped like a giraffe. At Eva's enraged cry, however, Niamh threw her hands up, declared that a few random germs would merely boost her daughter's immune system and abandoned the swap.

Rosie snuggled Rory, revelling in the softness of his pudgy cheek against her own. She stroked the tiny curls on his head and didn't mind at all as – in determinedly chewing on his own fist – he soaked her shoulder with a tidal wave of drool.

'Sorry,' Niamh winced. 'Let me grab you a muslin.'

Rosie shrugged. 'It's fine. If a bit of spit's the price I pay for a cuddle with this little champ, it's well worth it.'

'D'you want a coffee?' Niamh asked. 'I definitely need another. Sorry for starting without you but they've had me up since half four.'

'Urgh, that's awful!' Rosie said. 'You could have cancelled, I'd have understood.'

'No way,' Niamh said, standing up. 'Brendan's been away all weekend – work trip to Berlin – and at least if I'm here with you the ratio of adults to children shifts a little in my favour. Sorry if I look a state, by the way.'

'You look lovely,' Rosie said, meaning it. While Niamh was visibly tired and had a flustered, strained sort of aura, she was still effortlessly stylish in dark denim jeans and an oversized lilac sweatshirt.

'So do you,' Niamh said. 'I shall refrain from making any suggestion that you've dressed up for the sake of your new roommate. Flat white?'

Rosie made a glaring face that amounted to an admission, then said: 'That would be great. Would you order me some toast and jam, too?'

'Sure,' Niamh nodded. Rory began to whine as he watched his mother walk away in the direction of the cafe's counter. Rosie saw Niamh flinch at the sound.

'Now don't you worry,' Rosie cooed, reclaiming his attention and making a succession of funny faces at him until he gurgled a laugh. 'See? She's back already.'

'You're really great with them, you know,' Niamh said. 'You'll make a wonderful mum some day.' Then, seeming to feel like she'd put her foot in it, she cried: 'Argh, sorry, I shouldn't have said that – blame the early morning.'

'It's OK,' Rosie told her. 'I do want a baby one day – there's no point denying it. Did I think I'd be closer to having a family than this at thirty-two? Yes. But am I glad James decided to flounce off into the sunset before he knocked me up? Also yes. I'd feel a whole lot worse if he'd dumped me for someone else *after* we had kids.'

Two coffees arrived, followed by a plate piled high with granary toast, plus two ramekins filled with butter and raspberry jam.

Rosie put Rory down next to his sister in the play corner, then set about buttering some toast.

'I must say you're taking it all remarkably well,' Niamh said. 'If we ignore the unexpected yet obviously great quitting-your-job thing. And the nutty decision to let your hot, mysterious landlord set up camp in your spare room.'

Rosie threw her a withering glare and handed her some toast. 'So when you say I'm taking it *well* . . . ?'

'I mean the James side of it, I suppose,' Niamh explained. 'You seem almost philosophical about him leaving – even about this idea that he's hooked up with some other woman . . . If you'd asked me six months ago how you'd cope with something like this, I'd have said you'd be a wreck—'

'Gee, thanks,' Rosie put in, rolling her eyes.

'*No*,' Niamh exclaimed, 'I don't mean that the way it sounded. Can I please remind you I'm so sleep deprived it's amazing I can even function? I can barely remember my own name most of the time. What I mean is, you're OK. And I am so bloody relieved you're OK. I never thought of you as weak, but you've been even stronger than I could have imagined. It's like, despite James's gold-standard twattery, you haven't let this break you.'

'You're right,' Rosie agreed, pausing between mouthfuls of toast. 'I'm not broken. I'm a bit bashed up, though – I feel kind of like I've had a run-in with a life mugger.'

'A life mugger?' Niamh laughed.

'Yeah. Like, I've been knocked down and something I cared about's been taken away. But I'll survive. And . . . I dunno. Maybe the thing I lost was heavier and more unwieldy than I thought. Perhaps I'd just got used to carrying it.'

'And there you go, being all philosophical again,' Niamh said. 'You're amazing.'

'Thanks. Let's hope someone on the receiving end of one of my many job applications thinks so, too.' Rosie had spent much of her free time that week filling in forms and emailing CVs to other insurance firms, as well as several companies advertising for admin staff.

'They will,' Niamh said. 'You'll have something before the week is out, I'm sure. In the meantime, I guess you'll be setting up house with Nameless Neighbour – despite my very valid reservations about the idea.'

'His name is Aled,' Rosie intoned, 'as you well know. And we're not 1950s newlyweds. Honestly, he seems perfectly nice but I suspect I'll barely see him.' She tried to suppress her smile, and her pleasure at being able to talk about him. 'We're going to be flatmates, not friends. We both know he's only there because he needs somewhere to stay and I can only afford half the rent.'

'Right,' Niamh said sceptically. 'He's all moved in, though?'

'I think so,' Rosie said. 'It didn't take long – he wasn't kidding when he said he didn't have much stuff. It was a single suitcase, a few boxes of books and a guitar. Plus some artwork, his bed . . .' She trailed off, thinking of the items that had caught her attention. 'There were a few things that looked like he might have collected them. He had this beautiful sea shell – pearlescent pink, so pretty you could believe it wasn't even real.'

'Really?' Niamh murmured. 'The plot thickens. D'you think he's some kind of travelling troubadour? Or a deep-sea diver? He's got the looks for it – and the wetsuit.'

'Er – I don't know what he does,' Rosie admitted sheepishly.

'Does that not strike you as a bit bonkers?' Niamh demanded. 'I mean, he could have some really weird job. What if he's an embalmer or something? What if he's one of those people who puts makeup on dead bodies so they still look sort of alive at their own funerals?'

'Well then, maybe he could give me some tips on correctly matching my foundation to my skin tone,' Rosie said. 'You know I'm crap with cosmetics.'

'Laugh it off if you want, but you're kidding yourself if you think you'll be able to coexist with this person without getting to know him a little,' Niamh declared. 'You're built to befriend people. It's in your DNA. Hell, it might even be in *his* DNA to let you, since he's related to the grumpy old geezer he inherited the building from. The one you used to take home-made dinners and basically bullied into becoming chums with you.'

'I never bullied anyone!' Rosie insisted with mock outrage. 'And Aled and I will be ships that pass politely on our way in and out of the flat. There will be no relationship building, no cosy dinners, no looking after him of any kind because unlike his long-lost grandfather, he's neither old nor infirm.'

An image of Aled building his bed reminded Rosie just *how* not infirm Aled was, and she flushed slightly as Niamh checked on the twins. As she finished her toast, however, she privately resolved to at least find out what he did for a living – in the fervent hope that it had nothing to do with cadavers.

Rosie got home to a quiet, empty and beautifully fragrant flat. The scent she traced to a rustic bunch of sweet peas in a dark green ceramic vase on the table by the window. Definitely not supermarket flowers, she decided. Aside from that there were no signs that Aled had unpacked a thing – let alone spent the morning constructing furniture.

The sheer *neatness* of the place was almost enough to convince her that Aled had changed his mind and hightailed it back to the building's second floor. However, when she knocked on the door of the spare room, waited a beat and then opened it a crack, she saw it was no longer the vacant room

James had used as his dumping ground. The large wooden bed was neatly made with crisp white bedding and what looked like a hand-knitted, chunky oatmeal blanket. There were three or four books neatly stacked on the bedside table.

On top of a narrow chest of drawers sat a framed photo of Aled and two young children. Rosie noted, unsurprised, that he was ridiculously photogenic. It was a black and white shot, and he looked like an actor or a model in it – his cheekbones lit by the bright sun streaming in from a window to his left. Maybe he *was* a model? That would certainly be a more appealing profession for a flatmate than anything involving formaldehyde.

In the image he had a large, floppy-looking book in his hands. The children – neither of whom could have been more than about five – were staring up at him in awe, transfixed by whatever he was reading.

She felt curiosity alight inside her. Who were the kids? And was the loose-woven blanket that she felt tempted to run her fingers over some faux-authentic purchase from a posh shop, or was there a story behind it?

She caught herself before she stepped inside the room, pulling the door firmly closed so she couldn't start snooping. She didn't consider herself especially nosy, but she *was* fascinated by other people – and right now Aled was the sort of enigma Rosie found irresistible. She'd never admit it out loud – especially not to Niamh – but respecting his obvious desire to keep their relationship cool and professional might prove challenging for her.

'Rosie . . . ?'

She jumped at the sound of his voice.

'Oh dear god. You scared me! I think I've just aged about five years.'

'Sorry,' he said. 'I didn't mean to startle you.'

'I didn't hear you come in.'

'Yeah. I got that.' He looked at her quizzically. 'What are you doing, standing outside my new bedroom?'

Shit. What did she say to that?

'Oh. I, er . . . I knocked on the door and then I was waiting to see if you were in there. I was going to make dinner and wondered if you'd like some.'

Damn it. That wasn't even close to true – and it conflicted completely with what she'd said to Niamh little more than an hour ago.

'Dinner . . . ?' Aled asked. 'It's' – he looked at his watch – 'one forty-five in the afternoon.'

He arched an eyebrow at her, and she wished very powerfully that her mouth would stop saying things without putting them through some sort of brain-sanctioned quality control process.

'I was planning a slow cook!' Rosie invented wildly. 'Chilli, perhaps. You in?'

'O-*K*,' he said, drawing out the two syllables in a way that signalled both surprise and a degree of reluctance. 'Only if you're sure. I don't want you to feel like we have to eat together or anything . . . I'm pretty used to fending for myself.'

Oh, god. Had she coerced him into being sociable with her, just like Niamh had said she would? And how long had it taken? Easily less than half a day.

But she couldn't renege on the offer now . . . that would seem even weirder than offering to make a chilli roughly five hours before any sane person would want to eat it. After what felt like an eternity, she said: 'Duly noted. Consider it a moving-day treat. Oh, and lovely flowers, by the way!'

'No problem. It was the least I could do. And thanks, that would be nice,' Aled said, opening his bedroom door and stepping inside. 'I'll see you in a while? Just shout if you want help – or if you need anything picked up from the shops.'

'Absolutely!' Rosie cried, so brightly that she feared she sounded unhinged.

As Aled's door shut behind him, she stealth-ran to the kitchen and began a frantic fumble for ingredients.

* * *

Given that she'd thrown it together using store cupboard staples and frozen mince, Rosie thought her chilli wasn't half bad. Aled's clean plate implied he felt the same way.

As she mopped up a puddle of soured cream and spicy tomato sauce with a tortilla chip, she wondered what happened now. He'd spent the afternoon in his room, only emerging to use the bathroom or to make himself coffee; would he slink back in there so as to avoid making after-dinner conversation with her? The spare room was such a small space that it couldn't be comfortable to hang out in. Surely it felt claustrophobic, being boxed into an area that could barely accommodate a double bed?

She wondered if Aled whiled away spare hours scrolling on his phone or browsing the internet on a laptop. That was what James had spent most of his 'downtime' doing in the past few months, even when he and Rosie were in the same room. But – while she assumed he must have one – she hadn't yet seen Aled with any kind of mobile device in his hand.

To Rosie's surprise, Aled broke the silence that had descended when she served up their food. 'Thanks so much, that was delicious.'

He stood up to clear their plates and cutlery away, diligently scraping and rinsing everything before placing it carefully into the dishwasher.

Rosie followed him to the kitchen and began filling the sink with hot water. The chilli pan was large, crusty and needed to be washed up by hand.

'Nope,' Aled said, shaking his head. 'Step away from the Fairy Liquid. You made dinner – I've got this.'

Rosie flopped down on the sofa, struggling to identify the intense, almost uncomfortable feeling that was suddenly expanding in her chest. It was some combination of gratification – pleasure at feeling appreciated – and annoyance with herself for having gone so long without it.

James, she knew, would never have stopped her from cleaning up as well as cooking for them; she'd done it regularly, and mostly without complaint. Aled's attitude to this wasn't some show of enlightenment or superiority – he was simply treating her as an equal.

A lump rose in Rosie's throat at the thought that someone she barely knew had more consideration for her than the man she'd imagined she would marry. She swallowed it away and picked up the paperback she was currently reading from the coffee table.

It wasn't long before Aled had finished. Although she had tried to focus on her book, she'd found herself intently tuned in to the sound of pots and pans being put away, the spray of antibacterial cleaner on the work surfaces and then the whoosh of water hitting the inside of the kettle. For some reason, she refused to look round while he worked or even as she sensed him approaching. Given that he was a virtual stranger, it wasn't odd for her to be hyperaware of his movements, she told herself – but she didn't want him to feel spied on.

'Sorry to disturb you while you're reading,' he said. In truth, she'd got through barely a paragraph in the past fifteen minutes – but he didn't have to know that. She feigned studious absorption in the novel as she placed it face down in her lap and looked up at him.

'I just wondered if you wanted a tea, or anything? I'm making one for myself.' He shrugged awkwardly, and Rosie got the sense that – while he felt ill at ease about offering her a drink in her own home – he'd decided it would be stranger not to.

'I'd love one,' she said. 'Milk, no sugar, please.'

A few moments later, and with a battered-looking book tucked under one arm, he set her mug down on a coaster and turned as if to head back to his bedroom.

'You are allowed to sit on the couch, you know,' Rosie said, before she could stop herself. 'Or in that armchair, if you prefer.' She pointed at a weathered old leather chesterfield, which – apparently after some internal argument – Aled lowered himself into.

They sipped their tea in silence, and Rosie went back to her novel with determination to make some headway as Aled opened his own. She couldn't resist a look: *Jane Eyre*. She bit her bottom lip, her interest piqued almost beyond endurance.

It was one of her all-time favourites, but she knew very few men who liked it. Most of the boys who'd been in her A-level English class had considered reading the extracts they'd studied a form of slow torture.

Unable to concentrate on her cosy-crime paperback, she said: 'Can I ask a question?'

'Sure. As long as I get to ask one, too.' His smile was a fleeting, faint thing, but – in the split second before it faded – Rosie caught it.

She smiled back and nodded her agreement.

'If it's about the book, I'm reading it for work,' Aled said. 'Well. *Revising* it, I suppose.'

Strangely, Rosie had been preparing herself to ask about his job. It now seemed she might get two answers for the price of one.

'Oh, right. Why for work?' she asked, hoping she wasn't being too nosy.

'Because I'm teaching it,' Aled explained. 'A-level English. It's one of the set texts, as well as an old favourite.'

'Oh!' Rosie heard herself say, her voice several octaves higher than she'd have liked.

'Is it that much of a surprise?' he asked, amusement lighting his eyes and lifting one corner of his mouth. 'What did you think I did?'

Male model.

Movie star.

Funeral parlour professional.

'Erm . . . I don't know,' Rosie mumbled. 'Teaching hadn't occurred to me.'

Briefly, she wondered how many of his students were

harbouring continent-sized crushes on him – and whether he was aware of the passions he inevitably inspired.

Before she could ask how long he'd been a teacher or how he'd got into it, he said: 'My turn, now. How did you get to know my grandfather? It seems to me London isn't the sort of place where you regularly chew the fat with your neighbours.'

'Is that your excuse for never speaking to any of us before last week?' Rosie quipped, laughing.

'Maybe,' he said, with a smirk so brief she could have blinked and missed it altogether.

'Well, I used to check on him, like I told you that day you opened the door for me. I'd pop up and see if he needed anything, you know?' Rosie said. 'After a little while, when he realised I wasn't going to give up just because he found my "interference" irritating, he started letting me in so we could have a cuppa together. I'm not too proud to admit that this opening up neatly coincided with me starting to take him cake and biscuits.'

'So you just . . . knocked on his door? Until he let you in one day? Even though he was' – Aled looked like he was searching for the right way to put this – 'not receptive?'

Rosie couldn't decide if he was horrified or impressed.

'Pretty much,' she said, giggling nervously. 'I could tell he had a heart of gold beneath the prickly packaging. Niamh – that's my best friend – says I bullied my way into his life, which is a gross exaggeration . . . but she's not *entirely* wrong.'

At this, Aled actually grinned. The smile seemed to light him up from inside, like he was experiencing an upsurge of feeling too quick and bright to suppress. His full lips parted, his white teeth flashed in the dusky sitting room and his dark eyes danced. Rosie felt almost winded by the full force of his handsomeness, which she now realised she – and even Niamh – had vastly underestimated.

'So now I know,' Aled said. 'You plied him with baked

goods and relentless positivity until he was powerless to resist. Until he fell a little bit in love with you, I bet.'

Rosie felt her cheeks heat. She still wasn't fully recovered from the grin.

'I'm pretty sure he found my visits infuriating right up to the end,' she said. 'He used to tell me to stop mithering after him, and that he was perfectly capable of making his own dinner. I don't know about *love*, but I like to think the low-level griping was his way of showing me he cared.'

Aled smiled at her again, the expression softer this time but still powerful enough that she felt its impact somewhere around her solar plexus. *Crikey*. If this was what it felt like to have his full attention, she'd need to avoid attracting it too often in case it caused internal bruising.

'I'm sure it was,' he told her, holding her gaze to show that he meant it.

They turned back to their books, then, and said little else for the rest of the evening.

Chapter 12

On Friday of the following week, Rosie was home alone with a cheese and pickle sandwich and Jane Austen's *Emma* on TV.

It was only half past five, but she'd already settled down for the night. After a long bath with her favourite oils, she had her book print PJs on, and – given the weekend was afoot – she felt fairly confident Aled wouldn't be home any time soon to catch her in them. She was in desperate need of comfort after a week of bruising job interviews for roles that – if she was honest with herself – she didn't even want.

In between the leering older men who seemed more interested in what lay beneath her blouse than her professional experience, there'd been women ten years younger and significantly better qualified than Rosie, some of whom couldn't mask their pity for the thirty-something still looking for an entry-level position.

At one interview, she'd mistakenly mentioned that she started a university course, but gave it up after a single semester for 'personal reasons'. This, she realised, had been interpreted as code for 'I developed a substance abuse problem during freshers' week' – or perhaps 'I'm thick as mince and couldn't keep up with the work'.

When Rosie looked back on it, she didn't regret staying at home to take care of Grandpa George. She'd been within him during his final, increasingly infirm, eighteen months of life – quality time she'd have sacrificed if he'd gone into care and she'd continued her studies.

What Rosie hadn't banked on when she walked away from Queen Mary University, however, was the effect of grief – not to mention her family's repeated assurances that higher education was a waste of time and money – on her plan to return. By the time she felt equal to starting again, she'd met James. Things between them had quickly become serious, and they'd started to discuss living together when his degree course ended the following summer.

Although she'd talked to him about her psychology degree, and going back, James had made it clear to her from the start that he was done with student life. He'd landed an impressive-sounding graduate job, and as soon as he could manage it, he wanted to live as he imagined his fellow graduates would: a flash apartment, foreign holidays and the kind of nights out that Rosie's paltry student loan could never afford.

Though it was painful to admit, their relationship had taken precedence in Rosie's thoughts about the future. He'd left her to flat-hunt for them, and she'd fallen in love with the little garden flat in Walthamstow. Working full-time so she could afford to rent a place with James had felt grown up, and less daunting than striking out alone as a 'mature student'.

As Anya Taylor-Joy's Emma fumed at Mr Elton's untimely, on-screen proposal, Rosie heard the flat door open. She put down her sandwich and paused the TV.

'Hey,' Aled said, entering the sitting room and setting his satchel down with a dull thwack that implied it was heavy. His charcoal-grey pea coat was already hanging from a hook in the hallway.

'Hi,' Rosie said, a little flustered. 'You're home early. I didn't think I'd see you for ages.'

'School chucks out at three forty-five,' he said, frowning slightly in evident confusion. 'And after-school detentions end at five.'

'But it's *Friday*,' Rosie argued. 'I thought teachers – especially young ones – went to the pub on Friday nights to ring in the weekend and compare battle scars. You know, like, you'll never believe what that little oik Jimmy Brown did in my lesson this week . . .'

'Jimmy Brown? Little oik?' Aled said, arching a single dark eyebrow. 'You are aware that William Morris Academy is a school in present-day east London, not the Home Counties circa 1932?'

This shocked a laugh out of Rosie. She'd barely seen or heard anything of him all week – yet now the man who could probably win an award for reticence was making *jokes*?

'The point stands,' she told him. 'Teachers typically go out for a few jars at the end of the week. Yet here you are.'

'Maybe some do, I suppose,' Aled conceded. 'I'm a temp, though – I might only be there a term or two. Supply staff don't tend to get invited to much social stuff.'

'Hmmm,' Rosie said, squinting at him doubtfully. 'You're telling me *nobody* asked if you wanted a quick pint to celebrate getting through the first week of term?'

'I didn't say *that*,' Aled admitted.

Rosie shook her head and smiled at him. She was coming to the conclusion that, despite his Adonis-esque exterior, he was shy.

'How was it, anyway?' Rosie asked him, deciding not to tease him any further.

'School? OK, thanks. Some of the kids are amazing, others are tougher – but most of them are brighter than they believe they are. I think it'll be an interesting few months, at least.'

A little gingerly, as if scared to set himself down too close to Rosie, and with a side glance at the pyjamas that had felt so appropriate a few minutes previously but now seemed anything but, he sat at the other end of the sofa and loosened the already sloppy tie around his neck. It was a deep-red knitted thing, unshowy and sort of old-fashioned. Combined with his slightly rumpled oxford shirt and navy-blue V-neck – the sleeves of which he'd rolled up to the elbows – it gave him the look of a hassled professor.

He could definitely pass for the self-effacing mathematical genius in an action movie, Rosie thought – the guy who solves a critical equation and makes it possible for a troupe of stranded astronauts to come home. Or maybe the lead in a romcom about bookshops: some enemies-to-lovers story involving business rivalry and irresistible attraction. She cleared her throat.

'How was your week?' he asked. 'Or should I take the answer as implied since you're in your PJs?'

'Pretty dull and dispiriting, to be honest,' she told him, smiling wistfully. 'I had a few job interviews, most of which went well enough that I think I'll probably get something. I can't say I'm excited about any of the positions, though.'

'Have you applied for jobs like the one you were doing before?'

'Yeah. Insurance stuff, a couple of admin roles and some customer service positions.'

'I'm sensing pretty low levels of enthusiasm for all of the above,' Aled said, twisting his body around to face her.

'Guilty as charged,' Rosie said, holding her palms up – not entirely sure why she was being so honest with him when she hadn't even admitted this to Niamh.

'So . . . why not do something else?' he asked.

'I dunno,' Rosie mumbled, unsure how to respond to this simple and entirely reasonable question. It seemed to require a complicated answer she didn't have; it demanded justifications that she couldn't come up with on the spot.

In the end, she settled for: 'I've never really done anything else. I'm not sure what else I'm *capable* of doing, quite honestly.'

'OK,' Aled said. 'You're good with people – that much is clear. And I assume you can make decent coffee?'

'I guess so,' Rosie said, a small thrill shooting through her at his compliment.

'I know someone who's looking for a barista. You could probably do as many hours as you'd like, for as long as you'd like, while you figure out what kind of job you're *really* after.'

'That sounds . . . intriguing,' Rosie said, surprised to discover she meant it. 'Does it pay OK?'

'Well enough, I should think, depending on how many hours you want to do. It might not be quite as much as you're used to, but what have you got to lose? If you hate it, you can always quit and try something else – and it'll be easy to fit around your volunteering when you get started.'

Rosie was amazed that he remembered Gather even existed; she'd only mentioned it briefly, but he'd obviously retained the information.

'Is that what you'd do? Just give it a go?' she asked, not sure what difference this would make but keen to hear his opinion anyway.

'Definitely,' Aled said. 'This is why I do supply work. I like being able to move around, try new things. I started off doing TEFL – teaching English as a foreign language – so I've travelled a fair bit. I'm yet to stay anywhere for much more than a year.'

Oh. That explained his scant possessions, as well as the olive-gold glow of his skin. It had the kind of tone that even a Mediterranean complexion couldn't sustain under cloudy English skies; it spoke of days spent in brilliant sunshine and evenings on balmy beaches.

Rosie wanted to ask where he'd been, what sort of adventures he'd had, why he'd never put down roots. What had made him start travelling in the first place. She bit the questions back, aware they were too searching to ask someone she knew so superficially.

'So London will just be another pin in the map for you, then?' she said, her voice deliberately light. 'Are you renovating upstairs so you can rent it out and move on?'

Aled shifted in his seat, seeming uncomfortable. He cleared his throat, then muttered, 'Something like that.'

It was a strangely non-committal response, which Rosie

nevertheless felt was final. Something told her that picking at it – trying to strip away the ambiguity and uncover whatever meaning lay beneath – was a bad idea.

'Do you want me to put you in touch with the cafe? About the job?' he asked, effectively shutting down further discussion of his own future.

'Please,' Rosie said, refocusing on her situation and smiling gratefully at him. 'That would be great.'

'Sure, give me your mobile number and I'll pass it on. Now, can we un-pause the TV? I love this film.'

'You do?'

'Absolutely. *Emma* is Austen's best, in my opinion, and this version slaps.'

'*Slaps?*' Rosie dissolved into a fit of giggles. 'Oh my god. I'm not even sure what that means.'

'It's what the kids say when something's really good,' Aled grinned. 'Which this film is. Though I prefer Jonny Lee Miller as Mr Knightley. He plays it just right, I think: like the man's a smart arse who can't help himself starting arguments with the woman he secretly loves, because he *also* loves being right about everything.'

Rosie gaped at him. First, this was probably the longest run of sentences she'd ever heard him utter. But he also seemed to be telling her, with no agenda, that he'd seen multiple TV and film adaptations of *the same novel*. Her stomach flip-flopped involuntarily, the way it always had over handsome boys with bookish tendencies.

'How about I get some drinks? Beer? Wine?' he asked.

'A beer would be great, actually. There are some in the fridge.'

He reappeared a moment later, two ice-cold bottles clutched between the fingers of a single large hand. Rosie found herself oddly transfixed by the sight.

'What are we waiting for?' Aled demanded, grinning. 'I want to see Miss Woodhouse put that snooty vicar back in his box.'

Rosie shook her head, as if the motion might settle her thoughts into a more coherent order. Aled was . . . *confusing*. Full of light and shade. Cool and aloof one minute, then warm and funny the next.

Smiling back at him, Rosie accepted her bottle of Asahi and experienced a brief rush of *something* as his hand brushed hers.

Whatever it was, she was not going to obsess about it.

Resolute, she picked up the remote and pressed play.

A few days later, Rosie found herself outside the cafe-slash-deli Aled had directed her to. It was the same one he'd visited on the day he'd found her locked out of the flat – the sort of place that sold incredible bread, to-die-for pastries and bottles of balsamic vinegar that cost as much as champagne.

She'd never been in, even though it was within walking distance of the flat – mostly because, had she succumbed to any of the temptations on offer, James would have refused to join her in enjoying them. Now, in the early-evening cold, the smell of baked goods and freshly ground coffee beans – powerful enough to drift through ancient gaps in the door and window frames – made her stomach grumble.

The sign on the inside of the door, visible through a large pane of glass that was foggy with condensation, said 'Closed', which she had been told to expect. She rapped lightly on the painted wood. No answer.

Swallowing, she tried again, but louder.

A clear, rich voice boomed, 'Coming! I'll be there now!' from somewhere Rosie couldn't see.

Seconds later, a tall, statuesque figure bustled into view, unlocked and then opened the door. It was a woman – pretty and red-haired – with a tea towel thrown over one shoulder and a biro pushed into the bun on top of her head. Rosie guessed they were around the same age.

'You'll be the girl about the job, I take it? You'd best come in.'

The woman's tone was brisk but warm, and her accent, like Aled's, was decidedly Welsh. Rosie nodded and followed her inside.

'I'm Rhianne,' the woman announced.

'Rosie.' She considered trying to shake Rhianne's hand, but chickened out before her arm was fully extended and ended up waving her right palm in a weak greeting she immediately regretted. *What a dork.*

'Coffee?' Rhianne asked, able to sense Rosie's nerves.

'Please,' Rosie replied. Why was she so jumpy?

Perhaps, she realised, it was because she already liked this place – actually felt interested in working here. Also, she felt as though she'd been recommended for this position – like she'd be letting Aled down if she made a bad impression on the owner.

'Cappuccino? Flat white? What d'you fancy?'

'A flat white would be great,' Rosie said. 'Thanks.'

Rhianne smiled, her generous, red-lipsticked mouth opening a little to reveal a row of straight white teeth. She gestured for Rosie to pull up a stool at the polished wood counter, then moved to its other side and began flipping switches on a gigantic chrome machine.

Self-assurance seemed to roll off Rhianne like wafts of spicy perfume. She was taller than Rosie by several inches, and curvier too. She clearly saw no need to make amends for her plus-sized proportions by tenting them in the sort of 'flattering' garments Rosie often reached for. Instead, she wore blue skinny jeans with a patterned shirt tucked into the waistband. It was unbuttoned to display at least two inches more cleavage than Rosie herself had ever revealed in public. All of which was to say, she looked *fantastic*.

'Relax,' Rhianne said a minute or two later, grinning as she placed a cup and saucer in front of Rosie, who had unconsciously begun gnawing on her fingernails.

'This isn't an interview – more a quick once-over before you get started. That's assuming you *want* the job?' Rhianne went on. 'I hear you've spent years dealing with people who are pissed off because their insurance policies won't pay out. Handling the odd customer who's picky about the temperature of their latte should be a piece of cake by comparison.'

'I hadn't thought of it like that,' Rosie murmured, suddenly feeling more sure of herself.

'Well, maybe you should start,' Rhianne said, with a smart nod. 'I wasn't sure what you'd be like,' she went on, eyeing Rosie and then necking the last of her espresso. 'For a man obsessed with words, my cousin is shockingly inarticulate.'

'Your cousin?' Rosie asked, looking up sharply.

'Case in point,' Rhianne said, rolling her eyes. 'I gather he didn't tell you we're related. All he said to *me* was that he had a new friend who'd had a rough time lately, and that this person would be up for working here a bit while she sorted a few things out.'

Rosie nodded. 'All true.'

'His way of returning me a favour, as well as doing you one,' Rhianne went on. 'I put him in touch with the builders who are working on the flat. Same team as did this place.'

'Right,' Rosie said. 'I've met some of them, Tim, Richard and Amit? Nice guys.'

Rhianne smiled in agreement, then said: 'It was only after some aggressive questioning that Al informed me he was living in your spare room.'

'Ah. Yes,' Rosie said. 'It's a marriage of convenience, for want of a better way of putting it.'

Immediately, she wished she *had* found a better way of putting it. Her face flushed at what the phrase implied, and she looked intently at her coffee cup as she tried to will the redness away.

'A rough time means man trouble, I suppose?' Rhianne asked, seeming not to have noticed Rosie's embarrassment. 'Bad break-up?'

Still reeling from the revelation that Aled had described

her as 'a friend', Rosie was further thrown by this woman's directness. She found herself saying, 'Uh, yeah. My boyfriend dumped me after almost ten years. He swore he hadn't met anyone else – which I'm now pretty sure was . . .' She frowned, searching for the right word. 'Bullshit.'

Rhianne wrinkled her nose, evidently disgusted. 'Well,' she said bracingly as she picked up their empty coffee cups, then put them through a hatch into the kitchen. 'Let's hope his knob falls off, shall we?'

Rosie let rip an involuntary peal of laughter. She *liked* this woman – felt lifted by her no-nonsense positivity – and while working here would no doubt mean busy days and blistered feet, she knew instinctively that it would be fun.

'So, you're in then? When can you start?' Rhianne asked, grinning at her widely.

'Tomorrow, if you want me,' Rosie said, smiling back.

Chapter 13

Over the next few days, Rosie worked harder than she had in years. Her new job was physically demanding in a way her role at Cover 4 U had never been – but she loved every minute she spent in the stylish yet homely deli, steaming hot milk, slicing freshly made cakes and serving up mouth-watering salads.

It was a smallish space, but it had *grace*, in Rosie's eyes. Like its owner, it seemed authentic, unapologetic – justifiably proud of itself. There were exposed brick walls, spaces with dark grey wood panelling and rows of low-hanging pendant lights. If this was the sort of work Rhianne's preferred builders were capable of, Rosie couldn't wait to see how they'd transform Mr Bettini's old flat.

The deli's furniture was simple and sturdy, with some chairs upholstered in well-worn patterned fabrics and others in leather. None of it matched, but the overall effect was harmonious – and as a self-confessed interiors obsessive, Rosie knew that this required care and judgement.

Bright artwork hung from the walls, and bookshelves dotted here and there displayed dog-eared Penguin Classics. The cups and saucers were handmade, Rosie guessed, and haphazardly glazed in shades of mustard, teal and maroon so they looked like 1970s relics.

It was comfortable here, and Rosie could understand why some of Rhianne's regulars set up camp for hours, bringing books and laptops with them so they could work in the deli's cosy, coffee-scented corners. Surrounded by Rhianne's chatty customers and the rest of the staff team, she felt happier at work than she'd been in . . . pretty much *ever*.

Best of all, within a few days of starting at the deli it was clear that Rosie's bank balance wouldn't suffer too much for her shift in employment. Rhianne paid her team a decent wage, there were plenty of shifts available and Rosie's natural friendliness meant she earned extra money in tips. With a little trimming of her budget and perhaps the occasional dip into her savings account, she'd be fine.

She was already popular with her co-workers, too. Marcus, Yaz and Becky had patiently shown her the ropes during her first few days, explaining the various idiosyncrasies of the espresso machine, taking her through the cafe's opening and closing routines and pointing out which customers were likely to be particular about their orders. She was a quick learner and, as she vaguely remembered writing on several of the job application forms she'd recently filled in, a team player. When Yaz – a shiny-haired twenty-something with an array of arty tattoos – said she was happy Rosie had joined 'the cafe fam', Rosie had no trouble believing her.

Rhianne split her time between the kitchen, the counter and the tiny upstairs office, from which she managed ordering, accounts and other necessary paperwork. Within a couple of days of starting at the deli, Rosie had discovered that Aled's renewed proximity to his cousin was entirely accidental. Rhianne had been living in this part of London for several years, without any inkling there might be a family connection to the area. Aled's willingness to move into the building he'd inherited was, to some degree, bolstered by the unexpected nearness of someone he considered a close friend as well as a relative.

Rosie could understand this. She liked Rhianne more and more, but also wondered how a single family could have produced two such different people within one generation. She and Aled were like creatures from different planets; his inscrutability was the exact opposite of Rhianne's plain-speaking openness.

Even though they lived under the same roof and relations between them were cordial, Rosie felt Aled still weighed every word he spoke with precision – either to ensure perfect articulation of meaning, or to avoid giving too much away. On the other hand, Rhianne spoke at a rate even Rosie found hard to keep up with. Words were free and came easily to Rhianne, so she used them in abundance – never afraid of giving an opinion, offering an idea or sharing her thoughts honestly.

To Rosie's relief, her boss's frankness never veered into unkindness, and while she was brisk and down-to-earth, Rhianne was also empathetic. Rosie saw this in her warm relationships with several elderly customers who often spent long periods at the deli nursing single cups of tea, which were topped up on the house. She was also insistent that no food should ever be wasted, donating anything that couldn't be stored overnight to local community groups who shared it with people in need each day.

When Niamh popped into the deli to share a post-shift coffee with her, Rosie admitted that she felt rather inspired by her new friend. To her relief, Niamh didn't scoff at this. Instead – after Rosie had made brief introductions – she declared she could understand the feeling entirely.

Elsewhere, in a twist that Rosie hadn't dared dream possible, Ellie's most recent text message had left her whooping with joy. Martin's ACE metric had – in Ellie's words – 'gone down like a cup of cold sick' with senior management, and he'd been 'asked' to accept some sort of severance package. In his place, and to her colleagues' satisfaction, Ellie had been elevated to team leader. She'd made it clear that Rosie could have her old job back whenever she wanted, but Rosie had politely declined. As much as she liked Ellie, going backwards felt like the wrong decision now – so instead they made plans for a post-work catch-up sometime soon.

James, and the crushing feeling that accompanied thinking

about his betrayal, remained the single dark cloud on Rosie's horizon. However, after arriving home one evening to find he had taken his final few possessions from the flat, Rosie discovered that she felt more liberated than depressed by their disappearance.

Her clothes now colonised his wardrobe space, and she gloried in having two bedside tables on which she could place books, scented candles and fresh flowers. At Aled's suggestion – in line with his duties as landlord, given her ex-boyfriend had thoughtlessly hung onto his keys – the locks were also changed less than forty-eight hours later.

When she put her shiny new key into her old front door for the first time, it felt to Rosie like a red line had been drawn through her relationship with James. She'd thought they would last forever, but, little by little, loving and losing him felt less like a tragedy and more like an important life lesson – one she was more than ready to embrace.

'So how are you finding it? Living with Al?' Rhianne asked, as the clock ticked towards closing time one Friday afternoon. It was the last day of the month – pay day – and the whole team was in predictably high spirits.

'It's . . . fine. Nice,' Rosie said, not sure what kind of response was expected. In truth, there was little to comment on; she and Aled had spent barely any time together since the accidental 'welcome' dinner she'd made him and their quiet but companionable enjoyment of *Emma*.

Rhianne snorted. 'Oh god, is he letting the introvert in him win? Spending lots of time in his room like a surly teenager?'

Rosie groped for a diplomatic response. 'Erm . . . I think he's just really busy.'

'He's also a natural recluse in need of a self-esteem injection,' Rhianne said sagely. 'He's not great at making new friends – which is just one of a few reasons why he's spent so much time among people who can hardly speak English during the past few years.'

Rosie's eyebrows lifted at this. Aled was definitely the quiet type, but – what with there being several mirrors in the flat – she doubted he had a dearth of self-confidence.

'I'm serious,' Rhianne insisted. 'I know it sounds ridiculous because he looks like North Wales's very own Aidan Turner' – Rosie was reminded of Niamh's 'love child of Poldark' comment, as Rhianne grabbed a fresh tea towel – 'but really, it was *not* ever thus. He was a gawky thing when we were kids: skinny, rubbish at football, mouth full of braces – the whole works. He didn't get good-looking until we were about sixteen. I didn't even notice it because we were together all the time, but when we went back to school for Year Eleven, everyone, even the teachers, kept saying *how much he'd grown* over the summer. How nicely he'd *filled out*.' She made finger quotation marks in the air to emphasise her distaste.

Rosie nodded as if she understood, though she'd never experienced anything like this herself. She'd sometimes wondered whether, one day, like a butterfly emerging from a chrysalis, she'd awake to discover she was the slender, beautiful, un-clumsy woman she was surely meant to be. At thirty-two, however, she'd pretty much given up hoping for such a spontaneous transformation.

'It takes him a while to open up to people,' Rhianne continued, 'and he doesn't let many people in. But I think he will with you.' She eyed Rosie shrewdly, and Rosie got the sense that – just this once – Rhianne was choosing not to say out loud whatever was on her mind.

'We'll see, I suppose,' Rosie murmured, not sure what else she could say to this.

'We will,' Rhianne agreed. 'Now,' she said – louder, so the whole team could hear her – 'let's get this place tidied down and cleaned up so we can get to the pub. First round's on me.'

When Rosie started work that morning, she'd had no intention of finishing the day with an adventure in what Rhianne – and the rest of her staff – called 'rough pub karaoke'. In fact, she'd never heard of such a thing, only later discovering that it was an end-of-the-month tradition.

A heady combination of peer pressure and genuine fondness for her new colleagues meant that, by 6.30 p.m., she was nevertheless clutching a pint of ice-cold cider. The Dun Cow – the team's pub of choice – was an establishment that felt like it belonged in a soap opera or kitchen sink drama. Dark and old-fashioned, it had windows that looked painted shut and boasted air that – presumably because little of it was fresh – still smelled faintly of decades-old cigarette smoke.

The place was carpeted throughout, the pile richly decorated not only with its original Wilton pattern, but with stains left behind by the many drinks that had been spilled over the years since it was laid. It was slightly sticky underfoot, and Rosie thanked god – and Rhianne – that the deli had rules about wearing closed-toe footwear.

This was, Rosie mused as she took a tart, refreshing drink from her glass, the sort of place James would have refused to set foot in. It wasn't a gastro pub – there were no pan-seared scallops or posh pork scratchings in sight – but this didn't worry her.

'It'll all make sense when the singing gets going,' Marcus said, following Rosie's gaze as she took in her surroundings. 'It's not pretty, but this is the best pub in London – and the drinks are dirt cheap.'

This, Rosie could happily concede, was true. 'I can't remember the last time I went anywhere that a round wasn't almost double that price,' she agreed. She'd helped Rhianne ferry various glasses to their grateful recipients and done an involuntary double take when she'd seen the bill on the tray.

Marcus was tall and thin, with reddish hair, wire-framed glasses and a ready smile. Rosie had begun to suspect he had a thing for Becky – a dark-eyed, curly-haired northerner with a penchant for slogan t-shirts. Today's was a hot-pink number with 'A WOMAN'S PLACE IS WHEREVER SHE BLOODY WELL WANTS' emblazoned across the bust – a message

Rosie could definitely get behind. Marcus's eyes frequently followed Becky's progress around a room, though she seemed unaware of his fascination with her. As he looked at her, his features settled into the soft, adoring sort of expression that – now she saw it up close – Rosie had to admit she hadn't seen on James's face in some years.

'Rhianne is a legend in here,' Yaz said, appearing as if from nowhere and holding a glass that, Rosie guessed, contained some approximation of a pina colada. The drink was fluorescent yellow – so vividly bright that its provenance couldn't possibly have much to do with real pineapples. Yaz seemed totally unbothered by the likely presence of a raft of e-numbers, however. She sipped the concoction through a pink-striped straw, studiously avoiding the paper umbrella lest it poke her in the eye.

'A legend how?' Rosie asked. But before Yaz could answer her, the high-pitched whine of microphones and amps being switched on cut through their conversation.

'You're about to find out!' Yaz shouted over the din.

There was a tiny stage in the far corner of the pub's central space, which a thick-waisted, shiny-suited man now mounted. He spoke into the microphone directly in front of him.

'WELCOME, ladies and gentlemen, to the Dun Cow's monthly music night! With *your host*, Ian Barker!'

The man gestured at himself expansively, garnering lukewarm applause and several 'just get on with it' groans. He reminded Rosie of the cabaret singer from *Phoenix Nights*.

'First up tonight is a Dun Cow icon – a favourite from last month, and the month before,' Ian bellowed. 'And also, let's face it, the month before that as well. Please give it up for Rhianne – *the Red Fox* – Thomas!'

At this, there was genuine, thundering applause – not least from Rosie and her co-workers. A not inconsiderable number of people were chanting, 'Red Fox, Red Fox, Red Fox' as Rhianne made her way to the mic.

Seconds later, she began belting out a note-perfect rendition of Cher's 'Believe'. Within moments, the atmosphere in the pub had shifted; people were up on their feet, dancing and singing along, as if the woman on stage was fronting an international arena tour rather than doing karaoke in a backstreet east London boozer.

Rosie felt her mouth drop open as Rhianne hit the song's bridge and pointed directly at her. The sentiment of the track wasn't lost on her; it was the late-1990s equivalent of 'I Will Survive'.

'I see you weren't given sufficient warning about this place, or what happens here,' said a deep, sardonic voice from somewhere to her left.

Rosie jumped and – before she could register she was doing it – smiled in sincere delight at the sight of Aled. 'None whatsoever,' she told him, 'although I'm not sure anything could have prepared me for this . . .' Rosie waved a hand in Rhianne's direction as she took a bow and the crowd clapped again. 'How . . . how is she not famous? Her voice is *insane*. How is she not, like, Adele or something?'

Aled shrugged. 'No idea. But she definitely bears a good chunk of the blame for the "all Welsh people can sing" stereotype. At least around here.'

'Do another for us, my darling,' Ian was saying to Rhianne as she turned to leave the stage. 'Get this crowd properly warmed up for us.'

'One more,' she said, as a ripple of applause swept through the room. She whispered something into Ian's ear and he fiddled with the computer keyboard to the right of the microphones.

'That last one was for my new friend Rosie. And this one's for *her* new friend.' Aled groaned as the opening bars of 'You Can Call Me Al' by Paul Simon started up.

'Nobody could accuse her of being subtle, could they?' he said wryly.

Rosie laughed. 'Absolutely not. I'm guessing you hear this one a lot?'

'Frequently,' he nodded. 'You all right for a drink? You look almost ready for another.'

'Ah, go on then,' Rosie said, grinning. She couldn't remember the last time she'd had a night out like this. It seemed there were surprises round every corner. 'Thanks. Cider, please.'

'Coming up.'

She watched him squeeze past rapt patrons as he moved towards the bar. It was a credit to Rhianne's charismatic performance that the crowd wasn't parting like the Red Sea around the hot man; people were too distracted by her vocals to notice that a god walked among them.

He had the 'dishevelled academic' thing going on again, and Rosie had to admit it was working for him. Where a tie had once been was an unbuttoned shirt collar – cream, with a pale blue stripe. This exposed a tanned neck with a prominent Adam's apple, which for some reason was weirdly fascinating. His hair had been cut recently, she observed, and the shorter length made it more inclined to stay stuck up and ruffled after he raked a hand through it.

Without actually deciding to, Rosie realised she'd begun cataloguing his physical features and behavioural tics dispassionately – the way a scientist might log the antics of a mouse in a lab. It was almost like working through an equation backwards: she knew the answer was 'he's stupidly good-looking', but she was trying to find the formula that made this true. If this intellectualising was an attempt to swerve the chances of Aled attracting *her* – sparking the sort of lustful longing he must easily ignite in others – she wasn't conscious of it.

The notion of being interested in anyone romantically felt anathema after the James disaster. The near-farcical manner of his departure, and her subsequent discovery that he'd likely been playing away, had attached blinkers to Rosie's eyes. There were more important things to focus on – and Aled's incredible looks, as well as the way he inhabited the flat without dominating it, always asked if she wanted tea, *and* was the most considerate bathroom-sharer she'd ever encountered, were merely bonuses in their convenient flat-sharing arrangement.

As Rhianne sang about bodyguards and long-lost pals, Aled reappeared next to her. Yaz – no longer swallowed up in the crowd – side-eyed him, then mouthed '*Fit, or what?*' at Rosie, whose face immediately heated. Aled handed Rosie her pint, then apologised for missing Yaz out of the round.

'It's fine,' Yaz said. 'I should slow down, anyway, I can't take the pace – not built for heavy drinking.' She gestured at her slight frame, and Rosie felt a wave of loathing for her own lumpen fleshiness threaten to drown her good mood.

No, she told herself, *that wasn't a dig at you.* She reminded herself that other people didn't think or care about her body shape nearly as much as she did – that they were more interested in their own lives than her dress size. It was a refrain she was having to repeat more often than usual after the upheaval of the past few weeks.

'I didn't know you'd be coming,' Rosie said to Aled.

'Whereas *I* knew you would be – there was no way Rhianne was going to let you off your first-ever rough pub karaoke.'

'That was the impression I got when she said, *You will come out with us tonight if I have to tie you up with squid ink spaghetti and drag you down the street*,' Rosie laughed. 'The whole thing feels a bit left-field, though, based on how smart and stylish the deli is. I'd never have picked this place as her choice for Friday night drinks.'

'I think it's the vibe she likes,' Aled said. 'The singing, the raucousness – the fact everyone talks to, and over, everyone else. I suspect the general sense of drunken goodwill reminds her of home.'

'Home? As in, Wales?'

'Yep,' he nodded, taking a sip of some golden-coloured ale. 'We grew up in a small town on the north coast. Right by the sea. It's not the most exciting place, but it's the sort where people all know one another: a community, I suppose.

Living there, you always knew that if someone caught you smoking in an alleyway or whatever, news of what you'd been up to would get home even before *you* did. You'd arrive back to find your mam already irate, lecture fully loaded and ready for unleashing.'

'Are you speaking from personal experience?' Rosie asked, smiling. She was amazed – borderline intoxicated – by the easy way he was chatting to her. Perhaps he felt more comfortable talking about other people than he did about himself? This tallied with his willingness to debate the qualities of various on-screen Knightleys, Rosie supposed.

'No,' he said. 'I don't think it'll shock you to hear I was the quiet one.'

Rosie laughed and shook her head.

'But Rhianne was constantly in bother for one thing or another,' Aled went on. 'She was well ready to spread her wings by the time she left. I think she misses the old place more than she lets on, though.'

'Oh,' Rosie said. 'Do you think she'll ever go back?'

'No.' He shook his head. 'Her parents have both passed, now – I think it'd be a different place to her than the one she remembers, so in a sense she's missing something that doesn't exist anymore. There's a word for it in Welsh. *Hiraeth*. It doesn't translate properly into English.'

'Herrr – what, now? What does it mean?' Rosie asked, on tenterhooks.

'*Hiraeth*,' Aled repeated. 'It sort of means longing. Wistfulness. Yearning, tinged with nostalgia. It's like a special, specifically Welsh homesickness, muddled with grief for lost things that can't ever come back.'

'Wow,' Rosie breathed, around the lump that had suddenly risen in her throat. 'That's . . . beautiful. And so sad.'

Before Aled could reply, Rhianne emerged from behind a wall of burly men and threw her arms around him. 'You're here!' she cried. 'Talking and everything! I knew you'd tag along and be sociable if I got Rosie out.'

'Hi, Rhi,' Aled said, disentangling himself from her embrace and looking slightly abashed. 'Week all right?'

'Of course, now I have this one on my team,' Rhianne said, jerking a thumb at Rosie. 'She's a marvel, just like you said she'd be. Write this down for posterity, because the chances of me ever saying it again are slim: you – were – right.'

Aled rolled his eyes and Rosie laughed. The banter that ping-ponged between him and Rhianne was witty but warm – the sort of bickering that only close siblings were usually capable of.

It was the kind of dynamic she'd never had with Michael, whose status as their parents' favourite had made his every gibe at Rosie genuinely hurtful. He could mock her with little fear of retaliation or consequence beyond, 'Now come on, Michael, play nicely with your sister.' If Rosie had been given a pound for every time one of his insults had been dismissed as a 'boys will be boys' misstep, she wouldn't have needed a flatmate.

As the night unfolded, Rosie fully relaxed – and gave herself up to chaotic fun in a way she hadn't for as long as she could remember. Marcus treated the crowd to a surprisingly excellent rendition of 'Lose Yourself' by Eminem, while Becky and Yaz tag-teamed an admirable 'Shallow' from *A Star is Born*. Becky yodelled tunelessly through Lady Gaga's elongated 'ohhh's as the song swelled towards its apex, and Rosie genuinely thought she might die laughing.

She and Aled were the sole members of the group who point-blank refused to expose themselves to public humiliation – though Rhianne insisted that Rosie was only being given a pass because she was a rough pub virgin. 'Al's a law unto himself – simply not for turning – but I've got my eye on you for next month,' she said.

Predictably, Rhianne performed the night's final number. She was swept back onto the stage by what Rosie had come to think of as her army of fans, and a still-fawning Ian Barker handed her his microphone as though it was her rightful property.

'They say it's not over until the fat lady sings,' Rhianne quipped, grinning broadly. She was in a scoop-necked, skintight body, leather-look leggings and heeled black boots tonight, with a silk scarf tied around her neck like one of the girls from *Grease*. 'Well, here I am,' she said, shimmying for the crowd so her bosom bounced and her bottle-red hair gleamed in the pub's yellowish light. 'Though I prefer the word *voluptuous*, if I'm honest.'

The audience whooped and cheered, only quietening down as a familiar pattern of echoing, maudlin piano notes signalled the beginning of 'Total Eclipse of the Heart'.

'Oh yes, she's going there,' Aled said from right behind Rosie. She felt his warm breath hit the shell of her ear and shivered, then shrugged off the sensation and laughed. 'She might as well be singing "Bread of Heaven" and waving a flag with a dragon on it,' Aled quipped.

'She's incredible,' Rosie said, with total sincerity. 'An absolute force. I wish I could be like her.'

'Don't do that,' Aled said, with the half-smile she'd come to think of as uniquely his. 'You're great. Exactly who you're supposed to be. And more of a force than you know – if a slightly clumsy one.'

Rosie had no idea how to respond to this, so she smiled and threw herself into singing along with the rest of the Dun Cow's rowdy patrons. Even Aled – predictably tunefully – had now joined in.

Borne aloft by several more drinks than she'd usually imbibe, as well as the uniquely uplifting sound of many voices coming together as one, Rosie felt how far she'd travelled in a few short weeks. Rhianne sweetly sang the gentle plea, 'Turn around, bright eyes', and Rosie's gaze found Aled's in the semi-darkness.

Understanding bloomed between them, and Rosie felt un upsurge of gratitude that he'd brought her into what she knew, instinctively, was his small circle of friends. It was a generous gesture he needn't have made, and at this moment it meant the world to her.

Though Rosie was only a mile or so from home, she had no map for the place she was suddenly in. But as a swaying Becky seized her left hand, a whooping Yaz took her right, and Marcus and Aled stood behind her, still singing, she revelled in being there.

October

Chapter 14

For some time, Rosie had suspected that she wasn't the only person feeding the neighbourhood's stray cat.

She'd seen him on several mornings over the past few weeks, and each time he seemed no less hungry than usual – but there was no doubt he'd got bigger during the summer. He now had the look of a greedy chancer, rather than the sad mien of a malnourished scrounger. He was less Oliver Twist, more Artful Dodger.

Rosie's theory was confirmed when she walked up the alleyway to the rear of William Road. As she passed the fence that separated the alley from her garden, she stumbled across a shiny metal bowl, still half full of a strong-smelling, gelatinous mass that could only be cat food. Rosie didn't much use this cut-through, but time was incredibly tight this morning.

Concerned that she hadn't appeared before he left the flat for work – and aware she was due at the deli by nine – Aled had knocked on her door to discover she'd slept through her alarm. To his credit, he'd managed not to laugh as Rosie freaked out at the prospect of being late and bolted for the shower. When she emerged, he was gone – but she discovered that he'd made her a strong coffee in a travel cup and left it on the kitchen counter.

She smiled and sipped at the drink, then pulled her soft woolly scarf closer into her neck. Something in Aled had loosened, Rosie thought – and there were moments when she even thought she could see it in the easier set of his shoulders, the readiness with which his trademark tentative smile appeared. In turn, this had released some tension in her. It made the flat feel like home again, in a way it hadn't for longer than she cared to admit.

In the months before James's departure, she'd forgotten what it felt like to live with someone who seemed genuinely interested in her – and despite his shyness, Aled seemed to enjoy her company. Since their night of 'rough pub karaoke', something like friendship had begun unfurling between them. They'd graduated from making one another cups of tea to regularly sharing meals; it turned out Aled was a capable, creative cook, and his experience of cuisines from far-flung locations made for some interesting – and delicious – food.

They'd text one another if they were close to running out of milk or bread, and had fallen into the habit of sending occasional messages during the day. Aled would bring Rosie news of his students' most audacious behaviour –

Preposterous excuse of the day goes to Umair Ansari in Year Eight, who claims his homework sheet was stolen by an owl 🐯 🚓 😳

and in exchange, Rosie would report her day's funniest or most heartening moments:

Good Looking Latte Drinker finally asked Sleek Haired Writer if he could buy her a coffee!!! 😄. Have been watching him try and work up the courage for weeks

Admittedly, this dynamic was nothing like the 'strictly business' set-up Rosie had described to Niamh when Aled moved in. She supposed her best friend was right; she'd become chummy with her flatmate-slash-landlord because she didn't know how *not* to – and, as Niamh had predicted, his reserve was no match for her sunny effervescence.

When she got to work she was greeted by Rhianne, who had a pretty, very nervous young woman by her side. 'Ah,

Rosie! This is Tobi,' Rhianne announced, gesturing to the girl with huge brown eyes, incredible skin and an abundance of natural afro curls, which she'd gathered into a high ponytail.

'Pleased to meet you,' Rosie said warmly.

Tobi nodded shyly and shook the hand Rosie offered her.

'Tobi's joining us because Marcus's Master's course has started up again and he needs to drop some shifts,' Rhianne explained. 'Can I leave you to show her the ropes?'

'Course you can,' Rosie said, grinning. She'd been working at the deli for less than a month, but it felt like she'd been part of the team forever.

'Great, I need to go and kick the arse of our greengrocer – he's sent me turnips instead of parsnips, as if I can use them interchangeably. Whoever heard of spicy *turnip* soup? And who wants a maple-glazed *turnip* and bulgur wheat salad? It's utterly fucked up tomorrow's menus.'

Rosie made a clenched-jaw face and said, 'Eek,' in agreement with Rhianne, but also in sympathy with the greengrocer. By the time Rhianne had finished with him, Terry – the man about to get the full-length album version of her root vegetable lecture – was surely going to wish he'd moved to Spain with his ex-wife.

Rhianne flounced off, leaving a cloud of Chanel No. 5 in her wake. Tobi stared after her, as if she'd just seen Marilyn Monroe waltz away from a Hollywood film set.

'You get used to her,' Rosie said, smiling. 'Shall we get started?'

'OK,' Tobi agreed, still a little hesitant.

'I was new myself a few weeks ago,' Rosie told her. 'I promise you'll feel like part of the family in no time.'

Within a few hours, Rosie had taught Tobi most of the things Marcus, Yaz and Becky had explained to her on her first day. She'd also discovered Tobi was bright and articulate once she warmed up, but had recently missed out on a place at her chosen university.

She hadn't achieved the required A grade in history, so was unable to pursue the BA Philosophy course she'd set her heart on. It didn't take Rosie long to intuit that Tobi had been crushed by this disappointment – and that her family's lack of support for her desire to study had made matters worse.

Instead of picking herself up and trying to find an alternative course through clearing, Tobi had floundered. Now, as her parents piled on the pressure for her to do something productive, she'd taken this job at the deli.

'I bumped into Rhianne one day last week,' Tobi explained. 'Like, *physically* – I bashed into her so she spilled hot coffee all over her coat. I was so emotional and embarrassed I burst into tears, and when she asked why I was upset I ended up telling her about the whole uni mess. By the time she'd wiped the milk froth off her collar, she'd offered me a job.'

'Sounds like Rhianne,' Rosie said fondly. 'She's *a lot*, but she's incredibly kind. You'll love working here, I think.'

The afternoon rush saw them scurrying around delivering orders, wiping down tables and making endless espresso shots. As their crowd of customers began to thin out, Rosie caught Tobi in a quiet moment and told her, with full honesty, 'You've done *brilliantly* for day one. I think I'd have freaked out if I'd had to deal with queues that size when I first started here.'

'Thanks,' Tobi said, beaming at her.

Rosie poured out two glasses of iced water and handed one to Tobi. 'You've got a lot to offer, you know,' she said, unsure why her mouth had begun to deliver an inspirational speech her brain hadn't proofread. 'Don't let anyone make you feel like you can't do the things you want to do, the things that you feel are meant for you.'

Tobi looked at the floor. 'Thanks,' she said again. 'I just can't help feeling a bit . . . flat. Does that make sense? I had it all planned out – I knew exactly how the next few years were going to go. And now . . . now I'm here.' She smiled weakly and tried to look stoical.

'Here is good,' said Rosie. 'Here is great, actually. But you don't have to *stay* here. When you feel like your world's blown up, it hurts – but afterwards, you don't have to live in the place where you land.'

As she said it, she realised how true this was, for her too. Looking after and then losing her grandfather had left her bereft – but soon afterwards, she'd met James. Had she clung to him like a spar in the wake of a shipwreck? Had that felt easier than the other options, than pursuing what she felt truly passionate about?

'What about you?' Tobi asked.

'What about me?'

'Well, you seem like one of those "follow your dreams" sort of people. You remind me of one of my teachers. What do you want to do? Are you in training for something?'

Rosie coloured, embarrassed and a little angry with herself. Who was she to lecture a smart, ambitious eighteen-year-old on not giving up – on making the most of her life?

'Not at the moment,' she admitted. 'I've . . . well, I've not had the easiest time lately. I split up with my partner of ten years, left a job I'd been in for a long time and now I'm sort of . . . working stuff out, I suppose.'

'That sounds hard,' Tobi said.

'I'm lucky to have a few people on my side making it easier,' Rosie reassured her.

'Your family?'

'Ha! No. I haven't even told them what's happened, to be honest,' Rosie groaned. 'They love me – at least my parents do – but it'd be a stretch to describe them as supportive.' More than anything else, she realised, Rosie felt *lonely* inside her family. They didn't not care about her, but they didn't understand her – they saw what was lacking in her without recognising the qualities that her friends valued most.

'Sounds familiar,' Tobi said. 'My dad says I should go and get a job in an office. Work my way up. The idea of borrowing money to go to university was always crazy to him and my mum.'

'My parents said the same.'

'So did you not go, then? Do you regret it?' Tobi's dark eyes were wide, and Rosie saw that she had a strange sort of sway over this young woman. The Peter Parker principle popped into her mind, unbidden: *with great power comes great responsibility.*

Rosie knew she had lied to herself for years. At times, she had successfully convinced herself she had no regrets about abandoning university. But to lie to Tobi now felt somehow sacrilegious; it would be a shabby abuse of trust, and a poor foundation for the friendship she could already feel burgeoning between them.

'I did go,' Rosie admitted. 'Then my grandad got ill and I moved back home so I could take care of him. I was supposed to restart my course – I always said I would. But I didn't . . . And yes, I do regret that.'

She felt her eyes grow glossy and blinked the sudden wetness away. She'd never even told Niamh that, deep down, she wished she could go back and do things differently. Rosie had a strange sense of weightlessness – as if uttering the words aloud had lifted a burden she hadn't even known she was carrying.

Tobi's gaze was sympathetic. Rosie liked that she didn't feel the need to fill the silence between them with cheerful platitudes; it reminded her of the measured, calm way Aled approached conversations.

'Which is why,' Rosie said, characteristically unable to resist speaking, 'you should think long and hard before giving up on something you want. You can modify your plan, instead of chucking it in the bin. It isn't too late.'

Tobi nodded, then tipped her head to one side as if deep in thought. 'Is it too late for you? To go to uni, I mean? Are there reasons why you can't?'

'Maybe,' Rosie said, 'but I'm not sure how good they are at this moment.' In truth, her standard objections to studying seemed flimsier and less convincing than ever. Marriage and babies were off the table for now, as was the notion that her career could take a back seat to her more successful partner's.

'So does that mean you're thinking about it, then?' Tobi asked, smiling gently at her new friend.

'I could be,' Rosie nodded, smiling back. 'Anyway, we'd best get on. The dishwasher's not going to empty itself.'

When Rosie arrived back at the flat that evening Aled was sitting on the sofa, surrounded by what she could only describe as a sea of A4 paper. He was bent over a printout of what she assumed was a student's essay, his back to her, green pen in hand.

It was nice to see him there, using the space as though he had a right to. It had taken weeks, but he was finally behaving as though he *lived* in the flat – less like a troublesome house guest afraid to emerge from his room in case he irritated his host.

'Hey,' she said, gently breaking his concentration. She could tell he'd been so lost in whatever he was reading that he hadn't heard her come in.

He turned to say hi, and Rosie felt like a brick had dropped through her stomach. Her mouth went dry and her heart seemed to pause for a moment, then resume beating at double time.

He was wearing *glasses*. Spectacles with black, heavy frames that had begun sliding down his nose. It was like he'd one-upped himself, embellishing his sexy professor look with a finishing touch that should have come with a health warning.

'Secret glasses?' Rosie stuttered, nonsensically. 'Since when?'

He pushed at the bridge of the glasses with a forefinger, then made a confused smile-frown face. Rosie was increasingly convinced that he was woefully ignorant of his effect on women. And probably a decent proportion of men, too, come to think of it.

She added *looks insanely hot in glasses* to her internal catalogue of Theoretical Reasons Why Aled Is Inhumanly Attractive. The list was growing, but filing the information away in a drawer marked 'Factual Observations' felt safe; she could place it alongside gems such as *ribbons of vegetable are no substitute for pasta* and *no one ever wants 'just one bite' of your dessert if they didn't order their own.*

Collecting the information felt protective. Self-preserving. If she kept an accurate record of his charms, they couldn't take her by surprise. This, Rosie had decided, was important – as this afternoon's revelation proved. The last thing she needed, especially so recently after being dumped, was a sudden attack of the hots for someone so wildly out of her league.

'Since I was about twelve,' Aled said, reclaiming her attention. 'And not secret – just sporadic. They're readers: I wear them when my eyes are tired, though I should probably put them on more often.'

'Right,' Rosie nodded. 'Well. They're . . . really nice. Lovely, in fact. Specs-y, you might say.'

Oh. Sweet. Jesus.

'Thanks . . . ?' Aled was looking at her curiously, like he was concerned for her state of mind.

'What are you up to?' Rosie asked, realising the stupidity of the question only seconds after voicing it. It was quite clear he was marking students' work.

'Marking students' work,' he said, and she found herself wishing she could rewind time and live the last five minutes again, less idiotically.

'Upper sixth's timed essays on *Dr Faustus*,' Aled went on, 'some of which are making me wonder if their previous teacher even read the text with them.'

'That bad?'

'This one's pretty good,' he said, gesturing at the paper he'd set down on the coffee table. 'Zuli Anan's on course for an A for sure. However, Josh Holloway seems very confused about the doctor's relationship with Helen of Troy.' He pointed to another paper, handwritten in what looked like Sharpie ink. There was a coffee stain in one corner. 'Josh's essay refers to "the face that scoffed a thousand chips" – which suggests both a serious misreading of scene twelve and a deep-seated love of junk food.'

Rosie laughed, then reminded herself that *low-key witty* was already on her hot list. Before she could say anything else, a sudden movement in her peripheral vision made her jump.

'Oh my *god*,' she yelped, clutching her hands to her chest. A moment later, the shifting shape resolved into a form Rosie recognised.

It was the cat. Until he'd stood up to stretch, he'd been practically invisible – his silvery form blending perfectly with the throw blanket he'd been sitting on.

'*Ah*. About him . . .' Aled said, clearing his throat and looking sheepish. But Rosie had already crossed to the other side of the room, and was crouching down so she could pet the cat's head.

As he began to purr, Rosie said, 'Yes?' and arched an eyebrow.

'Well,' Aled continued, 'it was raining when I got home. And he was by the kitchen door. I didn't have the heart to leave him out there, getting soaked.'

The cat was now lying on his back on the same seat it seemed he'd occupied all evening – shamelessly showing off his fluffy belly to Rosie, who was obliging him by tickling it.

She looked up at Aled, penny dropping. 'It's you, isn't it?'

'What's me?'

'You're the one who's been feeding him all this time.' Rosie grinned, sure that she was right.

'I might have been filling in for you occasionally,' he said, scrunching his nose to push his glasses up again. 'He's been turning up while you've been at work the past few weeks. I couldn't let him starve, could I?'

'I *knew* you saw me in the garden that day,' Rosie said, feeling oddly triumphant.

'The day I rescued your apples? Guilty as charged. I knew from then that you were taking care of him.' Aled's cheeks were growing pink, and Rosie made another mental note: *blushes adorably.*

'Look at him,' Rosie said. 'He's a chonk. Easily twice the size he was when he first started appearing in the back yard. So, here's my theory: you've been giving him food *since the day you moved in* upstairs. The day of my major carrier bag malfunction was merely the moment you realised *I'd* been feeding him, too.'

Aled sighed and rolled his eyes. 'All right, Miss Marple. Fine. You've got me.'

'So why not just admit it?' Rosie laughed.

'I dunno,' Aled said, his face fully flushed now. 'I guess I didn't want to undermine the Rosie–Springsteen dynamic by pointing out that my Whiskas Fish Favourites sachets were just as appealing as yours. I got the impression your relationship with him was . . . special to you.'

Rosie chose not to dwell on this astute thoughtfulness, and instead asked: 'Springsteen?'

'Yeah. Sorry. It felt fitting. The first time I saw him he was prancing along the top of the fence, spotlit by a street lamp. Dancing in the dark?'

'It's perfect,' Rosie said, smiling. Then she remembered James's dire warnings about the stray's questionable hygiene. 'You don't think he's got fleas, do you?' She winced at the thought of having to fog the entire flat with pesticide.

'I'm sure he hasn't,' Aled said, with suspicious certainty.

'And you're sure because . . . ?' Rosie teased.

'OK, because I bought some of that Spot On stuff from the pet shop and treated him with it. And also a wormer. He's protected from vermin for the foreseeable future – as are your soft furnishings.'

'Incredible.' She laughed. The man was like a human

advent calendar – it seemed that behind every door, there was a pleasant surprise patiently awaiting discovery.

'Shall we keep him?' they said together. The answer came in stereo, too, before the word 'we' could echo too loudly: 'Yes.'

It was decided that they'd go to the pet shop tomorrow and purchase some essentials: a scratching post, a soft bed, some catnip toys and maybe even a cat flap for the back door. After picking him up for a quick cuddle, Rosie deposited Springsteen back on the chair that, already, he seemed to have designated Cat Territory.

She went through to the kitchen and made salmon teriyaki stir-fry for two while Aled marked the last of his upper sixth's essays. Jenna Marshall got an easy A, he informed her, while gifted-but-lazy Dimitri Adamos scraped a C.

If Aled recognised, as Rosie did, that taking on joint responsibility for an animal was an odd decision for two people who didn't intend to live together long, he chose not to mention it. Deciding to bask in this feeling of contentment for however long it lasted, Rosie didn't either.

Chapter 15

The following Saturday, Rosie sat on a stool at Niamh's vast, marble-topped kitchen island. Brendan had taken the babies for a walk in the park with one of the other neighbourhood dads, and conversation had rapidly turned to Rosie's living situation.

This was the first time she'd seen Niamh alone since the weekend Aled moved in – and Rosie was determined not to give her any cause to cry *I told you so*.

'He's very neat,' she informed her best friend over a cup of steaming hot tea. 'And very considerate. He always cleans the cooker after he's used it and never fails to replace the toilet roll when it's run out . . . All of which is to say, he functions like a responsible adult and meets basic flatmate expectations.'

'Wow,' Niamh said, smirking over her own mug. 'You're doing a great job of pretending to be underwhelmed.'

'What's that supposed to mean?'

'It means you can't fool me. After living with James for so long, cohabiting with a man who'll wipe his *own* scrambled egg remnants off the hob must be bliss.'

'Fine,' Rosie conceded with a small smile. 'It is. It's made me realise how much time I used to spend sorting out messes that weren't mine. He cleaned the bathroom the other day – *properly*, with bleach, and without being asked.'

'I am so jealous,' Niamh groaned. 'Seriously – if you carry on *I'm* going to develop a crush on him. Men who don't want to be mothered are like gold dust. I'm convinced that if I offered Brendan a grand to locate our mop and bucket, he wouldn't be able to do it.'

156

'Who said anything about a crush?' Rosie squeaked.

'You did. Well, your *face* did anyway. You look all gooey every time he's mentioned. Also, you're zooming in on the fact he's not a total slob to distract from the big picture – which is he's gorgeous, and it's clearly affecting you.'

'Rubbish!' Rosie protested.

Niamh rolled her eyes, signalling that this pathetic attempt at a rebuttal wasn't worth a response. 'You know,' she said after a minute, arching an eyebrow and looking altogether too pleased with herself, 'you get this faraway look in your eyes whenever you talk about him. I don't have my contacts in but I'm ninety-nine per cent sure your pupils re-form into cute little hearts.'

'Shut *uuup*,' Rosie complained. 'I do not. *They* do not.'

'I thought you might *melt* when you told me about the cat,' Niamh went on, enjoying herself. 'So much for *ships that pass on the way in and out of the building* and *no relationship*. He's been in the spare room a month and you've already become co-pawrents.'

'*Co-pawrents?*' Rosie said, with a horrified laugh. 'Wash your mouth out.'

'I read it in a book,' Niamh huffed. 'An excellent love story about two people who share a dog and end up shagging. A tale that feels VERY PERTINENT to this situation.'

'OK, all right, yes. We've become friends,' Rosie interjected. 'I said we wouldn't, and we have. Happy?'

'Not especially,' Niamh said. 'You're still in denial, and still celibate – which seems an awful waste, what with you fancying him rotten.'

'For god's sake,' Rosie moaned. 'Did I hit my head and wake up in 2006? Are we back in Year Twelve?'

'Nope, we're in a brave new world. One where you are single, free to mingle and – rather conveniently – have an incredibly fit flatmate.'

'A flatmate who, as mentioned, is *my friend*,' Rosie said. 'And a flatmate you told me was a really bad idea.'

'That was when I thought him moving in was a ploy to get James back! You remember James? He's the ex-boyfriend whose very existence has become a distant memory because you're obsessed with a brooding Welshman.'

'I am *not* obsessed,' Rosie insisted, feeling heat begin to creep up her neck.

'But you *do* fancy him,' Niamh crowed. 'And frankly, after meeting him properly the other day, I can't blame you. That *voice* . . .' she sighed. 'It adds a whole new dimension to the loveliness. It's so deep. So rich. He could make a killing narrating erotica on Audible.'

Rosie put her tea down on the countertop and buried her head in her hands. She knew it had been a mistake to introduce them at the deli the other night . . . Not least because he'd visibly steeled himself – swallowed the urge to shrink away and head home, instead sticking around to chat with her as they all shared an after-work drink.

Rosie's stomach flipped at the memory of how warm and welcoming he'd been. He wasn't naturally garrulous, but he'd clearly understood that Niamh was someone important – that it mattered to Rosie that they got along. This effortful friendliness had made Rosie feel like she mattered, too.

'Come on!' Niamh cried, prising Rosie's fingers away from her face. 'Why are you being so glum about this?'

'Why are *you* being so jolly about it?' Rosie demanded, suddenly aware that her temper was starting to fray. 'You were entirely against me having anything to do with him a few weeks ago. Now you're all in favour of me swooning like a schoolgirl while we live under the same roof.'

'All right, I'll stop,' Niamh said, her dark eyes wide with concern. 'I was just messing. But, you know . . . it's OK to feel attracted to someone else, if you do. You don't need to feel bad about it – you're not being unfaithful to anyone, which is probably more than we can say for James. And given that this living arrangement isn't going to last very long, a fling might even be fun . . . ?'

'I thought you said you were going to stop,' Rosie said, trying hard to smile and realising too late that she was grimacing.

'Yes,' Niamh said seriously, 'I will.' She mimed zipping her mouth shut, then immediately opened it again to slurp the last of her tea.

Rosie sighed and concentrated on her own drink, her insides writhing with discomfort. She felt rattled. Annoyed. With Niamh, but also with herself.

'Rose . . . ? What is it?' Niamh asked, her tone gentle now.

'It's just . . . well. Even if I *did* have a thing for him – which I absolutely *don't* – what would be the point? It's not as if someone that good-looking would ever be interested in me.' To her dismay, Rosie felt tears beginning to pool in her eyes.

'Oh love,' Niamh said. 'What are you talking about? You're amazing. Beautiful. The best person I know.'

'James literally dumped me for not being fit enough – in any sense of the word,' Rosie said, trying to stem the urgent flow of liquid from her eyes. 'He didn't find me attractive anymore. Just . . . didn't like me in the way you're supposed to like someone you live with. *Sleep* with.'

Niamh took a deep breath, then exhaled so forcefully that Rosie was almost surprised she wasn't breathing fire. 'I hate that man,' she said, through gritted teeth. 'But let's get one thing straight: he didn't leave because there is anything wrong with *you*. He didn't leave because he didn't like you, or didn't fancy you. He fucked off because, deep down, he doesn't really like himself.'

'What do you mean?'

'I mean that he was dissatisfied with *himself*, not with you. He bought into all the gym and diet stuff because it promised a fix – and because it made him feel superior, which we both know he enjoys. Think about it: how many times over the years did he make you feel deficient because he had a degree and you didn't? How much did he love it that he earned more money than you?'

Rosie sniffed. 'He did run me down sometimes. He'd talk about wasted potential but then list all the reasons why there was no point in me ever trying to go back to uni.'

'Lording it over you made him feel better,' Niamh said. 'I sometimes suspected it, but I never felt like I could say anything because you seemed so happy with him.'

'I was,' Rosie mumbled. 'Or at least I thought I was. It all seemed normal to me.'

'I've no doubt it did,' Niamh said, her eyes communicating what she wouldn't say out loud: that Rosie's own family treated her in a similarly selfish, thoughtless fashion. 'But listen to me,' she went on. 'There is no reason why that flatmate of yours wouldn't find you irresistible. You are *incredible*. You're allowed to want things, and you're allowed to go after them. You don't have to hide your light under a bushel because it makes other people more comfortable.'

Rosie took a deep breath and nodded. Not for the first time, she found herself thinking about Rhianne's bone-deep self-assurance – a fundamental personality trait that came with a shiny, protective carapace she couldn't help but envy. Now, though, she found herself wondering how hard won the other woman's boundless self-confidence had been. Had Rhianne faced childhood teasing for being a redhead? For being bigger than other girls? Based on Rosie's experience, she must have – yet she hadn't let other people's small-mindedness convince her to shrink herself.

Rhianne took up space, proudly and unapologetically. It hadn't occurred to Rosie until now that this might take work – that it required a commitment to loving herself that, while it might occasionally bend, was never broken.

'Do you know what I think you need?' Niamh asked, handing Rosie a tissue and pulling a packet of dark-chocolate digestives out of a cupboard.

'What?' Rosie asked, wiping her eyes.

'A biscuit, a shopping trip and a cocktail. Not necessarily

in that order. I'm going to phone Brendan and tell him to gird his loins for a full afternoon of solo parenting. You and I are going out.'

'We are?'

'Yes. No arguments.'

'I'm not sure I'm up for a makeover, if that's what you're planning,' Rosie said weakly. She gestured at her jeans, trainers and tunic top. 'We're working with questionable raw material here – She *Isn't* All That.'

'This isn't a makeover,' Niamh said, 'it's an intervention. It's about getting you to see yourself as worthy, not dressing you up for other people. But I can see I'm going to need reinforcements.'

She pulled her phone from the back pocket of her jeans, swiped the screen a few times and then put it to her ear.

'Who are you calling?' Rosie asked. 'Brendan?'

'No,' Niamh said, 'he'll keep.'

A moment later, she spoke into her phone: 'Rhianne, it's Niamh – Rosie's Niamh. Are you free?'

'This is going to be fun,' Rhianne announced as she ushered Rosie and Niamh through a door with 'Cleo's Closet' written directly above it in hot pink. 'Well worth the effort it took me to browbeat Marcus into pulling an extra shift.'

'Oh god, did he mind?' Rosie moaned.

'No, I think he was secretly grateful,' Rhianne said. 'Becky's on all day, so he'll get to moon after her for seven hours more than he was expecting this week – and get paid for it.'

'This place is heaven,' Niamh said, waving a hand to indicate the shop's array of brightly populated clothing rails, freestanding mirrors and shelves overflowing with accessories.

'It's a favourite,' Rhianne nodded. 'Rosie, your mission in here is to find items that make your heart happy. You are *not* to worry about what will "suit you", "hide a multitude of sins" or cover your arse.'

Rosie squirmed.

'I'm serious,' Rhianne insisted. 'Find things you like – stuff that brings you joy. This is dopamine dressing. It's about expressing yourself, flaunting your individuality – not putting on god-awful rags that claim they'll cover your belly or "balance out" your hips.'

'A-men,' Niamh said, turning to Rhianne for a high five.

'I'm still not clear on why you two have each other's numbers,' Rosie grumbled.

'I never meet anyone interesting without asking for their digits,' Niamh shrugged. 'I work on the assumption that they might come in handy. In this case, I thought about the deli potentially catering client events.'

'I didn't even know we did that,' Rosie said.

'Sometimes,' Rhianne explained, 'we do the odd bit of special occasion work. In fact, we have an after-hours party coming up in a few weeks – our first foray into hiring the deli out as a venue. I'll roster you on if you fancy the overtime.'

'Sign me up,' Rosie sighed. 'I have a feeling you two are going to make sure this afternoon bankrupts me.'

'We'll do nothing of the kind,' Niamh snorted. 'Anyway, your birthday's coming up – I'll get the first exciting item you find.'

'My birthday was two months ago,' Rosie protested.

'Whatever. I'm going to pretend it wasn't. Just stop stalling and start searching.'

'Seconded,' Rhianne said, pointing at a selection of brightly coloured dungarees. 'Let's crack on.'

'You two are a terrifying alliance,' Rosie said some hours later, as she, Niamh and Rhianne sat surrounded by shopping bags in the corner of a tiny north London cocktail bar.

She sipped her drink – a Bramble – through a shiny metal straw that sat between thick shards of ice. The combination of gin, lemon juice, blackberry and syrup was sharp but sweet. Opposite her, Niamh sipped an espresso martini and Rhianne nursed a negroni.

'We're the retail therapy equivalent of NATO,' Niamh said, crossing her arms. 'Nobody fucks with us.' Rosie rolled her eyes fondly but didn't disagree.

After her first few tentative selections, she'd given herself over to being handed random garments by her two friends, most of which were *wildly* different from anything in her current wardrobe. When she got over the shock of seeing her own cleavage in low-cut tops, her waist cinched in by colourful shirred dresses and her legs displayed in loud, patterned overalls, she began to enjoy herself.

She had even consented to visiting several cosmetics counters in the Westfield branch of John Lewis. Courtesy of Rhianne, Rosie had walked away with a red lipstick bolder than any she'd ever worn in her life. She'd also purchased an eyeshadow palette, highlighting powder and cream blush so she could recreate the look she was currently sporting at home. Carmel at the Bobbi Brown concession had cooed over her 'feline' green eyes, 'perfect pout' and 'flawlessly creamy skin' as she blended various powders and potions and applied them to Rosie's face. 'You remind me of the wee lesbian from *Derry Girls*,' she'd said. 'You know, the lass who's super glam in real life and best pals with the hairdresser from *Queer Eye*.'

Rosie sank back against the blue velvet banquette of their booth and felt almost euphoric – elated in a way that her half-drunk beverage alone couldn't account for. Bossy though they were, her friends had given up their Saturdays to boost her confidence. Their affection for her was palpable, and their sincere regard raised her opinion of herself.

It hit Rosie that years spent feeling unseen and unappreciated, often in ways she hadn't been consciously aware of, had blinded her to a simple fact. Being around people who loved her made liking, respecting and expressing herself that much easier. It was a truth she intended to hold onto.

'Thank you for today,' she said, lifting her glass to

clink it against Niamh's and then Rhianne's. 'It's been . . . important. More so than I expected.' While new clothes were only set-dressing for what Rosie knew would be an ongoing self-esteem improvement project, she now saw that saying goodbye to her collection of voluminous 'don't look at me' t-shirts and 'flattering' cover-ups was a vital first step.

She fiddled with the hair tie at the nape of her neck, then fanned her mid-length blonde hair around her shoulders. It was a pretty colour but it lacked volume, and it spent most of its life pulled back into a ponytail. Rosie's mum had sometimes said it was a 'hair grow' rather than a haircut, and – for once – she wasn't wrong.

'What are my chances of finding a hair salon that'll take a walk-in?' she said, to nobody in particular. Niamh and Rhianne exchanged excited glances.

'Slim,' Rhianne said, 'but lucky for you I know a hairdresser who owes me a favour.'

'Of course you do,' smiled Niamh.

Two hours – and two glasses of hair salon wine – later, Rosie was the proud owner of a wavy chin-length bob with face-framing bangs. Jules – Rhianne's own hairdresser and good friend – had convinced her it would look stunning, and supplied ice-cold Sauvignon Blanc for Dutch courage.

'Our girl's all grown up!' Niamh cooed, clutching Rhianne and grinning at Rosie as Jules added shine spray to her new do. 'You look *exquisite*.'

Turning her head from side to side in Jules's Hollywood-style mirror, Rosie noted a lit-from-within glow that had little to do with the 'pink quartz shimmer brick' she'd purchased. She felt good about herself.

On the bus back to Walthamstow, Rosie felt her phone buzz from inside her bag.

Aled: You in for dinner?

Rosie smiled and started typing.

Rosie: Yep. On way back now. Do we need anything picked up?

She caught her reflection in the drizzle-spattered window, beyond which the sky was turning a deep, darkening blue. She *did* look gooey, in just the way Niamh had described this morning in her kitchen.

Rosie thanked god, the universe, or whatever else might be out there that she was heading home alone. That there were no witnesses to her daft expression beyond the sleepy-looking woman across the aisle.

Niamh had caught a cab back to Wanstead, while Rhianne had matched with someone on one of the many dating apps she dabbled in. On a whim, she'd decided to head to Soho for a no-notice date.

Rosie sighed and shook herself, determined to wipe the hazy look from her face. She nearly jumped when her phone vibrated again.

Aled: It's Saturday night so I say we live a little. How about takeaway curry and a few beers? X

Rosie's stomach immediately rumbled at the thought of chicken dhansak, Bombay aloo and golden fried parathas. The realisation that she was famished almost masked the involuntary jolt to the heart that accompanied Aled's casual use of 'we' – not to mention the electronic kiss that followed it.

Stop it, she told herself. *Put 'sends nice texts' on the list.*

The problem was, the catalogue of things Rosie liked about her flatmate was rapidly swelling beyond the boundaries she'd set for it. She had no idea how to quantify the way he looked when he was bent over a pile of paperwork, painstakingly searching a student's essay for ideas he could award marks for. It was impossible to categorise the electric thrill of feeling his hand graze hers as she passed him a frying pan or bowl that she'd washed up, and which he stood ready to dry.

How could she file away the stomach-dropping, breathtaking sensation of simply being *near* him? The feeling that the air around her was denser and heavier than it should be; the clean, soapy smell that wafted from his t-shirts and made her palms itch to find the bare skin beneath; the simultaneous softening and sense-sharpening that always came with meeting his dark gaze and being brave enough not to look away.

She took a deep breath and messaged him back.

Rosie: Amen to that! Will get the drinks on my way and we can order when I'm home? x

As the bus neared her stop, Rosie remembered what Niamh had said earlier: *you're zooming in to distract yourself from the big picture.* Her best friend had no idea how right she was.

A little too late, Rosie was realising that, try as she might, the man she'd found herself sharing a flat with could not be broken down into individual components. The whole was greater than the sum of its parts, and she was losing control of how he made her feel.

Aled replied a moment after she alighted on the pavement.

Perfect ☺ x

The word seemed to shimmer too brightly from her phone screen, imprinting itself on Rosie's retinas. She knew she'd still be able to see it with her eyes closed.

Aled *wasn't* perfect, she told herself. Nobody was. But increasingly, she suspected he came pretty close.

Chapter 16

The following morning, Rosie awoke to find her mum had already sent her a text message.

> Mum: What time will U & James arrive 2day? Wd B gd if U cd get here 11ish, help me do the lamb, potatoes, mint sauce, etc x

Rosie groaned. She hated textspeak, and she knew that 'help' meant 'cook single-handed' – though it was always fun to predict what excuse her mother would make for disappearing during Sunday lunch prep.

Her grin at remembering the time she'd popped out in stilettos to 'help someone with a flat tyre' faded as she took stock of several key facts. 1. She'd completely forgotten about going to her parents' house today. 2. She was even less keen to make the trip to Essex than usual. 3. She still hadn't told her family that:

   a) James had dumped her
   b) She'd moved a man they'd never heard of into her
      spare room
   c) She'd quit her 'nice office job' and started working
      in a cafe

The idea that she was happier making cappuccinos and skinny lattes all day than she'd ever been handling insurance claims would be utterly lost on them – as would the unexpected discovery that losing James had wounded her, but not fatally.

Rosie dreaded the look she'd see on Julie's horror-struck face when she explained why she'd come to Sunday lunch alone. She could hardly bear to think of the doom-laden pronouncements that would be made about her chances of finding someone new 'at her age'.

Would any of them actually be interested in how she felt about everything that had happened? Would they listen if she tried to explain that – despite the cruelty of it – James's sudden departure, far from breaking her, had made her think differently about her whole life and the possibilities it might yet hold? Or would she simply drive away from her childhood home feeling worse than she had when she arrived?

The answer to these questions was unequivocal, and it made a lump rise in Rosie's throat. It hurt that her parents and brother would happily co-opt her as the free-of-charge family chef, but wouldn't do her the courtesy of considering her feelings before passing judgement on her life. Rosie might be a thirty-two-year-old barista with a live-in landlord, no boyfriend and no idea where the next twelve months would take her – but she was OK. *Better* than OK. For the first time in a long time, she was teetering on the edge of believing in herself.

Before she could talk herself out of it, she typed a message to her mum and pressed send.

Rosie: Sorry, Mum – I can't make it today. I've had a really busy week and I have loads to do at home. I'll see you soon, though x

This, at least, was true. Rosie's laundry basket was overflowing and the fridge was almost bare. If she spent the best part of the day having 'quality time' with her family by making roast lamb with all the trimmings, she'd come back to a mile-long 'to do' list and beans on stale toast for dinner.

Within seconds, her mobile began to ring. She should have expected this, but it still took her by surprise. Deciding that swerving the call would only make matters worse, Rosie took a deep breath and answered it.

'What d'you mean, you can't make it? You have to come! I haven't seen you in a *month* – and I've got all the food in now.'

Roughly translated, this meant: if you don't come, I'm going to have to do everything myself. While Rosie had some sympathy with this – it was outrageous that her dad and Michael found themselves unequal to wielding a vegetable knife or donning an oven glove – she had decided to prioritise herself today, and she stiffened her resolve.

'I'm sorry, Mum,' Rosie said. 'I've had a lot going on lately and I need to sort my own stuff out.'

There. That was vague but firm.

'You sound strange. What d'you mean, you've had a lot going on? *Oh my god*, are you pregnant? It's about time, I suppose – though your father'll do his nut that you've got yourself knocked up before you're married.'

Oh, god. Why hadn't Rosie seen this coming?

'Mum, *stop*. I am definitely not pregnant.'

'Well, what is it, then?'

For a moment, Rosie considered bluffing – cobbling together some excuse that would fob Julie off for another few weeks, and allow her to avoid the inevitable furore the truth would cause. But explaining what had happened wouldn't be any easier next month, or the month after. This was a little like peeling a plaster off a patch of sensitised skin: better to rip the thing off in a single, fluid motion and brave the sting.

'James and I have split up,' she said, 'he left a few weeks ago.' Then she added, entirely unnecessarily, 'It was a shock, but I'm doing OK.'

'What?!' Julie screeched. Rosie pulled her mobile away from her ear.

'This is a disaster!' her mother shrieked. 'Where did he go? What *made* him go? Have you tried getting him *back*?'

Rosie heard this barrage of questions burst forth from her phone, which she was now holding at arm's length.

Apparently in no need of a reply, Julie gabbled on: 'You want to try and make him reconsider, girl. You don't want to be back out there, single, in your thirties! Finding a man is pot luck at the best of times – and this is definitely *not* the best of times, is it?'

Rosie felt her mother's words like a kick to the stomach. Reeling and a little nauseous, she said: 'You'd rather I beg a man who clearly doesn't love me for a second chance, than go it alone?'

'Of course he loves you!' Julie scoffed. 'He's been with you for *years*, hasn't he? Unless you think he's traded you in for an upgrade . . . ?'

Ouch. The casual way her mother had thrown this potentially devastating verbal grenade staggered Rosie. Her mouth hung open in astonishment. If she hadn't already been fairly sure James had left her for Dylan, these words would have cut her to the bone.

'Rosie? Rosie! Are you still there?' came her mother's voice. She sounded tinny and far away, and Rosie realised that, in her shock, she'd dropped her phone on the floor.

With angry tears welling in her still-sleepy eyes, Rosie picked it up and said: 'Yes, I'm here.'

'Well, then. You'd best get yourself over to the house. We can do lunch and talk about how you're going to handle this situation.'

'*Mum.* I'm already handling it. In fact, it's handled – past tense.'

'It's not, though, is it?' Her mother sounded indignant now. Impatient. As though she thought Rosie was being wilfully stupid. 'You can't stay in that little flat all by yourself with only antique tat for company. Can you even afford it on your own?'

Rosie let this slight on her collection of vintage treasures slide. She had more serious beef with Julie today. 'Actually,

I'm very happy here and I've no interest in moving. I've got a new flatmate – so it's all fine, for the time being at least.'

'A new flatmate?!' her mother spluttered.

'Yes,' Rosie cut in, before she had to hear a list of reasons why living in shared accommodation in her thirties represented some kind of moral failing.

'Well, who is it?' Julie said. 'Some stranger you found on the internet, I suppose? Some weirdo you barely know?'

'Neither of the above,' Rosie said, with absolute honesty. Not only was Aled *not* an oddball she'd come across online – she was starting to feel like they really understood one another.

Last night's chilled evening in had been lovely: fun and relaxed in a way she'd never have thought possible a few short weeks ago. She'd eaten a mountainous plateful of curry with no fear of judgement, and they'd laughed like lunatics as Springsteen did his best to shove his nose in Aled's lamb pasanda. Characteristically reticent, Aled hadn't waxed poetic about her haircut; he'd simply said, 'New hair? It's lovely,' then passed her a bottle of Kingfisher. It was the simplest of compliments, but obviously sincere – and thus more welcome than any gushing, effusive appreciation might have been.

Conversation between them flowed naturally, now, but their spells of silence were equally easy – *soothing*, even. Being quiet with Aled, Rosie thought, was easily a hundred times more comfortable than talking to James had been towards the end of their time together. Aled's dark, watchful eyes and natural shrewdness had made her feel jumpy and exposed when they first met, but somehow, without her noticing, they'd taken on a different power. These days, the feeling of being seen clearly by him was warm and freeing. She felt like she had no reason and nothing to hide from him – with the obvious exception of her carefully curated 'Factual Reasons Why Aled Is Gorgeous' file.

None of these, however, were observations Rosie wanted to share with her mum. As a diversionary tactic, she volunteered yet more explosive information. 'While we're chatting, I might as well tell you: I've got a new job, too. I left Cover 4 U because my boss – for want of a better way of putting it – was a total idiot. So now I'm working with a lovely team at a local deli.'

The line went silent for a few seconds, during which Rosie genuinely wondered whether her mother had passed out.

'You mean, like . . . a cafe? You're a *waitress*?' Julie asked, aghast.

'I'm a barista,' Rosie said, 'for the time being, anyway. I enjoy it, the people there are great and it earns me almost as much as my old job.'

'Your father's going to go mad,' Julie announced.

'*Why*?' Rosie demanded, finally driving the conversation towards its crux. 'I've told you, I'm fine – not that you asked. So it isn't *my* welfare you're worried about, is it?'

Julie made a series of ill-defined, outraged noises, but Rosie didn't stop. 'Every shred of "concern" you've shown this morning is basic box-ticking. It's about whether I've checked off all the stuff you think I should do, or be. It's *never* about whether I'm happy.'

'Of course I care whether you're happy!' Julie cried. 'I'm your mother! I want to see you settled because I know it's what's best for a girl like you.'

'And what kind of girl is that, Mum?'

Her mother faltered.

'I don't even need you to say it,' Rosie told her. 'You think I'm nice. Simple. Not thick, but not that clever either. Average, if a little on the chubby side. You think I was *lucky* to have James. But d'you know what? He was lucky to have me. And I'm starting to realise there's more to me than you've ever seen – than any of you have ever bothered looking for.'

'Now, Rosie, come on,' her mum said, her tone softer now – almost wheedling. 'Come and see us today and we can talk about this properly. You and I can have a good old catch-up while we cook. Set everything to rights. Find a way forward.'

'I'm already moving forward,' Rosie said. 'Like I said, I'm doing pretty well. And I'm busy today.'

Julie's temper finally snapped. 'For god's sake, Rosie, what am I going to do with a 2.5kg leg of lamb and a fresh mint plant if you don't come for lunch today?'

'Oh, I don't know,' Rosie said, her own rage reaching its peak. 'Cook it yourself?'

She heard a sharp intake of breath from the other end of the line and immediately felt bad. Rosie was in the right, and she was hurting – but she knew that, for all her faults, her mother did love her.

'Listen, Mum,' she said. 'I'm not coming out to Braintree today, and I think we could both do with calming down. Why don't I give you a call next week? Maybe we could even arrange you coming to visit *me* for once.'

'Fine,' Julie said, sounding brittle. Rosie could tell she was already rehearsing a walking wounded routine in her head. When her mother recounted it, this conversation would be a story in which Rosie was the antagonist and Julie a hapless, well-meaning victim. Right now, though, that wasn't worth arguing about.

'I love you, Mum,' Rosie murmured – and she meant it, despite everything.

Julie merely sniffed.

'Don't forget to roast the lamb on a rack,' Rosie said, by way of farewell. 'And rub some chopped rosemary and butter into the skin, if you have it.'

After a trip to the bathroom, Rosie made her way to the kitchen. Aled was already in there, leaning against the countertop and dressed in damp exercise clothes.

She tried not to notice the way his t-shirt clung to his broad torso, or the defined muscles that corded his exposed arms. It took considerable effort.

There was a pile of mail next to him, obviously retrieved from the corridor as he returned from whatever workout he'd just done. One of the envelopes was huge: thick and A4-sized, presumably with a stack of important paperwork inside it. It was stamped with the logo of a law firm.

On top of that was a postcard – a pretty, vintage-style image of a beach. It was the sort of picture Rosie might frame and add to a gallery wall. 'You're popular this weekend,' she said, nodding her head at the pile.

Aled shifted from one foot to the other, suddenly self-conscious. 'It's just legal stuff. To do with the house.'

Rosie narrowed her eyes at him playfully. 'That's not from a law firm,' she said, pointing at the postcard.

'No,' he admitted. 'That's . . . from someone I never thought I'd hear from again.'

Rosie felt her blood turn cold. It was obviously from a woman: someone so cool and mysterious that they'd send a cryptic postcard to their ex – or possibly *future* – lover, instead of dropping them a WhatsApp, like a normal person.

'Are you OK?' Aled asked, stepping aside so Rosie could reach the kettle. 'You look a bit shell-shocked.'

Ah. Yes. She had been upset by the conversation she'd just had with her mum.

'Mostly OK,' Rosie said, sighing – glad of a reason for looking crestfallen that had nothing to do with fancying him. 'I've just had a phone call from my mother, who seems to think I'm a completely useless person and yet requires me to go to her house and cook dinner.'

'What?' He frowned, not understanding.

'I finally told her James had moved out. She always thought I was punching above my weight with him, I think – not least because she *also* thinks I could afford to lose a couple of stone. How's that for irony?'

'What?' Aled said again, gawping. 'You're joking.'

'I wish I was,' Rosie told him, rolling her eyes.

'If anyone was punching, it certainly wasn't you,' he muttered darkly. 'Surely your own family can see that?'

'There's no reason why you'd already know this, so I

understand the shock and horror,' Rosie said, managing a wan smile. 'But I don't have the best relationship with my family. For the most part they mean well – but when my brother and I were kids, he could do no wrong. I was always a bit awkward. Too bookish, a little overweight . . . I don't think they quite knew what to do with me.'

'I mean, it's pretty simple, isn't it?' he said, with a note of anger in his deep voice that she hadn't heard before. 'You have kids, you love them. For who they are, not who you imagine they should be.'

God. He somehow seemed more handsome than ever when he was being earnest.

Rosie swallowed. 'That's the theory, I believe. But, you know . . . what can you do?' Aled nodded sympathetically, but said nothing. She recognised this as an invitation to go on.

'A lot of it is rooted in Mum being a bit of a Stepford wife and me not fitting the mould,' Rosie continued. 'I've just done something Niamh would undoubtedly refer to as "setting a boundary". She's very into those.'

'Oh?'

'Yeah. I was supposed to go over there for Sunday lunch. It's a regular thing, and I *regularly* end up doing ninety-nine per cent of the cooking. And clearing up. It was the last thing I needed today, so I told her I was busy.'

Aled whistled, impressed. 'How did that go over?'

'Pretty badly, but I stood my ground. For the first time since I was eighteen.'

'*Whoa*. That's a big deal. Worth celebrating, I reckon. How do you feel about pancakes? American ones – the fluffy kind?'

'Very positive,' Rosie said, squinting up at him. 'Unless, like my mother, this is your way of asking *me* to make them.'

'It isn't,' he laughed. 'Now take your tea and sit down.'

Rosie did as she was told, and before long the luscious smell of browning butter and maple syrup filled the air.

She was more than halfway through a plateful of pancakes topped with blueberries – studiously avoiding the gluttonous gaze of Springsteen, who'd perched beside her in the hope of leftovers – before she realised she'd forgotten to add 'makes amazing breakfasts' to her list.

Chapter 17

In spite of her determination not to think about Aled's romantic life, living with him over the past six weeks had led Rosie to the conclusion that – if he had one – he kept it safely under wraps.

He'd never mentioned a girlfriend – or a boyfriend for that matter – and he didn't seem to be dating. Most of his evenings were spent at home: eating, reading, working or watching TV with Rosie. It struck her as implausible that someone this attractive, intelligent and likeable could be single.

She supposed it had taken her a while to see past his reserve and understand that her flatmate's cool manner was born of good old-fashioned shyness, rather than a superiority complex of the kind James had always suspected. Perhaps the combination of Aled's diffidence and other people's feelings of intimidation explained his not being in a relationship.

Now that she saw what lay behind his reticence, however, Rosie almost wished she couldn't. Her interest in Aled extended well beyond the bounds of what was normal for a flatmate, and convincingly bypassed what would have been appropriate for a friend. She was burning to know who'd sent the mysterious postcard. He'd taken it into his room, rather than pinning it up in the kitchen as Rosie would have done, so she'd had no chance to sneakily glance at it. Who was it from? Had he written back? Rekindled some sort of romance with the woman who'd reached out to him? The idea made her feel strangely nauseous.

She wondered about his family situation, how he'd grown

up, where he'd been to university. She wanted to know more about his travels, where he might go next and (although it made her stomach twist) when he might depart. Every time she met Tim, or a member of his building team, in the corridor, she found herself hoping they'd say 'slowly' when asked how the top floor renovation was progressing.

Worst of all, she imagined how Aled's full, soft-looking lips might feel against her skin – what it would be like to be embraced by someone so much taller and *larger* than herself. Would she feel protected? Impassioned? Overwhelmed? All three, she decided . . . and no doubt deliciously so.

As if to add to her general sense of confusion, James had been in touch. As Rosie finished her final shift of the week at the deli and prepared to head home for the evening she discovered a missed call and a text from him. His message simply said:

Hey. Just wanted to check in and see how you are. Hope you're doing OK. X

Fuming, she'd typed and deleted a succession of increasingly snarky responses as she walked home, eventually resolving not to send any of them. She had no idea what his game was, but her best guess was that, almost two months out from finishing with her, he was experiencing an attack of conscience.

In which case, bollocks to him. James hadn't given a fig for Rosie's feelings when he'd planned to end their decade-long relationship with a Dear John letter – nor when he'd shacked up with another woman and lied about it. It wasn't her job to soothe his guilty feelings. On a whim, she blocked his number – and the corresponding high she experienced was the sort she felt sure no drug, legal or illegal, could ever deliver.

To Niamh's delight, Rosie was more clear-eyed than ever about her tendency to pander to the sensitivities of people who wouldn't give her the time of day. This included her mum, who had called her several times since their Sunday lunch disagreement to inform her 'how worried' the whole family felt about her job/relationship/living situation. Newly impervious to such emotional blackmail, Rosie calmly explained that she was doing well, and that there was no need to be concerned. She also reminded herself that assuaging such concern was not her responsibility.

In what Rosie saw as a bid to raise the stakes, Julie had now changed tack and begun expressing fears for her husband's health – referencing his high blood pressure, refusal to exercise and enduring love for bacon sandwiches. While Rosie agreed her dad could afford to be more active, she couldn't bring herself to get wound up about it. Julie's fatphobia was no doubt at the root of her desire to see Colin take up jogging and shed the (relatively small) spare tyre middle age had bestowed on him – and this fear of excess flesh was something Rosie had no desire to reinforce.

When she got back to the flat Aled was on the sofa, a book on his lap and a glass of red wine in his hand. He was wearing his glasses again, and Rosie berated herself for her immediate, swoony reaction to seeing them.

'Good day?' he asked.

'Busy,' Rosie said, 'but fun. It was mostly Tobi and I today. She's a real sweetheart.'

'I guess I'll meet her at the next mandatory karaoke night.' He rolled his eyes at this affectionate reference to his cousin's pushiness.

'I should think so,' Rosie smiled. 'I can't imagine Rhianne letting her skip it, even if she has zero interest in alcohol or singing. What are you reading?'

'Dylan Thomas – collected poems.' He held up the book so she could see. It was a battered, well-loved old paperback that Rosie guessed had been all around the world with him. Its cover was faded and wrinkled, and she wondered whether he'd sat by some warm, faraway sea with his dark head bent over it – whether he'd read the verses one balmy night on a balcony beneath the stars. Then her brain supplied the image of the lithe, beautiful woman he might have recited them for, and she felt a little sick.

'Are you all right there?' Aled asked. 'I mean, I know it's a cliché – Welsh man reads famously Welsh poetry – but you look aghast. Are you that horrified?'

Busted, Rosie thought, as she tried to arrange her face and return his smile.

'I'm fine!' she said, her voice tight and shrill. 'Maybe just hungry. And no, not horrified at all.'

'I'm thinking of doing some Thomas at school – he's no relation, by the way.'

'I didn't like to ask,' Rosie said wryly, grateful for the opportunity to lighten the mood.

'I'm revisiting some favourites and thinking about ways into them that might seem relevant to a bunch of urban sixteen-year-olds,' Aled explained.

'Rather you than me,' Rosie laughed. 'Though I'm sure it's great stuff.'

'It is, and you'll definitely have heard some of it,' he assured her.

'Hmmm, I wouldn't bank on it,' Rosie demurred. 'I love novels but I'm not much of a poetry reader. I think the last time I looked at any was when I studied the stuff in my GCSE anthology, and we both know *that* wasn't recent.'

Aled sat up straighter and shook his head at her. 'You talk like you're some wizened old woman. What are you, twenty-seven? Twenty-eight?'

'Thirty-two,' Rosie said, wincing.

'Positively ancient, then,' he said. 'You're the same age as me. And regardless of when you did your exams, you *must* have heard this one:

'Do not go gentle into that good night
Old age should burn and rave at close of day;
Rage, rage against the dying of the light . . .'

Good god. Was he actually trying to kill her?

Rosie was convinced her heartbeat must be audible; it was hammering as though it thought it could thump itself free of her ribcage. This should have been cheesy and embarrassing, but instead it felt poignant. He was showing her yet another side of himself – sharing something that, somehow, she knew was important to him.

Every word Aled read aloud seemed to land on her skin like autumn rain – or maybe like the last rays of a golden afternoon's sunshine, wrapping her in early-evening warmth. She had heard the poem before, but she'd never *felt* it. She'd never felt *this*. The words were magic, or maybe he was.

Rosie didn't dare speak in case she broke the spell. It was only when Aled cleared his throat that she realised she'd closed her eyes.

'Well,' he said, smiling but sardonic. 'Perhaps I should rethink this idea. You look half asleep . . . The last thing I need is my Year Twelves reacting to this the way you just did. Half of them might as well be comatose as it is.'

'No!' Rosie cried. 'I wasn't – it was – I was just listening. It was . . .' She fished around in her brain for a word that would imply 'mildly enjoyable' rather than 'intense and intoxicating'. Failing dismally, she finished, '. . . *lovely*.'

'OK, all right,' he said, colouring slightly. He put the book down and asked, 'What shall we do for dinner?'

Rosie shrugged and said, 'I'll see what's in the fridge. I reckon some sort of pasta might be possible.'

'Great. Want me to chop?'

'No, I'm on it – any chance of a glass of that wine, though?'

As she pulled bell peppers, cherry tomatoes and a slightly sad-looking chilli from the fridge, Aled poured her a good-sized glass of red and set it on the counter next to the chopping board.

'I'm good,' she told him, 'honestly – finish your lesson planning while I cook. You can wash up later.'

As he left the kitchen area, something like relief flooded her chest cavity. Being physically close to him right now felt positively terrifying – like standing on a slowly crumbling ledge with no idea what lay beneath, in the full certainty that eventually she'd tumble into the void.

He was right about one thing, she thought, as she glugged olive oil into a pan and watched it start to simmer. If Aled's students responded to his reading poetry in the same way she had, the consequences would be disastrous. They'd all be half in love with him by the time the bell rang for break.

Rosie's cobbled-together pasta dish was satisfyingly tasty: a spicy combination of sweet tomato, rich red pepper, chilli and pan-fried bacon.

After eating and pronouncing it delicious, Aled tidied the kitchen while she relaxed on the sofa. Pleasingly full and a little wine-woozy, she flicked through various TV channels, struggling to find anything that wasn't depressing, half over or dull.

As she happened upon the opening credits of *When Harry Met Sally*, Aled sank onto the opposite end of the couch and said, 'D'you know, I've never seen this.'

'You've never seen *When Harry Met Sally*?' Rosie asked, incredulous. 'It's a classic.'

'So I'm told.'

'I am *shook*,' Rosie said, laughing.

She lifted and pointed the TV remote, keen to change the channel again. She loved this film, but sitting through its romantic 'friends to lovers' plot with Aled just inches away was the last thing she needed right now.

'Whoa, hold your fire,' he said. 'Let's watch it. Assuming it's not rubbish, of course.'

'It's great,' Rosie admitted, 'just . . .'

Just *what*?

Think!

Find an excuse to switch over.

'Just . . . ?' Aled asked.

'I dunno. It's a romcom.'

'So? I'm not some kind of cultural snob, if that's what you're thinking. In fact, I'm inclined to think there's a direct line that leads from Austen to Ephron. Now come on, let's watch.'

With great reluctance, Rosie set the remote control down on the coffee table and scooched as far back into her corner of the sofa as she could. It was small, and there was barely a foot between them – but it would have to be enough.

Before the film was even halfway through, Rosie felt she could confidently label the evening's viewing the worst cinematic experience of her life. As Meg Ryan gasped and moaned her way through the most famous fake orgasm in history, she found herself wishing the sofa would transform into some flesh-eating monster and swallow her whole.

While the movie was as good as ever, she lacked the capacity to concentrate on it. Her whole body was humming with a powerful *awareness* of the person sitting next to her. Illuminated by the dim light of Rosie's thrifted, 1970s-style lamp and the flickering images from the TV screen, Aled's face looked like a work of art.

Its clean lines, smooth skin and almost perfect symmetry made Rosie think of the marble busts she'd seen in museums. She could almost believe it would feel like cool, unyielding stone if she touched it, were it not for the warm, clean scent that drifted through the air each time he moved.

It struck her that Aled possessed gravity in both senses of the word. On the surface, he seemed serious – perhaps even solemn on occasion – but the more time they spent together, the more magnetically she was pulled towards him.

Just as a tearful Sally ranted that her ex-boyfriend's fiancée was supposed to be 'his transitional person, not the one!' everything stopped.

The TV went blank, the light from the lamp disappeared and even the street light outside was extinguished.

'Argh, power cut,' Rosie said.

'Shit,' Aled murmured, shifting uncomfortably and taking a deep breath.

'Are you OK?'

'I'm not great with pitch darkness.'

'Oh. Sit tight, then,' Rosie said, surprised but sympathetic. 'There are some candles and matches in the kitchen. I'll go and get them.'

She fumbled her way to the kitchen, located an ancient bag of tealights, and was back in the sitting room a moment later. She set a line of candles out on the coffee table, then struck a match and lit them.

'There,' she said, hoping to reassure him, gesturing at the array of orange flames. 'This could almost be deliberate, now. Romantic, even.'

Why, why, *why* had she said that?

Aled managed a short laugh, which made Rosie feel even worse. Clearly, the notion that there could ever be anything between them was absurd to him.

Through the gloaming, Rosie could see he was tense. The stiff set of his shoulders betrayed a visceral reaction to having been plunged into this sudden blackout, and she understood that he was trying to rationalise some long-held fear.

'You must think I'm ridiculous,' he said, feeling her eyes on him.

'Not at all,' Rosie promised. 'Is there anything I can do to help?'

'Nah,' he said. 'I've tried everything – even had hypnotherapy once. I had a . . . bad experience when I was a kid,' he explained. 'I had the piss taken out of me a lot. I was always a bit different. We were playing a game of hide-and-seek one day – I think I was about nine. The boy who lived next door to us, Robbie . . . he convinced me to hide in the potting shed on one of the allotments over the road, and they locked me in for a laugh.'

Rosie felt her breath catch in her throat.

'I was stuck in there for hours,' Aled continued. 'It got darker and darker as the day wore on. No windows. I remember freaking out when the last shreds of light disappeared completely. It was pretty melodramatic of me – my overactive imagination, I guess – but I started to feel like I'd never escape. I've never quite got over it.'

'That's not melodramatic,' Rosie said hotly. 'That's *awful*. What a bunch of little bastards.'

'They were just kids,' Aled said, resigned. 'And I was an easy target. Scrawny, bespectacled, fatherless . . . I started reading all the time when I realised that living in my own head was easier than trying to fit in.'

'Sounds familiar,' Rosie said. 'Can I ask . . . How did you get out of the shed in the end?'

'Rhianne found me. Heard me yelling, knocked the rusty old padlock off the door with a trowel she found and then threatened to beat the living shit out of Robbie and the others if they crossed me again.'

'God,' Rosie said. 'I wish I'd had a Rhianne in my corner when I was growing up.'

'How d'you mean?'

'I was always the butt of the family jokes,' she told him. 'My brother was pretty evil to me at times. I remember he nicked my favourite Barbie at one point and made it part of some Action Man war game. He staged an execution – she was court-martialled for espionage, if I remember rightly, on very thin evidence. Anyway, he beheaded her with my mum's bread knife.'

'That's dark.'

'Yeah. And when I ratted on him I got the usual "it's just laddish larks" fob-off. I can't remember him *ever* being held accountable for crap behaviour. If I'd taken something of his and destroyed it, there would have been hell to pay. When I look back on it we were held to wildly different standards, though I know our parents loved us both.'

'No wonder things are a bit sticky with your family,' Aled observed.

'Nope,' Rosie said. 'No wonder at all. What are your lot like? I mean, I know Rhianne, obviously . . .'

It was a question she'd been burning to put to him for weeks, but something about sitting in near darkness made asking it easier. Moreover, she told herself, moving the conversation on might prove a useful distraction for him.

'Mam is a bit like Rhi,' he said fondly. 'Strong, kind, honest – a little fearsome. She got pregnant with me after a summer fling. My father wanted no part in raising a baby and tried to convince her it was crazy to go through with it – as did her own parents, I think – but she wasn't having any of it. She stuck to her guns, even though she was young.'

'What a cool woman,' Rosie said, shrugging off the thought of a world without Aled in it. 'What does she do for work, your mum?'

'She runs a guest house. Rhianne and I grew up by the sea on the north coast, so there were always tourists. I helped out with everything that didn't involve speaking to scary strangers from the minute I was old enough.'

'Is that how you learned to cook?' Rosie asked.

'Pretty much, yes. But it was only years later that I learned to make massaman curry and all the spicy stuff you like. There wasn't a lot of call for it in Conwy County in the 1990s . . .'

'Shed imprisonments aside, it sounds like a pretty nice way to grow up,' Rosie said.

'It was,' Aled agreed. 'People thought it was weird, and sometimes took the piss that I didn't have a dad, but I never felt deprived. I suppose you don't miss what you've never had, and there were enough big personalities in my family that there never seemed to be a father-shaped hole.'

'I take it Thomas is your mum's surname? Otherwise you'd be a Bettini.'

'That's right,' he said. 'She said that if she was bringing a child up alone, he or she would have her family name. I always respected that, and it made me feel closer to Rhianne, too. Her dad was Mam's brother.'

'Did your mum never find someone else? Or get married or anything?' Rosie asked.

'She did, when I was about thirteen. For years she said she couldn't be bothered with anyone male except me, until she met Mal. He wooed her like they were in some old Hollywood film, and eventually she let him get close enough that she fell for him, too. They got married a year later and Mam had the twins.'

'Oh, wow,' Rosie said, swallowing back the words *so they were the kids in your photo* before they could incriminate her.

'Yeah. Gethin and Tiegan. They're brilliant. I stayed close to home for uni so I could see plenty of them while they were little.'

'So what made you decide to start travelling?' Rosie said. It was a bold question – the sort she probably wouldn't have asked by daylight – but her urge to understand more of him made her reckless.

Aled stared into the candlelight for a moment, then turned to Rosie with a rueful smile and said, 'The same thing that makes all homely, bookish types resort to drastic action. I had my heart broken.'

'*Oh*,' Rosie said, almost breathlessly. She was desperate to know more but unsure of her permissions. Could she really ask him to elaborate when the story she wanted to hear might cause him pain?

'It was a long time ago,' Aled said. 'She was my girlfriend from our last year of school up until I finished my English degree.'

'Crikey,' Rosie said, 'that's a long time to spend with someone when you're so young.' Involuntarily, she remembered what Rhianne had divulged about teenage Aled: *he didn't get good-looking until we were about sixteen.*

She found herself wondering – without foundation and very uncharitably – if the girl in question had only deigned to notice him when he became tall and preternaturally handsome.

'Yeah. Her name was Ceri. I was besotted with her.' He shook his head, almost embarrassed. 'We stuck together even though I went off to study. Mam told me I was crazy, of course – that I should have fun, throw myself into uni life, enjoy the independence of living away from home . . . Honestly, I think she knew Ceri better than I did.'

'But you were in love,' Rosie said, her heart squeezing in her chest.

'I was. Foolishly so. And I thought *she* was, too, until I graduated. When I was suddenly around all the time, she announced she wasn't ready to settle down. A week later, I spotted her out on the town with – wait for it – Robbie. Of locking-me-in-the-shed fame.'

Rosie gasped in horror. '*No way.*'

'Yes, way. In the end, I think she found me interesting and mysterious from a distance but boring up close. I decided then that I had to get away. Going somewhere I'd barely even heard of with nothing more than a backpack was kind of a 'screw you' gesture – an attempt to prove I wasn't the dullard she'd pegged me as. I've kind of drifted along from place to place ever since.'

'She sounds awful,' Rosie said, 'and you are *not* boring. I think you're one of the most interesting people I've ever met.' She felt herself grow pink and was grateful that he probably wouldn't notice in the candlelight.

'Only because you know I've lived in Russia and spent a summer at an Italian monastery,' Aled laughed.

'Actually, you hadn't mentioned the monastery,' Rosie said, arching an eyebrow. 'But the globe-trotting isn't what makes you interesting anyway. There's a lot more to you than that. You have . . . layers.'

'Layers, like an onion? Like *Shrek*?' he asked, grinning.

Rosie made a face at him. 'I mean, maybe? What would be wrong with that?'

'He's bright green, Rosie. He's a literal ogre.'

'He's the eponymous hero of four films!' she cried indignantly. 'And you've just proved my point. If someone had told me two months ago that you had a sense of humour, I'd have asked them what they were smoking.'

'Gee, thanks.'

'Come on,' she said. 'You have to admit you were a bit standoffish.'

'I'm rubbish at meeting new people,' he admitted, looking sheepish. 'Also, your boyfriend hated me from the moment I moved in, and I got the sense he was the jealous type.'

'*Ex*-boyfriend. Yeah, so jealous he binned me off for another woman!' Rosie hooted.

'He's an idiot. It's very much his loss,' Aled said, with such feeling that Rosie's stomach seemed to trip over itself.

She didn't know what to say. Rosie felt the silence between them stretch and grow taut.

Aled's eyes were ink black in the darkness, and they were fixed on her in a way that made her wonder if he had X-ray vision. She almost wished he could see all the way through her – right down to the part of her that was screaming for him to kiss her senseless.

As though he could read her mind, his eyes dropped to her lips. She pressed them together; a nervous tic she'd never been able to shake.

'Do you think she was right? In the film, I mean,' he whispered.

'Who?' Rosie asked, her own voice low and confidential. 'About what?'

'Sally. About the transitional person. The person who comes after a big relationship being someone who usually doesn't last.'

'Oh.' She frowned, then said: 'I don't know. Surely you're

in a better position to answer that one, if you and Ceri broke up years ago.'

'You'd think. But there's barely been anyone since then. It's not often I meet someone I feel at home with.'

The words weighed heavy in the air. They seemed laden with significance, but Rosie couldn't make full sense of their meaning. The idea that he'd ever be short of female company was ludicrous to her – yet that was what he'd implied.

Unable to resist asking, Rosie said: 'Was it Ceri who sent you that postcard?'

Even in the dark, she could see Aled's expression of surprise that she'd remembered it. 'Yeah,' he said, a little grudgingly. 'Her way of making sure I know that *she* knows I'm back in the country. According to Rhianne, she's newly single – and considers me significantly less boring than she did ten years ago.'

Before Rosie could organise her thoughts, let alone formulate a response to this, the TV – now showing some late-night news programme – burst back into life. The sitting room lamp lit up and the street light outside glowed yellow.

'Power's back,' she observed, pointlessly. 'D'you feel better?'

'Better than in a long time,' Aled said, smiling at her softly before standing up to take their empty wine glasses to the dishwasher.

Chapter 18

Over the next week or so, Rosie reran the power cut conversation approximately five thousand times.

The more she thought about it, the less sure she felt of what it had all *meant*. He'd told her about a childhood incident so unpleasant it affected him more than two decades on, and yet she couldn't be sure how significant this was. He might well have related the story to *anyone* he happened to be sat next to seconds after the lights went out. He'd been vulnerable and panicked, and while baring his soul seemed out of character for Aled, Rosie understood why he'd done it. In that moment, he'd felt the need to explain what lay behind his sudden nervousness – and for all she knew, he would have offered a total stranger full disclosure.

Then there were the revelations about Ceri – a woman who'd apparently bewitched him, then broken his heart so thoroughly that he'd had to leave the country in hopes of getting over her. Perhaps it wasn't surprising that, a decade on and with Aled in possession of a valuable London property, the woman seemed to have changed her mind about him. Rosie tried to comfort herself with the thought that, at least so far, Aled had showed no sign of softening towards his ex-girlfriend.

It was what he'd said about feeling at home – feeling better than he had in a long time – that she'd tucked away in her memory for safekeeping. She fetched it from her mental storehouse more frequently than she should, re-examining it like it was a precious artefact or a puzzle she couldn't quite solve. It meant he liked her, she supposed – that he felt comfortable with her in a way that was unusual for him. Even after her mini-makeover, though, she couldn't bring herself to believe he had anything more than friendly feelings for her. No doubt he'd bring some tall, skinny, highly intelligent girlfriend home any day now. Through gritted teeth and with a roiling stomach, Rosie would shake her hand and chat pleasantly, all the while secretly wishing for the woman to be struck by lightning.

It was half-term, and she had a day off from the cafe. Aled had spent the morning finishing some school work while Rosie had done a few rounds of YouTube yoga, and there was a vague plan to head out for a walk and a cheeky afternoon pint if the weather held. It was bright but cool, the sun breaking through thin white clouds in a way that made everything look pretty but proffered little warmth.

Rosie emerged from the bathroom after her post-workout shower and detected what sounded like an argument drifting down the corridor from the flat's front door. *Weird*. As she tuned in she quickly realised that was *James's* voice – and Aled was remonstrating with him.

Forgetting that she had a towel on her head and was wearing nothing but underwear and a knee-length dressing gown, she marched towards the increasingly heated conversation.

'. . . not going to let you in here unless she says she wants to see you,' Aled was saying, his deep voice firm but calm.

'I'm not being funny, mate, but since when did you become her keeper?' James snapped sourly, his Cheshire accent strange to Rosie's ears after so many weeks without it. 'I think I know better than *you* what she might want,' he went on. 'We were together for almost ten years.'

It was funny, Rosie thought, that he'd invoke the length of their relationship when it suited him. It hadn't meant all that much when he'd finished with her, leaving her high and dry in a flat he knew she couldn't afford.

The moment she came into view, James clammed up. He

stared at her, round-eyed, taking in her near nakedness and her proximity to Aled, who she'd deliberately stood right next to.

'James, what are you doing here?' she asked.

'You've not answered any of my messages or calls. I wanted to see how you were,' he said sullenly.

'Why? I told you when you left that we weren't going to be friends – that once you were gone, we were over for good.'

'Please, Rosie, there are some things I want to say. I'd really like it if we could talk. *Alone*,' James added, with a murderous look at his former neighbour.

'Do you want to talk to him?' Aled asked, looking down at Rosie with sincere concern in his deep brown eyes.

'I am *here*,' James put in, sounding like a sulky teenager whose parents were openly discussing his most recent misdemeanour. 'Don't talk about me like I can't hear you, please.'

Aled rolled his eyes and placed a gentle hand on Rosie's shoulder.

Thrilling at the contact, she took a deep breath and then turned to her ex-boyfriend. 'You've got no *reason* to be here, James. But you can have five minutes to get whatever it is off your chest,' she said. 'And before you even *think* it, let alone ask: I will not be making tea.'

'You sure you're all right?' Aled asked, his hand sliding down her cotton-covered arm and then brushing her own. He gave her fingers a squeeze, as if to reassure her that he wouldn't leave her alone with James if she had even a shred of doubt about seeing him.

The gesture was kind, empathetic and not in any way sexual – but the feel of his warm skin touching hers was electrifying. She felt a jolt of *wanting* more powerful than anything James had managed to elicit in her during the decade they'd spent together.

Rosie glanced up to see that her ex's eyes, narrowed and lit with resentment, had taken in the sudden flush she could feel lighting up her cheeks.

'Follow me,' she said to James. Aled went into his room – which, at this oddest of moments, Rosie realised she no longer thought of as in any way 'spare'. He shut the door to give them privacy.

They reached the sitting room, and James moved towards the armchair he'd often sat in when he and Rosie lived together.

'Watch out,' she warned, pointing as James lowered his backside towards the seat. 'You'll squash him.'

'What the—' James yelped, as Springsteen uncoiled himself and stood up from the cushion he'd been lounging on. He glared at James with accusing yellow eyes, hissed imperiously and then leapt to the floor. After throwing a final withering glare at his would-be assailant, he trotted in the direction of the recently installed cat flap.

'Is that the mangy old stray from the alley?' James demanded. 'What are you thinking, letting it in?'

'*He* is called Springsteen,' Rosie informed him. 'He lives here now – and there's nothing mangy about him.'

James looked around the flat, taking in the cat food dishes on the kitchen floor, the obviously masculine jacket and boots that occupied the rack by the back door and the two empty coffee mugs that sat next to the sink.

'Seems like *Springsteen* isn't the only one who's got his paws under the table,' James said with venom. 'What the hell is the bloke from upstairs doing in our flat? And why the fuck don't my keys work?'

'*Our* flat?' Rosie scoffed. 'You moved out, James, remember? You don't pay rent anymore. Which is also why you no longer have keys for the place.'

'You changed the locks?'

'The landlord felt it was the right thing to do,' she said, trying to stop a smug smile from creeping onto her face. James still had no idea Aled owned the building, and keeping the information back felt like a small but significant victory.

'And what about Tom Jones? Your lad from the valleys?'

he said, jerking a thumb in the direction of Aled's bedroom door. 'What's he doing here while you're half-naked? Isn't there some coal that needs to be dug up in his homeland?'

Rosie was suddenly incensed. Nothing James said or did should have surprised her at this point, but resorting to cheap, insulting stereotypes felt beneath even him.

'He lives here,' she said, simply– allowing the statement to reverberate in the tense silence that followed it, then land with maximum impact.

James boggled at her, lost for words.

'I don't know why you're so shocked – or even interested, really,' Rosie said. 'You must have known that, unless I was prepared to pack up and live *chez* Colin and Julie, I'd need to find a flatmate. Or did none of that occur to you when you were working on the lovely letter you wrote me?'

'You're living with *that* guy? The bike fascist? Oh my god, are you *sleeping* with him?'

Rosie's temper threatened to erupt, and she took a steadying breath. 'What business of yours would it be if I was?' she asked. 'It's not as though you're living like a monk in the aftermath of our break-up, is it?'

James looked down at his feet, flinching away from her gaze. Following his eyes, Rosie saw that he was wearing a pair of unutterably ugly trainers. They were bright white with prominent black branding and looked incredibly uncomfortable: his recent 'style over substance' approach to life epitomised by overpriced footwear.

'What was it you wanted to say, James? Why did you come here today? Because I'd really like to get on.' She gestured at her state of undress.

'I wanted to . . . I don't know . . . reach out and try to fashion some sort of *friendship* with you,' James said, his voice quavering in a way that Rosie couldn't help but feel was studied. Deliberate. 'It just feels *wrong* not having any contact at all,' he went on. 'Surely you can understand that, after all the years we were in one another's lives? I wouldn't have turned up on your doorstep like this if you'd returned any of my texts.'

'I didn't get your texts,' Rosie said, not wanting to be cruel but unwilling to take part in what he evidently hoped would become a pity party.

'You blocked me?' James asked, his mouth dropping open.

'I did,' Rosie admitted. 'I don't have to talk to you anymore, James. I don't have to let you back into my life because you suddenly want to be back in mine. You made the decision to dump me in the least respectful way possible – and to lie about why. After ten years together you let me find out by accident that you were seeing someone else – living with her, I guess.'

James stared down at his hideous trainers again.

'I'm sorry,' Rosie said, feeling a prickle of sympathy for him that she immediately stamped on. 'But you hurt me. I haven't forgiven you yet, and I can't be sure I ever will. Right now, I don't want to be your friend.'

'Wow,' James said, his voice hardening. 'That's harsh, given that it seems to have taken you only a week or two to start shagging the handsome hermit from the second floor.'

'It really isn't harsh, James,' Rosie pointed out. 'It's not like I've gone out of my way to contact you and declare I don't want you in my life. *You* came to see *me*,' she continued, '*uninvited*. And it seems that what you're really bothered about is the fact I'm not some quivering wreck – which is no doubt what you were expecting. Would you have felt better if you'd found me sobbing, snotty and mainlining Ben & Jerry's in my joggers?'

'Of *course* not!' he yelped, with practised emphasis. James's words insisted he didn't want her to be miserable – but his eyes said he'd have much preferred it to finding her unclothed and cohabiting with someone much better-looking than himself.

'I think you should go now,' Rosie said, keen to get rid of

him before he could wind her up any more. Thus far, she'd resisted yelling or screaming at him – but her resolve would snap if this conversation went on much longer.

'Why? So you can get back to business with lover boy? Or should I say *boyo*?'

'What I might do, and who I might do it with, is no longer anything to do with you,' Rosie hissed, her patience wafer-thin. She stood up and pointed towards the flat door, hoping he would take the hint and leave.

She couldn't bring herself to refute James's accusations; on principle, it shouldn't matter to him if she and Aled had struck up a relationship, but there was a bit of her that relished his obvious dislike of the idea. A still deeper part of her – one that was far less sanguine – knew that telling the truth would hurt. There was only friendship between Rosie and her flatmate, and she knew she would put that in jeopardy if she allowed her already sizeable crush to spiral out of control.

'Fine,' James said, heaving himself up off Springsteen's favoured armchair to rock back and forth on the soles of his horrid sneakers. 'I came here today to extend the hand of friendship – to try and salvage something from the years we spent together. I can see I was wasting my time.'

Rosie saw red. How dare he try and cast himself as the magnanimous ex, only here for the sake of ensuring the lover he'd cast aside hadn't gone mad with grief?

'D'you know what?' Rosie asked as she opened the door to wave him through. 'I think you came to see me today for your own ego. You wanted to reassure yourself that I was unhappy without you – that I was just waiting to be picked back up like some discarded toy, in case dumping me doesn't work out so well for you.'

James made an exaggerated frown face – schooled his features so they were the very picture of righteous outrage – but Rosie knew him too well to miss the shock that had passed over them a moment before. She'd hit the nail squarely on the head.

'Instead,' she said, 'you've found me getting on with my life. Unfortunately for you, I'm not wallowing in self-pity or composing sad ballads about how much I miss you. I'm actually OK.'

'I . . . I'm glad you're OK,' James murmured. 'Truly. I just . . . I never imagined things would go this way.'

This was the first fully honest thing he'd said since turning up, and Rosie had the grace to agree. Then, in an echo of their first parting, she said simply: 'Goodbye, James,' and shut the door behind him.

Regarding herself in her bedroom mirror, Rosie couldn't help thinking that – as 'revenge looks' went – hers left a lot to be desired. If she'd had any inkling that James would appear on her doorstep this morning, she'd have been sure to greet him in her tightest, brightest, lowest-cut t-shirt (recently purchased with an insistent Rhianne right behind her).

She'd also have dried and styled her bob, concealed the hormonal zit that had blossomed on her chin overnight and donned a slick of fire-engine red lipstick. That said, she felt she'd achieved impressive hauteur for a woman in a slightly stained waffle robe from Tu at Sainsbury's. She'd stood her ground, and it had felt fantastic.

An unfortunate side-effect of agreeing to speak to James was the fact that her hair, still in its towel, had now dried in a Mr Whippy-shaped cone on her head. However, with the aid of some leave-in conditioner and her GHDs, this was a punch Rosie decided she could roll with.

She put on a thin cotton vest and rooted in her drawer for a soft knitted pullover that Niamh had bought her two Christmases ago. It was a vivid bottle green and clung to her curves in a way that had distressed her so much she'd barely worn it until now. Today, emboldened and determined not to hide, she pulled it on.

As she instructed herself not to panic about the way the jumper's wide V-neck confidently announced her breasts, she couldn't help noticing how its colour complemented her eyes. Niamh had been right when she said it was exactly the right shade for Rosie – but it had taken her until now to see it.

She fastened the button on a pair of high-waisted 'mom' jeans – still with no real understanding of why they were called this – and heard the soft rap of knuckles on her door.

'One sec!' she cried, urgently trying to flatten her hair. Once she'd reduced its bushy height by a centimetre or two, she opened up.

God, but Aled was massive. He practically filled the doorway, and the glossy, white-painted architrave around it made Rosie think of a picture frame in an art gallery. He was the portrait of a handsome man come to life.

For just a second, she let herself look at him: the shiny mass of dark hair, the expressive eyes and the sharp, stubbled line of his jaw. He had the sort of looks that translated across time and space, Rosie thought; he'd look right depicted on the wall of some eighteenth-century National Trust stately home, but could be just as comfortable on the cover of *GQ* magazine. As this occurred to her, she rather wished he wasn't seeing her with what looked like a haystack on her head.

'Are you all right?' he asked. 'I heard the door go a while ago. Thought I'd best check in.'

'Thanks,' Rosie said, smiling. 'I'm fine. And James, despite being an utter twat, remains unmurdered.'

'What did he want?'

'To be *friends*, if you can believe it,' Rosie said scathingly. 'I'm pretty sure he was just here to make sure I was falling apart in his absence. You can imagine how happy he was to discover that, in fact, I'm doing fine.'

'He was ecstatic, I suppose?'

Rosie laughed, but stopped short of telling Aled that it was his presence in the flat that had fanned the flames of James's indignation. She didn't want to reference the assumptions her ex-boyfriend had made, or her refusal to deny them.

'D'you still fancy a walk somewhere when you're ready?' he asked. 'Blow a few cobwebs away?'

'Definitely,' Rosie said. 'But you know, I think we need to up the ante a bit. Do something more exciting? Or else I'll always remember this as the day I had a confrontation with the man who left me while wearing a dressing gown with ketchup on the sleeve.'

'We can't have that,' Aled laughed. 'What did you have in mind?'

'I dunno. Where have you never been in London that you like the sound of?'

'God, loads of places,' he said. 'I've only ever been here and right into the centre – for plays and touristy stuff, when I was a kid. I like the idea of exploring the parks, but never know which one to start with.'

'OK, so how about Primrose Hill? It's lovely. The views are gorgeous, there are loads of blue plaques and some excellent pubs.'

'Sounds great,' Aled said. 'But what about you? We should go somewhere you've never been, too – or do something you've never tried before. Any ideas?'

Rosie thought for a moment, then said: 'This is stupid, but I've always wanted to try roller skating.'

The moment the words were out of her mouth, she wished she could stuff them back in.

'*Roller skating*?' Aled repeated.

'Yep,' Rosie nodded, reddening. 'Told you it was daft, but when I was about twelve, Lucy – the girl next door – had this amazing pair of roller boots. Proper 1980s-style things with four wheels in a square. They were turquoise and pink, with big sparkly stars on the back.'

'And . . . ?'

'Well. I was painfully jealous, of course. Desperate for some of my own. Mum was worried I "lacked the physical dexterity" to skate without injuring myself. By which she meant I was too chubby to try it.'

'That's shit,' Aled said. 'No offence, but your mother sounds like a real piece of work.'

'You're not wrong,' Rosie said. 'I think she thought she was helping – that I'd lay off the cheese sandwiches and Walkers Smoky Bacon if I believed a pair of roller boots might be on the horizon.'

'I have no doubt you were a lovely child who absolutely deserved access to glittery, eye-wateringly colourful footwear with wheels,' Aled insisted. 'We are going to right this wrong today, Ms Butler.'

Rosie laughed. 'Thanks, but no – I was just being silly. I can't go roller skating for the first time at thirty-two.'

'You *can*, and you will,' Aled said, his face alight with determination. 'This is not going to be the day you had an awkward confrontation with your ex – it's going to be the day you got the wheels you always wanted.'

'I don't know where you can even *do* roller skating nowadays,' Rosie protested. 'It's kind of old-fashioned, isn't it? It's probably not even possible.'

'If there's one thing I've learned since coming to London, it's that very little is impossible in this city,' he said sagely. 'You finish getting ready and I bet by the time you're done, I'll have found us a place to go.'

'Are you sure you want to do this?' Rosie asked, taken aback – not to mention slightly swept away by his sudden dedication to the cause.

'As sure as I am that Josh Holloway won't hand in his *Dr Faustus* homework on time,' Aled said. 'Leave it to me.'

Chapter 19

Half an hour later, Rosie was putting on her trainers and her new winter coat. She'd retired the navy blue number in favour of a checked wool jacket in autumnal shades of orange, red, black and beige. Aled was ready to go and stood waiting in his charcoal-coloured pea coat and leather lace-up boots – both of which looked so good she could easily have believed he'd been paid to model them.

Rosie felt a pang of worry about what she'd got herself into here. The undercurrent of attraction she'd recently been feeling towards Aled felt increasingly like a wave that might swell to twice her height, then pull her below the surface. At this thought, a bolt of excitement went through her: what would it be like to just *give in* to it, she wondered?

Hideously embarrassing, she chided herself a second later. *Epically humiliating*. The sort of *I only see you as a friend* mortifying that there's no recovering from.

As he locked up, Rosie riffled through the envelopes on the post table for the sake of hiding her pink face. There were several letters for Val and Pat, some sort of catalogue for James (which she immediately chucked into the recycling bin) and several things addressed to 'A. Thomas'. Rosie shook her head in wonder as she piled them up. It seemed slightly mad that until very recently she'd had no idea what the 'A' signified – yet now she was having to talk herself out of trying to jump him in the minutes before they embarked on a joint roller-skating adventure.

She noted that several of the letters for Aled had local estate agents' logos stamped on them. He'd told her not long ago that he'd been asked to have valuations of the building done for insurance purposes; property in their neighbourhood was so sought-after that every firm was doubtless keen to handle managing the building on his behalf.

'Crikey, you're popular,' she said, stacking his mail into a neat pile he could pick up later.

'Oh,' he murmured, frowning. 'I suppose so. I'll have a look at them when we get back. Just . . . leave them.'

'Sure,' Rosie said. He looked almost rattled, and seemed on the point of offering an explanation for his sudden stiffness when Rosie decided not to push for one. It must be weird to feel suddenly responsible for the roof over a bunch of strangers' heads, so instead she asked: 'Am I allowed to know where we're going yet?'

'If you insist,' Aled said, seeming to recover himself. He gave her his trademark half-smile and opened the building's front door. 'Regent's Park. As luck would have it, there's some kind of outdoor festival happening there this week – for the school holidays, I guess. There's a company renting out roller skates by the hour, provided you're willing to sign seven different disclaimers that mean you can't sue if you break your leg.'

'Oh my god, really?' Rosie cried, not sure whether to feel excited or terrified.

'Really,' Aled confirmed. 'We can skate around for a bit, then walk on to Primrose Hill. It's all planned.'

Rosie's heart skipped a beat at his use of the word 'we'.

'You're going to roller skate with me?' she asked, looking up at him in disbelief.

'Why not?' he said, pointing at the bus stop they needed to head for. 'At no point on my travels have I attached wheels to my feet and tried not to fall over, so I think now's the time.'

'Bravo,' Rosie laughed. 'I'm impressed.'

'I'd hold back with the praise if I were you,' he said grimly. 'I've got a feeling it's not going to be pretty.'

'Ha!' Rosie grumbled. 'You strike me as one of those effortlessly sporty people – the sort who's good at athletic things but doesn't make a song and dance about it. I, on the other hand, am truly graceless – as you well know. I'll be on my arse within minutes, but sod it. You only live once.'

'Too true,' Aled agreed, smiling. '"Loveliest of trees, the cherry now".'

'More poetry?' she said, squinting at him and grinning.

'It is,' he said, colouring a little. 'Sorry, bad habit.'

'I like it,' Rosie said, realising it was true. The random quotations could have been pretentious and grating, like James's tendency to rattle off technical computing terms she couldn't understand – but Aled's delivery of them was unstudied and spontaneous. She wondered whether other people's words came more easily to him than his own.

Either way, the sharing felt special; he'd memorised these lines because they meant something to him, and he was letting Rosie in on their secret. At least, he would be if he explained them.

'What does it mean?' she asked, eyeing the bus shelter's electronic display. 'You've got two minutes to enlighten me.'

'Oh god, don't make me.' He made a tortured face. 'I promise, only prose from now on.'

'Come on now, Mr Thomas – share with the whole class,' Rosie quipped.

He bit his bottom lip and said, 'Fine. It's from an A. E. Housman poem – the opening line. The TLDR summary is that we should enjoy life in the moment. Drink in all the beauty we can.'

His eyes swept her face, then, and the intensity of his gaze sent a shiver through her. A second later, as the bus pulled in to their stop ahead of schedule, she was almost sure she'd imagined it.

To Rosie's delight, she was surprisingly graceful on roller skates. After a couple of false starts she got the hang of gliding along, changing direction successfully and coming to a stop when needed.

Aled, on the other hand, was more ungainly than she'd imagined possible. Like a newborn foal, he stumbled and cursed, struggling to remain upright. It was as if his sheer height and heft made the whole thing harder, his large frame requiring superlative balance and total control of his suddenly wheeled size 11 feet.

Rosie hooted at the sight of him clutching the black metal gate they'd entered the park through, which stood wide open and adjacent to the mobile skate rental stand.

'Come on, you can do it!' she trilled. 'I believe in you. Just try and let go!'

He threw her a look that was half furious at her piss-taking, half thrilled that she seemed to be enjoying herself so much.

'Easy for you to say, Tinkerbell,' he said, his voice wry and amused. 'I must have at least a foot further to fall than you do.'

'Easily,' Rosie conceded, skating over to him, emboldened by the discovery that she wasn't half bad at this. 'However, you said you'd do this with me, so let's be having you.'

Gingerly, he removed one hand from the railing he was holding. He wobbled and bellowed '*Shit!*' the word barely audible above Rosie's burst of laughter.

Without thinking, she extended her arm and offered him her hand. He hesitated. 'Are you sure about this?' he asked. 'If I go down, I'll take you with me.'

'It's a risk I'm prepared to take,' Rosie said. 'Besides, you've saved me from breaking bones before, remember?'

'Of course I remember,' he told her, sliding his large warm hand into her smaller, cooler one. Within seconds, Rosie realised her error.

The contact with him had immediately rendered her knees weak, and it took every shred of her core strength not to collapse onto the dusty path beneath her. There was something strangely paradoxical about Aled's effect on her. At the same time as feeling completely safe with him – finding the sensation of touching him almost like a relief, or a homecoming – being around him was totally destabilising. Her heart thumped as her lungs struggled with the simple act of breathing.

With some effort, she restored her own balance and pulled Aled away from the fence so they could skate slowly along in tandem.

'Dear god, this is terrifying,' he said, a little breathlessly.

'Oh, come on,' Rosie scolded, hoping that teasing him would restore her equilibrium. 'Surely you've done scarier things than this on your grand tour? Bungee jumping? Sky diving? Fire eating?'

'Nah,' he admitted. 'I was always more about the landscape and local cuisine than potentially life-threatening leisure pursuits.'

'Fair enough,' Rosie laughed. A second later, she couldn't resist asking: 'Is there anywhere you still want to go?'

'Honestly? I don't know,' Aled said, straightening his spine slightly as he grew more confident that he wasn't about to keel over. The motion drew Rosie closer towards him, and her breath caught in her throat. She ached with the need to be nearer still.

'I dunno if I'm maybe a bit tired of wandering,' Aled continued. 'When I first came to London I thought it'd be a short stop on the way to somewhere else. Then I realised the flat needed work, which I decided to stick around for . . . Plus Rhianne's here, and now school are asking if I'll consider staying on.'

'Really?' The word came out high and shrill, and Rosie worried it betrayed an unreasonable degree of excitement on her part. Fortunately, Aled was concentrating so hard on not collapsing that he seemed not to have noticed. He was still holding her hand, his grip firm but warm.

'Yeah,' he said. 'The person whose job I've been covering is on maternity leave. Apparently she's confirmed she's coming back, but in the meantime someone else has resigned. The head grabbed me last Friday to say the position's mine if I want it, which is obviously nice.'

'Wow,' Rosie said. 'Definitely flattering. What did you say?'

'That I'd think about it,' Aled said, cautious and a little cagey. 'It would be quite a commitment. And a major change of plan.'

The words were cold water on Rosie's rapidly burgeoning hope that he might stay.

'D'you think you can manage now?' she asked him, not wanting to drop his hand but knowing that – for the sake of her sanity – she had to.

'Oh. Yeah. Probably,' Aled said, as if it hadn't occurred to him to let go.

Seeming to sense Rosie's desire to put distance between them, Aled soldiered on and skated alone for the rest of their allotted hour. He meandered along behind her, narrowly avoiding several elderly pedestrians and a handful of bolshy teenagers who seemed to find his clunky movements singularly hilarious: 'Lol – look at Grandad! Are you wearing those things for a bet, mate?'

The same gang of RP-accented ne'er-do-wells, all of whom were sporting Jack Wills hoodies, entirely failed to notice Rosie skate by. This was unsurprising, given the speed and confidence with which she was now whizzing around.

She felt alive, exhilarated – almost as if she was flying. Her heart felt fit to burst with the sheer pleasure of being here, *now*, with the cool October breeze ruffling her hair and eddies of falling leaves swirling on the wind.

'We should probably head back,' Aled called from somewhere behind her. 'Our time's almost up.'

'Race you!' Rosie shouted back, turning in an easy arc on the pavement and heading in the direction from which they'd originally come.

'What? No!' Aled yelled, trying and failing not to laugh. 'Cheat!'

It took him several moments to stop his forward motion and about-turn – by which time Rosie's head start was significant.

He gained on her as they neared their destination, finally throwing himself into skating as fast as he could. As he reached for Rosie to try and arrest her progress, she squealed and pirouetted away.

In the end, she won easily. They both collapsed on the grass next to the skate stand, breathless and giggling.

'That was *not* fair,' Aled panted, grinning.

'Nonsense,' Rosie declared. 'Your stride's much longer than mine when you man up and dare to use it. I had to get the edge somehow.'

'Daring generally isn't my thing,' he said ruefully, and Rosie wondered what he meant. Then, before she could argue that solo backpacking around the world was surely pretty daring, he said: 'Pub? Loser buys the first round . . .'

After handing in their skates and putting their own shoes back on, Rosie and Aled began the walk north through the park towards Primrose Hill. It was a comfortable half hour stroll, though the dark clouds gathering overhead made Rosie wonder if they'd make it before it began to rain.

As they ambled past newly naked trees and flower beds that showcased the fading remnants of summer splendour, Rosie frequently felt the eyes of fellow walkers snag and fix on them. No doubt, she thought, these people were wondering what this broodingly handsome romantic hero was doing with the dumpy, girl-next-door character. In the movie of their lives, this would doubtless be the scene where he confessed undying love for some taller, thinner, prettier woman – and it would probably only make the director's cut.

The heavens finally opened as they crossed Prince Albert Road. A sudden deluge of thick, heavy raindrops splashed from the sky, as though buckets of chilly water were being emptied directly onto their heads.

'Oh, *fuck*!' Rosie yelled, laughing as her immediately

sodden hair stuck to her scalp and water dripped from the tip of her nose.

'I say we run for it!' Aled said, raising his voice above the sound of the rain pelting the pavement.

'Agreed!' Rosie laughed. She jogged around the edge of the park and Aled followed. Soon they were running down a residential street towards a crossroads, at the end of which was a cosy-looking pub. Its double doors were painted some shade of Farrow & Ball grey, and gold letters above it spelled out 'Princess of Wales'.

They burst inside, laughing and out of breath. Puddles immediately formed where they stood.

'Nice out there, then?' the barman said sardonically. 'Take a seat over there – radiator's on.'

'Thanks,' Rosie sighed, grateful.

She took a moment to gather her wits before looking up at Aled. She'd learned that it paid to be prepared, and the sight of him rain-soaked and flushed from their run was bound to be A Lot.

In fact, it was all she could do to avoid cardiac arrest when she looked up at him. She had to remind herself to keep breathing as she took in the moisture that clung to his long, dark lashes and the wet shine of his hair.

God help her, there was a bead of water on his bottom lip, which – oh yes, *of course* – he deftly licked away. She was transfixed, motionless, *undone* . . .

'Pint, then?' he asked, tipping his head to one side and eyeing her quizzically.

'Yes! Excellent!' she squeaked, pushing her wet fringe out of her face and wondering how terrible she looked. She swept two fingertips across the skin beneath her eyes, and they came away sooty. So much for her 'waterproof' mascara.

She heard Aled laugh softly, presumably at the appalled expression on her face. 'On a scale of one to "rodent who's been flushed down the toilet", how bad is it?' she asked, before she could stop herself. She waved a hand in the direction of her almost certainly ruined makeup.

He gazed down at her in a way that made her toes curl inside her damp Converse high tops, then tentatively, delicately raised his hand to brush a raindrop from the edge of her jaw. She stifled a noise that might have become a whimper if she'd let it, but before she could lean into the touch, it was over.

Apparently embarrassed, Aled thrust his hands into his pockets and said, 'I wouldn't change a thing.' Without letting his eyes meet hers, he made for the bar.

A little dazed, Rosie peeled off her sodden coat and hung it over the pub's vast, Victorian-style radiator. What had *that* been about?

Was it possible he liked her? The idea seemed absurd.

Then again, she couldn't imagine that Aled of all people would go around touching random women's faces for no reason. Everything about him was deliberate, thoughtful and intense. For a moment, she let herself imagine not just kissing him, but being kissed *by* him. She had no doubt the experience would be world-altering: deep and urgent and insistent. It would be the kind of kiss that involved clashing hips, fingers stroking up and underneath t-shirt hems to find bare skin, and lips caught teasingly between teeth. The sort of kiss that happened in books and on film, and maybe in real life – but never to her.

Rosie exhaled heavily, then made herself confront the painful truth she'd been avoiding all afternoon. Just as she'd intended, James's am-dram performance of penitence felt like it had happened a thousand years ago – not merely this morning. His unexpected appearance had paled into insignificance beside the fulfilment of a long-forgotten childhood wish . . . but mainly beside the euphoric feeling of Aled's hand closing around hers.

Niamh had warned Rosie it would be impossible to live with such a gorgeous man and not end up smitten. What she hadn't foreseen was how much Aled would start to *matter* to Rosie – that whatever physical attraction he inspired would give way to genuine attachment.

Rosie wasn't sure how or when this had happened. Perhaps there'd been a tipping point she missed – some key moment that tilted her in a direction it now seemed impossible to change. Either way, it hit her that the feeling she'd been staving off for weeks was now flooding her, filling her from top to toe in the brief minutes it took Aled to buy her a drink. The dam had burst, and she thought of a phrase that had struck her when she'd studied *The Sun Also Rises* at school. Asked how he went bankrupt, one of Hemingway's characters replied: *gradually, then suddenly.*

Aled reappeared, all enigmatic face-touching forgotten. More inscrutable than he'd been in weeks, he set a pint of Aspall cider down in front of her, then produced a packet of Scampi Fries from his coat pocket. 'The Marmite of pub snacks,' he said, by way of explanation. 'Thought I should find out: are you a lover or a hater?'

'A lover,' Rosie answered, feigning composure she wasn't anywhere close to feeling.

'Damn it – me too,' he said, with a tight smile. 'I should have bought two packets.'

As they ate and drank in companionable silence, Rosie took fries from the torn-open bag at rare intervals – an act of self-preservation, lest her skin brush against Aled's and cause her to spontaneously combust.

After a second drink and a drizzly potter around Primrose Hill, they were both ready to head home. Neither of them fancied a long, cold walk in the dark that was falling, so they ordered an Uber.

It stopped at the end of their street, and their breath misted in the evening cold as they got out of the cab. Rosie felt consumed by the need to say something – *do* something.

This was the best 'date' – and actually one of the best *days* – she had ever had, but she had no idea what any of it meant. Aled seemed to have shut down, retreating into himself in a way that reminded her of how he'd been when they first met. Yet what she'd felt when his fingertip met her cheek earlier had been real. *Electric.*

Yes, Rosie was generally short of self-confidence – but she couldn't quite believe he hadn't felt it, too. And there was tenderness in the way he treated her. There had been from the start. There was understanding between them: a sense that each recognised the other, could see qualities that most people would miss.

The air between them was dense – thick with things unsaid. Rosie longed to reach for his hand: to lace her fingers through his as they strolled towards home. Somehow, on some elemental level, she felt sure that if she did so, he'd know why.

Just as she resolved to act, he stopped walking abruptly. 'Rosie,' he said, turning to her. His voice was low. Urgent. 'There's something I need to say. Something I have to tell you.' He sounded almost nervous.

'OK . . . ?' Rosie said, feeling like her heart had just tripped over itself. 'What is it?'

'I . . . um. When I first moved in with you . . . Argh. *No.* What I mean to say is—'

'Aled? Al, is that you?'

The voice that cut through the twilight was female. Accented. The figure that went with it was tall, slender and dark-haired.

The woman wore a black, belted coat, high-heeled boots and indigo skinny jeans. Her hair was threaded with tiny beads of moisture that glimmered in the light from the street lamp above. She was beautiful, as Rosie had guessed she'd be: large blue eyes were set above a slender nose and a pretty, petal-pink mouth. Even from several metres away, Rosie could tell her cheeks were flushed with cold. She guessed this meant their visitor had been outdoors for a while. Waiting.

'Ceri?' Aled said, his tone surprised but not displeased. 'What are you doing here?'

'I wanted to see you,' she said. 'I hope it's OK.'

'Er . . . sure,' Aled replied, running a hand through his damp hair, tugging at it in the way he always did when he felt awkward. He turned to Rosie. 'I didn't know she was coming,' he said helplessly. Confidentially. 'We'll go round the corner to the pub and catch up there.'

'Who's your friend?' Ceri said. She'd walked towards them and was close enough to look Rosie up and down in a way that reminded her of her mother. In the split second it took Ceri to conduct this assessment, Rosie authentically hated her.

'This is Rosie,' Aled said. 'She's my flatmate.'

Not even a friend, then? Rosie thought. *Or not enough of one for you to admit it.*

Ceri's perfectly threaded eyebrows briefly pulled together. 'Ah. I see.'

What do you see? Rosie wondered. What do you *want*?

Reluctantly, Rosie remembered what Aled had said earlier: that he'd grown tired of travelling, but wasn't sure about accepting a permanent role at school. 'Rhianne's here,' he'd said – and she'd assumed he meant 'in London', but maybe he meant 'in the UK'. It could be that the homesickness he'd said Rhianne occasionally suffered had hit him, too. He certainly had plenty to miss: a mother who adored him, a supportive stepfather, and two half-siblings he doted on.

What had Ceri interrupted? Had he been about to say he was moving back to Wales? That he and his ex were trying to work things out? The thought made Rosie feel like her stomach had dropped through a trap door.

After a brief handshake with Rosie and a moment's insincere small talk, Ceri tugged on Aled's sleeve and led him away.

Back inside the flat, Rosie leaned against the front door and tried to regulate her swift, shallow breathing. She felt irrationally angry – blazing with resentment that, when she looked at it head-on, seemed mostly like it should be directed at herself.

Aled had done nothing wrong. In fact, he'd gone out of his way to help her start rebuilding her life. He'd promised her nothing and – regardless of Ceri's reappearance – they'd always said their period of mutually convenient cohabitation would finish at the end of the year.

It was only now that Rosie realised this prospect had become more painful to contemplate than the grim reality of James's departure. *Gradually, then suddenly*, she thought again. *That's how these things happen.*

Slowly, then all at once.

November

Chapter 20

Over the following week, Rosie saw less of Aled than she'd become used to. She couldn't help thinking this was a likely side-effect of his encounter with Ceri, though he'd shared precious little about what they'd discussed.

All Rosie knew was that she'd appeared in London – newly divorced and keen to catch up. Rhianne had grumbled darkly about Ceri attempting to 'get her claws back in', bemoaning Aled's 'intensely romantic' nature as just the sort that might let her.

To Rosie's relief, Ceri's stay in the capital had been short-lived. Rhianne reported that she'd gone back to their home town within a week – though she couldn't say what promises, if any, Ceri had extracted from Aled before she left. Though it killed her not to ask him herself, Rosie couldn't face questioning Aled about his affections for the woman who broke his heart. Ignorance wasn't bliss, but it was preferable to hearing a potentially painful truth.

Upon starting back at school after half-term, Aled had also been informed that an Ofsted inspection was imminent. The late nights and early starts this necessitated meant that, at most, he and Rosie crossed paths in the kitchen while waiting for the kettle to boil.

In a show of support, Rosie continued making dinners for two and left large portions in neatly labelled Tupperware containers so he could eat on the go. She also made several batches of her favourite chocolate-chip cookies for him to take and share with his over-caffeinated, sleep-deprived colleagues.

This was nothing more than she'd have done for a close

friend, but it was a far cry from what common sense informed her was appropriate for a short-term flatmate. The voice of reason, however, was drowned out by the low, insistent hum that reminded her, very inconveniently: *you miss him.*

Since the 'accidental best date in history', which – in the privacy of her own head – was what she'd begun to call their afternoon of roller skating, she'd felt the pull of him more powerfully than ever. On the days when he was absent, she felt the loss of him keenly. The bathroom smelled of his shower gel in the mornings, his book sat unread on the coffee table and more than once she made two morning cups of tea, forgetting that he'd already have left for work.

She'd said nothing to Niamh about the mess of her feelings, and felt grateful that a run of high-profile projects was keeping her best friend so busy they'd cancelled their last couple of meet-ups. As soon as Niamh saw her in person, Rosie knew it would be game over. It would be useless to deny that her feelings for Aled had progressed from 'noteworthy but manageable crush' territory to take up residence in a dangerous place that might be labelled 'sexually spellbound and emotionally invested'. She was in no rush to admit this to herself, let alone anyone else.

It annoyed her that, on the Saturday after the school inspectors departed, Rosie was unable to take Aled up on his offer of a 'thanks for looking after me' lunch. 'I've got to drive out to Essex,' she moaned. 'I have a christening to go to, my cousin Mandy's baby.'

'Oh, nice.'

'Not really,' Rosie grimaced. 'I RSVP'd months ago, when James and I were still together. I'll be on the receiving end of some major sympathy-trolling when I turn up alone.'

'Sympathy-trolling?' Aled raised a single dark eyebrow, which did strange things to Rosie's stomach.

'Yeah. You know, where people say things like: "So how *are* you, really? I mean, *honestly*? Are you *managing* since the split?"'

Aled simply stared at her, so she ploughed on. 'What people really mean when they lay it on like that is, you look like shit, it's no wonder you got chucked and good luck finding another partner – you'll definitely need it. The crappier your situation, and the more they backhandedly reinforce its crapness, the better they feel about themselves.'

'Ouch,' Aled murmured. 'Will your parents not have prepared the ground for you at all? Warned people that James won't be there, that it's a sore subject?'

'Absolutely not,' Rosie said, barking a laugh. 'Not in a million years. My mother would rather eat full-fat cheese than admit her daughter's been dumped by the man they all hoped she would marry.'

'That's rough.'

'Yep. Wish me luck. If I'm not back by six, assume I've pulled into a lay-by on the M11 to rock slowly back and forth while contemplating my lonely, loveless future.'

Oof. She wished she hadn't said *loveless*. She could feel her face heating.

Aled smiled softly, his soulful eyes thoughtful. Then they lit with a glint that could almost be described as mischievous. 'I could . . . come with you, if you like? I mean, no pressure, I just have nothing else on today. If you could use a friend . . . ?'

Rosie felt her mouth drop open. His garbled thoughtfulness made her heart squeeze, even as the word 'friend' echoed unpleasantly in her ears. She told herself it was an improvement on 'flatmate'.

'Er – isn't this sort of thing your worst nightmare?' she asked him. 'Like, tons of people you don't know – most of whom, I won't lie, are pretty awful . . . Not to mention a church service, during which the baby will cry and my uncle Jim's mobile will go off at least five times. He gets a lot of Betfair notifications.'

'I'll manage,' Aled said, grinning. 'I'd like to help. You've been amazing to me all week – why not let me do something nice for you in return?'

Rosie writhed internally, her instinct to say yes at war with the knowledge that it would only complicate things. She couldn't deny it would be tremendously satisfying to show up for a family occasion with Aled in tow, but it would inspire speculation – and it would be a one-time only deal. When he never came to another christening, wedding or funeral, she'd be sympathy-trolled worse than ever: *he was a looker, though, wasn't he? Shouldn't have expected him to commit, really. It was always going to be hard for Rosie to hang onto a man like that.*

Rosie cringed, then told herself to knock it off. She knew she looked good today, in the floral midi dress Rhianne and Niamh had helped her pick out. It was bold but classy, with bracelet-length sleeves and a square neckline that showed a hint of bosom. She'd paired it with thick black tights because bare legs, November weather and draughty English churches didn't mix.

Aled, meanwhile, was still in a pair of pyjama bottoms and an old grey t-shirt that did wonderful things for his broad shoulders. *Gah.* He could come dressed in those and still be deemed too attractive for her. Her entire family would take one look at him and wonder what on earth he was doing with her. God, what if they thought he was an *escort*? That she'd paid for a fake date? That would be mortifying.

'Earth to Rosie . . . ?' Aled said, waving his arms to get her attention.

'Sorry. I was . . .'

'Spiralling? Catastrophising?'

'Both,' Rosie admitted. 'Honestly, this isn't going to be enjoyable. You don't have to do this.'

'I want to, though,' he said, with such sincerity that Rosie couldn't find the words to rebuff him. 'I can be ready to go in fifteen minutes. Does that work?'

Rosie nodded, mute, unable to resist – and not at all sure whether spending this afternoon with Aled would make it better or worse.

* * *

When Rosie pulled her VW Polo into the car park of St Catherine's C of E Church and Community Centre, her heart sank. Her mother was standing outside the old arched door, lying in wait for her daughter and surrounded by a cloud of what Rosie identified as vape smoke.

Up close, it was a cloyingly sweet steam that smelled powerfully – and synthetically – of peach. It reminded Rosie of the scented disinfectant she sometimes bought for cleaning out the wheelie bin, but she decided to keep this to herself.

Julie was wearing a satin sheath dress in deep navy, cut just below the knee and so tight it looked like it could have been sprayed on. Her feet were in heels that might have doubled as stilts, and Rosie wondered how on earth she could stand in them, let alone walk. Her mother's face was flawlessly made-up, presumably with her own TrueYOU products; shimmery taupe eyeshadow highlighted her hazel eyes, and her lips were glossed bright red. She looked amazing – though arguably her outfit said 'off to collect a BAFTA' more than 'suburban church service followed by finger sandwiches'.

'Rosie!' she cried, through a final plume of fruity air. 'And who is *this*?'

Rosie felt her soul wilt at her mother's tone, which managed to sound simultaneously surprised, intrigued and somewhat lascivious.

'This is Aled,' Rosie explained. 'My . . . erm. My . . . He's staying in the spare room.'

God, she was an idiot. Why couldn't she just have said friend, like he did earlier? *Because the word's too small for him*, a voice inside her said. *It doesn't contain enough.* She instructed it to shut up, then realised her mother was frowning at her.

'So, he's your flatmate?' Julie said, like she was a foreign language student testing the correct application of a word she'd recently learned.

'Yes. *Flatmate*,' Rosie repeated, trying to pack as much meaning as possible into two syllables.

'Pleased to meet you, Mrs Butler,' Aled said, offering her a very large hand to shake. Julie visibly thrilled at this deference, looking up at him coquettishly from beneath lowered lashes and purring, 'Likewise.'

Rosie rolled her eyes. 'Shouldn't we be going in?' she said, before Julie could start asking questions or – god forbid – flirting heavily.

Her mother looked at her shiny, gold-plated wristwatch. 'Oh. Yes. I just came out for a quick not-ciggy break, ha ha. Aren't I good?'

'You do know vaping isn't that great for you, either?' Rosie said in a low voice, as they entered the building and found seats on the same row as Michael and Colin.

'Rubbish,' Julie hissed. 'It keeps me slim. And it tastes nice.'

Rosie's eyes found Aled's in the dim light, and they exchanged the sort of nonplussed looks that couples sometimes share in the presence of eccentric extended family. It made her chest hurt.

Soon the vicar – a surprisingly young, hapless-looking fellow who genially invited the congregation to call him Father Simon – was at the front of the church. The service unfolded in the usual way, with Mandy, her husband Karl and a gaggle of godparents all swearing to reject a devil that Rosie was fairly sure none of them believed in.

When they got to the part where Father Simon sprinkled water on the baby's head, Rosie realised she'd forgotten to warn Aled about her name. She winced as the vicar's voice rang out: 'Crystal Khaleesi Turner, I baptise you in the name of the Father, and of the Son, and of the Holy Spirit.' To the celebrant's credit, he managed not to laugh.

Beside her in the church pew, Rosie felt Aled stiffen and knew that he was holding in considerable mirth. If they looked at one another, they'd corpse.

With great difficulty, she resisted glancing at him and

instead focused on a man two rows in front of them – one of Karl's uncles, she thought. He appeared to have dyed his greying hair a sort of orangey-brown colour that resisted definition. The closest descriptor Rosie could land on was that it resembled one of Rhianne's signature soups: curried sweet potato and coconut.

The christening came to an end, and a low murmur of voices began as people filed out of the church and into the community centre next door.

'Khaleesi?' Aled said in Rosie's ear, and the feel of his warm breath on her skin sparked thoughts that were definitely *not* church-appropriate.

'Yes,' Rosie whispered back. 'Sorry, I should have said. Mandy and Karl are big *GoT* fans.'

'Not big enough that they've watched the final season, it seems. Daenerys burns a city to the ground with dragon fire. She goes *mad AF*, as Year Eight's Umair Ansari might say.'

'Oh, they've seen it,' Rosie assured him. 'Mandy's take is that, although slaying civilians isn't cool, Dany's look is *on fleek* right up to the end. She has – and I quote – *mad respect* for a woman who can win a war and never have a hair out of place.'

Aled shook with silent laughter as they made their way to the after-party.

'Don't say you weren't warned,' Rosie said as they reached the bright green door of the outbuilding. 'Once we're inside, there's no turning back – and I seem to remember you claiming that bravery was not your speciality.'

'You're worth manning up for,' he told her, and she glowed. She should be satisfied that he considered her a friend, she told herself; it was enough. It would have to be enough.

'Rosie!' called an imperious voice from a plastic chair in the corner. It had been strategically positioned next to the vol-au-vents.

'Oh god, it's Great-Auntie Maud,' Rosie groaned under her breath. 'Hide. Seriously. Get behind that display of kids'

Easter drawings – she'll never see you. I'll take this one for the team.'

Aled glanced at the months-old display of crayoned crucifixions, several of which were alarmingly graphic.

'Forget it, Spartacus,' he said, smiling. 'I'm with you. "Once more unto the breach, dear friend".'

'Poetry, at a time like this?' Rosie smirked, trying to ignore the word 'friend'. 'Really?'

'Shakespeare,' he whispered. 'Sorry.'

'Rosie AND BOYFRIEND!' Great-Auntie Maud shouted, as if to confirm that they had *both* been spotted and neither would be suffered to escape. Maud was the sole northerner in Rosie's family – a migrant from Rotherham who'd come south but had clung to her accent like Japanese knotweed to a building site.

'Hello, Auntie Maud,' Rosie said when they reached her. 'This is Aled. He's my, er—'

'Friend,' Aled put in. Every time he said it, something inside Rosie shrivelled. He was like the children in *Peter Pan*, inadvertently killing fairies by saying they didn't believe. She stifled the urge to clap her hands.

'HA!' Auntie Maud huffed. She turned to Rosie. 'I never had a friend who looked like that when I was young. If I had, there's no way I'd have married your great-uncle Gerald. AWFUL man.'

Aled valiantly turned a burst of laughter into a coughing fit, and Rosie looked around the room in the hope that someone – *anyone* – would rescue them. No such luck. The only person who caught her eye was Michael, and he merely saw fit to smirk at her before stuffing a sausage roll into his mouth.

'They reckon you shouldn't speak ill of the dead,' Auntie Maud went on loudly, in the manner of elderly people who might be hard of hearing but, on the other hand, perhaps just have no more shits to give. 'To which I say, POOH,' Maud continued. 'He was a miserable sod, wasn't he, Rosie?'

'Erm . . . I don't really remember, Auntie Maud,' she said, round-eyed. Maud threw her a withering, disappointed glare, as though it were Rosie's fault she hadn't been born until two years after Uncle Gerald's stroke.

'Don't say much, do you?' Maud barked at Aled, changing the subject entirely and gesturing at him with her walking stick. 'Good job you're pretty. Where are you from, lad?'

'Wales,' he told her. 'The north coast.'

'Hmm,' she grunted. 'At least it's north of *here*, I suppose. I don't understand these flashy southerners, with their fake tans and false eyelashes and breast augmentations.'

'I don't think every woman who lives south of the Watford Gap has had a boob job, Auntie Maud,' Rosie said reasonably.

'Perhaps not,' Maud conceded. 'Some of them are still saving up. You can go on holiday and have it done now, you know. Fly to Turkey and come home with new tits as well as a tan.'

Rosie wanted to die. Aled was staring fixedly at a spot on the ceiling, his huge shoulders shaking with silent laughter.

'Well, it's been lovely to see you, Auntie Maud,' Rosie began, not quite able to believe she'd just witnessed an eighty-seven-year-old woman utter the word 'tits' in a community centre maintained by the Church of England.

'Not so fast, young lady,' Maud interrupted. 'I've not finished with you yet. What about that lad you brought to your brother's thirtieth? Jonathon, was it?'

'*James*,' Rosie said. Michael's thirtieth was a sore point; her parents had organised a big family get-together for him earlier in the year, having done precisely nothing to celebrate Rosie's big birthday two years earlier.

'Didn't like the look of that one,' Maud continued. 'Superior sort. You're better off with Andrew, here.'

'*Aled*,' Rosie said. 'And we're not . . . we aren't . . . It isn't like that.' It hurt her to admit it, and Maud could apparently read the scowl on her face with alarming accuracy.

'That's what they all say,' Maud declared. 'That's what David Tomkinson told his wife, Gladys, when she accused him of throwing one up the woman who worked in the betting shop. Load of horseshit, as it turned out, but Gladys had the last laugh.'

'How d'you mean?' Aled asked, as Rosie desperately prayed for this conversation to end.

'Well,' Maud said with relish, 'after that fall he had, it was all up to Gladys.'

'What was?'

'The decision to turn off the oxygen,' Maud said, smiling sweetly.

It wasn't often that Rosie could say she felt relief at the sight of her mother. However, as Julie beckoned her from across the room, she was intensely grateful for the excuse to leave Auntie Maud with a fresh cup of tea, a plateful of snacks and her fond memories of Gladys Tomkinson's revenge.

'You had your hair done, love?' Julie said, immediately zooming in on the all-important matter of her daughter's new look.

'Oh. Yeah,' Rosie said, patting her bob self-consciously. It had been a big change, but she had zero regrets; her shorter cut felt good – bolder, somehow.

'It's quite nice,' was her mother's verdict. Rosie almost choked on her cream cheese and cucumber sandwich; faint praise it might be, but this was hands-down the nicest thing Julie had said about her appearance in years.

She felt her mother's eyes slowly scan her outfit – an act which yielded no comment. Again, in the context of previous assessments, Rosie could consider this a win.

'So, how did you meet this new *flatmate* of yours?' Julie asked. She gestured at Aled, then said to Colin and Michael: 'This young man is living in Rosie's spare room, if you can believe it.'

Rosie cringed, wondering why Julie was referring to Aled as though he were a new pet or a piece of furniture.

'*Ah,*' Michael smirked, his eyes roving from Rosie to Aled and then back again. 'That makes more sense.'

Rosie was too needled to resist demanding an explanation for what was obviously a barb, even though this was precisely what Michael wanted. 'More sense than what?' she asked.

'Than you two being an item, obviously,' Michael said. 'I know you're back on the market, but – as I always say to my clients – when you're on a budget, there's no use looking at penthouse apartments in Spitalfields. Shop for what you can afford.'

Rosie experienced a rush of anger that, for once, she didn't feel like quelling. Perhaps unwittingly, Michael had hit an already raw nerve. 'And what's *that* supposed to mean?' she demanded.

Michael grinned, gleeful that he'd riled her so easily. 'Ooh, does Roly Poly Rosie have a thing for – what's your name again?'

'Michael,' Julie cooed indulgently, 'be nice to your sister. Don't start an argument and ruin Mandy's day – she's put this lovely spread on.'

'What about his impact on *my* day?' Rosie said, growing steadily redder and more furious. She wondered how many of her days, in the three decades since he'd been born, Michael had been permitted to ruin with no fear of reprisals. Even one more felt like too many.

'Oh, calm down, Rosie,' Julie said. 'There's nothing to ruin – you're not the one with a beautiful new baby to show off, more's the pity.'

'Jim says he's going over the road for a pint,' Colin interjected. 'Only booze Mandy's got here is fizzy wine. I'll be back in a bit.'

Utterly mortified, Rosie found herself wishing for a rogue meteor to land precisely where she stood and put her out of her misery. Then she changed her mind: far better for it to hit the rest of her family, leaving her free to live out her days in peace. At the very least, the universe could oblige her by obliterating her rancid little brother with a giant space boulder.

She took a deep breath, as if she were working up to something – though she had no idea what she could say. Arguing with Michael was like throwing petrol on an already out of control fire – while Julie, as always, was indifferent to any damage it might do so long as it didn't burn her.

As Rosie arrived at the realisation that angry tears were pricking her eyes, she felt a large, warm hand at her back. It was bracing her, almost – supporting her stance and stiffening her resolve. She let Aled's touch ground her and blinked the moisture away.

Before she could say or do anything else, Aled had turned to Michael. He leaned forward a little, as if to make sure Rosie's brother noted the difference in their height and bulk; at least five inches, and probably a couple of stone.

'Since you ask, my name is Aled,' he said. 'Your sister and I are friends.'

That *word* again. It went through her like a knife.

'However,' Aled went on, 'I'd consider myself lucky if she did have a "thing" for me. Don't make the mistake of assuming that just because you don't recognise her value, other people won't see it. Plenty of us do, myself included.'

His hand was still hot, comforting and solid at the base of Rosie's spine. She wanted to turn ninety degrees, press herself against him, bury her face in his broad chest. She wanted to breathe in his clean, soapy smell until everything else in the world disappeared entirely.

Instead, she looked at her mother. Julie's crimson-lipsticked mouth had fallen open and her false-lashed eyes were wide. 'I think it's time we were going,' Rosie said. 'We can say goodbye to Mandy and Karl on the way out.'

'Whatever you want,' Aled said, letting her shift their position, orienting them towards the exit.

They walked on together, his hand at her back all the way.

Chapter 21

Rosie's heart fluttered erratically in her chest the entire way home. Neither she nor Aled said much, and it seemed easier simply to listen to Taylor Swift and watch the evening draw in. She had no idea how to bring up what Aled had said without embarrassing both of them – particularly as she suspected he'd oversold his affection for her in seeking to shut Michael down.

Somehow, though, she needed to tell Aled how much it had meant that he stood up for her – that nobody had ever spoken out for her that way. James had always shrugged off Michael's gibes in the same way Julie did – gladly accepting this tacit permission not to defend the woman he supposedly loved, and thus avoiding conflict. This was especially convenient during their Sunday lunch visits to Braintree, when James's friendly relationship with Michael assured him a seat at his usual table in the White Horse, the pub they typically decamped to while Rosie took responsibility for the cooking.

As she parked the Polo, a crackling sound overhead reminded her it was Bonfire Night. Through the windscreen, she saw a smattering of pink and yellow sparks lighting up the night sky above the town hall.

'I'd forgotten there'd be fireworks tonight,' Aled said.

'Me too. D'you think Springsteen will cope all right?'

'Cats tend to just hide from stuff they dislike – a habit I empathise with, to be honest. He'll probably slink under the sofa until it all stops.'

Another bang sounded above them, followed by a powerful burst of lilac, blue and green light.

'So pretty,' Rosie said softly.

'D'you want to go and take a proper look?' Aled asked. 'We can pop in and check on Springsteen, lock the cat flap and then walk over, if you like.'

'Oh. I don't know . . . I mean – it's pretty cold, and we should probably have something to eat. I'm not sure three tiny sandwiches are going to see me through.'

'You won't be cold when you're stood next to a roaring bonfire,' Aled argued. 'And I'll buy you a toffee apple. Come on,' he pleaded, his face young, hopeful and open in a way that made Rosie's insides ache. 'It's years since I've had a proper Bonfire Night. Nowhere else in the world celebrates it, if that's even the right word.'

'It is a bit grim,' Rosie laughed. 'Literally burning a likeness of some bloke who tried to blow up the king. Celebrating his grisly execution.'

'Let's be honest, though, that's less important these days than the high-quality snacks involved. There might be baked potatoes,' Aled said, knowing the promise of piping-hot, buttery carbs would almost certainly convince her. 'Maybe hot cider. Mulled wine . . .'

'You had me at toffee apples,' Rosie admitted, shaking her head fondly. 'You check on Springsteen and I'll lock the car.'

The large field behind the town hall was busy; a sea of local people either huddled together to watch the sky, queuing at stalls for food and drink or playing fairground games. There was hook-a-duck, a tombola and a tin can bowling alley, as well as the opportunity to guess the name of the guy.

By the time Rosie and Aled got there, said effigy was already half burned on his pyre – but a photograph showed what he'd looked like before he was set alight.

'Hmmm,' Aled said. 'He has the air of a Quentin, I reckon. Or maybe an Arnold.'

Rosie laughed. 'Not a Crystal Khaleesi?'

'Ha! No. Nor a Khal Drogo. Doesn't have the requisite biceps.'

After a brief debate, they settled on Tarquin, duly paid £1 for their guess and moved on.

Rosie found her resolution to tread carefully around Aled weakening in direct proportion to the number of warm, boozy drinks she imbibed. The hot cider was spiced with cinnamon and spiked with rum, while the mulled wine hummed with clove, star anise and nutmeg.

After they'd both eaten baked potatoes so hot they burned their mouths, Aled procured the promised toffee apples. As he passed Rosie hers, their fingers brushed – the contact lasting just a second longer than was necessary. His dark eyes seemed to glow like hot coals, and as she looked at him through the smoke-heavy air her heart throbbed with a feeling she didn't want to name.

'Rosie!' a voice rang out from behind them, and she turned to see Tobi, Marcus and Becky emerging from the crowd.

'Hey!' Rosie said. 'You all having fun?'

'Absolutely,' Becky said, chugging what was left of her cup of cider. Since the weather had turned cooler, she'd swapped her slogan t-shirts for printed hoodies and jumpers. Peeping out from inside her parka were the words: 'IF YOU LISTEN CLOSELY, YOU CAN HEAR ME NOT CARING'. The black upper-case caption contrasted somewhat with the tight lilac sweatshirt it was printed on, but that was Becky all over: her petite size and sweet prettiness belied a steely core as well as a deceptively sharp tongue.

Realising she'd finished her drink, Marcus seized Becky's empty cup and immediately offered to get her a refill. Becky blushed and linked arms with him, and they ducked into the cider queue. Rosie raised an eyebrow at Tobi.

'Oh yeah, that's definitely happening,' Tobi said.

'About time,' Rosie laughed. 'Yaz not with you?'

'She's here somewhere, I think,' Tobi said. 'With a girl she likes. I think she's trying to avoid us in case we embarrass her. Rhianne's on a date, too . . . She's gone to some Michelin-starred place in Belgravia with Ethan.'

'Ooh,' Rosie said, genuinely intrigued. 'The chap she's been out with twice already? The one she met the day she took me shopping?'

'Yep,' Tobi confirmed. 'He seems borderline obsessed with her.'

'He wouldn't be the first,' Aled said. 'Rhi tends to have that effect on people.'

Must run in the family, Rosie thought. Then, as she felt her friends' eyes swivel in her direction, she realised she'd said it out loud. *Shiiit*.

'You must be Aled,' Tobi said smoothly, smiling at him. 'Rhianne and Rosie talk about you a lot.'

Embarrassed but abundantly grateful for Tobi's intervention, Rosie stared at her shoes.

'I am. And you're Tobi,' Aled said, smiling at her warmly. 'Rosie's mentioned you, too.'

It struck Rosie that he didn't seem anxious, despite his usual reluctance to meet new people. It might be the cider, she concluded – or simply the fact that Tobi was roughly the same age as some of his students. He'd told her once that while teaching seemed an odd profession for a self-confessed introvert, it worked very well. Adopting a stern persona wasn't hard for him; his physical size was an advantage and it was easier to relax with large groups of children and young people once you felt sure they'd stay in line.

'Rosie has been wonderful to me,' Tobi said. Rosie immediately blushed, and wondered if Tobi was a little tipsy herself.

'When I started at the deli,' she went on, 'I was pretty down. A bit broken, to tell the truth. Rosie's helped me put myself back together – get my confidence back. I was going to tell you this next time we were on shift, Rosie, but I've gone through all the university websites we've been talking about and drawn up a shortlist. I'm going to apply again, for next year.'

'Yes!' Rosie shrieked. 'That is *brilliant* news!' She drew Tobi in for a tight hug that almost sent her toffee apple flying.

'I couldn't wait to tell you and say thanks,' Tobi said, grinning, before her attention was caught by someone hollering at her from across the field. 'Oh, I know her from school – I should go and say hi.' Tobi quickly hugged Rosie again, then turned to go in search of her old classmate. 'See you next week!'

When Rosie glanced up at Aled, he was smiling at her softly. It was the sort of smile that turned her hot and cold at the same time, and made every inch of her skin tingle. It was a look that said, *I see you. I know you.* And she almost couldn't bear it.

'Have you given much thought to what you'll do next?' he asked, as they ambled past a bunch of teenagers writing their names in the dark with sparklers.

'How d'you mean?' Rosie asked, crunching the last shard of toffee from her apple.

'Well, you've convinced Tobi to follow her dream. What's yours? You know, it strikes me that you'd be an incredible counsellor. You're a fantastic listener, you're not judgemental . . . And based on what I've just witnessed, as well as how excited you are about volunteering next year, you're brilliant with young people.'

'I did always wonder about going into something like that,' Rosie said. 'I started a degree in psychology. Also, my old boss told me I was too nice to the callers – let them talk too much about their troubles when I should have been filling in forms. Feels a bit late to start training for something like that now, though.'

'"It is never too late to be what you might have been",' Aled said, with exaggerated formality.

'*Again* with the poetry.' Rosie elbowed him gently and laughed.

'It's not poetry, actually – it's one of those motivational quotes people put up next to their desks or stick on the fridge. Attributed to George Eliot. In any case, the point stands.'

They'd reached the edge of the field now and it was colder here, further away. They wandered up to an old wooden bench and Rosie sank down on it, deciding to watch the last of the fireworks in relative comfort.

'You're lovely,' she said, before she could stop herself – the words fizzing up to the surface like bubbles in champagne. 'Really, truly lovely.'

'And you are extraordinary,' he said, as another burst of brightness illuminated the sky.

Rosie nudged him again, shaking her head in self-deprecation. 'You don't have to say that.'

'Surely you know by now that, given the choice, I'll almost *always* say nothing,' Aled pointed out. 'I'm not in the habit of coming out with stuff I don't mean.'

Rosie nodded. Bit her bottom lip. Heart sinking, she said: 'I guess I should thank you, then. For earlier. For what you said to Michael.'

'Rosie, look at me,' Aled said. 'Please.' When she didn't move, he placed a fingertip under her chin and tilted her face so he could gaze directly into her eyes.

'I didn't say anything to your brother that wasn't true. Every word was sincere.'

Rosie swallowed. Dimly, she remembered reading once that the moment before a kiss could be just as magical as the kiss itself.

This felt like one of those moments. Aled's focus on her face was total, his pupils blown wide, his breathing rapid. This was promise, *potential*, suspended in a second. If she were Aled, she'd find a line from literature to encapsulate the feeling.

Rosie wondered if you could die from kissing – or from *not* being kissed. Surely she wouldn't survive, wouldn't be able to function for another second unless he touched his lips to hers.

A heady warmth bloomed through her, and her limbs went deliciously loose. Their faces were so close she could taste his air: sweet and spicy from the cider. Intoxicating. Beneath that there was familiar, clean soapiness – the pleasant, pervasive scent of his laundry, which somehow smelled like home.

She felt her eyes flutter closed. Let her head shift upwards, lifting her lips towards his.

Then, she felt him move away.

Shit. What had happened? What had she just *done*?

She must have misread the situation totally. Let her own wishful fantasising convince her there was something real here. *God.* For all she knew Aled and Ceri were back together, or working towards some kind of reconciliation.

Could she style this out? Perhaps, if she pretended to be drunker than she felt. 'That moment last night?' she'd say. 'You know, when I tried to snog you? Forget it. I was off my box.' The thought of lying like this, trying desperately to save face, made her feel suddenly sick.

'It's not you,' Aled said, after a pause that felt like an ice age. The words sounded strained, like they were costing him something.

He put his head in his hands, seemingly unable to look at her.

Rosie gulped again. 'Is it Ceri? I know she's been in touch with you, and Rhianne said—'

His head snapped up. '*God*, no. That's . . . that's not a thing, I promise. Rhianne doesn't give me enough credit.' He looked momentarily annoyed.

'But there's other stuff,' he went on. 'Stuff I'm still sorting out. I like you, Rosie. I want us to stay friends. And I know we won't if . . .'

'Got it,' Rosie said briskly, her terse tone totally failing to cover her embarrassment. 'Friends.'

He meant that if they kissed – or did any of the things Rosie's anatomy was telling her were urgent and *necessary* – it couldn't last. He meant he didn't like her in that way, or at least not enough. How had she ever let herself think otherwise? *Stupid, stupid, stupid.*

'Rosie, I—'

'It's fine,' she said, her voice clipped and efficient. 'We've both had a bit to drink. Let's say no more about it. I think we should probably go home – check that Springsteen's survived the night.'

'Right,' Aled said, uncertainly. 'OK.'

He stood up and offered Rosie his hand.

She didn't trust herself to take it, and pulled herself up from the bench as though she hadn't noticed.

They walked home in silence, only breaking the quiet when they discovered Springsteen lying on top of a basket of clean, folded laundry. Rosie's favourite jumper now bore a fine layer of silvery fuzz, which she'd have to scrape off in the morning.

They said goodnight and closed their bedroom doors, and it was only when Rosie had climbed into bed that finally she let a tear roll down her cheek. It was the first she'd shed since the night James had left her, and it pained her far more than any she'd cried for him.

Chapter 22

During the days that followed, Rosie kept waiting for her mortification to abate. Surely, if she was patient enough – fully committed to pretending that nothing of note had happened – the feeling would eventually disappear.

More than a week after the Bonfire Night debacle, however, she still felt a rush of embarrassment every time she looked at Aled. Typically, this was closely followed by the dull thump of *wanting* that the sight of him inspired. She felt like a pining teenager, caught between needing him to leave and never wanting him to go.

On the surface, both she and Aled carried on as normal: making each other tea and coffee, regularly eating together and keeping the cat in the sort of comfort he clearly believed was his due.

Predictably, Rhianne had noticed the change in them both. 'I have no idea what the bloody hell's going on between you,' she said to Rosie, 'but it's not working for anyone. Al looks like I felt when the Spice Girls split up, and every time you smile I worry your face is going to crack in half. It's forced, like a fear grin. It's not natural.'

Wednesday afternoon saw Rosie home alone in the flat. After doing the early shift at the deli, she fought through the windy walk home to get started on some long-neglected chores. Her concentration was hampered by frequent reminders of how settled Aled had become in a home that no longer felt just hers. At some stage, he'd stopped closing his bedroom door all the time – possibly when Springsteen moved in, so the cat could hop up on the bed and recline in the sunny patch cast by the small sash window. With Rosie's enthusiastic consent, he'd also started storing books in her antique dresser, and had made use of an old bureau she'd bought for a song some years ago. Rosie had never had need of it herself, and it pleased her to see it stacked with the set texts he taught, hastily scribbled lesson plans and piles of students' essays.

She sighed as she sorted through a clutch of her own paperwork, starting when she found a piece of thick, embossed card among her bills and bank statements. It was a wedding invitation, addressed to 'Aled and guest'.

After scanning it for details, Rosie concluded this must be from a colleague – an invitation to the evening reception, which was to be held this Saturday at a boutique hotel in Shoreditch. Determined not to wonder who he might take, or to have any feelings whatsoever about this, Rosie attached it to the front of the fridge with a magnet.

She proceeded to tidy, dust and vacuum – much to the dismay of Springsteen, who took one look at her trigger spray of kitchen cleaner and bolted for the garden. She was hot, sweaty and dishevelled by the time Aled got in, and cursed herself for not planning this better.

'Hey,' he said, his eyes sweeping over her too-tight vest top, cropped leggings and bare feet. Her exposed skin shimmered with perspiration, and she wished she'd had time to shower before he got home. It took her a few seconds to realise that he didn't seem revolted. If anything, he appeared embarrassed – as if he'd been caught looking at something he shouldn't.

'D'you want a glass of water?' he asked, as he moved towards the kitchen.

'Please,' Rosie said.

He set the kettle to boil, then went to get the water filter out of the fridge.

'Oh god, I'd forgotten about this,' he said, pointing to the invitation. 'It's a woman in my department who's getting married – she wants us all to go. Nice of her to include me, especially since it's not certain I'll be there next year – but I'm not sure I can face it.'

Rosie found she was irritated – partly because it seemed he was speaking in riddles again. It wasn't certain he *would* be staying at William Morris Academy, but nor was it certain he'd leave. What was she supposed to do with that information?

'Why wouldn't you be able to face it?' she asked him, unable to resist an eye roll. Ordinarily, she was understanding of his reserve – in fact, she found it sexy and compelling in a 'still waters run deep' kind of way. However, annoyance prompted her to point out: 'Won't you know a good chunk of the people there, if everyone from work's going?'

'Some, yes,' Aled conceded. 'But . . . it's going to be all couples.' He hassled at his hair, and Rosie realised he was genuinely agitated. 'I just . . . I don't want to go on my own,' he finally admitted. 'I'd been planning to ask if you wanted to go – as friends. And then . . .'

And then I practically begged you to kiss me under a shower of firework sparks, Rosie thought.

The tips of Aled's ears turned pink, and he shifted from one foot to the other in evident discomfort. He was trying not to look at her, and the pain of witnessing this reluctance snapped her self-control. She could cope with him not fancying her – or maybe with him fancying her, but not wanting a relationship, which was sort of what he'd implied. She *couldn't* cope with his pity: with him pulling further away in some misguided attempt to spare her feelings, when what really hurt was his not being close enough in the first place.

'I'll go,' Rosie said, with impressive self-assurance for a woman not currently wearing a bra and reeking of bleach. 'Why not? Unless there's any reason why I shouldn't?'

Aled was fully flushed, now – more flustered than she'd ever seen him. An agonised expression passed over his features, which then settled into a determined look that Rosie couldn't read.

'OK, then,' he said. 'Saturday. We'll go. Together. As friends.'

This oddly staccato summary of the decision confused her more, but all she said was: 'Right. Good. I need a shower, so would you mind feeding His Majesty?'

'Of course,' Aled said, recovering himself somewhat. 'And take your time – I'll cook dinner.'

As Rosie pulled up the zip on the same red dress she'd worn months before for James's company party, she asked herself what the hell she was doing. Saying she'd go to this thing with Aled was stupidly hubristic: an act of bravado that could only lead to a thoroughly uncomfortable evening.

In theory, her aim was to save face: to prove she could spend time with him without craving the sort of physical contact that tested, then comprehensively trashed the normal limits of friendship. It wasn't going to work. She'd set herself up for failure; it was like she'd given up chocolate for Lent the day before touring Willy Wonka's famous factory.

She sighed, eyeing her reflection in the bedroom mirror. She looked different, now, she decided, and it wasn't just because her hair was shorter. She stood taller – straighter and prouder – though she was as wobbly as ever in high heels.

Rosie felt like the woman who'd clambered into a cab with James, then let herself be ignored for half the night so he could suck up to his boss, was almost unreal. That Rosie was an out-of-focus phantom: a warning of what might have been ahead. For all the messiness of her current situation, she wasn't sorry she was no longer *her* – the person who'd staked her future on trusting and supporting a man who took her entirely for granted, and whose own priority would always be himself.

She applied a coat of vibrant red lipstick, straightened her spine and spritzed her favourite perfume behind her ears. She could do this. She was ready.

Or not, as it turned out. As she emerged from her bedroom

into the open-plan living area, the sudden rush and thud of blood in her ears reminded her she wasn't in full control of her feelings, or her biology.

Aled was leaning against the kitchen worktop, drinking from a tumbler of water. He looked, quite simply, devastating. While his usual, slightly unkempt academic aesthetic worked for him perfectly, the sight of him in a suit was something else. The dark fabric of his jacket hugged his broad shoulders, and for once his tie was properly fastened – neatly Windsor-knotted at the apex of his throat. Rosie felt her own go dry.

He was all long lines and easy grace; large, but never lumbering. The sight of his capable-looking fingers splayed against cold glass made her heart thump. How had Rosie not foreseen this?

'You look . . .' he began – but whatever words he'd been reaching for deserted him before he could utter them.

'So do you,' Rosie said, wishing she could see around whatever obstacle lay between them – wishing she understood what it was, and why it was there.

'Are you ready to go?' he asked. He sounded hoarse, like his throat was sore.

'Yep. Are we Uber-ing?'

'Yes. I'll sort that while you grab your coat. It's cold out there.'

Rosie nodded and busied herself with checking her handbag for essentials, then wrapping up warm.

'Cab's here,' Aled soon said, and they headed outside.

Seemingly without thought, he opened the door of the taxi and helped Rosie inside. At their destination, he was similarly gentlemanly, leaping from his own side of the car to offer her a hand out before she could exit the vehicle herself.

Maybe, she thought, *my previous form has him on high alert*. She guessed it wouldn't do for her to trip over and skin her knees immediately before meeting his work colleagues.

The hotel was an old industrial complex, lavishly

refurbished. Inside, it was modern and sleek: exposed brick and metro tiles were offset by polished metal light fittings and functional hardwood furniture. The wedding reception – for Cora, Aled's workmate, and her new husband Ed – was on the basement level. This, Rosie discovered as they descended the stairs into the space, was now a cavernous function room with vaulted ceilings, a marble floor and a bar twinkling with filled champagne flutes.

'This place is incredible,' Rosie breathed, unable to stop the interiors obsessive in her from gushing.

'Is it the sort of hotel you and James would have got married in?' Aled asked.

The question took Rosie aback. 'I never thought that far ahead, to be honest,' she admitted. 'I guess I was more focused on the idea of him proposing than on what a wedding, or even a marriage, might look like. Which might have been part of the problem.'

They made their way to the bar and each picked up a drink.

'Do you think you'll ever get married?' Rosie asked, deciding that the mood between them tonight was already so awkward, nothing she said could make it any weirder.

'I used to think I'd marry Ceri,' he said. 'Then, for a long time, I thought I wouldn't settle down at all.'

'Too much fun sowing wild oats?' Rosie said, sipping her drink and doing her best to sound nonchalant.

'Hardly,' he snorted. 'I just didn't think I'd meet the right person. Someone who'd feel like the other, better half of me.'

'Hmmm. As in, "you complete me",' Rosie murmured, quoting the end of *Jerry Maguire*. Aled's eyebrows shot up, and she realised he was desperately waiting for some sort of explanation.

'You're not the only one with a memory for a good line,' she said, cutting through the tension. 'It's what Tom Cruise says to Renée Zellweger right before she tells him, "you had me at hello".'

'You've lost me.'

'Oh my god, have you not seen *Jerry Maguire?*' Rosie cried. 'How many other cinematic triumphs are you ignorant of?'

'No end, I should think. That sounds like one I might like, though I've never recovered from seeing Tom jump up and down on Oprah's sofa.'

'Eek,' Rosie said, shuddering. 'Fair point.'

'We should go and say hi to Cora,' Aled said, pointing at her. She and her new husband were on the other side of the room, welcoming newly arrived guests. Her wedding dress was made from layers of lace, all slightly different shades in a palette of blush, cream and gold. The bodice was long-sleeved and belted at the waist, from which tiers of delicate fabric flowed. It was lovely – and unlike any wedding gown Rosie had ever seen before.

Up close, Cora was glowy and smiling – tightly clutching the hand of her new husband as she turned to greet them.

'You came! I'm so glad,' she said sincerely.

'I'm Ed,' said her husband, 'it's nice to meet you. Cora says they're trying to persuade you to stick around permanently.'

'That's right,' Aled said, a little uncomfortably. 'I'm just trying to work a few things out.'

'You must be Rosie,' Cora said, reaching over to peck her on the cheek. 'Please help us persuade him to stay. I'm sure you wield far more influence than the rest of us put together.' She smiled at Rosie warmly, yet somehow pointedly – her gaze skimming Rosie from head to toe in a way that implied said 'influence' was more to do with feminine wiles than wit.

'I'm not sure I have that kind of power,' Rosie said, waving the idea away. 'When you've been travelling for as long as Aled has I think it takes something pretty extraordinary to ground you again.'

'It does,' Aled interjected, catching Rosie's eye, 'but that doesn't mean it won't happen.'

'Keep trying!' Cora mouthed at Rosie, winking as she and Ed disappeared into the crowd to mingle.

'Another drink?' Aled said, inclining his head towards the bar, which had rapidly run out of complimentary bubbles.

Rosie nodded her agreement and walked with him, then found herself unable to resist asking: 'So why would it happen? You choosing to stick around somewhere, I mean. What sort of . . . *extraordinary thing* would need to occur?'

She'd been aiming for jocular, but her tone came off anxious – too eager for the information.

'I'll know it when I see it,' he said, evasive under pressure.

'Surely there's a poem for such a moment,' Rosie teased, a little giddier than she'd realised from quaffing champagne on an empty stomach. 'Some line you can quote.'

'There is,' Aled said, mock-scowling at her. 'But I'm not going to tell you if you're taking the piss.'

'Oh, go on, I promise not to be an arsehole about it. Pretty please? I'll buy the drinks!'

'*Fine.*'

After giving the bartender their order, she looked back at him expectantly. 'Hit me.'

He rolled his eyes, then cleared his throat. 'The poem you're looking for is "The Confirmation" by Edwin Muir.'

Rosie frowned up at him, eyes lit with outrage and amusement. 'You massive cheat! You're not going to recite it for me?'

'Absolutely not – not *here*, anyway.' His cheeks had turned pink. 'You can google it.'

Grumbling, Rosie fished her phone out of her clutch and did as he suggested. A lump formed in her throat as she took in the opening line: *Yes, yours, my love, is the right human face*. It was a poem about finding a home after seemingly endless travel – about stumbling upon a soulmate.

'Aled! Aled *and guest*! Get your arses over here!' a voice boomed from the nearby dance floor. Trying to swallow away the emotion that was making it difficult to breathe, Rosie looked up to see a gaggle of semi-inebriated teachers, none of whom looked likely to take no for an answer.

'I do love this song . . .' Rosie said, feigning composure and shimmying her shoulders to Arctic Monkeys' 'Fluorescent Adolescent'. 'Come on. A bit of bopping won't kill you.'

Seemingly unable to resist her enthusiasm, Aled allowed himself to be pulled onto the dance floor. Within seconds the song changed, and the opening bars of 'Sea of Love' by Cat Power filtered softly through the overhead speakers.

Rosie prepared herself to step away, but before she could move Aled had pulled her closer, his hands soft against the smooth fabric at her waist. One slid up her back, meeting the bare skin of her shoulder and settling there. Holding her. 'I thought you wanted to dance.'

After a second's deliberation, Rosie let her body go loose in the way it had been longing to. She allowed him to turn her in slow circles, to sway with her. She revelled in the sensation of being pressed against him – her soft flesh against his broad, muscular frame. Her blood felt hot, like it was moving through her too fast, kindling fires in all the places where she wasn't supposed to need him. It was intolerable, and she never wanted it to end.

She didn't know she'd laid her head against his chest until, with infinite tenderness, he nestled a hand in her hair. She breathed deep, pulling air that smelled of him, of *home*, down into the bottom of her lungs. She wanted to drown in it.

Rosie had never felt like this – never been so aware of another body, another soul. She'd never felt like that other was some missing part of herself: fundamental, undeniable, necessary.

She remembered what Rhianne had said about her cousin, her eyes rolling in indulgent amusement as she iced a freshly made carrot cake. She'd called him *intensely romantic* – and she'd meant that he was someone for whom love was all-consuming, a riot in the heart, the reason for existing. Wrapped in his arms, Rosie found she felt the same. With James, she'd obsessed about the milestones they should have been reaching: the boxes they should have been ticking, the events and experiences that signified successful adulting.

Now, she saw that none of it mattered. What were rigid life plans and her parents' expectations, set against the profound, unruly joy of feeling known and whole?

The song ended, and they drifted apart as if awaking from a dream.

Rosie knew Aled wouldn't kiss her, so she didn't gaze up at him, lean forward or part her lips in readiness, even though everything in her wanted to. She kept her eyes down until the roaring inside her had quieted, until she'd swallowed away words like 'I want you' and 'kiss me' and 'take me home'.

As the glow between them faded, they resumed talking, drinking and socialising – chatted as though it had never been. But Rosie could see it now: the shining, delicate thread that joined them. She could hear the refrain that powered her steadying heartbeat. *It's us. We fit. We're right.*

She knew what this was, and she wasn't afraid of it.

Because for the first time, she felt sure that Aled knew it, too.

December

Chapter 23

Things between Rosie and Aled weren't so much uncomfortable as *strained* after the wedding reception. They were scrupulously nice to one another, neither mentioning the moment of fierce attraction they'd experienced on the dance floor – but its after-effects were palpable in the low thrum of need that pulsed between them.

Accidental touches started small fires on Rosie's skin, and both she and Aled avoided prolonged eye contact. She lost count of the times she conversed with him while staring determinedly at the cat.

Rosie didn't know what scruple or fear was holding him back from her, and she didn't dare ask – but the wall between them felt shaky and insubstantial. She wondered what it would take to break it, and what might happen when it did.

On a Friday several weeks after Cora and Ed's wedding, Rosie was due to work late in the deli. It was the night of the private party Rhianne had mentioned back in October, and they closed early so it could be decked out with fairy lights, fresh flowers and a banner that read 'Congratulations!'.

'It's an engagement do,' Rhianne explained. 'Though it was originally booked as a birthday party. The woman is . . . *exacting*. Clear about what she wants: there's to be no mention of Christmas, or any remotely festive food, even though it's December and all right-minded people have boarded the good ship *Mince Pie*.'

'Oh right,' Rosie said, immediately nervous.

'She sent over a whole list of dietary requirements,' Rhianne went on, 'so I ended up building the menu around them. Gluten-free this, low-carb that . . . I'd never have agreed to host it if I'd known she was this difficult upfront. It physically pains me to create a buffet that doesn't include freshly baked sourdough and burrata.'

'I guess it's a case of taking a breath, then thinking about the fee she's paying?' Rosie asked.

'Indeed,' Rhianne agreed. 'Though I'd have doubled it if I'd known, to price in this much hassle.'

Yaz and Marcus were sticking around for the evening, too – Marcus manning the drinks station, which was to offer flavoured kombucha and smoothies instead of wine, and Yaz helping Rhianne in the kitchen. Rosie's job was to fetch, carry and ensure everyone was happy. Guests were due to start arriving from 7 p.m., and by 6.30 the team was ready for them. The deli looked perfect – elegant and romantic – and despite the limitations placed on Rhianne's culinary creativity, the food smells emanating from her workstation were mouthwatering.

Only minutes after the deli door was unlocked, people began to file in. Couples and small groups of friends gratefully collected their non-alcoholic drinks, then pulled up chairs around the large table that had been assembled in the centre of the room. Everyone looked smart and cool, Rosie thought, though perhaps with a slightly brittle quality. These were successful people with trendy hobbies, designer clothes, exclusive gym memberships and wholefood, plant-based diets; no doubt their lives were highly Instagrammable, but not all of them looked happy about it.

'Which one is the party organiser?' Rosie asked Rhianne at just after 7.20.

'She's not here yet,' Rhianne snorted. 'I guess she's running deliberately late. She's the sort who wants her audience in place before she deigns to make an appearance.'

Rosie nodded, then continued handing out canapés, refilling dishes of houmous, tzatziki and baba ganoush and ensuring that everyone had what they needed. Finally, a few minutes after 7.30, the bell above the deli door signalled the arrival of the soon-to-be bride and groom.

Rosie set down the jug of iced water she was carrying, straightened her spine and pulled her shoulders back in preparation for meeting the woman Rhianne had christened 'a proper fussy fuck'.

Nothing could have prepared her for the sight that greeted her. Rosie's mouth dropped open in horror, her lips forming an aghast 'O' that resisted all attempts at reform. The fussy fuck was Dylan, and the man standing next to her – the man Dylan was *engaged to* – was James.

Rooted to the spot, Rosie tried desperately to arrange her face into a neutral, indifferent expression. But her mouth refused to co-operate, remaining stubbornly wide with shock as her unblinking eyeballs turned scratchy and dry.

She had no idea what to do. By any measure, this was mortifying. The man who'd claimed he didn't want to settle down – who had pulled the 'it's not you, it's me' routine from the arsehole boyfriend playbook – was not only living with another woman. It turned out he'd asked her to marry him.

Rosie felt sick. Suddenly, the sight of Rhianne's usually irresistible olive tapenade made her want to throw up.

James's blue eyes found hers, widening in amazement. He turned and whispered in Dylan's ear, and she looked directly at Rosie – her expression pitying but grimly amused. It was the same look Michael had sometimes worn when, as children, he and Rosie had co-operated on some nefarious scheme that she alone was blamed for.

Not sure what else she could do, Rosie turned and fled for the kitchen.

'Whoa there, tiger,' Rhianne said, as Rosie burst through the swing door. 'I don't want to end up *wearing* this chickpea and feta salad, thank you very much.'

'Oh god, I'm sorry,' Rosie panted. 'I'm so sorry. I'm—'

'*Hey*,' Rhianne said, her tone entirely different now. She put down the large glass dish she'd been holding and took

Rosie's shaking hands in hers. 'What's happened? *Breathe*. Tell me.'

After taking several gulps of fragrant, spicy air, Rosie managed an explanation, upon which Rhianne's expression turned savage. 'Say the word and I'll take my best Santoku knife to his jugular.'

Rosie managed a watery laugh. 'That won't be necessary. It pains me to say it, but I don't think this is James's fault. He didn't know I worked here.'

'*She* did, though,' Rhianne said, her voice almost a growl. 'She came by to pay the balance for the room hire a few weeks ago when you were in. It was after your shift, and you were busy chatting with Al and Niamh. I saw her glance over at you.'

'Wow,' Rosie said, disbelieving. 'What a catch. James has clearly done well for himself.'

'I think you mean, what a *bitch*,' Rhianne said. 'D'you want me to chuck her out? Because honestly, I kind of wanted to even before this happened.'

'*No*,' Rosie said, shaking her head emphatically. 'This is your business – your livelihood – and none of this is your responsibility. I can get through it . . . Besides, I have the feeling she wants this to be some sort of massive drama. We'll be playing into her hands if we create a scene.'

'Are you sure?'

'I am,' Rosie said, determined. 'You don't have to do anything.'

'The least I can do is swap you and Yaz over,' Rhianne insisted, squeezing Rosie's hands before letting them go. 'You can work in here with me, and Yaz can deal with the fun sponges out there.'

'OK,' Rosie agreed. 'That does sound sensible.'

'Good. You dress this salad and I'll go and find Yaz,' Rhianne said firmly, handing Rosie a bottle of home-made vinaigrette. 'And Rosie? Screw this woman and the wellness wagon she rode in on. I hope she chokes on her chia seed pudding.'

* * *

As Rosie helped Rhianne put the finishing touches to twenty-five mini puddings, she couldn't help feeling that she'd hit a new low. Hiding from her ex-boyfriend in the kitchen of the venue where his engagement party was taking place felt so pathetic it beggared belief. It was like a scene from a sitcom, except that it wasn't remotely funny.

When she examined her feelings closely, however, she discovered she was more angry and embarrassed than hurt. She searched for the part of herself that wished she had a ring on her finger – a promise of forever from the man she'd once thought she'd grow old with. To her satisfaction, she couldn't find it. This situation was unpleasant, but not devastating. As long as she kept her head down, she'd survive it.

Yaz entered the kitchen and collected two large trays of desserts, throwing Rosie a supportive look. Both she and Marcus had been apprised of Rosie's sudden need to keep a low profile. Once the rest of the plates had been taken out and distributed, Rosie let out a long sigh.

Having discharged her responsibilities, she decided now was a good time to visit the bathroom. The crowd was concentrating on eating, and she could probably sneak from the kitchen to the toilets without attracting attention.

After using the loo, she washed and dried her hands, only to realise that the greater challenge would be getting back to the kitchen unseen, as people finished their puddings and began to refocus on their surroundings. She looked at her reflection in the mirror above the sink, fluffed her hair and applied a fresh coat of her new, favourite red lipstick. If she was going to be seen, she wanted to be seen with her new do on point and her war paint in place.

Seconds later, she was glad she'd thought of this. James was lurking just beyond the bathroom door – apparently waiting for her to emerge.

For a moment he simply stared, taking in her outfit (a

fun but functional pair of dungarees), her haircut and her makeup. 'You look . . . different,' he said.

Rosie shrugged. 'So do you.' *And not in a good way*, she thought. He had those awful trainers on again, and a skintight t-shirt designed to show off his burgeoning biceps – though Rosie couldn't help thinking it mostly served to highlight the narrowness of his shoulders.

'I . . . I'm—' he fumbled, struggling for coherent speech. 'I'm sorry about this.'

'I'm sure you are,' Rosie said blandly. She found she wasn't furious with him. Instead, she felt frustrated with herself: dismayed that she'd wasted so many years and so much affection on someone who was so wrong for her.

'The engagement – this whole thing – it's been a whirlwind,' James said. 'I'm not even sure how it happened, honestly.'

Rosie rolled her eyes but said nothing.

Seeming to take this as an invitation to continue unburdening himself, James went on: 'She's . . . Dylan's a bit of a force. Demanding, you know? And I'm sort of along for the ride.'

Rosie frowned at him, stunned into speechlessness. Was he really implying that his engagement to this woman was something he was merely going along with? A corner he'd been backed into?

'Anyway. I really am sorry about this whole situation,' James said into the silence. 'I know it must be horrible for you. Upsetting.'

Rosie's pride flared at this. 'It's awkward, James,' she said, 'obviously. But as you can probably see, I'm not sobbing into my apron about it.'

'Honestly, Dylan is like . . . a *hurricane*,' James babbled. 'I've been swept away. It's all happened so fast.'

Rosie felt her patience threatening to snap, and knew she needed to shut this down. She had no desire to erupt at him in her workplace.

'James, I really don't care,' she told him. 'All I can say is good luck to you – based on what I've seen so far, I think you're going to need it.'

She pushed past him, but before she made it back to the relative safety of the kitchen, Dylan's voice rang out – just high enough that every single person in the room could hear.

'Oh yes, that's his ex. The waitress over there with the thick thighs. *So cringe* that she's working here, but what can you do? He's just making sure she's not going to drown herself in chocolate milk now our news is out.'

There was a low ripple of laughter and some mild shock from the crowd. Tears of rage burned in Rosie's eyes.

Without looking, she knew that everyone in the room was staring at her – waiting for her to react. She needed to remove herself from view before humiliation overwhelmed her, but her feet wouldn't move. Amid the sound of murmuring and whispered questions Dylan spoke again, unnecessarily loudly: 'Oh yes, I know – he's traded up. *Way* up. Of course, he'll have to meet *my* standards now, ha ha . . .'

Moisture brimmed behind Rosie's closed eyelids, and she knew she was going to cry. *Fuck it all*. She didn't want this woman to know that her words had hurt her. Didn't want to give her the satisfaction of mistakenly thinking she'd won some kind of game – not when the prize was James, a man Rosie increasingly thought of as a weapons-grade wanker.

A large, warm hand closed around hers. Another settled on her shoulder.

Rosie looked up and saw Aled – his face in soft focus, shimmering beyond the gloss of tears in her eyes.

He bent and dropped a kiss to her right cheek, which flushed immediately. 'Ready to go home?'

Rosie nodded, leaning into him for a second – needing him to feel the depth of her relief and gratitude. He rubbed soothing circles on her shoulder, smoothed his thumb over the skin at the nape of her neck. She breathed him in hungrily, fortified by the heat and solidity of his body.

He kissed her again – a featherlight brush of his lips to her forehead. 'Let's go.'

Clinging to his hand – squeezing it as she tried to slow her rapid breathing – she let him guide her to the deli's front door.

Rhianne was there, ready and waiting with Rosie's coat and bag. With no need for explanations, Rosie understood: she'd called her cousin so he could be here for their friend – because she knew that Rosie needed him.

She dropped Aled's hand so she could shrug her jacket on, then hoisted her handbag up onto her shoulder. Still, she felt eyes on her – the watchful gaze of people who'd expected a pitiful meltdown, but instead were witnessing her make a dignified exit on the arm of a tall, dark and handsome man.

Without a moment's hesitation, she took Aled's hand again. She looked into his eyes, wordlessly communicating what she hoped he understood: that she was touching him for her own benefit, not theirs. Because she wanted to – needed to. Because she was so unbelievably tired of *not* touching him.

Out on the street where there was no one to see them, Rosie laced her fingers through his. She felt almost defiant – as though she was daring him to ask why, or what it meant.

Frost glittered on the pavement, making it slippery underfoot as they walked towards home. Winter was digging its heels in now, but the night was clear – the cold, cloudless sky filled with gently winking stars.

'Thank you,' Rosie said softly, as she and Aled made their way towards home.

'What for?' he asked, as Rosie pressed their palms together.

'For doing what you always seem to,' she replied. 'For breaking my fall.'

Back inside the familiar surrounds of the flat, nothing felt the way it usually did.

They stood in the hallway beyond the front door, not sure

where to go from here – or what to say. The air had that crisp, static quality that foreshadows a lightning storm, and every feeling in Rosie's body had narrowed down to a single point: the place where her hand still held Aled's.

He was waiting for her to let go – maybe even willing her to do it, since he didn't seem able to himself. She wasn't going to co-operate. Whatever mystery still lurked beneath the surface, Rosie knew Aled to be good. She trusted him. She wanted him. She wouldn't blink first.

Perhaps for the first time in her life, she was prepared to risk choosing rather than wait and hope to be chosen. Her fear of rejection was less important than her need to be honest about what he'd come to mean to her. Expressing herself – giving in to these feelings – wasn't something she believed she'd ever regret.

She was driven by instinct; tugged towards him by the gossamer-light string that connected them, that was urging closer, deeper coalescence. She could still feel the ghost of his lips on her face – the soft kisses that had been simultaneously comforting, soothing and possessive. She thrilled at the notion that he'd wanted James, and everyone else, to see them and understand: I'm hers and she's mine, so don't you dare fuck with her.

Aled shifted, twisting his body so he could look down at her. His eyes searched hers, penetrating and uncertain. She held his gaze, and his moment of hesitation felt like it lasted a million years.

When his self-restraint broke, it shattered. He bent down and kissed her, sighing his relief into her mouth. He pressed her back against the wall of the corridor, the length of his body flush against hers, the weight of him breathtaking.

She pushed up and into him, needing him to know how much she wanted this. She opened her mouth, tangling her fingers in his dark hair as the kiss deepened and became more urgent.

Aled trailed gentle kisses along her jawline, up to her left ear. 'I've been dying to do this since the moment I saw you in that red dress,' he confessed.

Rosie shivered, thinking about their dance at the wedding reception – the way his hands had lingered on the silk of her skirt, the way they'd set her skin alight without even touching it. 'Oh,' she murmured, '*yes*. Me too.'

His mouth met hers again, hungry and eager. He pulled her bottom lip between his teeth, and Rosie made a sound she'd never have thought herself capable of.

Aled's hands found their way inside her coat, then past the bib of her denim overalls. His fingers drifted across the hem of the long-sleeved t-shirt she wore under them, then found the hot skin beneath.

Not to be outdone, Rosie pushed her hands up and underneath his sweater. He groaned.

'Are you sure about this?' he whispered. 'It's so soon after James. Are you sure you want me to be . . . *this*, to you?'

With no real idea what he meant, Rosie could only say, '*Yes*. Yes, please.'

'All right, then,' he said, half resigned, half ecstatic. As if she weighed nothing, he lifted Rosie clean off the floor. She clung to him, wrapping her legs around his waist, arching closer and discovering that he needed her as much as she needed him.

'Take me to bed,' she breathed – words she'd never uttered before, and which she'd never felt the need to say. She was a mess of sensation, governed only by the desire to be closer to him.

She still had all her clothes on, but this was already the best sex of her life. As her mouth met his for the thousandth time, as they moved together, a voice in her head said: *This is going to ruin you. You'll never want another man again.*

Rosie knew it was right, but she also didn't care.

'Are you certain?' Aled asked, audibly grasping for his last shreds of self-control.

'Completely,' Rosie promised, burying her face in his

tanned, soap-scented neck as he walked them – seemingly effortlessly – towards what used to be the spare room.

As the door closed behind them, coherent thought deserted her – drowned in the tide of bone-melting kisses, overcome by the heady glide of skin on skin and the elation of being seen, known and desired.

Chapter 24

'So,' Niamh said, as she and Rosie sat on either side of her kitchen island the next morning. 'How have you been?'

'Er – good,' Rosie replied, feeling like she needed to warm up a little before she could say, *I'm marvellous, actually, on account of having slept with my hot flatmate three times in twelve hours.*

'You look good,' Niamh said, narrowing her eyes. 'Suspiciously good. Did you buy more new makeup? A different moisturiser?'

Rosie said nothing, but noted that Niamh, in unusual contrast to herself, did *not* look good. For the first time in as long as Rosie could remember – probably since Niamh's break-up with Christian, the pretentious wannabe actor who'd dumped her during her second year at university – her friend looked harassed. Drained. She appeared more than tired, somehow: as if she was weary in spirit, and not just knackered from juggling work, childcare and the everyday business of living.

'Ah. Thanks. I haven't, though. Are you OK?' Rosie said, changing the subject with all the subtlety of a sledgehammer.

'I feel like a cat who's been killed eight times and is merely awaiting the sweet release of death,' Niamh said. 'Or like I've been run over by a bus, which – for good measure – has reversed and then run over me a second time.'

'That good, eh?'

'Yeah. The twins' night sleeping – or lack thereof – is pretty much killing me. It's like they're *nocturnal*. And work is mad busy, too. But I'll be fine. It's just been a tough week.'

She waved a hand blithely, as if to indicate this subject was now closed.

Rosie couldn't help thinking that, with two babies to take care of, a husband who worked long hours and a very demanding job, all Niamh's weeks must be tough. She resolved to try and be a better friend – to check in more often, and perhaps take the twins out when she could for the sake of giving Niamh the chance to nap.

'How goes the flatmate hunt?' Niamh asked.

It took Rosie a moment or two to work out what she meant – not only because the question came out of left field, but because she genuinely hadn't thought about trying to replace Aled in weeks. Barely at all since he'd moved in, if she was honest.

'Well. It . . . doesn't. Go, I mean,' Rosie said, not able to bring herself to lie.

Niamh's eyebrows knitted. She compressed her lips into a flat, worried line. 'I thought the artist formerly known as Nameless Neighbour was set to move out after Christmas?' she asked. 'Aren't you leaving it a little late to find someone else? Surely the renovation's getting there now.'

Rosie bit her lip and stared at a particularly interesting pattern on the natural stone work surface. The thought of Aled moving out made her heart hurt, though she supposed there was no reason to think it wouldn't happen. No reason except every kiss, every touch, every whispered endearment they'd shared last night.

'*Rosie?*' Niamh demanded.

'Um . . . I haven't found anyone yet. I'm sure things will work out for the best.'

'What the hell does that mean?'

'I don't know yet.'

'You're talking in riddles,' Niamh declared, her temper fraying. 'What's wrong with you?'

'Nothing's *wrong* with me,' Rosie said, beginning to feel riled herself.

This wasn't how she'd imagined the morning's conversation would go. She and Niamh were supposed to drink coffee while the twins napped, eat a few biscuits and discuss – in gleeful tones – the incredible night she'd just had, as well as what it might mean. Rosie also needed to relay the revelation that James was engaged to Dylan, though this seemed far less important than the rest.

'Oh my god,' Niamh said, closing her eyes in understanding. 'You're shagging him, aren't you?'

Rosie's face was clearly all the answer her best friend needed, because she followed this up with: 'I *knew* that "just boffed" glow couldn't be down to cosmetics.'

'It's not like that,' Rosie said. 'It's . . . more than that.'

'Oh my god,' Niamh said again, wearily this time. 'This has disaster written all over it.'

Rosie felt stung. 'A few weeks ago we sat in this very kitchen and you *told* me I should sleep with him! You were all in favour of – and I quote – a fling.'

'But that's not what this is, is it?' Niamh asked. 'I can see it in your ridiculously radiant face. The train has left the station – you're well on the way to falling for him. I can't *believe* I didn't see this coming.'

'See *what* coming?'

'The impending disaster I just mentioned. I should have predicted you'd jump in with both feet, instead of keeping your next relationship casual. You need a transitional person, not something full on.'

Rosie racked her brain and tried to remember where else she'd heard the phrase 'transitional person' recently. She came up blank.

'It's like you're *asking* to get hurt,' Niamh went on. 'It's bordering on masochistic.'

At this, Rosie drew in a sharp, shocked breath. 'That's pretty harsh, in the context of everything I've had to deal with recently,' she said. 'And you don't know the half of it, as it turns out.'

'Maybe not,' Niamh snapped, in no hurry for any extra information Rosie might want to impart. 'But James treated you like crap for months. Maybe years. Think about what you put up with – the *people* you put up with.'

Rosie felt like she'd been kicked in the chest. 'Are you saying I'm weak? Some kind of pathetic yes-person? Because I don't think that's fair. I've come a long way in the past few months and—'

'And you're going to *ruin* all that progress by letting another man walk all over you,' Niamh almost shouted. 'A man who's been to twenty-five countries in the past ten years, has a temporary job and appears totally uninterested in staying anywhere for more than a few weeks. You've accommodated *his* needs without considering your own. You've started something with him, but you haven't asked for any kind of commitment in return. You're still pandering. You're constantly bending over backwards to be what other people want, and it's *exhausting*.'

Her rant over, Niamh looked up at Rosie, who now had tears rolling down her face.

There was some truth beneath Niamh's bluster, and it frightened her: she and Aled hadn't discussed his job, or their living situation. Did he want to stay with her? Did he plan on catching the next available flight to somewhere interesting and exotic? Would he leave her, or did he want to stay in her life? She knew what she'd felt between them last night, but nothing was certain. Nothing had been said out loud.

She eyed her friend from across the counter, taking in the deep, dark shadows beneath her eyes. She noticed Niamh's bitten nails, and finally recognised her pinched, nervous look as one that often accompanied too much rapid weight loss. Rosie's mother had worn it frequently in years gone by – usually after crash diets that made her thinner, but also rendered her so ravenous she could barely function.

Sympathy for her friend swelled inside Rosie. Niamh was

sinking, and she had been too preoccupied with her own troubles to properly realise it.

As she prepared to say something kind and calming, Niamh burst out: 'Your naivety is *astounding*, Rosie. I mean, when are you going to stop letting life just happen to you? When are you going to start living with *intention*?'

'For fuck's sake, spare me the fridge magnet bullshit,' Rosie retorted angrily. 'I had more than enough of that from James. I *am* living with intention. I intended to have some excellent sex last night, and I absolutely did.'

Niamh shook her head dismissively.

'And d'you know something?' Rosie continued, her ire now up and running away with her. 'You lecture *me* about bending over backwards for others – trying to be all things to all people without considering my own needs. Look at *yourself*. I think this is your stuff, not mine. As one of those LA life gurus might put it: you're projecting.'

Niamh's jaw dropped.

'Since you went back to work, you've been coming apart at the seams,' Rosie said. 'You won't even admit it's hard half the time – you just shrug for the sake of saving face. You want to be perfect for Brendan, perfect for the kids and perfect for your clients, no matter what it costs you. You think *I'm* exhausting? I'm exhausted just looking at you. I don't know why you can't admit you're struggling and *let me in*.'

'I think you've said enough,' Niamh murmured, her face a stony mask that didn't quite conceal how hard Rosie's words had hit her.

Rosie herself felt breathless, like she'd had all the air knocked out of her lungs.

She wanted to fix this – to wind the clock back and begin the whole catch-up again. She wanted to apologise for yelling, to ask Niamh what she needed and to offer her some support . . . But Rosie was hurt, too. Niamh's characterisation of her as a desperate walkover had cut deep, and she apparently had no intention of saying sorry.

'Maybe you should go,' Niamh said stiffly. 'Unless, of course, you think I won't be able to manage when the twins wake up.'

'I've no doubt you'll manage,' Rosie said, entirely honestly. 'I just worry about what all this *managing* is costing you, because I love you. I'll see myself out.'

Dazed and confused by her argument with Niamh, Rosie caught the bus back to Walthamstow. She ambled around the village's nicer shops, as though eyeing up designer stationery or artfully displayed house plants might reveal a solution to her troubles. She and Niamh hadn't argued since they were in their early twenties – and they'd never fallen out this badly.

When no magical answer presented itself from among the hand-knitted scarves in the shop next door to the deli, Rosie decided to pop in and see Rhianne. If nothing else, she could thank her for getting in touch with Aled last night – for saving her from a situation that would have been utterly humiliating, but for his unexpected appearance.

Almost every table inside was occupied, so Rosie pulled up a seat at the counter. Becky was there, in a t-shirt that read: 'FEMINISM IS MY SECOND FAVOURITE F WORD'.

'You all right, Rosie?' she said. 'You look sort of . . . down.'

'I'm OK, I promise,' Rosie lied. 'Is Rhianne around?'

'In the kitchen. Go through – I'll make you a coffee. Something cheering. Caramel latte?'

'That sounds perfect, thanks.'

In the kitchen, Rhianne was part way through slicing up a trayful of chocolate brownies. They smelled sinfully delicious, and the fudgy edge of each one oozed temptingly as they were loaded onto the tiered cake stand they'd occupy until lucky patrons purchased them.

'Hey you,' Rhianne said. 'Volunteering for an extra shift? I've got some biscuits that need icing over there.'

'No chance,' Rosie said, managing to crack a smile. 'I just wanted to say thanks for last night.'

'For calling Al, you mean? Least I could do. And once I told him what was happening there wasn't a snowball's chance in hell he wouldn't come for you.'

Pleasure fluttered through Rosie's chest, and she felt a lump rise in her throat. 'Really?'

Rhianne looked up from the brownies. She raised a single, sceptical, perfectly pencilled eyebrow. '*Obviously*. God knows he hasn't used his words to say this, but he's mad about you – and if I'm not mistaken, you're more than a bit fond, too. Surely the pair of you managed *some* kind of tryst after last night's romantic rescue?'

Rosie simply stared as Rhianne placed a final brownie at the top of her display. 'Er – well . . .'

'Good,' Rhianne said, clearly taking Rosie's vocal stumbling as confirmation. 'It's about time. All I ask is that you're careful with him. I know he's a grown man, but he's crazy sensitive below the surface.'

'I know,' Rosie said, affection warming her tone. 'That's one of the reasons why I . . . like him.'

Rhianne laughed. 'Well, rest assured he *likes* you too. It's a long time since I've seen him like this – I'm not sure I ever have, truth be told. When he first came to London he was all, I'll check this building out, get it on the market and be on my way. Then it was, I'll renovate it before I put it up for sale – spend some time here. And *then*—'

'I'm sorry, what?'

Rosie felt like she'd been doused with iced water, or hit from behind with a blunt object. The fuzzy glow she'd felt at Rhianne's earlier words evaporated. She was suddenly chilled to the bone.

Rhianne's face turned ashen. 'Oh, god. What have I said?'

'Nothing. At least, nothing that he couldn't have said himself,' Rosie replied, her cold, calm tone belying the frantic hammering of her heart. 'I have to go. I'll see you later.'

Without looking back, she marched out of the kitchen and then through the deli's front door into the frigid December air.

'Rosie! Your coffee? It's here for you!' Becky called. But Rosie didn't hear her.

Chapter 25

By the time Rosie got back to the flat, she was brimful with emotion. She felt naive. *Foolish*. Angry and confused.

She couldn't bring herself to believe Aled had set out to deceive her, nor that whatever was unfolding between them wasn't real. Yet the fact remained, he hadn't been honest with her.

Fully aware of how badly James had betrayed her trust, Aled had let her believe that their living together would keep her in her home – that it would save the haven she'd built while everything else around her crashed and burned. Now it seemed his occupancy of the spare room had only ever offered a stay of execution: a temporary reprieve for this comforting corner of the city she'd carved out for herself.

She found him in the sitting room, ready for an onslaught of accusations. Rosie surmised that Rhianne must have messaged him some sort of *mea culpa* – an apology for letting the cat out of the bag.

This merely incensed her further. She loved this place: she'd poured herself into it, brought it alive with more than colourful paint and thrifted furniture. Why should she be the last to know she was likely to lose it?

'Is it true?' she asked, immediately annoyed that her voice was tremulous and scratchy. She wanted to be strong and intimidating, but she was coming off as grief-stricken.

'Not exactly,' Aled said, shaking his head. 'Rosie, I—'

'*Not exactly?*' she repeated scathingly. 'I know we live in an era of alternative facts, but I'm old-fashioned about these things. Something's either true or it's not.'

'It's true that I intended to sell this place when I first came here,' he said, sounding utterly miserable. 'I was going to stay for a few days, meet with some estate agents and then be on my way. It's also true that I started prevaricating pretty quickly – partly because the top flat was in such a state. I thought it'd help to fix it up before putting it on the market.'

'And you didn't think it might be fair to tell me what you were planning before moving into my spare room? Before befriending me? Before letting me—'

Her voice cracked, and she stamped her foot in frustration. Niamh had been right: she was fully gone for this man. With scant information, she'd opened her heart to him as well as her home, and now she was reaping the bitter reward.

'I told myself I *wouldn't* befriend you,' Aled said. 'That nothing would happen between us – but you made it impossible not to—'

'So this is *my* fault?'

'No, that's not what I mean,' he groaned, agonised. 'When I first moved in, I planned to stay distant. And I thought you wanted me here to cover the rent, but also because you knew it would piss off the boyfriend you hoped would come back. I convinced myself that *neither* of us was being fully honest.'

He had her there. While Rosie had never seriously believed James would come running at the news that she'd moved another man in – and although she'd quickly arrived at the conclusion that she didn't actually *want* him to – her motives for choosing Aled as a flatmate had been murkier than she cared to admit.

Shoving this thought aside, she said: 'We've been living together for *months*. You could have told me at any time. After everything I went through with James, did it not occur to you that I might value honesty?'

'I kept trying to bring it up, but something always got in the way. And the more time we spent together, the more I liked you. The harder it became to risk ruining everything.'

'What even *is* there to ruin?' Rosie demanded, feeling tears begin to trace their way down her cheeks. 'You let me think you genuinely cared about me, when all the time you were planning to sell this place out from under me the moment your sums added up.'

'It wasn't like that,' Aled insisted, agitated now.

'Was sleeping with me just an added bonus?' Rosie asked, her fury breaking. 'A last bit of fun before fucking off to some far-flung place for good? I mean, presumably you could live off the profit from selling this place for years. What's it worth? A million quid? Two? Good for you, I suppose. That'll buy you a lot of beers on Thai beaches.'

'You can't seriously mean that,' he ground out, his face flushed, pained with outrage. 'I held myself back from you for weeks – *months* – from the very first *day*. I've been terrified this whole time that you'd hate me for ever *considering* selling this flat, and simultaneously frightened that I'd become some stopgap between proper boyfriends – between James and the one you settle down with. It was weak of me not to put it all out there before starting something with you, I admit. I fucked up. But I did it because I was scared, not because I'm cynical.'

'But you seem to think *I'm* cynical,' Rosie retorted. 'What do you think I'd want a *stopgap* for? Revenge? Kudos? A confidence boost?'

'You wouldn't be the first person to find my "hidden depths" disappointingly dull,' he said, raking a hand through his hair in dismay.

'Oh, great,' Rosie said indignantly. 'So I'm shallow as well as selfish and manipulative.'

'I didn't say that.'

'You don't say much, to be fair – and I knew that from the beginning,' she snapped, unable to resist resorting to sarcasm. 'But there's a point at which being evasive segues into being dishonest. Into lying by omission.'

'You're right, and I'm sorry. Please can we just—'

'No. I'm really not sure we can,' Rosie interrupted. 'I trusted you absolutely. I never doubted a thing you said to me. Now I feel like an idiot – like I should have been thinking about all the things you *didn't* say, what the silences might have meant. All those letters from estate agents . . . The ones that came stamped with your solicitor's logo. You waved them away as if they meant nothing. What a *fool* I must be not to have put two and two together.'

'I've never lied to you, and I never will,' Aled said hotly. 'You haven't let me explain properly. There's still stuff you don't know.'

'And whose fault is that?'

As Rosie's near-shouted words hung between them, the trill of a mobile phone ringtone cut through the air. For a few seconds, she felt sure it couldn't be hers; this was some unfamiliar tune in a depressingly minor key, not the jaunty melody she was used to. Then, bewildered, she realised it was definitely coming from her handbag.

The penny dropped. This was the dirge-like tone she'd tipsily attached to Michael's contact details in her phone on a night out with Niamh. She'd been bemoaning his latest put-down and – having imbibed copious amounts of fizzy wine – Niamh had also encouraged her to replace his photo with a picture of a street sign that read 'Bell End'.

What the hell was *Michael* ringing her for? They never spoke unless forced to by close physical proximity.

All at once, her mother's rambling concerns about Colin's supposedly failing health came back to Rosie; she thought of all the text messages she'd recently ignored, imploring her to come home and encourage him to consciously uncouple from the sofa.

She scrambled to find the phone before it stopped ringing, and breathlessly swiped to answer it.

'Michael?' she said into the handset. 'What's wrong? What's going on?'

This wasn't melodrama – it was cutting to the chase. There was no way he'd call her unless something terrible had happened.

'It's Mum,' Michael said, his voice thick with emotion.

'*Mum*?' Rosie burst out, unable to keep the shock out of her voice.

'Yes,' her brother answered, sounding sadder and sorrier than Rosie had ever heard him. 'She's in hospital. She's asking for you. Can you come?'

'I'm on my way.'

Rosie drove to Chelmsford Hospital on autopilot. Later, she had only a dreamlike recollection of getting into her car, then navigating her way to this unfamiliar destination as swiftly as possible. She was pretty sure she'd left Aled open-mouthed, mid-conversation – but right now, she didn't have the capacity to deal with their argument as well as panic about her mother's collapse.

According to Michael, she'd complained of chest pain several times in the past week. Then, during this morning's mammoth house clean, she'd slumped over the Dyson cordless vacuum cleaner, clutched at her torso and toppled over to land, unconscious, on the sitting room carpet. It wasn't lost on Rosie that Michael and her father had been sitting on the sofa at the time, reportedly glued to some televised darts tournament.

She struggled to find a parking space, sent up her thanks to the universe when she did, then made her way to the A&E department. 'I'm here to see Julie Butler,' Rosie said to the woman behind the plexiglass screen at reception. 'My dad and brother are here somewhere. She's my mum.'

Rosie felt her eyes grow glossy at these last three words. She swiped beneath her eyes to catch her tears. What if she never got the chance to make things right with Julie? She'd spent weeks ignoring her for good reason, for the sake of self-preservation – but running away from the issues in their relationship wouldn't solve them. It just meant they couldn't repair anything.

The receptionist nodded briskly, seemingly used to sudden

displays of emotion from visitors. 'Take a seat just in there,' she said, indicating a door that led to an open-plan waiting room. 'She's undergoing tests, I believe. You should hear more soon.'

A minute later, Michael and Colin appeared in the waiting room. Her father was holding a paper cup of some hot liquid that doubtless claimed to be tea, while Michael was clutching two packets of Walkers Max Flame Grilled Steak crisps and a Yorkie bar.

Colin appeared sad and overwhelmed, while Michael looked haunted.

It seemed clear that neither was coping, and Rosie didn't know why she was surprised. It was inevitable that she'd have to be the adult in this situation – though, for once, she didn't resent it. She wanted to be the one who listened to the doctors, who made sure she and the rest of her family understood what was happening.

'What do we know so far?' she asked, addressing her father.

'Not much,' Colin replied. 'It looks like a heart attack. They're running tests.'

A heart attack? Rosie couldn't help feeling a little awestruck by the terrible irony of this, which flew in the face of Julie's certainty that staying thin was the only way to achieve health.

Michael motored through a packet of crisps as Colin sipped his tea, which Rosie now saw was the same unappetising colour as used washing-up water.

'D'you want a square of chocolate, Rosie?' Michael asked, to his sister's amazement.

'I thought Yorkie bars weren't for girls?' she said, referencing an old TV ad he'd quoted at her countless times when they were children.

Michael shrugged. 'Have some if you want.'

'I'm OK. Thanks, though.'

A tall, grey-haired doctor in green scrubs appeared before them, and asked, 'Are you the family of Julie Butler?'

'We are,' Rosie told him.

Colin's hands were shaking, and Michael had chocolate on his chin. Sensibly, the doctor focused his gaze on Rosie for a moment before turning to Colin and saying, 'Lovely. I'm Dr Copeland. Would you like to follow me?' Rosie understood that she needed to pay attention on behalf of her distraught father, who – quite understandably – might not remember everything that was said during the next few minutes.

At the doctor's words, Michael began weeping. He turned to Rosie and moaned: 'Are we being taken into a private room so he can give us bad news?'

Rosie couldn't imagine the word 'lovely' would precede such a step, so she shook her head soothingly.

'I'm sorry,' the doctor said a second later, 'I didn't mean to alarm you. Mrs Butler's in a room just up here – she's sleeping peacefully.'

Michael howled all the louder at this, and Rosie was reminded of the time Lucas Hale, an older lad from their street, had accidentally run over Michael's carelessly abandoned mountain bike in his Ford Ka.

They entered the room where her mother slept. Julie's body was connected to various monitors that appeared to show she was comfortable. She looked tiny in the hospital bed, but even in these dire straits her glamorous shine hadn't worn off. Her hands rested on top of her pale blue blanket, her long, almond-shaped nails gleamed bright red, and her diamond engagement and wedding rings were sparkling in the room's harsh fluorescent light.

Rosie turned to Dr Copeland. 'What do you know so far?' she asked. 'Was it a heart attack?'

'It doesn't seem so,' he said. 'We believe she has angina, which is a condition associated with severe chest pain. We're awaiting a couple more test results which should confirm the diagnosis. Angina can forewarn that a heart attack or stroke is likely, however – so we tend to encourage patients to treat it as a wake-up call. An opportunity to reset and reconsider their health – explore whether there are ways they could improve it.'

'I see,' Rosie said. 'And . . . will she be all right? Will she recover fully from this?'

'I see no reason why she shouldn't,' Dr Copeland said. 'Though I'd like to keep her here for a couple of days, and she'll need a period of rest and recuperation at home after that.'

'Understood,' Rosie said.

'I'll leave you to spend some time with her, now,' the doctor said, backing out of the room. 'Someone will be by to check how she is shortly.'

Rosie looked at her father and brother, each of whom had taken one of Julie's carefully manicured hands in theirs. She couldn't help thinking that her mum's 'period of rest and recuperation' would be a rude awakening for both of them – but she was determined to make sure Julie got it.

'Did either of you bring anything for her when you came in earlier? Toiletries? Nightwear? No worries if you didn't think of it, I probably wouldn't have either.'

'Oh, no love,' Colin answered, sounding anxious. 'D'you think she'll need much? What will she want? Where does she even keep it all?'

'If she's going to be in here for the next few days, she'll want her night cream, lipstick and best dressing gown at the very least,' Rosie said with a small smile. 'But don't worry, I can sort it. I'll go back to the house and pack her a bag.'

'You're an angel,' her dad said. 'Thank you.'

'Yeah. Thanks, Rose. You're solid,' Michael murmured. It was probably the nicest thing he'd ever said to her.

Chapter 26

Julie awoke a couple of hours after Rosie returned to the hospital with an overnight bag for her. Squeezing her daughter against her chest with unusual enthusiasm, her mother expressed sincere thanks for the gift of clean underwear, not to mention her favourite TrueYOU makeup essentials and a copy of that week's *Grazia*.

'I'm really grateful, love,' she whispered. 'And you know, your hair really does look good like that. It's funky. Confident.'

'Thanks, Mum,' Rosie said. 'I'm just glad you're all right.'

That evening, when visiting hours were over, Rosie, Colin and Michael returned home. Rosie slept in her old childhood bedroom – a boxy little space that now boasted shelf upon shelf of cosmetics and skincare products. She had no idea when it had become Julie's stockroom but made a mental note to hunt out anything that might suit her. *When in Rome,* she told herself.

She'd messaged Rhianne to ask if someone else could cover her shift on Monday and received an emphatic yes in response, as well as warm wishes for her mother's recovery. Rhianne also sent a grovelling apology, devastated that she might have caused a rift between Rosie and her cousin. Rosie didn't have the heart to fib, so she replied with no reference to Aled, a vague assurance that she was OK and a promise that she'd be back at work as soon as possible.

Aled had sent her several texts over the past twenty-four hours, and had tried to call her twice. Inside the hospital, her mobile signal was weak – and in any case, she didn't know what to say to him.

She was angry with him, but she didn't trust herself not to melt and forgive him within minutes if she heard his voice.

In the end, she settled for a brief, non-committal WhatsApp:

Mum's going to be OK, thank god. So will I x

What she really wanted, she realised, was for him to *be* here with her. She wanted to fall against him, to let him share the weight of all the worry she'd suffered in the past couple of days. She wanted him to kiss her hair, to tell her everything was going to be all right – to feel the safe, reassuring solidity of him. After their argument, though, she felt too proud – as well as too hurt – to ask. And it was too much to hope that he'd intuit any of this for himself.

On Sunday afternoon, an unexpected visitor did arrive at the hospital. As Rosie refilled her mum's water jug at the fountain in the corridor of the ward she'd been moved to, she saw James striding towards her.

Somehow, Rosie managed not to drop the plastic carafe in shock. She felt her mouth go slack and her brow furrow.

What the actual *fuck*?

'Er – hi,' she said, when he came to a stop directly in front of her – right next to the now full water jug, which she'd placed on the floor near her feet.

'Hi,' James said, imbuing the word with a gravity that implied he was here to say something important. Rosie's heart sank. The last thing she needed right now was more drama.

'What are you doing here? Are you here to see Mum? Because that's nice and everything, but it's probably a bit inappropriate now we've split up.'

'I wanted to see you,' James said.

'Oh. How did you even know I was here?'

'Michael posted something on Facebook about your mum

being ill. I knew you'd be here for her. You're always there for the people you love.'

Facebook? For the love of god. Rosie rolled her eyes, then scratched the back of her neck uncomfortably. 'So . . . what did you want, James? Only, I need to give Mum this water while it's still cold.'

This was a piss-poor excuse for fleeing, but it was the best she could come up with under pressure.

'I wanted to tell you that I've realised I've been wrong about everything these past few months,' James said in a rush, before she had a chance to bolt. 'I feel like I've woken up from a nightmare, only everything I did in the dream was real.'

He looked thoroughly sorry for himself, and Rosie almost felt bad for him.

'I've messed up my whole life,' James went on, his mouth turned down in an almost childlike expression. He looked tired. Disappointed. Desperate for someone to swoop in and make it all better.

'What about Dylan?' Rosie asked. 'Forgive me, James, but this speech is somewhat surprising given the last time I saw you was at your engagement party.'

'That whole thing was *her* idea. Her plan. I found out afterwards that she knew you were working at the venue. It was . . . cruel. It made me think about what sort of person she is. She's very driven – very impressive in a lot of ways, I suppose . . . but she isn't kind.'

'I can't disagree with you there,' Rosie said. 'But do you seriously expect me to believe you were duped into an engagement, then dumped your fiancée because she was nasty to your ex – who you yourself had tried to dump *by letter* just weeks before?'

'I've been an absolute shit,' James said, wincing. 'I know I have. But I love you. I see that now. I'd become so obsessed with peripheral, superficial stuff that I lost sight of the truth. And the truth is, you're my rock. My cheerleader. My safe place.'

Rosie couldn't believe what she was hearing. And yet . . . hadn't Niamh predicted this? She'd said something along these lines months ago – suggested that James would eventually realise Rosie was the person he relied on, rather than the person holding him back.

The word 'cheerleader' made her feel bilious. She didn't want to spend any more of her life egging someone else on, propping up their ambitions and – inevitably, in this case – washing their pants into the bargain. Rosie wanted to be her own champion. To be with someone who believed she was extraordinary and exciting, who wanted to be part of *her* adventure. To paraphrase a rough pub karaoke classic: she was not, and didn't want to be, the wind beneath anyone else's wings.

'So if I'm your safe place, what was Dylan?' she couldn't help asking.

'She was *harsh*,' James said. 'And I thought I wanted that. I thought I needed that kind of motivation to better myself. But nothing I said or did was ever good enough for her. She was constantly critical in small, backhanded ways. In the end, it was demotivating. Hurtful. Horrid.'

Rosie raised her eyes to the ceiling and pressed her lips together. There was a part of her that wanted to laugh. 'That sounds . . . familiar, James.'

'I get that,' he said, justifiably abashed. 'It made me see how badly I'd behaved. How I took you for granted. And it made me remember how *good* you are. I was a fool to leave you. If you give me another chance, I'll never let you down again. *Please*. I can't go on without you.'

This was getting out of hand. Moreover, James was right about her goodness: Rosie wasn't ruthless enough to take pleasure in seeing him brought so low that he'd publicly beg for her forgiveness. She was conscious of people milling around in the stairwell beyond the corridor window, of the lift going up and down. A few had already noticed something was happening. This scene was set to become embarrassing for both of them, and she needed to end it.

'James,' Rosie said gently, 'I can see you're sorry. I hear you. But—'

'Let me finish,' he interjected, holding a hand up to stop her talking. Then, to her amazement, he went down on one knee.

'Rosie, I love you. I want to be with you. We belong together, and I was an idiot to doubt it. I want to spend the rest of my life with you by my side – with you *on* my side. Please, make me the happiest man in the world and say you'll marry me.'

She stared down at him in speechless disbelief. Three or four months ago, she'd have given almost anything to hear him say these words. Now, they felt hollow. Meaningless.

He was holding a diamond ring out to her, waiting for her to pluck it from its plush velvet cushion and squeal with delight. It looked suspiciously similar to the ring Dylan had sported on the night of their party – the night Rosie had finally given in to how she felt about Aled.

'Get up,' she hissed. 'Please. This is *mental*.'

'Er. Is that a no?' James asked, scrambling to his feet and rubbing his temple.

'Let me ask *you* something,' Rosie said, pointing. 'Is that a second-hand ring?' James went scarlet. 'Either way, it's a very strong, unequivocal, *final* no,' Rosie told him, in the gentlest voice she could muster. 'You were wrong to finish with me in the way you did,' she went on. 'You weren't honest. But things weren't working between us – they hadn't been for a while. Splitting up was the right decision, executed in the worst imaginable way.'

'Rosie, come on – we were great together. We can get that back.'

'Things were great for you, because I made everything easy. I put you first in a way you never reciprocated. I don't want to go back to that. Relationships aren't like your office computers, James – you can't switch them off for a bit, then turn them back on and expect that everything will miraculously have started working again.'

'Well, then – I can change.'

'Maybe you can. Maybe you'll cheer on the next person you love – encourage them, empower them, instead of expecting them to be base camp for *your* exploits. But I've already changed,' she told him. 'And I'm sorry, but I just don't love you anymore. Everything's different for me now. I want to move forward, not go back.'

James nodded. To Rosie's horror, a tear rolled down his nose as he dipped his head. It was absolutely typical that she felt sorry for him mere moments after he'd tried to scam her with a recycled engagement ring.

'Is it . . . is it because of *him*?' James asked, spikily. 'The bike fascist? The guy from upstairs? Are you with him? Do you *love* him?'

Rosie's heart squeezed painfully. *No* and *yes*, she thought.

'It's because of me,' Rosie said, eventually. 'And I'm sorry if that hurts. I wish you the best, James – I hope that you're happy.'

'Thank you,' he said, through stifled sobs. 'That's probably more than I deserve.'

'I mean it,' she said, pulling him in for a quick hug.

'Only you could be this nice to me after everything. You really are wonderful, you know.'

'Thanks, James,' she said – and she meant it. 'Thank you for finally noticing.'

'Where on earth have you been?' Julie asked, when Rosie reappeared in her room. 'I was starting to wonder whether you'd run off to Gretna Green with a handsome doctor. Chance would be a fine thing, eh?'

Rosie emitted a high-pitched, nervous laugh. 'Ha ha ha, yeah – imagine being proposed to in a hospital corridor.'

'You'd probably say no anyway, wouldn't you? Right now

I can't say I blame you. Spending your life trying to catch a man, then looking after a man . . . It has its drawbacks. One of the doctors came to see me earlier – said I've got to slow down, reduce my blood pressure. That I can't run around doing every last little thing for your father and Michael like I always have.'

'I think that's good advice, Mum,' Rosie said, sitting down in the chair next to her bed.

'I'm probably going to get out of here tomorrow morning,' Julie said, 'and when I go home, you're to go back to London. Back to your life. My husband and son can look after me for a while – it'll do them good.'

'I agree.'

'Also,' Julie shifted in the bed, turning to face her daughter. 'Being in here – having this scare . . . It's given me time to think. Rosie, I want to say I'm sorry. Over the years I've given you a hard time – been judgemental. I haven't always been supportive, or even loving. I haven't always been the mum that you deserve.'

'*Mum*,' Rosie said, emotion stinging the back of her throat. 'Please don't upset yourself. You don't have to apologise for anything.'

'I do,' Julie said softly. 'My own mother raised me to be a useful ornament – never to know my own mind or follow my own path. I was to take care of my family, keep a spotless house, stay attractive and never complain. I thought it made sense to raise you the same way, but I was wrong. You're your own woman: strong and clever and beautiful, all in your own way. I'm proud of you. I'm sorry that I ever made you doubt it.'

Sobbing, Rosie stood and took her mother in her arms.

'It's OK, Mum, it's all OK.' And it was.

As they dried their eyes, Colin and Michael returned from their latest walk to the vending machine.

'Everything all right, girls?' Michael asked. 'Why are you both all weepy? George Clooney hasn't died, has he?'

'Of course not,' Julie snapped. 'We're fine. And Michael' – she waved at what must have been his ninth packet of crisps that weekend – 'you want to lay off the junk food. Start taking after Rosie here. Learn to cook from scratch.'

Chapter 27

When Rosie arrived back at the flat the following week, she knew immediately that something was wrong. There was no sign of life apart from Springsteen, who was lolling happily in his favourite chair. No laundry was drying on the heated rack near the back door; no coffee smell lingered in the kitchen; no mugs or plates were stacked in the dishwasher.

For the first time in a long time, Aled's bedroom door was closed. She knocked, fully expecting to get no response. After a moment, she opened it.

The bed they'd slept in together, curled into one another like two speech marks, was neatly made. His furniture was still in place, but there were too many things missing: books, postcards, the guitar she still hadn't heard him play . . . the framed photo of him, Tiegan and Gethin. Her stomach turned over, and a cool sweat began beading between her shoulder blades.

All night, Rosie waited and hoped he'd come back.

When he didn't, she went to bed in her own room, only falling asleep when the exhaustion of the past few days finally pulled her under. She dreamed of his hands, of his voice in her ear and his lips on her throat.

When she awoke alone, still in darkness, she cried.

'What are you doing here?' Rhianne demanded when Rosie turned up for work the next morning. 'I had it all sorted: Yaz was going to cover for you again.'

'It's fine, I messaged her last night,' Rosie said. 'I'm back now, Mum's doing OK and I knew I'd go out of my mind with boredom stuck at home on my own.'

'Are you sure you're up for this? You don't want to catch up on some sleep or watch three different versions of *Pride & Prejudice* back to back?'

'I really don't,' Rosie said honestly. Anything book- or romance-related would only make her think about Aled. She'd spent half the night going over what had happened between them, and she still had no idea where he was or why he'd gone.

Yes, they'd argued – and yes, she'd left in a hurry on Saturday afternoon. But had that single argument really torpedoed every hope for a reconciliation? Had it been enough to blow up everything that was good between them?

Rosie kept thinking about what he'd said right before Michael called: *You haven't let me explain properly. There's still stuff you don't know.* And now that she thought about it, there had been moments where Aled had seemed nervous – like he was teetering on the cusp of saying something scary and significant. Something had always interrupted them, claiming her attention or robbing him of his nerve. And he *had* resisted the pull between them: she thought about roller skating, Bonfire Night, Cora and Ed's wedding reception . . . He could have kissed her any time he chose, but he'd been reluctant to do so dishonestly – or at the risk of being anything less than the person she really, truly wanted.

Rather inconveniently, since she appeared to have lost him both literally and figuratively, he was *precisely* the person she wanted: now, and probably forever. She'd come to work today not only for the sake of escaping the emptiness of the flat – she needed to talk to Rhianne about what was happening.

If anyone knew where Aled had ended up, it would be his cousin and closest friend. Depending on when he'd left, Rosie also knew that Rhianne would have been drafted in to feed and fuss Springsteen while they were both away. There was no way he'd have asked local cat loather Mrs Beaumont to look in on him, even though she only lived next door.

After a busy breakfast time, however, it was Tobi that

Rosie found herself face to face with. She was also on shift all day, looking as happy and confident as Rosie had ever seen her.

'I've had a wonderful idea,' Tobi said as she wiped down the coffee machine, her big brown eyes shining with excitement.

'Oh? What's that then?' Rosie asked, trying to make sure she didn't sound as miserable as she felt.

'I will if you will,' Tobi said significantly.

'Will what?' Rosie replied, nonplussed.

'Apply to university!' Tobi exclaimed, beaming.

'What?'

'It's a great idea, right? We do it together,' Tobi explained. 'We can help each other with the forms, with the personal statements – through the whole process. It's something we both want, and something we've both been scared of. Let's not be scared anymore.'

'I . . . I don't know,' Rosie mumbled. 'I'm a bit all over the place right now. I'm not sure I can do it.'

'You absolutely can,' Rhianne announced from behind her. She'd emerged from the kitchen with a massive tray of freshly baked mince pies, which she now began to place inside the glass display cabinet on the counter. 'In fact,' she went on, 'you can do whatever hours you need to here while you study. You can go part-time, you can do weekends only . . . And if you don't at least *consider* this brilliant idea, I might actually have to fire you.'

'What?!' Rosie said again.

'You heard.' Rhianne pointed at her with a newly polished fingernail that Rosie now noticed had been painted to resemble a Christmas pudding.

She took a deep breath. 'Does this count as workplace bullying?'

'Definitely not,' Rhianne said, tearing a mince pie into thirds and giving a chunk of it to Tobi. 'This is *encouragement*. This is us saying we believe in you. Mince pie?'

'Absolutely.'

She handed Rosie a lump of warm pastry, oozing fruity filling.

'Oh my *god*, that's delicious. Why do we not eat these all year round again?'

'Because then they wouldn't be special,' Rhianne said sagely.

Tobi dusted pastry crumbs from her fingers, then held her hand out to Rosie. 'I will if you will,' she said again.

Rosie hesitated. Wavered. Then she thought about what she'd told James at the hospital. She had said that she'd changed – that she wanted to move forward. She needed to honour that no matter how hard it might seem, and with or without a man in her life.

She put her hand in Tobi's. Shook it. Tobi jumped for joy, pulling her into a hug that knocked the breath out of her and made her eyes shimmer with tears.

'I will if you will,' Rosie whispered, squeezing her back. 'And we're both going to be great.'

'Marvellous,' Rhianne said, bustling back towards the kitchen with her baking tray. 'God bless us, everyone.'

Chapter 28

At the next possible opportunity, Rosie cornered Rhianne – determined, despite the inevitable awkwardness, to ask her what had happened to Aled.

Rhianne looked pained when Rosie finally caught up with her by the recycling bins. 'I know what you're going to say, Rosie,' she groaned, 'and I think Mouth Almighty here has already done enough damage to your budding romance. I can't get involved – Al was very adamant about that. He says I'll only make things worse, and for once I completely agree with him.'

'That's ridiculous,' Rosie said. 'I'm worried about him. He's completely disappeared. He's not answering my messages. At least tell me if he's staying with you.'

'He isn't.'

'Would you tell me if he was?'

'Oh god, I don't know,' Rhianne said. 'Probably? I'm not clear what the rules would have been on that, he wasn't specific . . . Or maybe I'd just stopped paying attention by that point. In any case, he isn't at my flat.'

'Right. So where *is* he?'

'I'm not supposed to say. He seemed *broken*, Rosie – totally devastated. He doesn't want to see anyone, or be anywhere that reminds him of you. A suitably poetic reaction, I'm sure you'll agree.'

'Reaction to what?' Rosie said, balling her hands into fists. 'We had a horrible argument, but it wasn't so bad that he needed to run away. Is that what this is? Has he just *left*, sailed off into the sunset at the first sign of trouble? Is he even still in the UK?'

'In fairness to him, it was more than just one argument, wasn't it? What about the whole proposal drama?'

'What?' Rosie said, her frustration audible, her voice a low growl. 'What are you *talking* about?'

'He said he came to see you at the hospital. To check you were all right because you weren't responding to texts or calls. He said James was there, declaring his undying love for you . . . on one knee, with a ring.'

'Oh my god. Oh my fucking *life*.'

Rosie felt cold panic grip her as a vision of hugging James slipped into her mind – felt the mad rush of adrenaline as it seeped into her bloodstream and told her heart to kick faster, beat harder. 'What are you saying, Rhianne? That he thinks I'm back with *James*?'

'I told him it was unlikely – insane, even,' she said reasonably. 'I said he should speak to you before jumping to any conclusions. Did he not?'

'*No*, he did not!' Rosie barked. Rhianne's eyes widened.

'Rhianne, I adore you,' Rosie said, 'you know I do. But if you don't tell me where *the man I love* is right now, I might have to get violent with this potato masher.' She seized the shiny metal implement from a nearby pot of utensils, brandishing it as if to signal serious intent.

'All right, all right. Took you long enough to admit how you feel,' Rhianne said, nodding in approval. 'He's gone home to Wales. To his mam's. The school term was done, after all.'

'Who's gone to Wales? And why do you two look like you're re-enacting a scene from *Ramsay's Kitchen Nightmares*?' came a voice.

Rosie turned and saw Niamh. She was gesturing at the potato masher, still held aloft in menacing fashion.

'Brilliant – you're here,' Rhianne said with satisfaction. 'I knew we'd need you – though I had no idea this one would get so het up she'd start waving my equipment around.'

'Put the masher down, Rose, and let's talk about this

calmly,' Niamh said. 'At least lay off Rhianne. If anyone deserves a whack with that thing, it's me. I've been a total dick. Though you better believe I am *livid* that you didn't tell me your mum was poorly.'

'Sorry,' Rosie said, sliding the potato masher back into position between a fish slice, a pair of tongs and a pasta server. 'Did Rhianne let you know?'

'No,' Niamh said. 'I found out on Facebook. Michael really doesn't hold back on the personal updates, does he?'

'He does not,' Rosie said grimly, shaking her head. 'The good news is, Mum should be OK. She'll have to live with the angina but there's no reason to think she's in immediate danger. The more pressing issue is that I am madly, deeply, *irrevocably* in love with someone who thinks I'm either engaged to my idiot ex, or at least considering it.'

'Why on earth would Aled think you were back with James?' Niamh asked, scrunching her nose in distaste.

'Because James appeared in the corridor outside my mum's hospital room and proposed to me,' Rosie said, rolling her eyes. 'On one knee. And Aled – who had come to be with me, to see if I was OK – apparently saw enough of this that he thought, he genuinely thought . . .' Rosie's throat choked up, and her best friend filled in the rest for her.

'He thought you were hedging your bets, hoping to win James back the whole time.' Niamh winced. 'God, what a moment for that knobhead to make good on my prediction! Only he could finally try to win you back in a way that fucked up your *new* relationship.'

'Er – Rosie . . . ? I don't mean to interrupt whatever this is, but the lunch rush is starting and I might need some help,' Tobi said from the doorway, sounding a little flustered.

'Shit – sorry. I'll be right there,' Rosie promised. 'Though I might need to head off a bit early today. As soon as you can spare me, Rhianne. Is that all right?'

'Of course,' Rhianne said, grinning. 'Got somewhere to be?'

'I have,' Rosie replied, certain that Rhianne already knew the answer. 'I'm going to Wales.'

'How are we getting there, then?' Niamh asked an hour or so later, over her frothy cappuccino.

'We?' Rosie said.

'Obviously,' Niamh sighed. 'Unless you don't want me with you.'

'I always want you with me,' Rosie said, giving her a quick, tight hug. They were still at the deli, but Marcus had arrived for his afternoon shift and Rhianne had urged Rosie to get going.

'Do you think a train might work?' Rosie asked.

'I checked, and there'd be a fair few changes, I think – the nearest station to Aled's mum's guest house is Colwyn Bay, which is way up on the north coast – it'd be a long journey, which we'd most likely spend standing up.'

'Why?'

'Because it's three days before Christmas,' Niamh said. 'The trains out of London will all be packed.'

'Oh god, of course.' In all the drama of the past few days, Rosie had completely lost track of the date. 'OK, we'll take my car then. It's fine. I mean, I've no idea where I'm going and pretty much the only place I've driven in the past five years is to my mum's, but how hard can it be? This is what smartphones are for, right? We'll Google Map it or something.'

'*Exactly*,' Niamh said. 'We can do this. I'm ready when you are.'

'But what about the kids? Work?' Rosie asked, winding a soft woollen scarf around her neck and pulling on her gloves.

'Brendan has the kids until further notice, and work isn't an issue.'

'In what way *not an issue*?' Rosie said, mildly concerned but also relieved. Niamh looked much more like herself again – calmer and happier than Rosie had seen her since the summer.

'I'll tell you in the car,' Niamh said, swiping at the screen of her iPhone. 'We're going to have . . . ooh. A good *four hours* to talk about it.'

When she got back to the flat, Rosie put down some extra food for Springsteen and threw some essentials into an overnight bag. Whatever happened with Aled, her chances of getting back here before tomorrow were virtually non-existent – so it made sense to be prepared.

It was drizzling and already getting dark, and for the first time it occurred to Rosie that this journey was going to involve navigating unfamiliar roads in weather conditions that could only be described as less than ideal. She pushed the thought aside, dropped a goodbye kiss on Springsteen's head and made for the door.

Niamh had gone on ahead to grab her own pyjamas, toothbrush and change of clothes from Wanstead. Just as importantly, she had declared, she would pick up a selection of 'road trip' snacks before returning. When she arrived at Rosie's front door, she was proudly clutching a plastic carrier bag full of food and a cardboard tray holding two takeaway cups.

'Peppermint hot chocolate with whipped cream, sprinkles and crushed candy cane topping!' Niamh announced, brandishing the tray with pride. 'It's *amazing*, try it.'

Rosie took a tentative sip through the hole in the plastic lid and couldn't help grimacing. 'It tastes like type 2 diabetes,' she said.

'*Delicious*, in other words!' Niamh trilled happily.

With some trepidation, Rosie peered into the top of the bag Niamh was carrying. Inside was a box of mini yule log cakes, a bag of iced ginger biscuits shaped like Christmas trees, a sizeable sack of red and green marshmallows and a pack of 'Christmas pudding-flavoured popcorn'.

'Is this some sort of experiment?' Rosie asked, aghast.

'Are you trying to prove you can rot a mouthful of healthy teeth in the time it takes to get from London to north Wales?'

'You'll be glad of the odd energy burst when you're an hour or two into a monotonous motorway drive,' Niamh said. 'And I got us a Lindor Santa each. *Big* ones. They're in my overnight bag.'

'Touché – and well done,' Rosie conceded.

Getting out of London seemed to take forever. As Rosie's little car crawled through urban sprawl, they turned the heat up until they were toasty and listened to Christmas songs on the radio. Niamh tunelessly joined in with 'All I Want For Christmas Is You', holding a gigantic marshmallow in front of her mouth as if it were a microphone.

'So come on,' Rosie said when her performance was over. 'Are you going to tell me, or what?'

'I need to apologise for being a total bitch first,' Niamh said. 'I kind of haven't done that yet.'

'You admitted you'd been a dick,' Rosie said. 'Which you were. But I said some pretty harsh things to you in return. I'm sorry I was so brutal. I was angry, but I've also been really worried about you, too.'

'I know. It was hard to hear, but you weren't wrong about any of it. Since Rory and Eva were born I've been determined to do everything the way I'd always planned – to be a great mum, but also not to become one of *those* people: the people whose lives are turned completely upside down by offspring.'

'Isn't that *all* people?' Rosie asked, indicating to pull onto the M1.

'You're so wise, Rose,' Niamh sighed. 'It probably is. However, I had this idea that becoming a mum would be like learning a new skill. Like, it would add another string to my bow – as if it was the equivalent of becoming a qualified first aider or learning to play the piano or something. You know: here's another thing I can do now!' She did jazz hands, and Rosie laughed.

'I knew having the twins would change things day-to-day,' Niamh went on. 'The house would always be messy, we'd have to go to restaurants that served chicken nuggets, we'd become obsessed with Julia Donaldson books. What I wasn't prepared for were the changes it would cause in here.' She pointed at her head. 'Becoming a parent isn't about learning a new skill. It's more like learning to be a new person – or a new version of yourself. When I went back to work, I had to face the fact that I wasn't the Niamh I used to be. Not only could I not stay at the office until eight o'clock on a busy day, I genuinely didn't *want* to. I didn't want to win accounts that would take me away overnight, or organise corporate events that would see me miss five bath-and-bedtimes in a row. And it isn't that I don't want to work, or that I want to stay at home all day, every day with the twins – it's just that my old job isn't right for the new me.'

'Wow,' Rosie said. 'That's a lot.'

'Yep. And I don't think I'd have got there if it wasn't for your rant,' Niamh admitted. 'At the very least it would have taken longer. Brendan's been trying to talk to me about all this since September, but I kept refusing to engage. He's been super worried – it's driven a bit of a wedge between us.'

'But you're OK now?'

'Better than in months,' Niamh said. 'I resigned from the agency last week, and Brendan and I have agreed that in the new year I'll set up as a freelancer – work for myself planning mostly local stuff, and on a small scale to start with. If it goes well and I get to a point where I'm able to expand or take on employees, I'll be able to do it on my terms – and in a family-friendly way that will make it easy for other parents with young kids to succeed.'

'That sounds incredible,' Rosie said sincerely. 'I'm so proud of you. I haven't a shred of doubt that it'll go brilliantly.' She hesitated, and then decided to go for it – a bubble of excitement forming about her own decision, which had been somewhat eclipsed by recent events. 'Actually, on the career-slash-personal development front, I have some news of my own.'

'Spill the tea,' Niamh said, gulping from her minty hot chocolate cup.

'I'm going to apply to go back to university,' Rosie said, testing how the sentence sounded out loud. Saying the words felt good. 'I've no idea where yet – I need to do some research – but I think I'm going to look at psychology and counselling courses. Maybe do it part-time, so I can keep working as well.'

'YES!' Niamh cheered. 'This is AMAZING. This deserves a yule log. Or would you prefer a handful of Christmas pudding-flavoured popcorn?'

'Let the record show that I am very dubious about the popcorn,' Rosie said, pointing at the yule log packet in Niamh's hand. Niamh passed her a bite-sized chocolate mini roll adorned with white icing. Presumably this was supposed to look like snow.

'OK, so now the work stuff's out of the way and we're besties again, I need you to tell me about how you fell in love with Nameless Neighbour,' Niamh said. 'Start at the beginning and do not leave *anything* out.'

'I reserve the right not to answer graphic or anatomical questions,' Rosie warned her.

'Spoilsport. You must be really gone for him if you won't share all the dirty details.'

'As you put it, the train has left the station. I think it chuffed off a lot longer ago than I realised, to be honest.'

'I'm settled in for the full story,' Niamh said, snuggling down in the passenger seat and tearing open the odd-flavoured popcorn.

As she and Niamh joined in with Chris Rea crooning 'Driving Home For Christmas' through the car stereo, Rosie couldn't help thinking that was precisely what she was doing. She'd thought her flat was home: her vintage prints, her second-hand coffee pot, her antique furniture and charity shop finds. But without Aled there, it had all felt wrong. Empty.

It turned out home was a feeling – not bricks and mortar or bric-a-brac, but a sense of belonging, of being complete.

Now, on this dark and rainy motorway, she was on her way to find it.

Chapter 29

As her little Volkswagen Polo crossed the border into Wales, Rosie began to feel nervous. It was dark, wet and cold, and she was entirely reliant on Rhianne's directions – plus the internet – to get her to her destination.

So far out of London, it occurred to her that she might not be able to rely on a functioning 4G signal all the way to the guest house . . . And even if she could, this was Christmas time. What if, in line with tradition, there was no room for her at the inn?

She'd thrown some pretty awful accusations around last time she saw Aled – ones she increasingly felt he hadn't deserved, or at least not fully. And when he last saw her, he must have concluded she'd spent the past few months scheming her way back into a relationship with James. In itself, this was galling; but then, she hadn't been upfront about her developing feelings for him, always afraid that honesty might lead to heartache, as well as loss of face.

For so long, Rosie had assumed that someone like Aled could never be interested in someone like her. She'd wanted the reassurance of being selected – of him showing his hand first – before she put herself on the line.

Tonight, she was going to be braver. She was picking her own path. As it turned out, this was the A55.

'I wish we could see what's out there properly,' Niamh said. 'I bet we're passing through some lovely countryside.'

'Probably,' Rosie said. 'We're getting closer to the coast now, as well.'

Their proximity to the Irish Sea seemed to be affecting the

weather, which was worsening. Great gusts of wind shook Rosie's tiny car, and rain slapped the windscreen so hard that the sound drowned out the radio.

She slowed down, her ability to see where she was going seriously hampered by the furious swiping of her wipers, as well as the constant barrage of what she now felt could quite reasonably be called a storm.

'How much further?' she asked Niamh, who was in charge of navigation.

'Only about ten miles.'

'Thank god.'

It was around seven o'clock, but it might as well have been midnight. Rosie noted the lack of light pollution outside, in comparison with London. Big cities rarely got truly dark, she supposed – but here there were long stretches of pure blackness beyond the lights above the road.

The car rounded a corner and suddenly, on Rosie's right, was a vast expanse of churning sea. The water arched and crashed angrily, whipped into a frenzy by the gale. Further on, they saw stationary headlights – and as they grew closer, they realised that the road ahead was blocked. A police car had been parked across the carriageway, and beyond it Rosie could see there'd been an accident. Her stomach turned over, and she sent up a silent prayer that whoever was involved wasn't hurt.

'Shit,' Niamh said. 'They're directing everyone to get off at the next exit. That's going to put us on some small, local road – I'll have to rejig the route from there.'

'OK,' Rosie said. 'That's fine.' She drummed her fingers nervously against the steering wheel.

Guided by Niamh, Rosie drove through residential streets, past houses and a primary school, before finding the small cluster of country lanes that signalled they were near their destination.

'Just a mile to go now,' Niamh said. 'And it's pretty much a straight line.'

It was at this moment that a ferocious screeching assaulted their ears.

'What the hell is *that*?' Niamh cried.

'I've no idea,' Rosie gasped, as the car began to slow and judder. With some effort, she pulled over onto the grass verge at the side of the road, then cast her eyes over the various dials and lights of the aged car's dashboard.

'Oh *fuck*,' she said a second later, putting her head in her hands and accidentally beeping the car horn.

'What?' Niamh yelped, taken aback by the noise.

'We've run out of fuel,' Rosie moaned. 'We should have made a second stop when I saw the dial start dropping again . . . I'm an idiot.'

Niamh winced and said: 'Would it help if I pointed out this is *absolutely* something we'll be able to laugh about a year from now?'

'Maybe?' Rosie said. 'I can't believe this. I can't *believe* we've come all this way only to fall at the final hurdle.'

Niamh twisted in her seat, folded her arms and stared at her friend.

'What?' Rosie asked miserably.

'I'm just waiting.'

'For a miracle?'

'No,' Niamh said calmly. 'For you to do what you always do: dust yourself off and try again.'

'There *is* no try again – we've got no petrol. The only thing we can do from here is . . .'

'There you go,' Niamh whispered, a split second before Rosie said,

'. . . *walk*.'

Dubiously, Rosie looked out of the car window, which was still being battered relentlessly by rain. 'I can't believe I'm going to do this,' she said.

'You mean, you can't believe *we're* going to do this,' Niamh informed her. 'Safety in numbers. Just . . . tell me he's worth it.'

'He's worth it,' Rosie said, with feeling.

'Right then. Shall we?'

Disbelieving but grateful, Rosie got out of the car and pulled her rucksack from the back seat. 'I wish I was the sort of person who carried waterproofs and a torch in the boot,' she shouted to Niamh, her voice barely audible above the howling wind.

'It's good to have something to aim for,' Niamh yelled back.

Using Rosie's mobile for torchlight and Niamh's for directions, they staggered up the hill that led to the guest house. The road beneath their feet was slick and treacherous, and every tree they walked under seemed to gift them with a fresh dousing of chilly raindrops.

All hope of appearing at least moderately presentable lost, Rosie now simply prayed that Aled would *recognise* her when she arrived. She was soaked to the skin, her coat, scarf and gloves all dripping moisture, unable to absorb any more rain. Her limbs were shaking with cold.

The road before Rosie and Niamh curved, finally bringing the guest house into view. Twinkling fairy lights adorned its mullioned windows, illuminating the huge festive wreath that hung on the front door.

Galvanised by the warm, welcoming light that seemed to spill from every corner of the building – not to mention the thrilling sight of smoke curling up from its chimney – they trudged the final few metres towards it as fast as their leaden legs would carry them, then practically fell upon the doorbell.

A middle-aged, friendly-faced man with a glass of beer in his hand opened the door. At the sight of Rosie and Niamh, he scrambled to put the drink on a nearby window ledge – apparently fearful that shock might cause him to drop it. On an occasional table behind him, a mini Christmas tree glowed – and when the scent of sweet roast chestnuts reached Rosie's nostrils, her stomach griped hungrily.

'I . . . erm . . . How may I help you, ladies?' he said, his eyes scanning them a second time, as if he couldn't quite process what he'd seen on his first try.

His question, Rosie thought, was impressively polite under the circumstances.

'Are you Mal?' she asked, through chattering teeth, keen to cut to the chase.

'I am. Who's asking?'

'I'm Rosie Butler, and this is my friend Niamh. I'm here to see Aled, if he's in?'

Mal's eyes widened with what Rosie thought must be recognition. She couldn't decide whether this boded well or not.

Before he could say anything, though, a teenage girl poked her head into the doorway, grinning mischievously as Mal ushered them into the small entrance hall. She looked briefly at Rosie and Niamh, who were huddled together for warmth, then swivelled to face in the other direction.

'*Maaam!*' she shrieked, projecting her voice back inside the house. 'There's a girl here to see Al! I think it's a girl. It could be a sea monster. It seems to have two heads!'

'He's playing pool in the shed with Geth, thank god!' another voice yelled back. 'First time he's been out of his room all week, poor love. He'll not hear you – I'll go and tell him there's a kraken here to see him, will I?'

Rosie cringed, then found herself amused by the contrast between Aled and his witty, confident and very loud relations.

'Don't mind Tiegan – or Gwyn,' Mal said. 'You'd best come right in. You're drenched.'

'Thank you,' Rosie said. 'But I don't want to mess up your carpet. We're soaked to the skin.' At the mention of Aled's mother, she'd become acutely aware of the need to make a reasonable first impression – and destroying the floor of her house didn't feel like the best way to go about it.

'Come this way,' Mal said, directing them down the stone-floored hallway into a room where – mercy of mercies – a wood fire was burning.

'Can I get you anything?' Mal asked, as Rosie and Niamh fell to their knees in front of the grate, practically sobbing with relief. 'Towels? Tissues? A stiff drink? And let me take your coats.'

Gratefully, both women peeled the sopping garments away, only to reveal the equally wet clothing that lay beneath. Mal winced in sympathy as Rosie pulled the hem of her jumper away from her stomach and the motion sent a shower of drips splashing onto the hearth.

'What's all this about a sea serpent, Mal?' came Aled's voice from just beyond the doorway. 'I hope it isn't some plot to get me out of the shed so Geth can rearrange the table without me noticing, because I'm having a blinder.'

'Er – not exactly,' Mal said as Aled entered the room.

Rosie shot to her feet and pushed her water-logged hair out of her face.

'I'm the sea monster. It's me,' she said, newly amazed at her capacity for saying stupid things in front of this man she adored. 'Well. Me and Niamh. She's the second head . . .' She gestured haplessly at her friend, who was sitting on the tiled hearth of the fireplace like a house cat. Steam seemed to be emanating from her.

Aled's eyes didn't so much as flicker in Niamh's direction. Soft, dark and full of feeling, they were focused immovably on Rosie. She shivered under this intense scrutiny, then fought to gather her wits.

'What I mean is, I wanted to talk to you. I needed to see you,' she went on.

'*Whoa*,' another male voice said. 'Is this the woman he's been moping about all week? Did she *swim* here?'

This, Rosie guessed, was Gethin, who'd clearly been encouraged by his twin to abandon playing pool in favour of spectating.

'My car broke down,' Rosie said. 'We walked the last mile up the hill.'

'My god, you really are soaked,' Gwyn said as she entered

the room. Her reddish eyebrows knitted together at the sight of Rosie and Niamh, and she cast an appraising eye over Rosie – as if she were reconciling what she saw with things she'd already heard. Her shrewd gaze reminded Rosie powerfully of Aled's.

Seeming to decide that Rosie wasn't here to cause her son further emotional distress, she said: 'Mal, fetch these girls a large brandy and some clean towels – in that order. The rest of you, be on your way.'

'It's fine,' Rosie assured her, 'everyone can stay. I don't have anything to say that I'm in any way embarrassed by. Apart from the sea monster bit, obviously.' Aled stifled a laugh, and Niamh put her head in her hands. Gwyn's expression shifted, and Rosie thought she saw respect written there; it seemed her willingness to make a tit of herself was worthy of approval.

'Firstly, I'm not back with James,' Rosie said, her eyes fixed on Aled's. 'I did feel a bit sorry for him, but let's face it – he's an idiot. I told him that day at the hospital that there was no way I'd ever want him back because . . .' *deep breath, Rosie,* she told herself. 'Because I know myself better now. I want different things. I want *you.* Because I love you.'

'*Bloody Nora,*' Tiegan said.

Gwyn poked her and hissed, 'For god's sake, *hush.*'

'When I got home from the hospital that day – back to the flat,' Rosie went on, 'I was gutted to find you gone. And I realised something: it's just a building, a box. I've painted it and furnished it, but it isn't my home anymore if you're not in it.'

'Oh *my* . . .' Gwyn breathed, her hazel eyes shiny with tears. Then, realising she'd spoken aloud, she mimed zipping her own mouth shut.

'I didn't give you a chance to explain your reasons for thinking about selling the building,' Rosie continued. 'But I know they must have been good ones. I was angry, but I should have let you tell me.'

'If you had,' Aled said, 'I'd have told you it was for the people in this room. I'd got this idea that Tiegan and Geth needed university funds – that this was a way I could give back to Mam, after my father left her with absolutely nothing. It felt fitting that the money should come from his family, see? I'd hired a conveyancer to start organising the legal stuff before I even met you. And when I knew I was falling in love with you I instructed the firm to pause the process.'

Mal whistled.

Rosie felt breathless. Fireworks were exploding behind her eyes. She turned his words over in her mind, half convinced she'd imagined him saying them: *I was falling in love with you.* With some effort, she managed to regain her composure.

'Um . . . when was that?' she asked, her voice tremulous.

'A long time ago,' Aled said on a sigh. 'The day I admitted I'd been feeding Springsteen.'

'The singer?' Gwyn interjected again. She sounded thrilled.

'The cat,' Rosie and Aled said together.

'But that's . . . that was only a few weeks into us knowing each other,' Rosie murmured, incredulous.

'Yeah.' Aled dragged a hand through his hair and bit his lip. 'When you know, you know. I told you I was done for from the moment I saw you in your red dress. And I meant the first time . . . the day I met you, when you almost knocked me out and then started babbling about marriage proposals. You are beautiful and lovely, funny and bright and kind. You're extraordinary, Rosie. Like I said, it shines out of you. You warm everyone you meet.'

At this, Niamh emitted a sob. 'It's too much! It's just too lovely.'

'I can't believe you liked me from that first day,' Rosie said. 'I was a clumsy oaf. I was mortified!'

'I hid it well, but you made me want to laugh until my ribs cracked,' Aled said, with the half-smile she'd adored almost from the very first time she saw it. 'Here's something else you won't believe: I've seen *When Harry Met Sally* about fifty-eight times. I just wanted a reason to sit next to you that night we had the power cut.'

Rosie's mouth dropped open.

'Also, I made James put his bike in the outdoor shed because I didn't like how he treated you. He wasn't in any way wrong about me having a vendetta. *Also* . . . the renovation on the top-floor flat was finished two weeks ago. I just didn't say anything because I couldn't stand the thought of not living with you anymore.'

Rosie laughed. 'Is there anything else you need to confess? Because I wanted to ask you something. And since it turns out you *have* seen the end of *When Harry Met Sally*, you'll understand that I want to do it as soon as possible.'

Aled shook his head, smiling at her.

'I didn't come here to disrupt your family Christmas,' she said, 'but I wanted to ask what you were doing on New Year's Eve? And maybe . . . maybe for *all* the New Year's Eves afterwards. For the rest of our lives.'

He pulled her into his arms, laughing as her sopping-wet jumper immediately soaked his own. 'I'm doing this,' he said, dropping a kiss on her forehead. 'Always this.'

And then, as if he'd never been shy a single moment of his life, he pressed his lips to hers, kissing her like he'd been starved – like he'd been waiting for her. Like she was all his Christmases come at once.

Someone – Gethin? – wolf-whistled. Someone else coughed. A voice that sounded very much like Niamh's said, 'Dear *lord*. No wonder she was willing to drive all this way.'

Rosie leaned back a little, breaking contact with Aled before their kiss became too heated for family viewing.

'Maybe we could watch the odd Jane Austen adaptation, too?' she said, a little dizzy. 'Eat curry on Friday nights? Make each other tea and toast in the mornings. That sort of thing.'

'And fight over who gets to have Springsteen on their lap every night,' Aled agreed.

'As if we'll get a say in where he sits,' Rosie scoffed, raising an eyebrow.

Aled laughed and stroked her still-sopping hair. She relaxed against him, breathing him in as everyone else in the room cheered.

'I'm so glad your mum's OK, by the way,' Aled murmured, squeezing her tighter. 'I should have said before.'

'How did you find out?' Rosie asked, squeezing him back.

'Weird as it sounds,' Aled said, 'I saw it on Facebook.'

Epilogue

Rosie still loved the Walthamstow flat.

She loved the life she led inside it – but also the new understanding she'd gleaned that, for the most part, its crucial components were adjustable. Adaptable. Transferable.

She loved her quirky knick-knacks, the bookshelves stuffed with favourite stories and the many framed photographs of her most-loved people. Just lately, there were more of them than ever. A candid photograph of herself and Michael, snapped as she showed her terrified brother how to soak a Christmas pudding in brandy, then set it alight, had pride of place on the mantelpiece.

She loved the silver tabby cat who made it known that she and Aled were lucky to have him; who blessed them with his presence in exchange for belly rubs on demand, first dibs on his favourite chair and a daily diet of overpriced, extremely malodorous food. (She *didn't* love the lecture she'd recently had from the vet. Springsteen was bordering on obese, Rosie had been informed, and he needed to lay off the Dreamies with immediate effect.)

She loved being able to walk to the Red Fox Deli. She adored working there, just as she adored Rhianne and her crack team of coffee-making, karaoke-loving weirdos.

Most of all, she loved Aled. She loved his quiet steadiness, his thoughtfulness, his gentleness and intensity. She loved that when he laughed, he laughed with his whole body – and that he kissed that way, too.

She loved that they fell asleep together every night, dovetailed into one another like jigsaw puzzle pieces. Every morning, they awoke still connected: her head on his chest, or his arm flung around her. She loved that he could make her breathless with a single, careful touch; that he could tell her he adored her with no words at all, or with famous ones he'd found in poetry books.

She loved the desk she'd set up in what was once the spare room – the university text books stacked on top of it and the journal Aled had given her on the day she'd started her course: a cherry-red Moleskine with 'RB' embossed in gold on the cover.

She loved the room's recently painted 'gender neutral' yellow walls, the slightly wonky light fitting and its scratched-but-salvageable original floorboards.

It was a room with possibilities. With a future that hadn't been written yet.

Acknowledgements

Writing this book has been a true joy, for which I'm profoundly grateful. It's probably a poor show for someone who deals in words for a living, but I can't adequately express my thanks to the wonderful team who have been behind me as I've worked on it. From the moment Rosie and Aled appeared in my head, I've had kind and clever people cheering me on, encouraging me to bring their story alive in the sweetest, swooniest and most satisfying way.

To my editor, Jane Snelgrove: thank you once again for believing I could do it, and for the crucial part you always play in making these stories of mine more ambitious, more delightful and more amusing. Melanie Hayes, it's been marvellous getting to know you and benefiting from your expertise this past year. Here's to many more collaborations!

To my agent, Kate Hordern: you are the calm to my storm, the 'just stop for a bit and have a cup of tea' to my (frequent) moments of panic. I appreciate you!

Thanks to Anna Perkins and the wider Embla team. You make words more perfect, book covers more beautiful and marketing plans more effective. You are brilliant.

Gratitude, as always, to my amazing family and friends. Your support means everything to me – and I couldn't write about fictional love and friendships half so well if I didn't have an abundance of them IRL.

Finally, my deepest thanks to you, dear and valued reader, for picking up this book. It's a privilege to be trusted with the task of entertaining you for a while, and I hope this tale delivered on that promise.

Read on for an exclusive extract from
Rachel Ryan's Resolutions ...

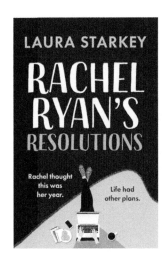

University of York

2009

The thorny branches of the bush she was wedged into scratched at Rachel's bare arms. As her oversized sunglasses slid down her clammy nose, she offered up a silent prayer that no one was about to pass by.

Like a character from one of the clichéd cop dramas her mum was obsessed with, Rachel was hiding in a hedge in broad daylight – transfixed by the sight of two people deep in conversation, sitting on a patch of yellowed scrubby grass a few metres away.

It was late July and, although only around ten o'clock in the morning, the day was already warm in the oppressive way that promises an evening downpour. The moisture now pooling at the small of Rachel's back and beneath her armpits, however, was less a consequence of the muggy atmosphere and more a result of her rapidly rising heart rate.

She was *willing* this not to be real. Hoping it might not be true.

It wasn't working.

They were too close together, too intimate. His hand was

resting in hers and their inclined bodies formed a graceful arc, lit from behind by bright sunshine.

He was wearing yesterday's clothes.

Rachel tasted the acrid flavour of impending vomit and wondered if she was going to be sick. *Not here, not now.*

Her stomach contracted, muscle and flesh tightening, curling inwards. *Just breathe*, she told herself.

She scrunched her eyes shut and gulped down lungfuls of air until the twisting sensation in her gut let up a little.

Always a sucker for punishment, Rachel made herself look at them again. He was kissing her now – the other woman.

Even from a distance Rachel could tell this was one of Jack Harper's special signature kisses: languid but delicious, rich with intent. She hated him for this, but for a split second felt her standard longing for him too.

She knew she would never forgive him, and yet, as his arms snaked around someone else's waist, she couldn't help admiring him. His overlong chestnut-brown hair shone in the sunlight, casting an ironic halo of copper-coloured light around his head. He opened his green-gold eyes as the kissing stopped, and his smile – a wide, lazy grin for this skinny girl with a treacle-dark mane – was a baseball bat to Rachel's stomach.

Misery ballooned in her ribcage. Her sadness felt massive – so big it might push vital organs out of place. A sensible voice from somewhere deep inside Rachel insisted that, awful as this was, it still didn't rank as the worst thing that had ever happened to her. But still, how could Jack be doing this? Today of all days? It was crushing.

And his doing it *here* – out in the open, on the lane she so regularly walked down . . . It was as if the location he'd picked sought to minimise his offence. The thoughtlessness of it implied that, to Jack, hooking up with someone other than Rachel was no big deal. There was cruelty in this, she realised, whether he'd intended it or not: it heaped humiliation on top of hurt, spoke of unequal affections. It made her feel stupid for letting herself care so much.

That word, *stupid*, clanged in her head. She should have seen this coming. Jack's Lord Byron Lite act, as she'd once called it, had seen him motor through girlfriends faster than she sped down their reading list of set texts. But her resolve to keep him at arm's length despite his obvious charms had crumbled when he'd told her she wasn't like anyone else, that she was different – that he'd fallen in love with her.

She had believed him.

Hot tears filled Rachel's eyes and she forced her thoughts back to the present, shoving down the hysterical laugh that was bubbling up her throat. This was a *ridiculous* situation.

She needed to get home. She couldn't hide in a hedge forever . . . Not even for another ten minutes, she realised, checking her watch.

Rachel's parents would be arriving soon and they were notorious for being early, particularly on special occasions. And for reasons that only a handful of people knew, including the cheating snake now casually fondling his latest conquest, today was a *very* special occasion.

She didn't want to crash back through her front gate flustered, sweaty and feeling like she'd been freshly disembowelled, only to find them waiting on the doorstep in their Sunday best. She needed to greet them happy, serene and smiling, ready to put the kettle on. The carton of milk she'd popped out to buy weighed heavy in her right hand.

Like the bile that still threatened at the back of her throat, Rachel swallowed her mess of feelings. Now, she decided, was *not* the time to throw them up. If she wasn't going to confront Jack, though, she somehow had to sneak past him and his new friend.

She wondered how long they were going to sit there, the bastards, alternately snogging and making moon eyes at one another. Then the bleak truth occurred to her: Jack and this girl were *utterly* wrapped up in the moment, and the lane was fairly wide . . . Rachel could probably walk by without them even noticing. The realisation stung, almost as painfully as everything else.

She took a deep breath, extracted herself from her improvised hiding place and walked – quickly, but not so fast that she'd make herself conspicuous – towards the main road.

Rachel had less than half an hour to get home, compose herself and start getting ready for the ceremony.

It was graduation day and her mum and dad were coming to watch her collect her First. They were proud of her. They wanted to celebrate.

London

2019

January 2019

New Year's resolutions

1. Consider exercise an act with actual benefits –
   both mental and physical – not merely grim
   punishment for pizzas consumed. Have a proper
   go at yoga.
2. Also re-download Couch to 5K running app and
   actually do the programme.
3. Apply for promotion at work at first chance.
   Move to bigger account and try to get pay rise.
   Avoid, if possible, further projects concerning
   dog biscuits, disinfectant, high-quality printer
   ink cartridges, 'miracle' grass seed, organic
   vegetables, etc.
4. DO NOT agree to further dates with Laurence.
   Remember: it's no use having a boyfriend who
   is good on paper if you do not actually fancy
   him.
5. Try to remember Mum means well, even during
   phone calls where she implies I am doomed to

a lonely life of penury because I am thirty with no partner, hardly any savings and no mortgage.

6. HOWEVER, do not (!!!) speak to Mum when suffering PMT. Set phone alerts for likely spells based on period tracker intel.

7. Try to address 'hardly any savings' situation. (If promoted, set aside extra earnings for future house deposit instead of spaffing it all on ASOS.)

8. Try to eat my five-a-day. (Remember horrid rule that potatoes do not count.)

9. Start using proper night cream with retinol.

1

Rachel sat on the cold, hard bus shelter bench awaiting the number 19 from Islington to Finsbury Park. Despite the best efforts of the manspreader next to her, both of her arsecheeks were still fully on the seat she'd claimed before the stop got busy. There was no way she wanted to stand outside; it was only just past six o'clock but already pitch-dark, and the air was a whirl of freezing drizzle. She watched her breath misting and mingling with it, enjoying her small victory.

Four minutes for the bus, according to the electronic display at the top of the shelter. Wincing involuntarily, she wondered if Jessica Williams would be on it this evening.

Rachel pulled her soft navy hat further towards her chilly ears, though her mass of dark-red waves prevented it from making effective contact. It was the second week in January and, as a worthy-looking man in Lycra leggings and fluorescent trainers jogged by, she reflected that her 'New Year, New Me' plans were off to a very slow start.

Unless you counted several panicked sprints towards trains and buses, she had done no exercise whatsoever. She had swerved several phone calls from her mother, eaten a lot of beige food and had yet to buy the retinol cream she was supposed to be applying each night.

Nevertheless, Rachel reasoned, she still had eleven and

a half months in which to keep the promises she'd made to herself. It was important not to be too self-flagellating in January, what with it being a month of general gloom and destitution.

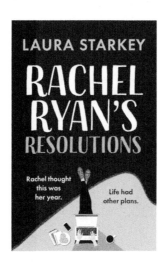

LAURA STARKEY

RACHEL RYAN'S RESOLUTIONS

Rachel thought this was her year.

Life had other plans.

RACHEL THOUGHT THIS WAS HER YEAR.
LIFE HAD OTHER PLANS.

As her mother likes to remind her, Rachel Ryan is thirty
with no partner, hardly any savings and no mortgage.
But when she makes her resolutions she's sure
this is her year.

By February things are not going to plan. Her career is
in chaos as the new guy at work is none other than Jack
Harper, who broke her heart at university – and despite
herself the chemistry is still there. Plus her best friend has
news that will change everything.

As life starts to fall apart around her, will Rachel be able
to move on from the past and make some very different
resolutions?

Maybe then she'll see what's right in front of her.

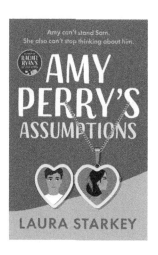

Amy Perry doesn't believe in fairy-tale romances. Smart, savvy and a little bit cynical, she's much happier keeping things casual. She thought her good-looking, wealthy boyfriend felt the same way. But here she is, 1,000 feet up in the air, watching him get down on one knee...

As if things couldn't get worse, after a messy break-up Amy is forced to relocate to her hometown to take up a new job opportunity - and runs into the last person she ever wanted to see again. **Sam Ainsworth**. Son of the local lord. The bane of her existence. Her first love.

Everything Amy believed about Sam turned out to be right when he broke her heart all those years ago. She's not looking to revisit the past. But everywhere she turns, Sam's there – with his irresistible molten brown eyes, wry smile and easy charm. Soon, Amy finds herself wondering: what if, after all this time, she's been wrong all along...?

About the Author

Laura was born in Warwickshire in 1982 and has been quite busy since then. After studying for a degree in English & Related Literature, she spent time as a secondary school teacher, a digital editor and a content designer. She decided to try writing a novel after a 12-month stint producing copy about central heating insurance policies. She hasn't looked back since. Despite her disbelief in real life 'meet cutes', Laura first encountered her husband on a Tube platform in London. It was a plot twist worthy of any romcom, and she has read and watched *a lot*. She now lives in a small village in the West Midlands with her family, her ever-growing book collection and a mini menagerie of pets.

Find Laura on social media:
X: @LauraStarkey
Instagram: @laura_starkey
Facebook: @LauraStarkeyAuthor

About Embla Books

Embla Books is a digital-first publisher of standout commercial adult fiction. Passionate about storytelling, the team at Embla publish books that will make you 'laugh, love, look over your shoulder and lose sleep'. Launched by Bonnier Books UK in 2021, the imprint is named after the first woman from the creation myth in Norse mythology, who was carved by the gods from a tree trunk found on the seashore – an image of the kind of creative work and crafting that writers do, and a symbol of how stories shape our lives.

Find out about some of our other books and stay in touch:

X, Facebook, Instagram: @emblabooks
Newsletter: https://bit.ly/emblanewsletter

Printed in Great Britain
by Amazon